I0824676

HALF WYLDE

Also by
Sabrina Blackburry

The Enchanted Fates series
Dirty Lying Faeries
Dirty Lying Dragons
Dirty Lying Wolves
Dirty Lying Sirens

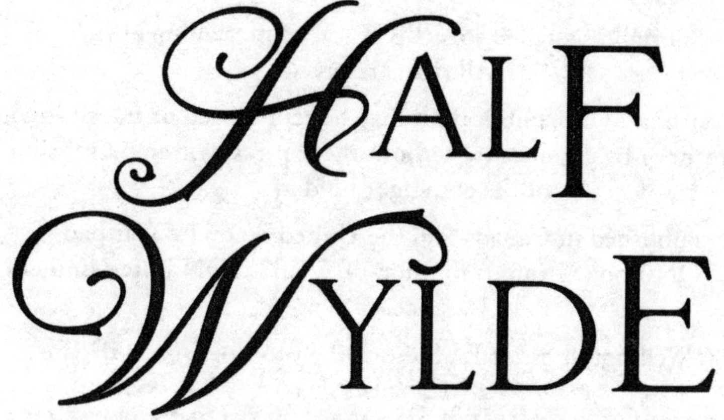

THE WYLDES
BOOK ONE

SABRINA
BLACKBURRY

An imprint of Wattpad WEBTOON Book Group

Copyright © 2026 Sabrina Blackburry.

All rights assigned to WEBTOON Entertainment Inc.
All rights reserved.

No portion of this publication may be reproduced or transmitted, in any form or by any means, without the express written permission of the copyright holders.

Published in Canada and the United States by Wattpad WEBTOON Book Group, a division of WEBTOON Entertainment Inc.

36 Wellington Street E., Suite 200, Toronto, ON M5E 1C7
Canada

5700 Wilshire Boulevard, Suite 220 Los Angeles, CA 90036 USA

www.wattpad.com

First Wattpad Books edition: May 2026
ISBN 978-1-83411-001-1 (Hardcover original)
ISBN 978-1-83411-002-8 (eBook edition)

Names, characters, places, and incidents featured in this publication are either the product of the author's imagination or are used fictitiously. Any resemblance to actual persons (living or dead), events, institutions, or locales, without satiric intent, is coincidental.

WEBTOON, UNSCROLLED, and associated marks and logos are trademarks of WEBTOON Entertainment Inc. or its affiliates. WATTPAD and associated marks and logos are trademarks of Wattpad Corp. or its affiliates.

Library and Archives Canada Cataloguing in Publication information is available upon request.

Printed and bound in Canada

1 3 5 7 9 10 8 6 4 2

Cover design by Bianca Bordianu
Interior image by Bianca Bordianu
Typesetting by Delaney Anderson

To the half children—stuck between two places, never fitting through the doorway to either one.

ONE
ASHES TO ASHES

I had always thought drowning would be a terrible way to die. Surely something quick would be better. A beheading, maybe. Or poison, if it were the right sort. But floating under the burning surface of the lake, it was hard to argue with the dark and comfortable sleep that beckoned.

My eyes, heavy and tired, closed. How much time had passed? My chest, which had seared with the strain to contain what air I could, was now numb, my lungs ready to let go. The fire overhead, a dancing watercolor of oranges and reds obscured by the rippling surface of the lake, promised no escape. Maybe wherever you went after death they wouldn't care that I was half monster. My lips parted, the water flooding in so hard that I couldn't change my mind now. I could feel myself fading. Leaving.

That was, until something splashed above me.

I tried to pry my eyelids open, but they wouldn't budge. The sway of the water around me pushed through my foggy consciousness as something took hold of me. The hard angles of an arm wrapped around me, fingers digging into my ribs as it pulled. Up I went. The water grew hot from the fire that floated on it, that burning oil ready to boil me alive if I was dragged too close. The heat on my face grew stronger as I got closer. A pause, then a motion that moved me around wildly as the water rushed in every direction, and for a moment the fire was gone. We broke the surface, and I blacked out.

I woke with a start, expelling all the water I had swallowed. Violently. The retching roared in my ears along with the blood trying to circulate once again after my cold encounter with the lake.

Still heaving, I strained to sense everything around me while I tried to lessen the swirling in my head, not yet able to sit upright. A warm crackle at my back soothed my frozen bones. A fire. I listened, but the clanking metal of the raiders no longer rang through the village. Screams had been replaced by cries of pain and loss. My head finally calm—or at least no longer threatening more sickness—I wiped my mouth with the back of my hand and sat up.

All around me, bodies huddled for warmth. The injured and dying moaned under the crackling of the fire. No sounds of fighting, no screams of terror; the raiders must be done with Silver Lake. Why was I here? Why were the villagers allowing me to sit so close? My only guess was that the shared horror of being caught in a raid had prevented anyone from bothering with me. I judged less than a quarter of the village sat here: the elders, the injured, and some women and children. But none of them were Bryn. The last thing I remembered was walking by the lake when the raiders came, then he'd thrown me into the water.

"Who has seen the woodcutter?" I asked. My voice crackled like the fire, my throat still raw.

Some of the people looked at me for a heartbeat, but I wasn't surprised to find that none of them met my gaze. Few of them spoke to me on a good day, and right now was certainly less than good. We might as well have been a pile of dogs crowding the hearth.

With no answer, I'd have to make a bolder move and find out for myself. Unsettled dread seeped into my heart. Standing slowly, a bit of a shake in my legs, I looked around and demanded an answer. "Where is Bryn the woodcutter?"

Some watched me from the corners of their eyes with shock and suspicion. I doubted any of them had heard me speak up before. Others just stared ahead, gray-faced and motionless, watching with hollow eyes as their world burned. And it did burn. I looked over my shoulder to see what remained of the settlement by the lake, and my heart sank. A once thriving fishing village was now blackened with ash in stark contrast to the dusting of snow around it.

"Everember oil, they called it," Shanna, a fisherman's daughter, whispered nearby. She had my full attention if she knew anything about what had happened. "It's on everything." Her body and voice both shook, stubbornness barely holding her in one piece. She glanced at me with those sharp eyes and then, as if she had just realized who she was talking to, she turned up her nose and stared ahead. She was clearly haunted by the sights before her, but the sight of me must have snapped her out of it. No one wanted to talk to the half monster. Especially not proud Shanna.

An old woman, Gerdie, I thought her name was, fell in a heap from where she'd been sitting on a sack of grain. The sound startled me, as well as most of the survivors of the attack. Almost immediately, I smelled the piss. The woman next to her leaned over to confirm what I suspected: her body was limp with death. They rolled her out of the way, and two more took her place by the warm fire without so much as a word. I said a silent prayer to the Mother. Gerdie hadn't been nice to me, but she hadn't been cruel either.

I reached up, lightly touching my arm. I would have a bruise where Bryn had grabbed me and thrown me into the water, and my lungs pained me from everything they'd gone through, but I was otherwise unharmed. There was nothing left for me at the fire but comfort from the cold and little in the way of answers. I walked away, and my place was quickly taken by other frozen bodies. So be it. I didn't need to sit by the fire; I needed to find Bryn.

Pieces of the puzzle fell into place as I walked the village. The blacksmith and his boys were pulling people from the lake who had tried to escape the flames. Most had jumped in. I had been thrown in right before that putrid oil coated the surface and was set ablaze. That couldn't have been that long ago; my clothes were still damp. So where were the raiders? Where was Bryn? My heart started to hurt as I walked, a bit faster as the moments grew longer.

My eyes drifted to a slow movement by the edge of the water. An old woman hunched over the lake, the villagers giving her a wide berth. An ancient raven perched on her shoulder, his one clear eye turned toward me. Mila the Witch. She rarely came to the village, but I was glad to have a friendly face here. One that would talk to me. I quickened my pace.

The smells assaulted me as I walked toward the water. A fiendish aroma of cooking meat seared my nose and watered my eyes. Tears fell, loosening the caked-on soot down my face. I tried not to look around me as I kept walking, not letting myself imagine what meat could be cooking right now. I focused on the watchful raven.

The witch shuffled a few feet and dipped back to the water as I drew near. Feathers and bones adorned her neck, and her hands rustled in the breeze over the lake. Her black dress billowed to her side as the wind tugged at it. The air around her was heavy with old magic.

"Wren, I see you survived." She didn't even turn to me as she collected a sample of the oil floating on the water. "Good. The Mother blesses you."

"Where is Bryn?" I asked, a tremor to my voice.

She turned to me now and looked me in the eye, her face soft. Wrinkled fingers reached for my hands, and she rubbed them gently. "You're chilled to the bone, child. You should have stayed by the fire."

My hands went numb. My heart tightened in my chest. "Where is Bryn?"

"I know he was as a father to you." Mila's words were slow, deliberate.

"*No*," I choked. My stomach dropped.

"He is gone, Wren," she said.

I fell to my knees, my legs suddenly losing whatever strength they had left. Tears welled and fell, distorting my vision as I scrambled to see where he had fallen. She couldn't be so sure of it, not in the chaos that had overtaken the village. Somewhere along the bank, near the dock but past the baker's house. That was where he'd pushed me in. Maybe he was still alive; Mila could be wrong. Maybe he needed help, or . . . or . . .

"Danger is still in the wind, and we need to prepare ourselves. Live now to mourn later."

"No! He can't be. He can't be dead." My throat tightened. My stubbornness held as the last dam of defense against the spilling of my grief. Keeping me in one piece, if only for a moment. Bryn was my only family, and without him I had absolutely nothing.

A fool. I was a fool not to admit it when I hadn't woken up to his smiling face. He wouldn't have left me alone by choice, and certainly not during a raid. Bryn was gone, and I could swear I heard my heart breaking as the first sob escaped me.

"Caution, child. Your danger has not yet ended," Mila warned. Her raven, Puko, cawed in agreement. Her voice might have been stern, but her warm hand rubbed my back even as she said it.

I tried to swallow the lump in my throat unsuccessfully. "What does it matter? My only family is dead."

"And Bryn would have you die as well?" Mila asked, more harshly.

I was numb. Empty. A coldness had settled over me that I wasn't trying to fight off.

"No," I whispered.

"Then get up." She grunted as she stood and dipped an empty bottle into the lake, a few steps down.

"I don't know what to do. Where is Bryn's . . . body?" I sniffed. *Body*. The word was disgusting to even think about. That it could be used to describe what was left of him.

"He will burn with the rest of the lost villagers," Mila said. "You do not need to see what remains of him. He would not want it."

I shivered. Her words promised a terrible end. "Still—"

"No. Not like this. Leave him a stone on his pyre later, but do not seek him out in this moment." Mila studied one of the vials in her hand, then looked down at where I sat on the hard ground. "Get up, child. To your feet. You should be moving soon."

"Why must I move? Why do you rush?" I asked.

Her aged face stilled, those eyes boring through me with deep sorrow and patience. Mila's words were never long, but she did attempt kindness in the moments when she remembered me to be the child she'd taught how to read and write and decipher the plants of the mountains. "This is a village of humans, Wren. And as much as you or I appear to be the same, they will remember our differences the moment they find their anger through their grief. Both of us must prepare to move on."

Our differences.

Still feeling numb, I stood up as Mila bent to scoop a new vial of oil, lost for any actions that weren't handed to me and ready to obey Mila's advice until I could regain myself. I wiped my face with my sleeve, eyeing the smoldering buildings behind me.

"Where are the raiders? How did any of us survive?" I asked.

Mila sighed, looking her raven in its blind eye for a moment.

"Something from the Wyldes came down from the mountains and slaughtered the raiders." Mila stood, brushing her knees. "It has been an age since I last laid eyes on a fae."

The numbness in my body subsided briefly, just enough to let in a jolt of fear.

"A *fae*?" My heart sputtered. "Here?"

"Do not bring fear of the fae into your heart, child." Mila came up to me and stroked the hair hanging over what remained of my left ear. "He killed only the raiders. If he wanted to do the same to the village he would have done it, not pulled you from the lake."

My body froze, but my eyes darted wildly. I looked at the lake, then at the path to the small fire for the injured. I looked to the remaining buildings, to the men scrambling to save what they could. The blacksmith still stirred the water for more people.

"A creature from the Wyldes carried me to the fire?" I asked.

Mila nodded.

"A *thing* from the north pulled me from the burning lake? Not one of the villagers?"

"They would not save you. The fae saw this and pulled you free himself." Mila rubbed her bad wrist. "They might have saved you last, but only after their own had been rescued. Is this a surprise to you?"

"No," I murmured. Numbness, emptiness, grief, all were replaced by a burning hatred in my chest. Clenching my fists, I took a calming breath. It didn't work. I turned and watched the people at work.

"Bryn would have saved anyone." My voice cracked as I spat my words at the village. At anyone who would listen, though none were close enough to hear me.

"I know, child." Mila reached to pat my arm. A tear trickled down my face. I ignored it and steeled myself.

"What am I to do now?" I cried, furiously wiping my face on my sleeve. "My . . . I can't hold him. I can't even see him."

"Bryn is gone, child. But the one who saved you is yet here, the fae. The villagers do not dare approach him." Mila scanned my face. "There is fear in the hearts of men of what is unfamiliar to them. *You* have no reason to fear him, and at the very least you owe him your gratitude."

I looked to where she pointed. South of the village, a dark figure moved among the dead. He walked slowly between the pile of horses and plainsmen, bending down on occasion, looking for something.

My eyes darted again to the village. Some threw worried glances behind them. They were staying well out of his way. Bumps coated my arms, and my breath came fast. The people of the mountains might not trust the fae, but they didn't trust me either.

"I thought you told me not to thank one of them," I said.

"Do not thank one needlessly, Wren," Mila said, her croaking voice sharp. "This is one instance in which it is a requirement. There are consequences to owing a debt to a fae, this is true. But to not thank one who saved your life would be far worse."

My hurting heart sank. I was trapped without a choice. I blinked away the fresh tears in my eyes, my throat tightening again as my body trembled to release my grief.

"Mila," I whispered.

"You are more than the fear of the humans in this mountain, child. Show him respect and then go home. Whatever comes of it, may it be for a day far from this one. The shock of this day will wear off, and I would have you warm in your bed when it does. Prepare your things. Times are moving, and soon so must I."

Mila gave me a rare smile. She wouldn't lead me astray. So be it.

I took a quivering breath and turned to approach the figure to the south. The pine needles crunched underfoot in rhythm with my beating heart. I drew the dotted circle of protection over my heart when I was only steps away from the creature.

"Hello, sir. Can you understand me?" He looked down at me, and my eyes widened as I finally looked at him from so close.

He was huge. His skin was blue as midnight. His shaggy hair, hanging loose nearly to his shoulders, was just a shade darker, almost black. Blood speckled him like stars, and beneath the blood a collection of scars told a long tale of violence. His silver eyes were as sharp as his teeth, and both looked ready to pierce me straight through.

My eyes flicked up to the telltale pointed ears of the fae, something I'd never seen in person before, then back to his face. He stared at me for a moment, then he gave me a slow nod. "I understand you."

The fact that he spoke struck me as unexpected. Something so beastly speaking the common tongue didn't seem to fit, yet he spoke all the same. I shivered at his voice, low and soft and demanding caution. The numbness of Bryn's loss was somewhat replaced by the panic I felt before this fae, if only while I was in his presence. I trembled like a rabbit before the fox.

"Thank you," I managed to whisper. "For saving me."

He narrowed his eyes at me and looked me up and down. "I accept your thanks, and on another day your favor."

Swallowing the lump in my throat, I waited for his next move. Some kind of trick, or a sinister laugh of triumph that he had fooled me. But instead, he turned his attention away from me and back to what he had been doing.

The fae studied each body and only occasionally stooped down to pull something free. I watched as he ripped a dagger from the belly of a horse, throwing it onto a pile of bloody weapons. The blade had pierced the animal's intestines; I could almost taste it in the air. It was lucky that my stomach was already empty or my last meal would have been on the ground. I resisted covering my nose. Something feral about the fae told me not to show any signs of weakness.

I watched as he worked, fascinated at his speed and precision but even more fascinated by his struggle. Something in this task was burdensome to him, I just hadn't figured out what that was yet. Should I assist in the task, or would I be underfoot if I tried? With my thanks given, I had nothing left to offer here, so I turned from him to see if I could find Bryn's body, despite Mila's warnings.

A hand shot out and grabbed my shoulder. I turned, my heart thumping. The fae's arm had stopped me where I stood, and I nearly fainted.

"Wait."

The look on his face was not a pleasant one, and he turned his nose to me like a wolf scenting his prey. He brought his other hand up, still gripping my shoulder, and delicately brushed the braided hair from the side of my face, exposing my ear. My shame.

The tips of both ears had been cut off in horrible, rough lines where there should sit two curved tips. Ugly and scarred, a glaring reminder that I was only half a human. The reason I'd been abandoned. The reason the village hated me.

Tears and hatred burned my eyes. Before they spilled over, I pushed at his chest, as deep an insult as I could muster. I hated him in that moment. Hated that he could tell I wasn't one of the people of the village. That even a complete stranger knew I wasn't one of the people here, not really. Tearing from his grasp, I ran for the woods, praying to anyone who was listening that he wouldn't follow. From what I could tell, he didn't, and while my prayers were working, I also asked never to lay eyes on another fae.

TWO
FLEE

There was still a gentle thread of smoke coming from the chimney when I reached home. Herbs dried on the mantle, a new bowl sat half formed in a pile of wood shavings on the table, and loaves of bread were rising on the windowsill. The cottage held a table, a hearth, and two beds piled with furs and quilts. As I stood in the middle of it, its warmth clung to my skin. A place filled with love. Little did the cabin know that its master was never coming home.

I wrapped myself in a blanket from Bryn's bed and sat on the floor and cried. Tears fell for my father, and for me, and for the destroyed patches of forest. None fell for the village.

The fae's face wouldn't leave my mind, and I hated him for that. It had been terrible but carved like a sculpture. My stomach twisted at the thought. He was a monster, not something to admire. But I couldn't deny he was beautiful too. They were supposed to be; that was how they lured in people for their terrible tricks. The hells could have him. He looked half animal anyway. And I'd likely offended him greatly. One of the rules Mila had taught me, and I'd broken it the moment I met my first fae. But he was awful for what he now knew of me without receiving my permission to know it.

It was little wonder humans didn't trust them. Trust me. Not that I had ever been among my fae half before, but it hadn't mattered then, and it hadn't mattered today. They hated me just as surely as they hated anything from the Wyldes.

Even when my tears finally dried up, I stayed on the floor. I didn't know how long I sat there. I traced the grain of the wooden boards. Small black patches were smooth where sparks from the fireplace had licked the floor. My fingers danced around a gouge I'd put in the oak with a spoon when I was young. I'd been trying to carve a bird. Bryn had scolded me for that.

Bryn. I hadn't dared look for his body. I was a coward. I wouldn't remember him mangled or burned or cut down, though. I would remember him as he was. Smiling, gentle, a large man with a large beard and a bigger laugh. He told the most wonderful tales, and he could carve anything with a knife and a piece of wood. He'd taught me the kinds of trees, and animals, and he'd taken me to Mila for reading and learning. But he was gone, and I wasn't.

I did what Bryn would have done to cheer me up, if he were here. I sang. I sang badly, with a broken voice and lyrics interrupted by sobbing, but I sang. I sang a sad ballad I had once heard at the fair. I sang through the few songs of the mountains I knew. Running out of things to sing, I even threw in a tune with bawdy lyrics I'd heard in the ale dens of Sulls when we went there on occasion. Everything I had to give, I gave through my voice in tribute and love and loss for my only family. The family of my heart if not my blood.

When I was done, my head ached. Next would be a stone of as much value and beauty as I could muster to set on his burning place. But with the tribute of song paid with everything I had, there wasn't enough of me to give any more that night. I lay down by the fire and slept, not waking until the fire burned out and the cold night woke me.

Blinking, I watched the moonlight cross the floor for a while. Eventually, I stood and let the blanket drop around me. My fingers itched for work, so I found things to do. I washed the mess I had become in the water basin. My dress, now ruined, lay discarded on the floor as I pulled on my doeskin pants and long green tunic. Dresses were for blending in with the people of the mountains, to make myself less different from them. Tunics were for working. I stoked and fed the fire's embers and put my coat around me. I laid the now risen bread by the fire and swept the wood shavings from the room.

Wet drops dotted the floor as I swept. Bryn was gone. Mila had hinted at leaving too. Without them, I wasn't sure there was a reason for me to stay.

Would the surviving farms around the forest accept me? I had helped chop wood and clear trees since I was big enough to hold an axe, and I could put up a new fence as fast as anyone, but my presence had only been tolerated because of Bryn. He was a friend to all. How long could I stay? And what would I do if the plainsmen returned?

Did I even need to see another human ever again? The only reason for money was to buy what I couldn't get for myself. Like clothes, I supposed. Food would never be a problem. But soap. I would miss soap.

A rustling that had no wind behind it whispered outside. My heart beat faster. Even now, a stray warrior could be lurking, waiting for a chance to strike. I grimaced and went to the wall by the door where the tools were kept. I couldn't see anything out the window, but that didn't mean nothing was there. Axe firmly in hand, I slowly opened the door and crept outside. I would not be cornered in a cabin in the woods.

"Mila." My shoulders dropped their tension as the hunched black form of the Witch of the Woods approached. Her raven sat on her shoulder, feathers ruffled. Usually his one clear eye stared back at me, but today it was the milky white eye that I had always assumed was blind.

"You need to leave, child," she wheezed.

My heart sank. "Why?"

"As soon as the fae left, the village turned sour. They hunt us whom they do not understand."

"The witches?" I whispered.

"They do not understand you either," she added.

The large bird perched on her shoulder flapped its wings a few times, scattering feathers on the ground.

"They say we brought the bad luck to them," Mila continued. "This is the final time I will be crossed by those who do not understand the Mother's love. We will not stay by people who do not want us."

"No," I breathed. "How could they? After all you do for them . . ." My eyes widened at the horror of a mountain so near the Wyldes without the protection of a witch. The Mother didn't guide her Daughters to watch over the wilder places for no reason.

"My sisters have been going home for the past few years. Times change, child, and whatever is on the horizon, we must all prepare for it. It won't be long before you will be sought out too." Her cold eyes studied me from head to toe. "You don't deserve what this mountain will do to you without the woodcutter."

"What will you do?" I asked, but already I had retreated to the cabin, where I could pack my belongings. Mila followed.

"The coven will gather where no man will find us. The question is what will *you* do?" Mila handed me the flint from the mantle. I put it in my sack.

"Can't I go with you? I could be of use." I didn't like the quiver in my voice as I gathered my comb and a small mirror. The skinning knife fit in the top of my boot with familiar ease.

Mila's stare weighed heavy on my back until I faced her somber expression again. "I cannot take you with me as you are now. The Mother does not answer my questions, and I do not know why her hand is closed to you. You cannot cross the borders I must cross, child."

"What does that mean?" I asked. "I can be useful. I'll keep your jars organized, I can carry bags and set traps for game."

"It is not about what you can do for me," she said. "The valley is closed off. Times are growing uncertain all over the lands, and you will not be able to pass through without magic of your own."

My shoulders tensed, and I turned back around to continue packing. "I know, I don't have witching magic like you do."

"And yet you do have something in you," Mila murmured. "There is a fog about you I cannot read. The Mother will show it when she wishes, I'm certain."

My hand strayed to the missing top of one ear. "I'm not one of her Daughters—"

"We are *all* her children," Mila corrected. "And you do have something in you not of these mountains. The Mother veils so much of you from my knowledge, dear child. If I could know more ways to help you, I would. But I cannot take you with me where I will go. I will travel with Gilly. Even now, she comes to me from the northwest. So I ask again, what will you do?"

It eased my worries that the old woman would be traveling with the much younger witch, but it didn't provide me with any answers. For a long time, my thoughts ran wild as I packed my clothes and a large store of food that we had been preparing for winter. The bird squawked, drawing my eyes to the wall beside him. I took the protection trinket Mila had given me from over my bed. I paused at the wooden cup Bryn had carved for me long ago. I put it in my sack too.

"There is nothing left for me here," I answered eventually. "I'll go further east. Maybe the people on the other side of the mountains can find a use for me." I looked around the cabin. What remained were not things I could bring with me, or they were things belonging to Bryn. My attention landed on the post at the foot of his bed. Bryn had worn his good coat into town, but that wasn't the one he used all winter. A dark leather coat hung ready, the inside lined with fleece, two pockets crudely sewn on in which to place warmed stones from the hearth. I shrugged off my own coat, nothing particularly special about it save for it being the nicest garment I could trade for at the Sulls markets two years ago, and pulled Bryn's around me. I took my own coat and hung it around the older woman's shoulders.

"Use your nose, your ears, and your eyes. Stop trying to be what you aren't. Ignoring what gifts you have will get you killed." Mila nodded slowly at me. "Do not consider every human your friend, and do not consider every fae your enemy. You are strong, child. Trust yourself. I will always watch out for you as best I can."

Her eyes shone in silent assessment. They seemed to look right through me, taking in everything she knew of me and everything I now carried with me. Mila patted my shoulder.

"I hope our paths cross again." I smiled, but it was a frail motion, ready to fall to pieces at the lightest push. Bryn. Mila. My home. All gone in one day, and I was still expected to keep the shattered pieces of me together enough to leave it all behind. The Mother was kind, but she could also be so very cruel.

"They will. The Mother wills it." Her eyes shone like moonlight, and a warm and frightening breath of air flowed through me. "A last warning: if you someday change your mind about your seal—and I hope when you are in a safe place you do—be very certain of whom you let remove it. Be well, Wren."

My back squirmed. I could almost feel where the seal was engraved down my spine, containing what magic my fearsome half granted me. The last lock keeping my fae self contained.

Pulling Mila close, I disturbed the raven on her shoulder, forcing him to find space in the beam overhead as I drank in her scent. I savored the feel of her hair under my palm as I stroked her back. Her thin fingers grasped me as she hugged me back. After a long moment of pressing every piece of Mila into my memory, we let each other go. Puko flew back down to his master's shoulder, and the Witch of the Woods turned to the door without another word.

She left. I grabbed the better axe, securing it with the cover looped on my belt, and I left too.

The sky was still gray with night when I began walking. Behind me, I pulled the sled that Bryn had used to carry wood in winter. It held my sack, the other axes, the bedding I'd brought, a hammer, and a bundle of cut maple that we had been drying for the winter solstice. On top of the whole thing, I'd thrown a bear pelt that would shrug off most of the rain or snow.

The oak sled was holding up well enough, considering the thin metal rails that made up the bottom were getting stuck on rocks and roots, but there was no way to carry everything otherwise. Luck found me when a muddy riverbed aligned with my path, letting me pull through the much smoother terrain. Soon the first snows would fall. Not this light crust sitting on the leaves but a real snow, and my pace with the sled could quicken. A bird cawed somewhere behind me.

Progress would have been even slower on other parts of the mountainside, but the lazy, ancient slope between Silver Lake and the small settlements east of it allowed for many level fields before tumbling down again. If I had gone south to Sulls and the sands beyond, I would have faced the downward trudge head-on. But there was no relief for me in Sulls, where the crowded city overwhelmed my senses and everything came at triple the price compared to the Wicked Spine, as the city dwellers liked to call our range after what lived on the other side of it. To the west I would have found more of the raiders that had just decimated the otherwise quiet fishing village. If it weren't for that fae—and I still didn't understand why he'd stepped in—the survivors would have been conscripted or killed. So, east I walked.

My belly reminded me to eat. I ignored it. Moving came first. When you move, you're useful. And when you're useful, you can ignore any thoughts that would crumple you into a heap on the mountainside for the bears to find. My arms burned, even rotating which shoulder I pulled the rope from. My face was tight and sharp where the chill in the air hit my wet skin. Leaves crunched and branches cracked. From the riverbed, I followed an old deer trail that was smooth enough for the sled to traverse. It would lead me to Pine Hollow by dusk. If I was lucky, word of the attacks wouldn't have reached the people there yet, and I might find a barn for the night.

Determined to heed Mila's advice, I turned my nose to the sky. A breeze carried the tanning yard's scent to me before it came into view. The first building of Pine Hollow.

At the first sign of men, I lowered my nose and turned my ears toward them, reaching up to ensure that my braids were in place over the missing points.

The people worked as they always had. No sense of worry tensed the air beyond the natural urgency that autumn afforded anyone who lived where the snow could pile high. Down the hill, a farmer was cutting hay. A babe cried. Goats played. I was nearly lost in the sounds when I caught the tanner watching me from his yard. Dipping my head down, I kept moving, my ears on constant alert for any sounds of being followed and possibly robbed, or worse. I could have been paranoid from the attack at the lake, but then, I had never ventured this far alone.

I continued toward the farmer. Just this summer, Bryn and I had felled the timber for his new fence. The grizzled man kept no wife, no family, and wasn't one to talk, which suited me just fine for making a deal tonight. He tolerated me, in a way—as much as he seemed to tolerate anyone. And I still needed to rely on the people of the mountains until I passed to the warmer lowlands.

"Ho, farmer!" I called. He glanced at me long enough to nod me into his field and then turned back to his hay. Bunches of golden straw lay at his feet. I left my sled but kept my axe with me.

"What brings you here alone, girl?" He grunted with every swing of the sickle.

"I'm leaving the mountains. I hoped to work in exchange for a night in your barn." He stopped cutting, standing up and wiping his wet brow with his forearm.

"We saw black smoke this morning from the west." He straightened his back with a grunt. "Where is the woodcutter?"

"Bryn is . . ." I swallowed through a tight throat. Lying now would do me no good. "Plainsmen attacked the people by the Silver Lake. We were there. Bryn is gone."

He stared toward the lake as though he could see through the rock and the trees all the way to its banks. Then he turned hardened eyes on me.

"One night. Cut from here to that post." He pointed. "Cover the pile and be gone before the sun rises."

I thanked him as he handed me his sickle. He walked down the hill toward the next field and disappeared. I turned to my task and mimicked the farmer's swing.

It was nothing like chopping wood. My arm bent in a way I hadn't used before, and it grew tired long before I was done. I gritted my teeth and continued. Bryn had always said I was stubborn, and stubbornly I cut the tangle of hay. It didn't stop me from cursing the goats in the nearby pen, though; they bleated and played as I worked to cut their winter meals.

With the last rays of light fading from the sky, I cut my final handful of hay and placed it in the pile. I hadn't been instructed on how to cover it, but I found a heavy tarp in the barn to throw over the whole thing so it wouldn't simply blow away in the night. A rock on each corner held it in place.

There was something peaceful about working myself so tired I couldn't cry. Leaning against the fence, the goats calling for attention I didn't give them, I watched the western sky. Smoke rose from the tree line, nearly swallowed up by the darkening sky. Funeral burnings, likely. Had they laid stones for Bryn? He had been liked by most, so I expected at least a few would be thinking of him today. That big laugh and easy temper had earned him more than a few seats at dinner. Hells and suffering, he'd been enough to have me tolerated by the people of the mountains, and that was no small thing. My lungs burned with the work I had just put in, which was well enough because if I had the energy I'd be crying through another lament. Singing was never a joy of mine, but it was for Bryn, who never walked without a tune to his lips.

Mother, I'd give almost anything to go back and lay a stone at his pyre. Offer him one more song and tell him what he meant to me.

I moved the sled out of sight, and by the time my head hit the barn loft, I was asleep.

THREE
FLEE

Whispers tickled me awake. It was not near dawn yet, and my muscles ached. I frowned and tilted my head slightly to hear better. A few words were clear enough to make out. *West. Soon. Smoke. Girl.* The wind had picked up, blowing the sounds away.

I sat up as quietly as I could, thankful for the fresh hay not quite dried out and crunching underfoot. The barn door was half open, but I couldn't see anyone through it. With luck, that meant they couldn't see me either.

I caught my lip with my teeth; my heartbeat quickened as my mind woke up to race through possibilities. Surely no one from Silver Lake had bothered following me for the sake of grief. Then again, I had faith in Mila's warnings. Could it be someone from Pine Hollow? The farmer didn't seem to mind me too much as long as I did my share.

I crept down the ladder, swearing to sleep with my axe from now on. My feet hit the dirt floor, and I tiptoed to the doorway to listen.

"Most of the girls in these parts match that description. You'll have to do better than that." It was the farmer, but who was he talking to?

"I smell her all over your fields. Does that bring someone to mind?" Faltering backward, I gripped the leather coat around me and kept my steps as silent as I could. Those words to the farmer weren't a question, they were a demand. The rumbling voice sent chills down my back. It was wild, something that didn't belong outside a barn but rather running through the trees or soaring in the sky. It was a voice of strength. It was low and dark and dangerous. And I'd heard it before, on the burned shores of Silver Lake.

"Let me think now. I had someone help in the fields, but she's done and gone from them now. She never said where she would go after that. Perhaps south, though, since there isn't anything in the other directions of much interest to a traveler." The farmer's drawl was slow, like he was thinking. Or buying time. I held my breath. They said the fae could smell lies. He hadn't outright said anything that was untrue, but he was most certainly pushing the boundaries. The old farmer might have been the bravest man I had ever seen. If it had been me, I'd have been shaking in my boots.

I dared a peek outside the barn door. It was him. The fae from the village towered over the human. I choked down a gasp. His back was to me, but the farmer could see me clearly. I ducked back into the barn.

"Yes, I'd go south if it were me," the farmer wondered out loud. "But I didn't watch her leave, so I can't be sure."

"So be it," the fae answered and stepped back from the farmer.

The fae's steps thundered. He ran with a frightening swiftness. I stuck my head out only to find he was already out of sight. The farmer stood in his doorway, staring open-mouthed after the creature from the Wyldes. Then he turned his head toward me and nodded once before retreating to the warmth of his house. I guess I ranked a little better than a fae from the Wyldes, at least to this farmer of Pine Hollow.

Fully awake now, and with every instinct urging me forward, I pulled my sled out the barn door. He had to be after me for my offense to him. I knew it was dangerous to offend them. Mila had told me so many times. But everything had happened so fast, I hadn't really known what I was doing until it was already done. I didn't regret pushing him, though. He'd put his hands on me and laid bare my most vulnerable secret. He'd deserved it, even if I now feared it would be the end of me.

North was tempting, the opposite direction of the wild thing that was looking for me. But the Wyldes were north of here, over the crest of the mountain range where the trails were said to slip down into dark places where the creatures of the Wyldes hunted one another. "We stay on the south side of the peaks," Bryn would say, "and they stay on theirs. By the grace of good luck that we aren't of interest." There were plenty of stories of humans who had gotten lost and become a plaything to the fae at best or a meal to the beasts at worst. Mila always reminded us there were never firsthand accounts, but Bryn could never turn down a full tankard and a willing storyteller, so we'd heard plenty of tales that told otherwise. I pressed eastward, if only for the fact that I'd told Mila I would be traveling that way.

The open fields in the hollow left me feeling naked. The trees were a welcoming cloak from the empty skies and the terrible growling voice I had left behind me on the farm. I tried to run, but the sled held me back, and the forest floor was a tangle of hazards, the snow too light. If only the deep snows had begun. I could already see several nicks in the metal rails where rocks had scraped the sled badly. Surely, it made too much noise. I debated abandoning it, but even with my natural strength and swiftness, I couldn't carry everything, and the weight of my sack would tire me sooner. Besides, with the now fully formed bruise from Bryn, my left arm was nearly as useless as it was sore. But the Mother smiled on my path, and I came across a brook. Unlike the muddy riverbed that had brought me to the farm, water trickled cold and unrelenting down the slope from the high places where the snow piled more readily. At least my burden could move through it.

Dawn came. I stopped to rest, drink, and eat. I tried to dry my wet boots. I cried again for Bryn. I set out once more. Worn deer trails and mostly dry creek beds aided me in moving the sled through what little frost lingered. I began to reach the edges of familiar forest, and glimpses of unknown landscapes danced ahead. I was tired, but I didn't stop again for rest or food until the sky turned red.

I ate a little more and soaked my feet in a trickling mountain spring. It was *cold* but refreshing. I chewed my lip and tore at my fingernails. Was sleep the right decision? But how long could I continue at this pace? I made up my mind to rest for only an hour, then I would move again.

A mighty oak with thick, low branches made a promising bed. I hauled my sack up with me and tied it off the ground, away from any curious animals. I sank the blade of my best axe into the trunk near where I lay. I would not let it leave my reach again. I devoured an entire loaf of bread before settling down to rest. For a long time, my ears twitched with sounds of the night. I jumped at owls, scurrying mice, and rustling branches. A bird cawed nearby. Finally, my weary body gave in, and I fell into a deep sleep.

I awoke at midnight. Much more time had passed than I'd wanted. My legs throbbed and my shoulders roared with hot aching, but I was far calmer than when I'd run from the barn. I let myself down from the tree gently, retrieved my axe and my belongings, and set forth again at a slower pace.

Wind howled down the mountainside. The chill bit into me, but my movement kept me from freezing. I found a gentle path, and another, and another, until I reached the bottom of the large slope. I ate an apple and began to climb. A few different muscles began to burn with the new motion of shifting upward.

Something pricked at the back of my mind. It was sleep, or nerves, or some primitive instinct to escape what was behind me. At times I could feel it, like an itch my hands couldn't reach. A tingle on my spine where my seal was. Other times it was all but gone. The feeling kept me going, and as it grew stronger with the rising sun, so did my fears.

And then I heard it. It was light, but it was footsteps. Definitely not an animal. How I could tell, I still don't know, but there was no doubt in my mind the fae was behind me.

My heart raced, and I gripped my axe. He wasn't close, but with his terrible speed, the gap between us would be a moment for him. Maybe he hadn't noticed I'd sensed him. Maybe he didn't care.

I went over every item in my possession in my head. My clothes, the food, my meager pocket of coin. I could survive without it; Bryn had made sure of that. I would cry for the things Bryn had carved for me, but I would live without them too. The only things that might save me now were surprise and every ounce of speed I had.

I took a deep breath and let go of the sled. It clattered down the slope behind me, hitting rocks and probably scattering my things. I ran.

Sprinting left, around trees and rocks, I hurled myself forward. A growl from behind shot chills up my spine just as a bear would have. My heart threatened to break through my ribs. I ran for what must have only been a minute when everything ahead of me stilled.

I skidded to a stop. An unearthly mist had covered the edges of the forest. Everything was darker, more sinister than it had been just a heartbeat ago, and I whipped my head back the way I had just come to see the strangeness had hidden the path back too.

Something felt off in the clearing. My skin prickled with it. I listened for anything I could hear from ahead of me where the mist began or behind me where something had chased me. I realized I couldn't hear anything at all. No birds, no insects. Not even the movement of branches overhead. The seal on my back burned like it would when Mila was crafting spells nearby, the angry roar of magic trying to escape and touch other magic.

A cold breeze, colder than a mountain winter, crept through me. The smell of a cave, wet minerals and stagnant grime, clung to the air and coated my tongue. Every hair on my body stood up as I pulled out an axe. Turning my head all around me, I heard nothing. Saw nothing. But I felt it, whatever *it* was.

"*Deliciousss*," a moist breath purred in my ear. I whipped my head around only to be met with empty clearing.

"Who's there?" I demanded.

"*It bites*." The voice laughed—it was not a happy sound. "*But ssso do I*."

I spun on my heels. There it was, a distance away in the trees. The air around it was dark and thick. A figure in a tattered robe with the hood drawn over its brow. The skin was whiter than the fresh snows. Even from where I stood, I could see black veins snaking under the skin. It had the body and voice of a woman, but the teeth between its red lips were narrow and sharp, like those of a fish.

"What do you want?" I gripped my axe. A tremor slipped into my voice this time, but I stuck out my chin and told myself I wasn't afraid of this thing. Disregarding the fact that I'm a terrible liar, of course.

"*It hasss been a long time sssince I have tasssted your kind*," it whispered. "*A long time indeed*."

I backed up, but I stayed in the clearing where I could move easily. The creature crept closer, its cold presence pushing in on my breath, burning my lungs. That feeling of wrongness threatened to strangle me.

"*No need to run, little one.*" It grinned, wider than a jawbone should have allowed. I wondered how quick a death this creature could provide. It glided toward me, even as I dug my heels into the dirt and moved my grip on the handle of my axe. I would like to say it was bravery that kept me there, but I was more afraid to show it my back than to face it. I wasn't going to give it the pleasure of an unguarded meal.

"*Don't be shy, ssstay there like a good girl. Yesss, that'sss it.*"

I swallowed as the thing drew close. My nose filled with its deep-cave stench, stale and cold. Its bony hands reached toward me, skin stretched tight over tendons and sinew. Fingers moved forward, a hair's breadth from running wet, sharp claws down my cheek, and I was frozen in place. The horrid thing before me, forever seared into my mind, smiled. One lone sound broke through the deathly still and sparked the life back into me.

"*Run*!" The fae, the very thing I had been running from up the mountainside, now thundered into the clearing and barreled toward me and the creature.

Snapping out of my stupor, I hefted the axe and swung it toward the creature; it was far too close for a natural attack position, but I tried anyway. As it shifted back from my clumsy swing, its eerie black eyes darting between me and the fast-approaching fae, a small opportunity presented itself.

Swinging again, not even righting the sharpened edge toward my target, I pulled the axe back and slammed the dull end against the creature's shoulder.

I ran just as a blur of deep blue collided with the thing now behind me. Tearing through the trees, low branches and tall grasses scratching at my skin and clothes, I put as much distance between me and that clearing as I could. My mind raced, recalling every story Mila had ever told me and trying to reconcile them with the predator that had nearly had me in its claws.

My legs ached by the time I finally slowed down. Stumbling to a stop against a large tree, I leaned against it as I slid to the ground and dragged as much air into my lungs as I could with each breath.

I dropped my axe next to me. It was a miracle I'd held on to it. That thing—that monster—was the stuff of nightmares. The shaking began as I replayed what had happened in my mind.

Running from the fae was one thing; I had thought I needed to be afraid of him. There was no understanding him or what he wanted. His nature was foreign to me, his ties to the Wyldes alarming. But this creature, the not-woman with those long, thin teeth who carried mist around her, that was truly something to fear.

The strain to hear what had become of their battle gained me nothing. The insects were buzzing again, my biggest sign that I had managed to get far enough away. But if the fae didn't win and that monster came after me again, I didn't think I'd make it out unscathed a second time.

My head pounded, my legs ached, my hands and face were scratched from pushing through the forest, draining all the strength I had left. Back to the tree, head leaning against the rough trunk trying to put pressure against the pounding ache, I closed my eyes. Insects, birds, rustling leaves, they had all returned.

The music of the mountains lulled me enough that when footsteps disturbed crunching leaves, I jolted.

The fae.

Something wet and black and smelling foul as rotten fish covered his hands—likely the blood of that creature—but the fae seemed otherwise the same as the day he'd killed the raiders.

Another thing I did not understand about him.

The clearing around me spun in a moment of vertigo as I shot to my feet, not wanting to be at any sort of disadvantage. My fingers curled around the handle of my axe, the steadfast tool now turned weapon. My stomach churned as he took slow, deliberate steps toward me.

What should I do? What does he want? What would my father do? Bryn would have asked already, and that realization, along with the terror of the last hour, amounted to one sob escaping me as I pressed my back against the tree.

He stopped in front of me, one hand moving overhead as he leaned against the same tree I had my back against. His expression was even, but his unblinking attention chilled me. Eyes on me were never good. It meant stares, whispers, and sometimes much worse. My mind was caught somewhere between Mila's advice to be open to the fae and a life among people who feared them.

And then he spoke, and my swirling concerns came to a halt as my attention was solely on him.

"You are frustratingly difficult to track down."

My mouth popped open, as though if I gave them the opportunity words would form and make a sensible response. Difficult to track down? He'd looked nothing but angry when I'd spoken to him at Silver Lake. He had clearly been agitated at the farm. Once I'd realized he might be behind me in the forest, I'd had every reason to be fearful. People did not chase me down with innocent intent.

"I shouldn't have pushed you," I finally said. Maybe that was what this was about.

His brows knit together, and he tilted his head before he seemed to remember. "And I should not have touched your hair."

If not for my transgressions against him, then what?

"A favor, then. You're afraid if you cannot find me, I cannot repay the debt I owe you." My chin rose, defying any lingering fears I still had. "I repay my debts, whatever you may think of humans."

Closing his eyes, he let out a heavy breath. "I do not care about that; I simply gave the formal response to your thanks."

"But the rules. I was taught—"

"An archaic practice." He waved the notion away. "From a time when humans were far less separated from the Wyldes."

Then what did he want? This maddening conversation was turning the feeling in my chest from concern to irritation. My body ached, my head pounded, I smelled foul, and all I wanted to do was make some sort of camp where I could clean the scratches on my skin and eat something. That *thing*, though. That thing was going to be fuel for my nightmares for a long time to come.

"Is that thing dead?" I asked.

"The wraith is dead," he answered.

Wraith. A shiver ran down my skin, crawling with the memory of how that monster made the very air feel like death.

Well, at least that takes care of that. One worry was gone, but I still needed to get to the bottom of this situation between us.

"Why is it you've followed me, then?" It was all I could think to ask.

"You smell familiar, and I needed to know why," he said gravely.

He could not be serious.

"If you are one of us—" he continued.

"I am *not* one of you." Biting, cold anger rose in me. I'd spent my whole life being punished for what might be in my blood. If I was truly one of them, they had abandoned me just as surely as the people of Silver Lake had shunned me. I couldn't be one of them, because if I was then . . . then . . .

Then neither side of my flesh and blood had found me worth keeping.

Two fat tears forged the path for streams to begin down my cheeks. Everything was too much; it was all too much at once.

Pushing off the tree, the fae stepped back and thankfully gave me some room to breathe. I moved to the side, putting a few more steps between us. Wiping furiously at the tears with one hand, I pulled Bryn's coat tighter around me. "Why are you here?"

He ran his hands through his hair, not minding the mess he had just made of it as my stomach flipped at the sight. He killed so easily, was so capable of ending the life of something that threatened his. Or others, I suppose. Some might consider it a good thing; I wasn't so sure yet.

"You are clearly of the Wyldes," he tried to explain with slow, calculated words. "The entire population of the courts is accounted for. No one slips through the cracks. No one. Everything of the Wyldes stays within its borders, and everyone else stays outside."

He had every chance to elaborate, but when he didn't, I realized I was going to have to prod every word of this conversation out of him. "Are you saying that I shouldn't exist?"

"No." He frowned. "I'm saying that you should not be unaccounted for. Why were you in that human settlement?"

"Because I'm part human. Look at me." I held up my hands. Their fingers were more pointed than a human's, but against this long-limbed and nimble creature before me, I felt stubby. Blunt, somehow. The differences in our details were as noticeable to me as the differences I'd grown up noticing between myself and the people of the mountains. I was built sleek and narrow, capable of running more swiftly and jumping further than anyone else around me. But compared to this fae, I felt like a toddler just learning to navigate the world with my body.

"Perhaps you are part human, but that is not what I asked. Why were you *there*?" he said.

By now, the threat of him was diminished enough that I tucked my axe back into the holder on my belt. If he wanted to harm me, my axe wouldn't do me any good anyway. Crossing my arms, I frowned back. "I lived there. Or near there. Why does it matter to you?"

"Because you were outside of the Wyldes." He said it as if this was something obvious that should make sense.

"Babies found in the woods tend to live wherever their guardians raise them," I snapped. "Please, for the sake of my sanity, what do you want with me?"

He shifted his weight to one side, taking me in as if for the first time. Whatever he had seen in me before was shaken into an entirely different shape in his mind. "Come back to the Wyldes with me."

"What? Why? I don't even know you," I said.

"Those people left you to die," he replied. "My kind will want to know you."

"Those people . . . Do you mean the villagers? They had other things on their mind. Like a force of angry horsemen throwing fire across the town," I argued.

He shook his head. "The men pulling people from the water saw you and turned around. They knew exactly who you were when they abandoned you to the water's depths."

Of course they'd left me. The wild girl that Bryn dragged around with him wasn't worth saving. I knew this, had always known this, and yet the sting of hearing it from this fae, this outsider, still bit.

"Why were you there that day?" I shoved the subject off me and onto a question that might help me gain perspective.

He shrugged. "It's my job to watch the doings of humans too close to the borders. A raid is of interest, so I followed it."

"Why intervene? I'm not stupid enough to think the fae have an interest in keeping the humans there safe."

"No, but then I sensed you." He said it so casually, as if it were the only obvious answer.

Me?

Me, because I was part . . .

Everything shifted. The fact that this fae had been there might have been coincidence, but when he'd acted, it was because of me. Because he saw me as one of his kind. Aside from Bryn's big heart taking in a lost baby, that was the kindest thing a stranger had ever done for me. Ever. It was surreal, and foreign.

"Because you sensed me," I repeated. "As one of you?"

He nodded. "Those people do not care for you. Come with me to a place where they will."

That almost made me sound wanted, and I was not a wanted presence. Aside from Bryn or the kindness of the Mother's Daughters, I wasn't a welcome sight. No village had wanted me there, but my labor was tolerable as long as it was next to Bryn. No farm, no homestead, no traveling camp, and no city. Bryn had even arranged our rooms in Sulls while I'd waited outside the inns, keeping my head hidden as we navigated the crowded streets. And now this fae was suggesting, simply by virtue of being of their blood, that I would be wanted in the Wyldes.

A place where they would care. I'd only ever been an outsider; I'd never been able to picture a life where I wasn't. My mind reeled with the possibilities but shied away from the unknown.

Do not bring fear of the fae into your heart, child.

My safety was at risk if I ventured into these strange and unknown lands, but I was at risk just about anywhere now that I was alone. Could I do it? Could I find peace with the other half of me?

"Come with you," I said, slowly, "just like that?"

He nodded again. A few strands of midnight hair fell into his face as he did, and he brushed them away. There he stood, a bloody mess from saving me from death—for a second time, I reminded myself—with no demands or expectations on his face. Just a possible welcome for a girl who had nowhere to go anyway. It was a strange sensation. Not that the fae knew that, but that might have made him even more persuasive. He didn't even know this was my last resort, a hand reaching out when I didn't have anywhere else to seek safety. But the tentative trust of one fae was still not quite enough to push me over the edge.

"You said your people would want to know of me," I asked. "Why?"

His brows lowered. "First, because you are one of our kind, and it is difficult to fathom why you would be apart from us."

Tension rose back into my shoulders. "And second?"

He grimaced. "Your story may hold a clue to an answer we have been seeking for a long time."

A reasonable person would have elaborated, but once again this short-worded fae did not.

"An answer to what?" I prodded.

"You are not the only one our kind has lost," was all he said. Perhaps the subject was difficult to talk about, but it did succeed in making me more curious. Lost. Were there others like me wandering around the mountains? It didn't seem likely, and the way he'd said *lost* carried a heaviness that indicated a more forlorn use of the word.

"How would this work?" I asked slowly. "If I say yes, that is."

"There is an outpost another day north of here, in the space we call the borders," he said. "That is where my triquetram is serving our rotation of watch. In a few days, we will leave, and another group will arrive. When we leave, we can take you with us to our city."

Too fast, too much information, too many things to keep track of. "Your tri-what? An outpost? There's a whole city of you?"

He blinked slowly, reminding me of a cat. "My triquetram, my bonded team. You truly don't know what that is?"

"No," I said, more defensively than I had intended.

"The others would be better teachers," he murmured.

"Others, your tri-ket-rum." The feel of the strange word in my mouth slowed me down. "Wait, so the first step would be an outpost. How many of you are there?"

"Three," he said.

Three fae. And beyond the borders, a whole city of them, at least. Taking a deep breath, I sent up all the thoughts I had for the Mother's guidance and hoped Mila had been right to have me trust this fae.

"I would like to come with you," I said, the words unlocking something in me. Hope? Relief? "I can work. I can find wood and forage."

He held up a hand. "That is not a worry, I'm happy to have you come with me. I promise we have everything we need at the outpost, no work needed."

My fingers tingled; I felt funny all over. The whiplash of going from being frightened by this fae to agreeing to go with him. Was I truly going to try my hand at finding a home among his people? *My* people? Could this possibly end better than it had with the humans?

"We will move soon," he said. "There could be other unexpected things nearby, now that the wraith is dead. It may even have attracted witches."

That stopped me in my tracks. "You make that sound like a bad thing."

His expression hardened, just enough for me to notice. "Our history is a difficult one. There are no conflicts with them now, but I don't want to run into them regardless."

What did that mean? There had been conflicts? Had Mila told me that? Did I not remember? It was as though the seal written down my back in violet markings, holding something within me from bursting out, now burned. My heart pounded. Was this a mistake? But I wasn't a witch, I just carried their work on my skin and Mila's years of teaching me as a girl in my mind. It wasn't as though I had any knowledge of their craft or ability to use it. Surely this wouldn't be a problem, right?

"They're unwelcome in the Wyldes?" I asked.

"I can't imagine why one would venture into our lands, but I know the lands I am from would be more than wary of one," he answered.

The truth, I had to tell the truth or this would eat me alive with worry and guilt. "There was a witch, I grew up near her, and she treated me well—"

"You are welcome to come with me." He stopped the beginning of my ramble before it began. "Whoever you've known, wherever you've lived to survive until now, I hold nothing against you. You are of the Wyldes, and you are welcome there."

I hadn't gotten as far as mentioning the seal, but I found relief in his words. Besides, Mila had told me to ensure I fully trusted whoever helped me remove the seal one day. If I never planned on removing it, if I didn't know this fae enough to have that amount of trust, it should be fine to continue as I had all this time. Only Mila and Bryn had known about the seal in the first place, and nothing had come of it for over two decades now. And I could venture back out of the Wyldes to find my old teacher someday, once I had learned everything I could about the people there and the other part of my blood.

"I'm Wren," I said, realizing we had come this far and still hadn't introduced ourselves.

"Thain," he offered.

Thain. It seemed to suit him. "Okay, Thain. I would like to come as far as the outpost and meet the others first."

He smiled, the first genuinely positive emotion I'd seen from him, and it finished disarming the tension in my shoulders.

"Welcome to the Wyldes."

FOUR
THAIN

Our first step was to collect my things. The plan was to skirt the area where the wraith had been and collect what had fallen down the slope, which was good enough for me as I had no desire to see any of the aftermath. Thain led, I followed. He moved like a cat; even through the simple tunic, I could see the muscles of his back shift. He had honed his body to that of a warrior, or maybe all fae were like that by design. If so, I certainly wasn't blessed with it. Bryn had had to help me shape my arms for woodwork through many seasons of labor, and even now I had added little size to show for it.

Thain stopped to pick up the splitting axe and guilt echoed in my head, hearing Bryn say, "Don't ding my axe or I'll make you take it all the way to the smith this time," with his half-serious guffaw. My gut twisted. I righted my sled and searched for what had fallen from my sack. Thain picked up the bundle of wood I'd brought in the event I was without dry firewood and found a length of rope that had uncoiled itself as it slid down the slope.

"We can still make good time before finding someplace to make camp." He ignored the rope I'd used to pull the sled and simply lifted it to carry. Still clutching the bundled wood under one arm, I was nearly running to keep up with his long strides.

"I can pull that," I insisted, reaching for the dangling rope.

"No need," was his only reply, and he didn't so much as slow down.

Everything about him was fluid. The unbreaking motions he used to pick things up. The way he moved nearly silently, even while making our way through the landscape littered with pine needles and dry leaves. My cheeks burned with the realization that every noise he had made for me so far was completely for my benefit. That would take some getting used to.

Before departing the area completely, he stopped to wash himself in a stream that was fighting a coating of frost at its edges, and then we went north. We had walked for at least an hour before I realized two things about Thain. First, he was painfully quiet. The effort it had taken me to pull our last conversation out of him should have been enough of a hint, but it would seem he had no problem walking in complete silence. Bryn had done nothing of the sort, always singing some song he'd learned, misremembering half the lyrics and trying to get me to sing along. It brought a small, aching smile to my face, the first I'd mustered while thinking about him since that day. But Thain was nothing like Bryn in that regard, and our travels consisted primarily of peaceful silence, something that was more akin to my habits than Bryn's.

The second thing I noticed about the dark fae that walked before me was that the tension had left him. There had been something utterly frightening about him at our first encounter. He'd said even fewer words then, and he'd seemed disturbed by something. My eyes drifted to his hands, and I recalled another detail from that first meeting.

"Your gloves are gone." I hadn't meant to mention it; it seemed like such an insignificant thing. But the moment the words left my mouth, I also realized that his primary method of fighting, as much as I could guess, at least, was with his hands. Particularly the fact that his fingertips ended in—

"And where are your claws?"

Thain looked over his shoulder, still not stopping. "The claws come when needed, and the gloves were for the iron."

What on the Mother's fruitful earth did that mean?

"Iron, like from the smith's?" I asked.

He grunted, shifting the sled from one shoulder to the other, though more out of awkwardness of the shape than burden of the weight, it looked like. "Iron burns. Does it not burn you to the touch?"

"No." I looked down at the axe on my hip in wonder. "Should it?"

Thain didn't answer for a long stretch. "Who knows. For anyone else in the Wyldes, it would."

Ah. Another difference for my long list. Though this one seemed beneficial, at least. Mila had never mentioned iron hurting the fae, but after all her lessons I very well could be forgetting a detail. Especially knowing I'd resisted any information about the Wyldes for a long time.

"Now that I think of it, why were you collecting the iron back then?"

"Tossed it in the lake. Don't need more humans waving around iron."

A laugh escaped me. This substance could burn the flesh of him and his kind, and yet he made it sound more like a nuisance than anything else.

"My axes, then," I said, a bit defensively. "No one will ask me to get rid of them."

A hand drifted to the solid head of the axe still on my hip, curling around the autumn-cooled metal head of it.

"No," Thain answered with ease. "But I don't recommend swinging them toward anyone once you arrive in the Wyldes."

"More than fair," I agreed. "I would never misuse my tools like that."

A corner of his mouth snuck suspiciously upward before he turned his head and I could no longer see it. "The wraith may beg to differ."

And then the image of my axe swinging at the creature came flooding back to mind. "That was life or death! I had no choice."

"No, you didn't," Thain said. "And yet, you didn't freeze as so many would. You did well."

As I followed his broad back through the trees on whatever path he had chosen for us, we returned to silence. His unexpected praise was more acknowledgement than anyone but Mila or Bryn had really given me in twenty-five years, and it gave me a warm feeling inside that left me with much to think about.

"We will need to camp tonight before we reach the outpost." Thain broke the quiet of the evening as we stopped next to an outcropping of rock that would afford us some shelter from wind or rain. It was hard to argue with the suggestion when my entire body ached and my stomach growled in demand.

"Is it safe here?" There were plenty of dark places behind the trees, and I wondered how many upcoming nights I would find the wraith slipping into my nightmares.

"Safer than we were back there," he said. "Do you see the brook that split and flows down either side of us now?"

"Yes." It wasn't big, but it was definitely there. The right arm was much larger than the left.

"Dark things from the Wyldes do not like to cross running water. Unseelie things, like the wraith. If something happens tonight, remember that." He gathered branches for a fire. "Some also don't like flame, though it can attract others. We're close enough to a patrol route here that I doubt we'll run into so much as a wisp. If we do, I'll take care of it."

With a grimace, I pulled a blanket from my sack. He had already gotten a spark to catch on his pile of wood and was working on lighting the thickest branches. Finding a good medium between the fire's heat and the evening's chill, I laid out my blanket. I tucked both axes close by.

"Wren." Thain broke the silence. "I will listen, if you need to talk."

"Talk about what?" I tossed a stick from under my blanket onto the fire, then eyed Thain, who had found nothing more than a broken stump to lean against. Small lines strained around his face, and I recognized that awkwardness. The entering of uncomfortable territory, doing something you rarely did.

"About everything. About the first time we met. About moving your hair."

"Don't," I started. "Don't worry about it."

Thain nodded, staring into the fire as it danced between the offered branches. An orange glow cast his face in warm light but made his expression no less unreadable. "Some encounter terrible things and require an outlet for what they have seen. Just know I offer it, though Eberon is much better at it. But I am the one who is here."

My fingers curled closed. He could have meant the raid at the lake, he could have meant the wraith, he could even have meant himself, and I wasn't sure what the normal reaction was supposed to be to that. All I offered him was, "I will recover; I always do." Thain nodded, laid a pile of branches nearby to feed the flames that licked high into the air, and busied himself with pulling the smaller kindling pieces out of the pile. We split portions of food from my supplies, though he had offered to hunt his own. There was no sense in spending the energy when I had more than enough with me. Considering we were heading to this outpost of his, I likely wouldn't need it all for much longer anyway.

After making a decent-sized dent in my supply of apples and the last bits of stale bread, the evening quieted down, and we settled where the heat of the flames was comfortable.

From where he was propped up against the stump, he nudged one of the branches with his boot until he could flip it with practiced ease into the fire without causing a mess of ash and embers. "You must have questions."

The fire crackled between us for a while. Talking had already been painfully awkward, so what was the point? But this was my chance to find out more about him, or the places we were going, or the fae people.

Sighing, I lay on my back under the blanket, pulling one of my arms up to act as a pillow.

"Do you often watch the borders of the Wyldes? That's the task you're here for now, right?"

He shrugged. "Every few years. The courts rotate who they send, and we stay for a few weeks at a time. Mostly I keep an eye on the darker creatures of the Wyldes that would come too close to the lands I'm from. My king asks, and I go."

A king. I should have expected something like that. The humans might think of the fae as wild and fearsome, but knowing Thain even for just the few hours since the wraith, I could tell there was much more to his people than that. Was his king anything like the sultana who ruled over Sulls? She was rarely among her people on the streets of her city, but maybe the king of the fae would be different.

"What about you?" Thain interrupted my thoughts. "What did you do with your days by the humans of the lake?"

Settling back down, I let the pain throb through my chest in a way I had evaded for hours. Even that made me feel guilty. Maybe everything would make me feel guilty, since I had lived and Bryn had not. Swallowing the mounting feelings, I threw my focus into answering. "Most days I split firewood. Felled trees. Planted more trees. Helped with simple buildings. A few animal shelters over the years. Fences. Many, many fences. Bridges. I've helped clear fields for homes to be built. It's peaceful work. Just you and the axe. And we'd trap. Sometimes fish. My old teacher, Mila, she would have me reading and writing. We'd practice learning the plants of the mountains and beyond too."

"It sounds like you enjoyed it," he said.

The fire crackled, the breeze played with the tops of the pines, and a wet streak fell down the side of my face. "I did."

He glanced at the rising moon. "We should probably get some sleep."

He stood, stretched, and walked silently to the edge of our little campsite, taking the watch. I let him. I had enough to think about, but my questions could wait until morning. A few insects buzzed around us outside of the fire's reach. A bird cawed in the distance. It reminded me of Mila, and my heart tightened anew at my loss. But even with my tangle of grim thoughts, I fell asleep quickly, the scent of Bryn that still clung to his coat comforting me into the night.

FIVE
THE NATURE OF FAE

I was in the cabin. Where had Bryn gone? He usually took me with him on errands. I shrugged and placed a pot for dinner by the hearth. I was dicing up carrots when the chill hit. The light in the cabin went dark, even the fire dimmed. A horrible shriek filled the air. The door slammed open, and Bryn ran in with panic in his eyes.

"Wren, get out of here!" he boomed. A motion from behind him froze him in place. Then the wraith woman stuck her terrible clawed arm right through his chest. Blood poured down the front of him as I screamed and screamed . . .

"Wren!" Someone was shaking my shoulder as I jolted awake. "Wren, wake up. It was a dream."

I had tossed my warm blanket off. My vision was blurry and dark. Sweat soaked my neck and forehead. The caw of a bird snapped in my ears, and I looked around the forest.

Thain hovered over me, his brows knit together and a frown on his face. My heart was pounding from the nightmare; it had been so real.

The smell of rabbit cooking in our fire hit me. I looked around to see the gray of pre-dawn peeking out from the trees on the horizon. I turned back to the dark fae still kneeling over me. At some point in the night, he had finished cleaning up. His hair was still damp as it hung lose around his face. His silver eyes pierced through me, and I realized he was waiting for some kind of response from me.

"I'm fine," I croaked. He let me sit up and handed me a waterskin.

He tried to steady me with a hand at my back, but I flinched at the touch. Could he sense the seal?

"Who is Bryn?" he asked softly.

When I didn't answer right away, he clarified. "You were calling his name."

Swallowing the tightness in my throat, I found enough words to answer. "My father. He's gone."

"I'm sorry," Thain whispered. He left my side long enough to deal with the rabbit over the fire. He returned with a leg on a spit. "Try to eat something if you can."

I took the meat silently. Despite the nightmare, despite the swelling sorrow, I ate. Thain offered more, but I didn't take it. I couldn't have a full belly when Bryn would never have one again.

The dark fae watched me closely as we packed up the camp. There was no mistaking his eyes on me as we scattered debris on the ground to hide any marks we might have left, and his concern was an unfamiliar film on my skin. Other than Bryn, Mila, and a select few visiting witches, I was not used to attention. The kind words, the food, the promise of a safe place to learn more about the Wyldes. It overwhelmed me, made me want to run. Suffocated me.

"Tonight you can sleep in a real bed." Thain drew me from my grim thoughts. "Nothing lavish, but not a blanket on the ground."

A blanket on the ground didn't bother me in the least right now, but I didn't say as much. "How far are we?" I asked.

"We will be there well before dinner." He gathered my things and stood. "If you change your mind at any time, tell me."

Just the offer, the choice in the whole thing, made me cling to my decision. The need to know more about them burned in me, and if these partners of his were better suited to teaching me, then I would go learn from them. The contrast between me and the humans around me was so noticeable, and now I craved to know what the other side of my blood looked like. Just how short I fell in that direction, or if I could truly find some peace with them.

I stood with him and followed as he led us further up the mountain. After a few minutes, we fell into a comfortable pace.

The mountains were smooth with age, and the slope was never terrible, but the further north we went, the steeper the peaks became. My legs ached from the days of hiking. My arms were a little better off, since the weight of the axe was familiar in my hand, though I still had a large, fading bruise on my left bicep. The air grew crisp, and my breath left trails of steam to brush my face and fall behind us.

Even with the cold, I broke a sweat after a while. Bryn's coat was too efficient, and I'd now spent several days walking long distances. Thain seemed wholly unaffected. He carried the bulk of my things, and still I was the one struggling. He had given me my silence, despite obviously having some question that clung just inside his mouth then disappeared when he tried to open it. There was a reason he was almost excited to have met me, and I couldn't figure out what it was, but I knew he wasn't giving me the whole story. Maybe that should bother me more than it did. Maybe he thought I'd run off if he explained.

Maybe it was my turn to make an effort.

"Why don't you travel with supplies?" I asked.

He shrugged. "Apart from a few essentials in my belt? I sleep in the trees, I hunt and forage for my meals, and the less I carry, the less I have to keep track of on the move."

"Oh." I looked at my heavy sack on his back. He must have sensed it somehow, because he stopped and turned to me.

"Don't for one moment regret bringing these things, Wren. I travel with nothing, but I have a home to return to. Don't regret any of this." He paused. "You survived something terrible. Don't regret that either."

He moved on without another word, and the silence echoed around us. The understanding wasn't something you could imitate, and it begged the question of what he had seen in his time.

The trees grew thinner, and I could almost reach up and run my fingers through the silken clouds. Were Mila and Gilly still under this vast blue sky, or had they already arrived at their coven somewhere out of reach?

We stopped for a midday meal when the sun was at its highest. The air was still crisp, but we sat in a patch of warm light, and I was as comfortable as I could have hoped for.

"What does one do for work in your city?" I prodded once we were back on the path north. Thain's enthusiasm was all well and good, but an outcast is the same no matter where she goes. Not everyone might feel the same way he did.

"Take up a trade, or don't. Work. Meet others. Travel the Wyldes. Laze around in bed, if that's what you think would fulfill you," he said, not looking back at me.

"Surely you jest," I scoffed.

"No one is going to dump you on the streets the moment we arrive. Not after finding you. It's been so long since we've seen a new face—" His head snapped slightly to the left, his eyes taking on the wicked glint of something that caught the scent of prey. "We aren't alone."

My shoulders tensed as I looked around. I couldn't hear a thing. I couldn't smell anything either. Thain pressed a finger to his lips and slid behind a thick pine tree. After a moment, he had completely disappeared from sight, and I was alone. I stood and continued to watch for movement around me.

"Are you truly leaving right now?" I hissed. "What are you leaving me to face?"

A branch snapped, and I whirled to face not a monster but something I was equally unprepared for: another fae.

If Thain was the dark blue of midnight, this one was the high noon sun in all its glory. He was elegant, far less feral than Thain. His skin was honey-gold and his hair a vibrant red, falling to his collarbone and framing his face. His matching red eyes danced over me, taking in my worn coat and disheveled hair, which I hadn't bothered to remove from my braids in days. He must have thought me a rabid thing with all the cuts and scrapes on my face and the caked-on dirt I had to be wearing. His own clothing was extravagant, with an embroidered shirt that tied at the sides and polished leather boots dripping with tooled designs. If there was an opposite to Thain's plain black tunic and pants, this was it. This golden fae wore the same curious obsidian ring on his thumb as Thain, and a gold bracelet.

"What in the Stars . . ." His voice was soft as a harp; a small crease between his eyebrows formed the only flaw on his smooth skin.

With a small, sharp breath, I stilled, but not before my fingers brushed the axe at my hip. Who was this? Why would Thain hide from him? How was he so incredibly different from Thain? Everyone I knew from Silver Lake dressed, looked, and spoke much the same. Was this a trick? An enemy?

"You aren't a human, are you?" His words were careful, caressing, and not a true question so much as a statement spoken softly enough to not frighten away a cornered animal. His approach was deliberately slow, his hands held in front of him with empty palms that showed no weapons, though the sheath that glinted at his gold-clad hip promised a blade. My lips sat in a firm line, and I held my ground. When he was only heartbeats away, a ferocious blue blur pounced on him.

"What in the hells?" snarled the new fae. "Thain, you bastard!"

Thain's deep laugh boomed through the thin air as they tumbled over each other, rolling several yards down the slope. Soon enough, teeth and claws flashed as they fought, and I backed up until I hit a tree. Eyes wide, I watched the ferocity of the scuffle, which ended almost as quickly as it had begun. This new red-and-gold fae pinned Thain to the ground, one hand on his throat.

"Yield!" the new fae demanded.

"Nice of you to come meet us, Eberon." Thain's expression eased back down into something closer to the stony face I'd gotten to know, ignoring the other fae's words.

"I was looking for *you*." The newcomer—Eberon—smacked Thain's shoulder with the back of a hand. "You spouted some nonsense about humans with iron on the move and then disappeared for days."

Thain moved his attention to me. "I found her in a lake."

My mouth dropped open as I glared at him. Of all the introductions he could have made, he'd chosen this? And while pinned beneath the golden fae as he said it.

"I apologize for this brute." Those red eyes fixed on me with a dignified gaze. "The rest of us know how to behave in polite company."

Thain moved in a flash, sitting up and throwing Eberon off with ease, and I wondered if he couldn't have beaten the other fae effortlessly to begin with. They stood, brushing off dirt and running fingers through their hair. One looked like a mildly inconvenienced cat, the other a preening bird.

"Wren, this is Eberon. It would appear he has abandoned our post," Thain said.

"Who abandoned it?" Eberon quipped. "Schula is keeping an eye on things while I came to track you down. And where could you possibly have found a young fae all the way out here?"

Thain shrugged, exasperating Eberon, who then turned to me.

"Wren, it is a pleasure to meet you." Eberon bowed low, sweeping his long arms gracefully and never taking his eyes off mine. "I am at your service, if you ever need to be rid of this oaf."

"Understood." I bowed back, a clumsy comparison to Eberon's. "It's nice to meet you as well, Eberon."

Thain's eyes played between us. "So, what do you think?"

The golden fae scented the air. "She's definitely from the Wyldes. What do we do, bring her back to Thanantholl?"

A trill of panic straightened my back, hoping that if Thain couldn't sense anything of the seal that no other fae would be able to either. "It's lovely to meet you. I appreciate the hospitality offered by Thain to see this outpost."

Eberon's brows shot up into his hairline, and he exchanged a look with Thain, who confirmed with a nod.

"How old is she?" Eberon whispered. "Is she not young?"

"I'm not a child." The insistence in my voice offered more offense than intended. "I've been an adult for years now. I'm twenty-five."

"No, no, of course not. I did not mean young as in a child, I meant young as in . . . How do I put this?" he murmured, turning to Thain. "Did you tell her nothing?"

Thain crossed his arms, shifting his weight to one foot. He was still taller than Eberon, but the way they spoke to each other was so comfortable, so familiar. The golden fae had been able to pull more expression out of Thain in a matter of minutes than I had in a matter of days.

"Well." Eberon recovered, turning back to me. "Then our hospitality you shall have. I could not fathom living outside the Wyldes. How anyone can breathe properly here is beyond me."

"Eberon . . ." Thain warned.

"That is," Eberon corrected himself, "a perfectly fine place to live, perfectly fine. For some. Anyway, I can't wait for you to experience the other side."

Thain sighed but said nothing further.

"What do you think, little bird?" Eberon winked at me.

I think you're a shameless flirt. My face surely relayed my feelings, because Thain's mouth turned up at the corner as Eberon faltered.

"Let's keep going, I want to be back well before it grows dark," Thain mused, patting Eberon's shoulder as he passed and leading us in the direction we had been heading.

We walked, but the usual quiet peace that had fallen between me and Thain was not what accompanied us now. Eberon liked to *talk.* He talked about the sights in Thanantholl, the Wyldes, the parties of the courts. Thain bristled at the mention of them.

"Don't mind him, he can't stand to have a good time," Eberon explained, a wicked smile on his lips. "The only time you'll find him at one of the court parties is when he's ordered to be there."

I didn't blame him. A room filled with that many people was bound to be uncomfortable.

Eberon quickly filled in the space with more chatter. The current fashions of the different courts, the horses he bred on his family estates. A whirlwind of information I couldn't possibly absorb. It was clear that Eberon enjoyed the luxuries of high society, and he had more money than I would see in several lifetimes in the mountains. But it was nice, in its own way. Not the endless chatter but to feel the conversation of someone who wasn't more worried about my ears than my thoughts.

It took another few hours to arrive. As we rose over another peak, further north than I'd ever been in my life, we spotted the outpost. I stayed silent as we approached a stone building that was as big as my cabin and Mila's combined. Smoke wafted lazily from the fat chimney. There was a clearly marked yard around the structure where no grass thrived.

At the far side of the yard was another fae, who must have been Schula. Dripping with sweat, she pounded on a wooden pole with her wrapped fists over and over again. Her practiced rhythms entranced me until I realized we were still walking and I'd fallen out of step.

"Here it is. I'm sure you're ready to sleep under a roof again," Thain said. Eberon led the way to the stone building, and Thain trailed behind.

The fae in the yard stopped. Her crystal eyes, such a pale blue they were almost as snow-white as the rest of her, snapped to me as we entered the yard. She stood unnaturally still, her long white hair tied in a braid that blew gently in the wind behind her. Her figure was curved, and she looked strong and stunning. Even in her plain tunic, she was the most beautiful being I had ever seen. The delicate points of her ears were tipped with silver filigree ornaments, and on her wrist hung a matching bangle, but she was otherwise unadorned. She didn't need it. Even standing safely between the two large fae, I thought she breathed with the capability of taking on anyone and anything she wished.

Now *that* was a presence I would have killed to have growing up.

I watched her with a combination of awe and a healthy dose of caution.

"Schula, this is Wren," Thain said. "I found her in one of the human settlements that was being raided by the ones from the west."

Embarrassment suddenly struck me. Bryn's coat was old and worn, my boots were scuffed and dirty from travel, and I hadn't been able to properly wash or braid my hair in days.

"What . . . how?" she whispered, leaning in to get a better look at me.

"I'm sure we will have a night of stories ahead of us," Eberon said. "From both sides."

Thain nodded, his usual response.

Schula's eyes softened as she spoke. "I can only imagine how one of us ended up past the borders. Welcome, Wren."

Swallowing the lump of nerves that had suddenly begun to plague me, I recovered enough of my voice to say, "I'm grateful for your hospitality. I can help around the outpost."

Schula's head snapped to Eberon. "What kind of offer did you extend that she thinks she needs to *work* for a bed?"

Eberon's palms shot up in front of him. "I made no such claims; ask Thain."

Thain had no visible response when Schula's glare landed on him. "I convinced her to come, that's as far as I got."

Schula closed her eyes, letting out a slow breath before meeting me with a smile. "I know exactly what you need, even if these two don't. Come, let me show you to the bath. Which you do *not* have to earn the right to use, by the way."

A *bath*.

I couldn't afford to be a nuisance here. I desperately craved answers that only the fae could provide. But possibly more importantly, I had to hide my back, and a bath sounded complicated for that.

"You don't have to trouble over me. I'm fine." I fumbled around my own tongue. "I can find a spring later."

"A *spring*? You most certainly are *not* fine. You are a guest here, that means we take care of your needs."

"You can take my room," Thain said. "Follow me."

"I'll start dinner," Eberon offered.

"I'll get the water ready," Schula said, and she followed Eberon to the outpost.

Thain, still carrying my things, walked toward the building. I followed before he left me behind.

When I stepped inside, he paused just long enough to let me look around.

The building was two levels with the second floor half open to the floor below. A set of stairs led up to a balcony with three doors. Below was a fourth door, a hearth with cushioned chairs around it, several shelves stocked with more things than I could keep track of, and a large table that commanded the room. Eberon was at a counter near the shelves, pulling vegetables from somewhere. Schula had disappeared into the door on the lower level. I stumbled trying to walk while looking at everything. If this was camping, I could only imagine what they called a house. I'd never been in a building this tall before, save for the giant public places in Sulls. You'd have to be a rich merchant to live in something this big.

Upstairs, Thain opened the middle door for me to find a large bed. I gaped at it. Bryn and I would have both fit easily, and he tended to toss and turn a lot when it got too warm outside. There was a mirror larger than a dinner plate and a private washbasin on a small desk. A window with real, clear glass was framed by red curtains, and sunlight curled up on the wool bedding. My lips parted as I drank in a luxury that I'd never been close enough to touch before.

"Thank you. I owe you another boon," I said. And I meant it. One day I truly wanted to repay Thain for everything he had done for me.

Thain took up much of the doorway as he leaned against it. His expression was softer, but there were still questions behind his eyes. He shrugged. "I hope it's comfortable enough."

A breath escaped, almost a laugh as I looked around the room. "You know this is nicer than my home, right?"

He moved his gaze away, instead choosing to look out the window across from the door. "No amount of nice things will replace home."

True. Very true. "Where will you sleep?"

"Eberon has plenty of room," he said. "Before I go, I wanted to make sure you're all right here. New places, new people."

Of course I knew what he meant, and I was able to meet him with a smile. "I can handle a little bit of overwhelm. They seem like they mean well."

That allowed him to relax his posture a bit. "The bath is downstairs. Schula should be done soon, by the time you've laid out your belongings." And with that, he left the room. Staring after him, I wondered if I'd ever be able to predict him. Moving to my things, I pulled out a clean set of clothes and spent time pulling out anything I wished to check for travel damage. After setting a few items around the room, I moved downstairs.

Schula was coming out of the door just as my feet hit the bottom step. She smiled and waved me over. Eberon looked over his shoulder from the kitchen, then went back to cooking.

"Let me show you the fixtures, in case you haven't used one of this kind before," Schula offered, urging me inside the room. Steam hit my face, and I cleared my throat.

"What about the others?" I asked. "I can be quick or wait my turn."

"I'm sending them to the creek," Schula said merrily. "They can rough it a little longer; we're on duty, after all. Duty that Thain left for me and Eb to handle, and then Eb left to be a nosy little prick, and I was here alone. This is their punishment."

"I didn't mean to be the cause of anyone leaving their post."

"No, no." Schula placed a hand on my shoulder. "They could have done this a dozen different ways, but Thain is a big boy. If he chooses to wander off without telling me or Eberon why, that's on him. They can handle a little bit of cold water in retaliation."

"Still . . ."

"Enjoy the bath," Schula insisted. "I don't know what Thain told you, and I don't know what you've been through, but believe me when I say you are about to have thousands of people overjoyed that you're with us. The least we can do is welcome you with a hot bath before figuring out what to do next."

What does that mean?

She didn't elaborate.

Schula pointed out how everything worked, and perfumed steam engulfed me the moment she closed the door. Rising from the floor like the bottom half of an enormous barrel was a tub of water. The concept in here was confusing. It was like a public bathhouse in the city, but the tub was only big enough for one or two people. The ladle for spilling water over my head and the slatted corner of the floor where excess water could escape was familiar enough, even if I had only done this a few times in Sulls. After you washed, you got into the tub, right? But there were shelves of soaps, oils, and salts that must all have been for special occasions: we never added expensive oils to the lard soaps back home unless it was for a holiday, a wedding, or a burning. Sometimes Mila would mix mint into hers to chase off the bugs, but that was about it.

After looking for far too long, I selected a soap that smelled of the wild mountain roses that bloomed in the summer. At least that I could come to terms with as something common, though the idea of using it to bathe with still seemed excessive.

The door had a lock, which I was thankful for. I undressed and laid my fresh clothing on a stool in the corner. After washing as carefully as I could with the soap, carefully maintaining its shape and setting it back on the shelf to dry, it was finally time to enjoy the hot water. A stepping block helped me over the edge to sink into the luxurious heat. High above the tub was a half-sized window that could be opened for air, but the wavy glass prevented seeing in or out otherwise.

The bath was unlike anything I had experienced. I usually washed in springs and ponds, but we had a small washtub at the cabin for the cold days of winter when we heated water to make it bearable. This was something else entirely.

I sank to my neck in the water and *moaned.* A shiver ran through me with the release of my screaming muscles. I let the heat seep into my bones for as long as I could until I had to pinch myself to keep from falling asleep. I let myself savor it for a few minutes before I had to drag myself out of this bliss.

Two wet drops fell from my face, landing in the smooth surface of the water. Swallowing through the lump in my throat, I scrubbed my face.

Standing in the tub, the cool air bit my now pink skin. Fingers and comb worked swiftly to regain my preferred braids, ensuring my ears were hidden once again.

Clean, but still juggling how this new situation made me feel, I dried off and brought my dirty clothes out with me. It was time once again to face the fae.

SIX
CLEAN

Something smelled amazing. Stew gurgled in the pot on the fire. Eberon was seasoning it while Thain and Schula sat at the table in hushed conversation. The former hunched over a steaming cup of something, and the latter tipped back on two legs of her chair with her feet propped on the stones by the fire. Thain turned his head to me just before the other two did.

Eberon grabbed a handful of dried green sprigs from a bowl. "Was everything satisfactory?"

"Very much so, yes."

"Wonderful," Eberon said. "The stew will be done soon."

"But take your time," Schula added.

I padded up the stairs and tucked my old clothes in the room I would be using. I shoved my boots back on and listened for the others. I could just hear them murmuring downstairs. If I was going to make an effort to get to know the fae, I might as well start now. Taking a deep breath, I crept out my door and went to join them.

"You look refreshed, little bird." Eberon smiled. "I can just picture you in the fashions of Thanantholl. We should take you straight to Pearl Street when we get there; I know all the best tailors."

"She can do what she wants," Thain grunted. I took a seat at the table as the golden fae stirred dinner over the fire.

"Of course, of course," he sang. "But can you blame me for wanting to show her the best our city has to offer? We haven't had a new fae in—"

Thain shook his head sharply, and Eberon cut off his words.

I cleared my throat, and they both turned their attention my way. "Exactly how much does lodging cost in the city? I have a little savings, and I can work after that."

"Nonsense." Eberon dismissed my words with a wave of his spoon. "You are a guest, and it would not put any of us out one bit to host you."

"If the king himself doesn't offer her hospitality the moment he sees her, she is under *my* protection," Thain insisted. "I have more than enough room."

"Easy, Thain," Eberon hissed, and I almost wanted to say the room grew warmer in that moment. "You do her no favors keeping her hidden from the court. I, at least, could prepare her for what's to come."

Thain stared daggers at Eberon. A breeze ruffled through the room, flickering the cooking fire.

"*Enough*." The sharp scolding of Schula, wearing only a thin white tunic that fell above her knees, her hair still damp from her earlier bath, pulled everyone's attention. After a long, tense breath, Eberon had the decency to turn back to his task, though Thain still looked annoyed.

"You can stay wherever you wish," Schula told me, pulling out a chair next to her at the table. "The offer for my own home stands as well. But I believe before we get much further, it's time we all sat down for a talk."

"Agreed," Eberon said, albeit somewhat reluctantly as he lifted a ladle and filled a bowl with a flourish. "But not on an empty stomach. And, with impeccable timing on my part, the food just so happens to be ready."

A steaming bowl was placed in front of me, along with a glass of sweet pink wine. It wasn't strong, and I drank deeply from it after seeing Schula do the same with her own glass. The stew was laced with herbs I had never encountered, as well as carrots, potatoes, some kind of root vegetable, and tomatoes.

"Decent," Schula announced, taking a spoonful as Thain snorted.

"I'll take that as a compliment, not that you barbarians know anything about good food." Eberon turned to me as he sat down with his own bowl. "I'm more interested in what Wren thinks."

I turned to my own meal and lifted a spoonful to my mouth. I nearly choked. We *never* had flavors this rich in the woods. Not even on the rare occasion when we'd gone to a city for specific goods had we eaten this well. There were more ingredients available south of the mountains, sure, but it didn't taste anything like *this*.

"It's *wonderful*," I said and immediately took another spoonful. Eberon smirked, throwing his golden arms open as though he were a performer receiving praise, and Thain rolled his eyes.

"You'll give him a bigger head than he already has," Thain said, leaning my way with a nod before turning to his bowl. "Anyone can cook with a pantry this well stocked."

"Could I?" I asked between mouthfuls. Ruby eyes snapped to me.

"There are markets in Thanantholl that have just about anything available. I can take you when we arrive," Thain offered. Smiling into my next spoonful, the first sparks of excitement seeped into me. Something to look forward to, something specific. We ate quietly for a moment, and I savored it. Dinner with three other people was almost as much as I could handle. What I would do in a large city, I wasn't sure yet.

"Any word from the fresh guards?" Thain asked, breaking the silence.

"They should be here in the next two days," Schula said. "Do either of you know who's got the next watch?"

"Galavan," Thain said.

Eberon grinned, not a happy expression, baring his full set of teeth. "Is that so? I'd love to show that Spring Court bastard what I thought of his remarks at the equinox."

"Then it's too bad I'm sending you ahead with Wren," Schula said. "I don't need you starting a fight between courts right now. Set up a camp in the usual place and *stay* there."

He sent a red glare her way but kept quiet. Whatever decision-making power she carried in the group seemed to go unquestioned. At the same time, the dynamic wasn't quite right. There was nothing obvious, and I couldn't really explain why I felt that way, but there was something not entirely authentic about it. Questions arose that weren't really my place to pry into.

This wasn't the first mention of the courts I had heard. Mila had told me once that the fae were ruled by factions of the seasons. I realized now that I had never bothered to ask more, but Thain and Eberon had both mentioned these courts, and it seemed like something I was going to have to deal with.

"So, you all aren't Spring Court? Which court are you?" I asked, trying to break the tension.

"We serve the Autumn Court's King Baeleon," Thain said.

Schula scraped the bottom of her bowl with her spoon. "The courts take turns watching the borders; it just so happens we were the lucky ones to be here to meet you."

"What does this watch duty entail? Is it all right for you all to be here at once?"

"Centuries ago, wards were put in place to alert us of anything crossing into the Wyldes that shouldn't be," Eberon explained. "Or out of it, I suppose. A few of us are always at this post to quickly respond to alerts from those wards, but we really don't need to walk the borders much anymore. It's more of a formality these days, but once in a long while something interesting might happen."

It occurred to me to ask about the wraith that had clearly crossed into human territory, but a tremor ran down my spine at the thought of the grotesque creature, and I decided I didn't want to know more. Not yet. "What happens to the fae that aren't with one of the courts?"

"Almost none of the fae live outside the courts," Schula said. "The ones that do are powerful, or foolish. To live in one of the realms is to be of that court. The Unclaimed Wyldes are for the shunned, dangerous, or mad."

"Oh." I was no court fae, so what would that mean for me?

"You are welcome to stay with us until you find the right place," Eberon added. "Baeleon will almost certainly command that you visit all the courts; the collective royals would have a fit otherwise. However, the final choice will be yours."

For creatures from the Wyldes, beings I had been taught through stories would chase you down and eat you for amusement, these fae seemed very concerned with allowing me to make my own choices.

"Could I not simply choose your court and be done with it?" I asked.

"While that would make us quite happy, it doesn't work that way. When you are amongst your court, you will *feel* it. It will be right," Thain said.

"Hells, half of the southern lords have that smear of freckles," Eberon added, looking at my speckled cheeks. "Perhaps you belong in the Summer Lands."

"I don't know," Schula said, "those smoky gray eyes aren't uncommon for the Autumn Court either."

"Do looks matter that much?" I could see how Eberon seemed the part of autumn, red and golden and smelling of spices by the hearth. And *maybe* Thain could be an autumn night sky, a wind through the trees and smelling of campfire. But Schula was ice and cold and winter incarnate.

"I'm a special case." Schula seemed to read my mind. "Some of us have become misplaced over the years."

"Well, none of this is a matter for tonight," Eberon said finally. "Don't let it worry you, little bird. No matter what, you will have friends in Thanantholl."

"We'll have several nights of camping before we reach the Autumn Lands," Thain said. "When we get to Thanantholl, we'll introduce you to King Baeleon."

My body stilled. "Right away?"

"I suppose we could delay it a day," Eberon told Thain. "Give proper reports first. You know Baeleon, he'll want some flourish to it."

"Why do I need to be introduced at all?" I asked. "I'm not even wholly a fae creature, nothing significant in the Wyldes. Surely, we don't need to bother a king."

The room grew quiet as Schula and Eberon scrutinized Thain under matching scowls. Thain stared ahead, ignoring them.

"You didn't tell her." Schula shot an accusatory glance at Thain. "That whole trip through the mountains, and you never explained? Why you were so excited? Why we welcomed a stranger while we're on a job for the king? It's a wonder you got her to follow you at all!"

"While I agree completely, this isn't the time, Schula." Eberon sighed then composed himself before turning to me. "Wren, there are certain factors that you haven't been enlightened about that make your presence . . . significant."

He exchanged looks with the other fae. "Some years ago, there was a plague in the Wyldes. It spread for seven terrible years. The older fae grew sick but recovered easily."

"The younger ones did not," Schula finished with a somber tone.

Eberon looked out the window, Thain at the floor. Schula took a breath and folded her hands on the table. "Our youth are dead. All of them. Anyone younger than fifty was wiped out within days of the sickness touching them. A few of the older ones survived, but almost none of our fae born in the last century are left to us."

Pulling in a sharp breath, I asked, "How many?"

"Hundreds. And many suspect magic in the plague. Foul play," Schula added, her tone just louder than the crackle of the fire. "Faelings aren't born so easily. Not like humans. We've been lucky to see a dozen born across all four courts in the last decade. Well, eleven and one on the way in the Summer Court."

"Nothing like that happened in the mountains." I straightened my back as the seal burned.

"That is the curiosity, isn't it?" Eberon murmured. "I can only assume it's because you were within the human lands. Or perhaps it had something to do with your human blood. Regardless, you, little bird, are a miracle."

The whole world tilted, and my breaths came in shallow beats. No wonder Thain had been so bewildered to find me. It explained everything. Maybe even my displacement to the mountainside, if my birth parents had died of illness. It didn't explain my ears, or the seal, but it was a lot more than I'd had until now. There weren't any survivors to this tragedy they had gone through as a society, except for me.

"I'm sorry to hear of the losses." There was no way to wrap my head around the numbers I had been given. Hundreds dead. The only number I could grasp easily was the twelve babies born in one year at Silver Lake. It seemed so few. Some of the homesteads around the forest had more children than that, but not by much. That would be like losing all the people of Silver Lake that day in the raid. Perhaps we would have, if Thain hadn't interfered. The number was just so . . . so . . .

"I didn't mean to keep anything from you," Thain finally spoke. "I never wanted to make you decide anything; it had to be your choice. If I'd told you all this, it might have forced your decision."

Schula reached out to place a cool hand over mine, her fingers wrapping gently around my balled fist on the table. "And no matter what court you fit with, we will support you. This is not about political games or acquisition of numbers. This is an entire people finding one of their own."

And there it was. The acceptance Thain had offered that I hadn't wholly absorbed or even understood until now. Words weren't coming to me; I couldn't force them through my tightened throat even if they had. Eberon offered a gentle smile as he lifted my bowl from the table. Thain and Schula stood at the same time and began cleaning up as well. My offer of help was politely refused, which left me uncomfortably without a task.

"Go," Schula said, wiping her hands on a towel at the counter. "Take all the time you need for yourself. I'll bring up a cup of tea later."

Nodding, I followed her advice and moved up the stairs while they busied themselves.

The bed was soft, the sheets cool to the touch. I took off my boots and pants and slid between the layers. As I lay on the down pillow, it smelled of maple. I cried again for Bryn. I knew he would want me moving on, but I couldn't help it. Dry of tears and exhausted, I slept deeper than I had in days.

Panic jarred me awake; the wraith still haunted my nights. Tonight, it had hunted me down and killed all the people I knew in horrific ways. Even though the men of the mountains had been cruel, they didn't deserve the fates I dreamed about.

I sat up in bed and wiped the sweat from my face. My stomach churned as I felt my legs swinging over the edge and running for the door. Keeping my steps light, I opened my door and was down the stairs in a heartbeat. Running outside, I threw up at the edge of the yard, still wearing nothing but a tunic and stockings.

Panting, I wiped my mouth and slumped to the ground. Sweat

glued my shirt to my back. Dew had gathered on what grass was brave enough to grow in the yard, turning to frost and poking my bare legs. My stomach continued to heave long after it was empty. When I had cooled down, I pulled myself off the ground and stumbled back to the warmth of the stone outpost.

The bolt on the door slid smoothly into place. The fire was low, so I put another log on it so it wouldn't go out before morning and climbed the stairs toward my bed, but something stopped me. My ears twitched. Mila *had* said to make use of them. I paused at the top step with my head tilted.

". . . probably connected to the wraith we saw." Thain's voice crept from under the door to Eberon's room.

"Who would be undoing the wards like that? Who *could* undo them?" Eberon sounded tired, and not because of the late hour.

"It may not be intentional. It could simply be from age. The witches created it, and for all we know it's meant to fail without them." Thain grunted. "Not that they would come back now."

His words shocked me, and the disgruntled tone he used at the mention of witches froze me in place. The witches had made this ward around the Wyldes? Mila had never mentioned it. Was it from before her time? But they were known to document everything.

"I'm going to walk the perimeter. Something doesn't feel right tonight." The floor creaked, and I slipped to my open door just as a shirtless Thain emerged. His shaggy hair was loose, and his silver eyes shone in the night. But no matter how quietly, how quickly I'd slipped away, he still caught me in the doorway before he passed by.

His brows knitted as he spotted me. "Is everything all right?"

"Couldn't sleep," I said, not a lie. His shoulders lowered a fraction as his tension eased.

"Do you need anything?" His eyes slid to my bare thighs and immediately back up to my face. "Is it too warm tonight? Do you need a thinner blanket?"

"No, I'll be fine." I tugged the hem of my tunic down further, an embarrassment I'd never felt before creeping across my cheeks in a flash of warmth. "I think I'll be all right now, I just needed air."

Before he could say more, I slid through my door and closed it tight. I covered myself with the bedding as soon as I could and buried my heated face in the pillow. Soft footsteps continued down the hall to the stairs, and I sighed. Then I scowled at myself. I'd played naked in streams as a child; I'd danced in only a nightshirt with Mila and sometimes other visiting witches on the solstice. It was just a body, everyone had one, and there were bigger things to worry about than Thain seeing my legs. And if it wasn't a sudden bout of modesty that had gotten me flustered, that meant it was Thain.

I rolled over in bed, tossed that line of thought aside, and contemplated what I had overheard instead.

These wards that were so important to the Wyldes. If someone was destroying them, it was none of my concern. If that sort of thing couldn't be left to these fae soldiers, who could it be left to? My attention roamed the room, landing on the now-cold mug of tea that Schula had promised to bring up after dinner. I already cared about these people; their worries would be my worries. If I wanted to keep up with them, the next thing I needed to focus on would be learning as much as I could about the Wyldes. Gray pre-dawn light was the last thing I saw before sleep finally found me again.

SEVEN
A PURPOSE

Nobody else was in the common spaces of the outpost when I awoke. Someone had built up the fire, but there were no other signs of activity. A light rain pattered on the roof as I decided on some distraction to fill my time.

Opening the door revealed an icing of fog that clung to the valleys between round mountain peaks. Bright drops from the sky misted my face as I made my way to the trees.

There were large branches that hadn't taken in much water yet, and more dead branches in the trees I could reach to cut as well. The rhythm of the axe was music to me, and I hummed one of the old mountain tunes Bryn would sing as we worked. Work felt good, right. The fae were kind but made me feel as though I were a novelty. Or perhaps it was my own discomfort at attention that made me feel that way. Regardless, I needed a task, and the forest always provided me something to do. The misty rain didn't stop until I had tied my bundle and started the walk back.

Fog still clung to the edges of the mountains, but the yard was clear and sunny. Even from a distance, I could see Schula at her post again. She was striking it with cloth-wrapped fist and booted foot in precise jabs. Her strength was enviable and her movements graceful. All three of them were like that, and I had to sigh that the human parts of me had robbed me of the same.

The rough handle of my axe weighed heavy in my hand. It had done nothing against Thain. It would do nothing against any of them. Not that

I thought I needed it here, with them, but the wraith was a thornbush prickling at the edge of my mind.

Schula nodded as I entered the yard before continuing her exercise. Her chest heaved, pulling air through her with practiced ease at the same arc of motion each time. Sweat glistened on her pale skin. Her efforts were as plain as day, and I scolded myself for assuming any of it was easy. Dropping both the bundle of wood and my lingering fears at the side of the yard, I headed toward the icy-white fae. It was time to do something about these feelings.

A corner of sturdy fencing made for a good perch where I could watch Schula while resting my aches. She didn't pause for me; she just continued in a trance. Everything was a pattern. Left hand, right hand, left foot, right foot. Again. Now reverse the order. Now again. I watched for some time, mesmerized by her movements.

In a heartbeat, so quickly I didn't register at first, she stopped. The only motion that remained was the rise and fall of her chest, hungry for air. She walked over to a waterskin hanging on a fence post. She turned and settled her icy eyes on me, sending a chill down my spine. So friendly, so welcoming, but still so foreign a sight. "Did you need me for something?"

"I didn't mean to disturb you," I said.

"Nearly done anyway," she panted, reaching for the waterskin and drinking deeply.

Shrugging, I dove right into the question. "Could you teach me how to do that?"

She turned back to look at where she had been, hanging the waterskin back up absently. "How to hit a wooden pole in the ground?"

My mouth formed a tight line, wondering if I had said or done something stupid. But her eyes danced with mischief, and I realized she was teasing me. Just as Bryn might have, except Bryn had the subtlety of a rockslide.

"Yes, I could show you the basics. Why the interest?"

"When Thain caught up to me, we encountered something monstrous," I said.

Schula frowned. "He did mention a wraith," she murmured.

"We came out of it unscathed, but only due to Thain. If I had been alone with it, I wouldn't have been so lucky."

"You want to protect yourself." She scanned me with a measured concentration: arms, shoulders, a glance at the wood I'd brought, the axe at my side.

"Not that Thain isn't capable," I started, "but the only one I can guarantee to be with me at all times is me."

"Well put." She closed the gap in a few steps. "I'd be happy to show you a few things. I train my body, but not in weapons. A solid body is the foundation of any form of self-defense, and an excellent place to start. If you would like to go beyond that . . ." She shrugged. "You look pretty comfortable with that axe."

"This isn't the same, I'm sure." My hand fell to the familiar handle. "Nothing so grand as a soldier's tools."

"A soldier's tools?" Schula mused. "The fae tend to rely on the magic of the Wyldes, but some magics don't suit every situation. You've probably noticed Thain can call wind, while Eberon can call fire. But wind can't do everything, and in some situations fire would do more harm than good. Some, Thain and myself included, would rely on our bodies for combat. Others, like Eberon, use swords and such. But a stick in Eberon's hand is better than a sword in the hands of the untrained. It isn't the tools as much as the person using them, and I think you'd be more formidable than you expect, given a few lessons. But I can at least start you off with your body."

"I would love to learn from you," I said. "If you have time."

"Thain told us about you trying to hit the wraith with your axe." Schula smiled, arms crossed. "That's some bravery, and I can't grow that in a person. That's all you. I can't promise you'll be as strong as a full-blooded fae, but I can at least teach you enough to get by. And that inner strength is what will help you through your training, if you're serious about it."

"I'll work as hard as I need to," I promised.

"That's unexpected." I jumped at Thain's voice to the side, throwing a hand over my pounding heart.

"You big oaf," Schula scolded. "You've frightened her right out of her skin."

Cool, silver eyes moved between us. "I didn't mean to startle you," he said.

A slow breath hissed out of me, and I dropped my hand. "I'll be fine. Apparently, this is something I need to get used to."

"Did you find anything on the wards?" Schula asked quietly.

"No, nothing. I can't even see where the wards are failing, but things are definitely slipping through." Thain scratched his neck. "I can't find the problem, so our next step is to report it."

"What exactly are these wards?" I asked cautiously, remembering last night.

"Witching magic," Schula explained. "There was a time in which the witches were in the Wyldes, and a barrier of sorts was constructed to prevent some of the darker things of our lands from seeping into the human territories. The details aren't as clear as they once were, given how long ago this was, but the wards have remained intact in their absence."

"Until now," Thain finished. "If there is a connection to the witches, we'll need to find out."

There isn't, is there? But Mila had no obligation to tell me her business. She'd taught me so many things, but there had been no reason to teach the ways of her sisterhood to me. Still, she lived her life in quiet, doing good for the mountain and the people. She did nothing maliciously. Right?

Schula sighed then turned to me. "We start tomorrow. I'm going to go clean up, and you should get another day with three full meals and plenty of sleep. You'll need it."

Even covered in sweat and tired as she must have been from her routine, Schula's stride was firm and alert as she retreated to the warm outpost. She overflowed with confidence, and it showed in her every movement. I wanted that. Mother's grace, I wanted that. Maybe if I were more like Schula I wouldn't worry so much about what in the Wyldes could kill me.

Thain shifted his weight next to me, a subtle reminder that he was still here. "For what it's worth, you would do well with an axe made for fighting. It would be a familiar weight in your hand, and I know you've built up the right muscles for it. Schula's a good teacher; she will start you off right. Eberon knows much about weaponry."

"Maybe," was all I managed, but I'd never been ready to brawl with anyone before. The few times I'd tried after being teased by village boys, Bryn had stepped in quickly. At the time, it would have done more harm to the tolerance everyone had maintained toward something from the Wyldes living nearby. If I'd started sending their sons home with bruises, things would have been far worse.

And yet, those skills might have been helpful if I'd had them when I needed them. Hopefully Schula could set me on the right path.

Schula was a demon. Another horror of the Wyldes, sent to torment me under the guise of helping. My morning had started with three quick raps to my door, followed by shoving strange clothing in my arms and pulling me outside to the yard. She had to help me tie the wrappings that wound around the middle of the tunic, and she told me their purpose was to help keep loose fabric out of the way while working. Apparently, many garments in Thanantholl had this feature, so I did my best to watch how she tied them.

Once I was dressed to her standards, she walked around me in silent observation.

"We'll straighten your posture," she listed out loud. "Good structure in your arms, though you're still so sleight. You'll need to be able to judge your weight against your opponent's, that's a key part of what I have to teach you."

After a list of assessments, she stopped before me and clasped her hands together. "Let's stretch you out." She grinned, her sharp teeth lending a sinister aura to her smile.

For the rest of the morning, Schula contorted my body. She pulled and pushed. She made me move in ways I never had before. I didn't so much as look at the pole I had asked to hit yesterday; my arms probably would have fallen off if I'd tried. Schula, on the other hand, moved like water. She demonstrated every stretch, every pose that she asked me to do, and she made it look as simple as breathing. By the time we were done, even breathing wasn't a simple task.

"I want you to take a bath, and I want you to stay in there for as long as you can stand it. Soak those muscles so we can do this again tomorrow, all right? I'll see you at lunch."

"Tomorrow?" I groaned. "That is . . . I appreciate everything you're doing for me. Truly."

Schula laughed, patting my shoulder as I winced, and led me inside.

Eberon and Thain sat at the table, smiling as I dragged my body through the main room. I wanted to make a rude gesture, but I was too tired. I heard Schula close her door upstairs as I entered the bathroom below.

The bath was more marvelous than it had been the last time I'd used it. Empty and scrubbed, it took a while to fill the tub, which I didn't mind as it gave me plenty of time to slowly scrub out the aches with the rose soap, though I did chance a smell and a swipe with a rich-scented, earthy soap that made me sneeze. Cleaned, and with the hot water almost full, I eased into the water with a groan. Once it finally covered me, I turned the faucet off and laid my head back. In the warm tub, everything relaxed fully after the morning of movement. It took only a little time for me to doze off.

EIGHT
AN OLD FRIEND

Tapping snapped me awake. It was faint but constant. The water sloshed around me as I stood. It was only warm; I must have been out for a while. I looked to the door, but the tapping wasn't coming from that direction. Over the tub, near the ceiling, something black tapped on the window.

There was nothing near me that could function as a weapon, and I cursed at myself for not having an axe with me, bath or not. Bracing myself, I stood in the side of the tub under the window.

Tap. Tap. Tap.

With a bar of soap in each fist, I was ready to throw whatever I could reach if need be. Holding my breath, I unlatched the window. The window fell halfway open, a chain catching it before it could hit the wall. A large black bird scrambled through and flapped down to the edge of the tub in a flurry of feathers and claws. In my panic to get out of the way, I dropped both bars of soap and sloshed half the water out of the tub.

When all was settled, I blinked. A giant wet, black bird was perched on the tub in front of me, making an annoyed clicking sound.

"Puko?" I stared at the ancient bird that never left Mila's shoulder.

He cawed loudly and looked at me with his one clear eye.

"Wren?" Eberon's muffled voice called through the door. "Is everything all ri—Where is this water coming from?"

"I'm fine! Don't come in. Everything is fine, and I'll clean it up."

A moment later, a firm knock sounded on the door.

"Wren, it's Thain," he boomed. "We need to know you're all right, will you let Schula in?"

My eyes darted to the door; in my exhaustion, I hadn't locked it. I cursed at myself. Puko seemed to agree.

Caw.

"Oh, shut up," I hissed.

"Is that a *bird*?" Eberon said, muffled by the door. I tried to grab Puko, taking him by surprise, and he squawked as I lifted him toward the open window. He struggled, not willing to leave. I was twisted, half climbing out of the bath to reach higher, when the door opened.

"*Bear shit*," I hissed.

"What is happening in here?" Schula shut the door behind her and stared. My back was exposed, seal and all. A wet, half-blind raven was clawing and pecking at my arms as I attempted to stuff him through a window. In a panic, I whirled around and slipped, dunking myself and Puko into the tub. I shot out again and gasped for breath. Water sloshed over the side, spraying Schula and flooding the bathroom even more.

We stared at each other for a moment. A *long* moment. She looked between me, dripping wet with hair clinging in odd clumps around my face and shoulders, and the giant black bird in my arms, still as a statue and staring at her with his good eye and beak open, then she slid out the door without a word.

I sank in the tub and let Puko free himself to perch indignantly on the side again. He ruffled all the water he could off his back and began preening himself. This was it. Whatever reaction this might earn me was coming. Mila had been certain it was a witch seal, and after Thain's earlier words, I wasn't confident this would end well. Best case scenario, they would send me away. Worst case . . . What was the worst case? My head went to a place I'd been in many times before, of staring, mockery, sneering, and shunning. Being offered the worst produce at market, having doors and windows closed as I passed by. And I'd seen in many eyes that they wanted to do far worse than that. My head swam to a darker place, where the threat of something violent lurked in my future.

A soft knock came a moment later, and it might as well have been a blow to my chest as I froze. This would be it, whatever was to come.

"It's Schula. I'm coming in." She entered with an armful of fabric, my sack, and two large towels.

Ice stabbed through my heart looking at the pile in her arms. So, this was how it would end. I would be asked to take my things and go. Any promise of a place with peace was too much for me to hope for, and I was a fool.

"Schula," I croaked, "I'm sorry. I'll go as soon I can."

"Go?" Lifting the sack, she pulled out one of my spare tunics. "I'm here with your clothes."

Staring at the worn fabric in her hand, then down at the clean towels, then back to the white fae before me, I was at a loss. "You mean for me to go . . . after I dress?"

Schula sighed, setting the items down on the stool and pulling one towel free. "You're not being sent away. I will admit this is . . ." She scrunched up her nose. "Complicated. But let's get you dressed first."

She held up a towel for me, and I took it, wrapping myself in it as I left the tub. She pointed at the stool, a silent order to sit, and then began combing my hair. I hissed as the teeth hit the scar tissue on my ears. She paused, and I let her draw back my wet locks.

Shame and embarrassment bubbled up in me as she stared silently, first at one side of my head and then the other.

"Thain told us as much," she offered softly. "I'll be more careful from now on."

And that was it. She combed my hair and let me braid it, all in silence with no damning weight in her gaze. She drained the tub and handed me fresh clothes. Then, with my towel, she mopped up the floor while I dressed.

"This is for the bird. If it will let you." She handed me the other towel.

"He will," I said. Puko, to his credit, sat still while I dried him off. He fluffed out his feathers when I was done, inspecting himself with his good eye.

"I'd like to talk to you upstairs, please," she said, hanging up the towels on a bar meant to air them out. "I want to clarify a few things."

"Have you told the others about the marks?" I whispered.

Schula pulled her lips between her teeth, eyeing the door. "No, but I should."

"Please!" I still held Puko in my arms, but even the bird seemed to sense it was time to keep quiet. "I'll tell you everything, I swear."

The snowy fae blew a huff of stress and pressed a hand to her forehead. "Let's go upstairs. I'm not promising anything yet, but let me at least try to wrap my head around what's happening here."

"Thank you," I said, piling one more favor on my shoulders. Unless what Thain said was true and it was no longer a practice. Either way, I owed Schula for this moment.

She gave me a grim nod and went out the door first to shoo the others away. They weren't in sight when I left the bathroom, and she led me upstairs.

We arrived in the room, and Puko wrestled himself out of my arms to perch by the window, settling his good eye on Schula as she sat on my bed. She patted the blankets next to her for me to join her. My gut twisted, and everything felt cold despite the hot bath I'd just left. This was a moment that would've had me chased out of Silver Lake by humans, and I didn't know what the fae would do. Their finding out might just cost me the new place I thought I'd found.

"So," she started, "I saw witch markings on your back." I grimaced. Puko chirped, clicking his beak. "And I would love to hear the story behind that. You smell of the Wyldes, so why the witching marks?"

"They found me with them. As a baby, I mean. This mark isn't something I put on myself, but just as you said, it's witchcraft all the same. This will cause a problem, won't it? Thain said they aren't welcome."

Schula hummed. "You aren't wrong. It's certainly complicated. And the marks haven't done anything to anyone else?"

"No," I answered. "It only affects me." I gave her everything I knew about the seal, telling her about Mila and touching briefly on the time we'd tried to remove it only to be met with a backlash of fire that still haunted me. Keeping it sealed up was for the best.

Schula had stood and started pacing slowly, back and forth between the door and the window while I spoke. My stomach churned watching her, watching my fate in measured steps as she came to whatever conclusion she was going to find.

"Okay," she said, stopping before me. "I'm not going to say anything. We can pretend I was helping you with the bird over there. But these markings, you need to deal with them eventually. Agreed?"

"*Thank you.*" I could have melted into the bed. "But do I really need to remove it? It's done the job for twenty-five years now."

"Yes, you must. It's keeping a part of you from yourself. Besides, questions will arise when you don't show signs of magic." Schula offered a tight smile. "I'm sure there are people in your life that have already tried to make you feel bad for things about you that aren't in your control. I can see that this is another one of those things, and no matter how others will view you for those marks on your back, I will not judge you."

Puko ruffled his feathers, shaking out a few more drops of water as he groomed himself. She looked over at the raven with tired eyes. "Now, about this bird."

The breath whistled out of me, the tension deflating in my rigid shoulders. Good. This was good. The seal was as much a part of me as my hands or my eyes. It was just . . . there. Keeping something at bay. Something I couldn't quite explain. Something wrong, something I didn't want to be and didn't want to let out.

Now, Puko I could explain. Sort of.

"Puko belongs to a friend, and it appears he followed me north." I looked over at the bird in my window. "He's harmless."

"The witch?" Schula watched Puko as he preened.

"Yes." At this point, I owed her complete honesty, and I remembered some of Mila's last words to me: *I will always watch out for you as best I can.* "I think Puko is here to look after me, actually."

"I see." Her eyes slid smoothly from the window back to me. "As long as he can't do any witchery himself."

"No, no," I assured her. "Even Mila said as much."

She nodded. "Can I ask about . . ." She touched her own ears.

Shrinking in on myself, just a little, I took a moment to meet her eyes.

"Like the seal, I was found like this. We aren't sure who did it or why I was left there, but the most likely story is because of what I am."

Her eyes darkened. "Is that so?"

"As far as I've been told. Bryn—my father, that is—found me as a newborn. He lived outside of the village but not far from Mila. Between the two of them, they got together what would be needed to take care of a baby." Swallowing, I closed my eyes, abruptly cutting off the rambling boiling over as I noticed. I'd never had anyone to talk to about it before. Everyone else in my life had already heard the story a dozen times over before I could even walk. Whispered around tables, muttered by strangers as my small hand was wrapped in a much larger hand's warmth while we strolled down the market lane. Even any visiting witches were informed by Mila so they would not make an unintended comment about me. I didn't know if Mila or Bryn knew that I was aware, but I was. Sometimes I hated it, other times I appreciated it. But regardless of how I'd felt about it before, I was now in strange new territory in which I had to be the one to explain.

Cool fingers wrapped around the fist in my lap, and my eyes popped open. "I'm sorry, Wren. For all you went through. But I promise I'm here for you now. We're here for you. And I know it takes time to build trust, so take your time. I want you to know you have someone to talk to, no matter what." Schula draped her arms around me in a loose hug that I could have brushed off if I didn't like it. "We will find you a place to call home."

Words caught in my throat. I could feel the tears trying to rise, but I pushed them down. Schula stroked the back of my head, something Bryn would do when I was a small girl. She didn't pull away again until my breathing steadied.

"Now, you're probably hungry. You can come downstairs and be subjected to the males, or I can bring you a plate and you can take a nap," Schula offered, standing and stretching.

"I think I would like to eat from the food I brought, just one more time." I looked at the pile on the desk. "Can we add what I have here to the stores for this outpost? I want to contribute, and I need to let it go."

"Of course." She smiled and helped me pick out a meal. Once I had settled on smoked ham, the last apple, and a small round of soft goat cheese, Schula took what was left downstairs. The room was big and empty without her.

I ate my lunch, stroked Puko's feathers, and slept.

To their credit, Thain and Eberon welcomed Puko and didn't ask any questions about what had happened in the bath. Schula piled strips of venison and spicy herbed potatoes on the table for dinner. She didn't say anything while the others made introductions, but she did give the old raven a sliver of uncooked meat. I took him to the door and let him fly off to find food and do whatever bird business he might have.

"The next patrol will be here tomorrow," Thain said, sitting down at the table. "Tonight we pack, and in the morning Eberon can take Wren to set up camp."

"Schula and Thain will meet us tomorrow once they hand over the patrol." Eberon spooned potatoes on my plate. "We don't need to go at a hard pace, and I can show you a first glimpse of the Wyldes."

"Am I the cause of you splitting up for the day?" I asked, putting down my fork. "I don't want to cause any changes for anyone."

Schula and Thain exchanged a look, then she folded her hands under her chin. "We thought you'd rather keep your entrance low-key. The next patrol is rather boisterous and would almost certainly send the latest gossip back home, possibly before we even reach Thanantholl. This way, you can move in peace as you learn a little bit more about the lands as we travel through them."

It felt as though all warmth drained from my face. "Yes, that. That one, please."

Eberon chuckled, spooning his own potatoes while Schula managed to hide a smile behind her next bite.

"How early do we leave?" I asked, trying a potato, my eyes popping wide at the new flavors.

"Right after you and I stretch just a little bit." Schula grinned. "Unless you no longer want to, in which case I understand."

"Stretching is code for torture," I muttered, and Eberon snorted into his tea. Clearing my throat, I said, "I would be delighted."

"Perfect." Schula laughed. "Might as well get it in before we arrive in Thanantholl. There will be excitement over your arrival, and the crown will have a big fuss that will interrupt our routine, I'm sure." More eyes would be on me, powerful eyes, but if that was what I had to endure to enter the Wyldes, so be it.

"I'll meet your king, and whatever others I must."

Thain inclined his head. "We want nothing more than to welcome you home. We all lost someone in that plague, and it will do everyone good to see someone who survived it."

One could only hope that would be true, because jealousy was an ugly thing, and surely the fae weren't completely immune to it. I wondered who Thain had lost to the plague but kept my questions to myself. The rest of the evening was spent avoiding the topic of the sickness and readying for tomorrow's journey.

NINE
THE WYLDES

Eberon led the way through the mountains. Puko flew overhead or sat on my shoulder as we walked. The unexpected weight of him dropping onto my frame nearly had me toppling over more than once in surprise, but his new habit of using me as a perch, as he once had with Mila, became easier as we traveled. Out of concern for Bryn's coat, I did wind a rope around my shoulder so Puko's talons couldn't cause any real damage to the weathered leather. My sled had been abandoned at the outpost, and I carried most of my belongings on my back and an axe on each hip. With the food stores gone and the thick bear pelt going with Thain, it wasn't too heavy. The rises and dips of the mountainside were not foreign to me; the ancient, rolling shapes filled with morning mist and afternoon sun had always been a part of my home. But as we traversed north and Silver Lake grew more distant, the feeling of the unknown prickled down my arms.

When we sank into thicker woods down the slope, I had a hard time keeping up. Eberon, for all his fine clothes and neat hair, was as much a part of the mountains as the towering pines were. He didn't stumble, he avoided every branch, and he picked his way through the trees as easily as if a road was laid out before him. If that was what it meant to be full fae, I had to admit I was a little jealous.

"Come here, little bird. I want to show you something." Eberon held a branch out of my way so I could stand next to him. Puko landed on my shoulder as I drew even with the fae, and I grunted with the unexpected weight of the huge bird. I looked up to scold him, but as my eyes hit the view below us, I lost my breath.

A winding valley, greener than the mountains in full summer bloom, swept below us like lush carpet. A crystal river cut through the hills and poured into delicate springs dotting fields full of dancing willows and rich with wild roses. Creatures I had no knowledge of grazed on the hillside, unaffected by the beauty around them. It could have been a painting. I couldn't believe it even seeing it with my own eyes.

"Charming, isn't it?" Eberon spoke beside me, but I still couldn't tear my gaze from the valley.

"This is the Wyldes?" I breathed.

"It is. Once you set foot in it, you feel its pull every time you leave," he said, his tone filled with sentiment.

This wasn't our destination; they'd already explained the travel ahead to me. Still, if the rest of the Wyldes was this beautiful, I would be in awe the entire way. "We're still in the southern borders of the Summer Lands, quite a bit of travel from home. Here it will remain summer for as long as there is a fae seated on the Summer Throne."

Puko made a croaking, chirping mess of notes in my ear, and I shooed him away until he took flight. Hungry for the sights before me, I had to pull my eyes from one to the next with deliberate effort.

"We'll be to camp in a couple hours," Eberon said, looking up at the position of the sun. "Not much more than that." Puko cawed his contentment overhead.

The twisting hike down the end of the mountainside was all the harder knowing what I was so close to. Maybe some fae part of me longed for it too. Some part that hadn't started to awaken until I'd met Thain and the wraith. When sprigs of bright green began peeking out of the leaves on the ground, my heart skipped a beat.

"We won't have the luxury of hot water again until we reach the city, but if you'd like to take a dip in one of the springs near the camp, you are more than welcome to. The current is slow and harmless, and there aren't any creatures to worry about in this part of the Wyldes," Eberon offered. "Once we cross into the Unclaimed Wyldes, that will no longer be the case."

I honestly couldn't have cared less if I had hot water so easily accessed ever again if it meant exploring a place like this for all my days. "I want to see everything."

Eberon's laugh crackled like a bonfire. "If the Summer Court impresses you, I cannot wait to see you set foot in the splendor of Autumn."

"Are you sure your opinion isn't biased?" I asked. I was ready to dance and sing and *live* again. I still mourned Bryn, and some part of me knew I always would, but something about the Wyldes touched me to the core. If I could ever find a home again, it would be here. The seal on my back was alive with the power of this place, and a mild burning like I had sat too close to the fire warmed the strange lines I knew ran down my spine.

The last pine crossed my vision, and the emerald fields opened up. Eberon held back and watched my face as I whirled around, trying to look at everything at once. "Do you see that small cliff under the oak tree? That's where I'll be setting up camp. I suggest you enjoy yourself for a while until the others arrive, release some of that energy. It feels as though you're about to burst with magic."

I stopped. My seal crackled to life on my back. Would the very nature of this place open me up like a box of fireworks? Mila had never said anything about the Wyldes, but why would she ever have assumed I'd come here? I couldn't stop the look of horror that crossed my face, and Eberon was instantly on edge.

"What is it?" He rushed to my side, one hand on a small horn at his belt.

"Nothing!" I almost screamed at him, then swallowed to calm my voice. "Nothing is wrong. I need to lie down, I think, or maybe soak in a spring. I'll be at camp soon."

"Wren—" Eberon's concerns trailed away behind me as I took off for a pool of water not too far away, but not too close to the oak tree. Eberon didn't follow me, but I could feel his eyes until I ducked behind a willow.

Heart pounding for several long minutes, I sat in the shade. When I was certain I was alone, I stripped my boots and stockings off and plunged my feet into the cool spring. I flopped on my back and stared into the sway of the willow branches, which offered a latticed window to the sky overhead.

"What have I done?" I threw an arm over my eyes. The flapping of wings overhead told me Puko watched me from the tree. I *knew* my magic fought the seal. I *knew* the Wyldes would be full of magic. I'd let myself get far too excited in this place. I didn't want the magic to come out. Mila had tried to unseal just a small part of it for me when I was ten, and it had ended in disaster. I never wanted to go through that again.

One calming breath. Then another. Then I kept breathing slowly, relaxing the part of me that pushed on the seal. Eventually, I was ready to see the world again. I moved my arm; Puko sat above me and gave me an indignant caw as he looked down with his good eye.

What are you moping for? Look around, you dummy; you're in the Wyldes!

Propping myself on my elbows, I turned to the clear water. I would keep myself under control. I wanted this place. My magic wanted this place. I just needed to figure out that happy medium where I could have friends here and not chase them off by firing magic all over the place. The day was too warm to have Bryn's coat on, and I carefully folded it into a pillow filled with familiar scents and many memories. It was a long time of lying by the water, eventually tucking my feet up on the grassy bank and letting the sun-warmed air lull me to sleep. I wasn't ready to face Eberon. Wasn't ready to face any of them. Reality came looking for me when a shadow fell across the water near my feet.

"Can I sit here?" Schula's cool voice washed through me. Sitting up, I nodded and scooted to make room on the patch of grass. She sat down gracefully and removed her boots, putting her own feet in the water. Stretching my legs, I joined her.

"Eberon told us what happened. Are you all right?" she asked, a softness rounding her words.

"Yes," I managed. "My back."

"Has this happened before? Does it hurt?" she asked.

Watching the ripples in the water, I collected myself. "Back at the outpost I told you we tried to remove the seal once. It didn't end well. I must have too much human in me or something, but it overpowered me. And I can't, I *can't* remove it. But I also know I must remove it at some point. I'm scared. I'm terrified right now that it's going to burst open, and I can't do anything to stop it."

Schula, to her credit, listened quietly, stroking her cool hands up and down my back. When I was done, she pulled her feet from the stream.

"Every fae has magic, Wren." She ran a hand over her wet skin, the drops freezing enough that she could brush them off before putting her boots on dry feet. "You can't help what you're born with any more than the rest of us. I can't imagine being separated from mine, let alone sealing it away. But I understand how you feel, so here is what we can do. I'm going to put a little more power in the seal. I won't tamper with it or read into it, just put a little reinforcement on it. You won't lose control here, and you won't be sick. And once we're settled and I can find out how to safely do it, we'll remove the seal. You have no idea how much a part of you your magic is; it's like you're cutting one of your limbs off. All right?"

I nodded. I wiped my face off and pulled my own feet from the water.

"Good." She smiled. "I won't say a word to Eb and Thain. It will be just like the bath. I'll just tell them you were feeling overwhelmed with your first touches of the Wyldes today. We can keep it secret for now; just remember that no one else can find it before you deal with it. Now, would you mind if I lifted your shirt so I can reinforce your seal?"

I let out a long breath.

"I'm ready," I said. Puko clicked his beak overhead.

"I'll start, then." Schula used cool fingers to glide under my shirt and up my back just enough to touch the markings. The first frost that snowflaked on the windowpanes, that was what it felt like. Her magic crawled up my back, only touching where the marks were. She was pulling my shirt back down before I knew she was done.

"Thank you." I turned to see an odd look on her face. She stared into the space between us without really seeing me, then she blinked and met my eyes.

"It was no trouble," she murmured. "This is not by fae magic. It's not any magic I know. Though, the witches have been gone from these lands longer than I've been alive, so I wouldn't recognize the feel of it, just the markings. But this witch of yours isn't the one who put them there, so I wonder who did."

"Mila never specified. Many nights I've lain awake wondering who could have done it, but I'll probably never know."

Schula and I just stared for a moment, neither having the answer to such a question, until Puko took off with startling wingbeats, drifting back to the campsite.

Schula shook her head. "Come on, we're not going to gain any answers by standing here, and I'm starving."

Shoving my boots back on, I scrambled up and followed her back to the others.

The cliff curved gently inward and made for some cover from the weather. A fire was already dancing in a pit that had the black marks of hundreds of fires before it. There were signs of previous bedrolls, notches dug into trees for who knows what purpose (possibly past campsite boredom), and a few sizeable stones placed in a circle, likely for some kind of game. Three logs had been positioned near the fire, and Thain sat on one, stretching out his long legs.

"Where is Eberon?" Schula asked.

"Out getting something to eat," Thain said, then settled his intense gaze on me. "Are you all right?"

My face burned, but a cool hand pressed against my back. "All is well," Schula answered for me. "The Wyldes are overwhelming for someone who has never been in them before."

Thain watched me for a long moment, one of his stretches of unreadable assessment, then nodded. "If you are both finished at the spring, I think I'll head over there now."

"We'll watch the fire." Schula sat down on a log and stretched. Thain left, and I sat on another log.

Thain's dark shape moved with ease, his black tunic against the green, grassy fields an easy thing to spot as he moved until he was out of sight. Shame stabbed through me like a hot rod of iron. His hand, rough and worn from his life here, had been the first to reach out to me. Ever. And I knew I was keeping a secret from him. On some level, I wondered if he knew it too.

"Would you like me to tell you about the Autumn Lands?" Schula interrupted my thoughts. I nodded, hungry for more now that I'd gotten a taste of the Wyldes. This place was full of shock and wonder, but I wanted nothing more than to make it as familiar to me as the mountains I'd grown up in. Craving to know it as a place I could call home.

"Please," I begged. "Tell me everything."

The evening came and went. We talked well into dark about the sights I would see, the people she knew, the foods she had eaten in Thanantholl. Thain and Eberon added their own opinions as the night wore on, until finally I fell asleep leaning against the log.

TEN
THE AUTUMN LANDS

The journey through the Summer Lands so far had been uneventful, unless you counted seeing the Wyldes for the first time. The days were warm, and the evenings were filled with a cool breeze. Travel, it would seem, did not prevent Schula from rousing me early each day to make me do her odd stretches. She had me pulling and twisting and moving muscles I didn't know the body contained, but despite the aches that protested throughout my limbs, I was thankful for the distraction from the near-constant itch on my back.

The rest of our days went at an easy pace, and every day was easier than the last until I became used to the routine and content with Schula's companionship. There had never been a time I could relate to the village children that had siblings, watching them walk hand in hand picking herbs or quarreling over something as petty as borrowing a ribbon. But with Schula, it was easy to imagine friendship with another woman who wasn't my teacher. Outside of our stretches, at least. She had taken a liking to braiding my hair and would whisper small secrets with conspiratorial mischief when the others weren't looking. I was better off for having met her, having met all of them. Even Eberon's stories, which were filled with nothing of consequence besides the opportunity to hear himself talk, became something to look forward to in the evenings. He was a charming person, and he knew it, but he used it to uplift or cheer up his friends more than anything else. It was easy to picture him at court, though the details were muddled with the only idea of crowds and status that I could muster up, looking more like the sultana and her advisers on the private balconies of Sulls, where people wearing silks and jewelry were free to lounge on hot days.

The only one I hadn't grown any closer to was Thain. Quiet, strong, watchful Thain. I knew almost nothing about him, really, except for the place in his heart that would reach out to help a stranger in a lake. Maybe that was all I needed to know about him. Bryn would have liked him. For that, if nothing else, I decided that I liked him too.

The days blended together. I was accustomed to sleeping outside on pleasant nights, so it didn't bother me that we had no shelter as we traveled. We crossed through the Summer Lands for days before reaching its edge, where the fear gnawed at my bones, beginning as an uneasy pull in my stomach before my heart began to race as it had when I first saw the wraith. Something ahead was unsettling in the air. And then I got my first glimpse of the untamed reaches of the Wyldes.

Terrible nightmare creatures danced through my head. Stories the parents of the mountains told their children to make them behave. Bryn hadn't told me many of those sorts of stories, but Mila had. And when Mila the witch told you a story, you would be wise to know her monsters were real.

We stood at the top of a grassy knoll, the warm sun on my back. A trickle of sweat slid between my shoulder blades. In stark contrast to the lush Summer Lands we stood in now, below us lay a much darker landscape. Gnarled gray trees and dry, rocky terrain reached out in ugly tendrils. The most prominent thing covering the ground was the massive tangle of dusty blue vines and thorny brown brambles. It sprawled out like that for miles.

"The Unclaimed Wyldes." Schula rolled her shoulders back and stretched.

"Is it all like that outside the courts?" I whispered.

"Not all of it, but most," Eberon said. "We've been skirting the edge of it, in accordance with a longstanding treaty for the patrols to travel back and forth from the outpost. The Summer Court allows us to stay within an hour's stretch of their borders as we move north."

"And there is no other way to Thanantholl?" I wavered.

"No." Thain shook his head. "None of the court lands touch each other. It's best that way."

I couldn't see how two bordering lands would be worse than having to travel the Unclaimed Wyldes when you needed to go somewhere, but I stayed silent.

"The span of Unclaimed Wyldes is the thinnest here. If we move as fast as we can, we can make it in two days. Let's get on with it." Schula walked past the rest of us, heading down the hill into the grim landscape. "I only want to spend one night in it, and that's only going to happen if we get a move on."

"We're sleeping in that place?" I whispered out loud to no one in particular. Of course, they all heard me, but none of them answered. I gripped my pack, resolving to follow Thain to Thanantholl no matter what. Even if it was through this nightmarish forest.

We walked for hours at a brisk pace. The weather here was cold as it should be for the season. The warmth of the Summer Lands no longer eased the journey, and I slipped Bryn's coat back on within a few minutes. None of my companions were willing to break the silence in the stagnant air; instead, I watched as their ears twitched at sounds that I couldn't hear. No breeze rustled the ugly trees, no animals roamed the landscape. Even Puko stayed close, choosing to perch on my shoulder more often than not.

We stopped to pull out some portions of cured ham and herbed crackers for lunch, but we walked as we ate. I suspected we wouldn't have paused for food at all except the three of them seemed determined to put some weight on me, having gained the habit of sneaking me extra bits of food when they thought the others weren't looking. It reminded me of Mila's friend Gilly, who would visit on occasion and act as a doting aunt more than anything else. Still, I was grateful for the distraction of food as we crossed the bleak landscape. My legs were aching from the faster pace we traveled at, but I didn't want to complain. The faster we got through this part of the journey the better.

When night was upon us, we stopped as we usually did, the end of our day signaled by Thain stopping at a spot and nodding to the rest of us. Eberon looked on edge, but Schula and Thain just seemed more alert than usual. They were probably better at hiding their feelings than Eberon was. Or me; I was sure I looked terrified.

"Aren't we camping off the path?" I asked.

"Do you think that would be wise?" Thain looked at the thick, gnarled trees just a short distance from us. The overgrowth whispered promises of nasty surprises within.

I shuddered. "No."

"Don't gather any firewood tonight," Schula said. "No fires. Not here."

I just nodded and began unpacking my blanket. Firewood was usually my job, so I didn't know what else to do.

We ate in silence and went to bed. Schula kept the first watch. We hadn't kept watch overnight while traveling in the Summer Lands, but I was glad we did so here. They didn't ask me to take a shift. I would have, but I didn't know what to look for, and I was no trained warrior. No more use than a child, as far as the task of taking watch was concerned. A lost dog they were leading home that didn't do anything but slow them down. I sighed and rolled over, trying to get comfortable. My thoughts were depressing, and they wouldn't stop. It took a long time before I could fall asleep.

I woke up in the pink air of dawn. Eberon and Schula were talking in hushed whispers, and they stopped when they noticed I was awake. They both stared at me for a moment.

"Good morning," I mumbled.

"Good morning," Eberon answered. "Have an apple, we'll be packing up and leaving shortly."

He tossed the red fruit to me, and I caught it, but the motion startled Puko, who had opted to sleep on a fallen branch at my back. He settled, but I eyed him and then the trees that provided high branches I would have thought a bird should prefer over a branch on the ground. Puko was an odd bird, that was not in doubt, but even he seemed wary in this bleak place.

"Where is Thain?" I asked.

Schula simply moved from where she and Eberon were talking and began removing traces of our stay on the road. "He will meet us soon. Eat and pack, we need to go."

That alarmed me, but I took a big bite of apple and did as I was told, rolling up my blanket.

We were on our feet and walking quickly. My eyes darted around as we went, ready to see some horrible thing jump out at us. I felt vulnerable without the presence of the quiet, strong fae.

It was about an hour later that we heard the rustling of the trees, which I was sure was for my benefit and no one else. Still, my hand flew to the axe at my right hip before dropping away when Thain appeared.

"There you are," Eberon said, moving to his side.

Thain came to us from the dark woods, covered in nasty scratches and the scent of blood. His eyes shone bright like silver fire, his fingers ending in sharp points, his teeth a little longer, mouth a little wider.

My heart sped up a little. I recognized this, recognized the small ways he was different when he had been in a fight. Something a little more beast than fae showed not just in his features but in his movements; it was the same way he had looked at Silver Lake and with the wraith. The time I'd spent with these three had muddied my memories of this part of their world, the things about them that were wholly not human. Mila's voice came to mind, scolding me for putting fear between me and Thain, who had saved me twice now. My nails dug little crescents into my palms as I willed the uncomfortable feelings away, and Eberon brought the usual Thain out of the beastlier version in front of us.

"Trouble while I was gone?" Thain grunted, pressing his eyes closed a moment while Eberon rubbed his back.

"Not as much as you, apparently." Schula eyed Thain up and down. "Is everything taken care of?"

"Yes, but we should keep moving." Thain brushed some dirt from his clothes, shifting to take the lead again.

As much as I wanted to ask what he had found out there, I was too afraid of the answer. The unknown was going to drive me mad in this place, and not for the first time I found myself wondering if I'd made the right decision. But I kept my mouth shut as we all began walking a little faster.

Thain kept to the front, and I moved myself up until I was closer to him than the others. We had so few opportunities to talk, and he was always so guarded. I took a moment to look at him in a different light.

He did not look tired so much as weary. Weathered, perhaps. With every step he took, he seemed to find himself just a little bit more. What was it like to be so different when danger was near? A blessing, sure, but there must be some downsides as well. Eberon and Schula sometimes insisted on taking the lead, but for the most part he didn't allow it, and something in that made me sad. When did he rest? When did he allow this mantle of watchful protector that he wore to fall away? In the end, I said nothing. This was not the place to distract him, and as someone he had only just met who wasn't much help on this journey, I had no right to do so. I fell a few steps back without having said anything, just being led along with the others.

We didn't stop for lunch that day, and we walked right until sundown. A vibrant strip of grass shone like a beacon in the moonlight, and I could have cried from the joy of seeing it.

The second the Unclaimed Wyldes were out of sight, Thain stopped us, and we all dropped where we were. Few supplies were pulled from bags; we barely passed around strips of some kind of salted meat and rounds of dried fruit for dinner. I didn't even unroll my blanket; I just laid my head on it like a pillow and passed out.

Warm sunshine roused me in the crisp air. The ground was wet with dew, and I noticed that at some point a fire had been built nearby. A pang of guilt hit me for not gathering the firewood last night; I thought we had all gone to sleep right away.

"Good morning." Schula crouched next to me. "How are you feeling?"

"I'm well enough." I sat up, accepting a slice of stale bread from her. "Are we in the Autumn Lands?"

"Yes." She smiled and stood, stretching. "Finally."

Stuffing the bread in my mouth (and regretting it when the dry crumbs had me coughing), I took a long swig from a waterskin and put away my already rolled blanket. Puko cawed happily as he glided in lazy circles overhead, as if urging us to hurry toward Thanantholl.

The entire day went like this, riding on an anticipation that seemed to be carried on the wind. The foliage rustled in an endless breeze, glittering like jewels of orange overhead. Eberon stopped us once when he spotted a patch of leaves I'd never seen before growing no higher than my calf. When he pulled several fat lumps from the ground, I realized it must be food, and I was pleasantly delighted that night to bite into a sweet, starchy mouthful after they'd been roasted in the campfire. Sweet potatoes, they called them, and it was yet another wonder I'd seen from this place that had so much abundance. Even Sulls would be hard-pressed to compare.

The day passed, and then another. On the third day, we began to see signs of other fae. My eyes stayed wide, staring at small movements on distant paths where patrols could be seen winding through the countryside amid the vibrant leaves. We spotted a farm, and I saw someone wearing fine clothes I would reserve for a festival to tend her chickens. Growing closer to the city, my stomach stirred with a mixture of curiosity and anxious anticipation.

There were very few other people traveling the roads we were on, but they were closer than any other strangers we'd come across so far. They all stared, every time. Watching one wagon, hitched to a horse and laden with crates, I nearly jumped out of my own skin when a cool hand landed on my shoulder.

"Is everything all right?" Schula asked.

"Yes." My voice cracked, and I cleared it. "Yes. They're just staring, and I . . ." And I what? How do you explain to someone that a lifetime of eyes on you made your chest tight and your palms slick with sweat? That eyes meant trouble, possibly danger, and that it was time to leave?

Thain paused, eyes landing on me and then drifting to the wagon that came closer as it traveled in the opposite direction on the same path we now stood on. He moved himself between the wagon's path and me, all of us shifting to the side as it passed. A solid hand pressed to my back over the leather coat, and a sense of grounding fell over me. Once the wagon moved on, so did we.

"We're nearly in view of the city." Thain pointed to the crest of a small hill, and our collective pace quickened. We thrust up the hill, and a breeze swept through us as we crested the top. Autumn rolled into view, and my world shifted.

Thanantholl was a garden, veined with blue rivers and cobblestone paths. The buildings and the trees were so intertwined it was impossible to tell from the top of the hill where one began and the other ended. What wasn't in bloom was orange, red, or yellow. Purple bushes speckled the ground between trees, and dusty blue vines with prickly-looking thorns crawled along the side of the roads that guided travelers to the city within a valley. Where the Summer Lands had been hills and streams, the Autumn Lands were forests as far as the eye reached. Trees, bigger than any I'd seen in the mountains, grew thick around us. Some trunks were as wide as a horse was long. We slowed as I took in a breath of autumn.

"Beautiful," Eberon said.

"Home," Thain added.

There were no words I could add to the sight, and I was happy to stay paused looking down at the landscape. Eventually, they dragged me away, and we trickled down the slope to the large gates at the tip of the valley. Thain nodded at the fae guarding the gate, and they nodded back. I almost didn't notice, I was so enchanted with the city as we stepped through a giant archway.

Maple leaves of every color littered the ground. They floated in the pools of water and clung to the damp rooftops. Every building was made from clay bricks, sculpted to shapes complementing the gnarled trees around them. The wood on the doors and windows was painted with bright colors and detailed embellishments.

Wind whistled through the trees and lanterns swayed over doors and in shady pockets under the canopy. So many people flowed through the streets, while smoke and the smell of roasting food drifted lazily over us. The citizens were strange to see, but familiar in the ways I was familiar with the Mother's creatures. Some appeared with animal features but walked upright like the rest of us. Others were more like my companions, with odd colorings and unfamiliar movements but appearing mostly fae-like. Yet more were covered in every manner of skin from scales to bark.

"Here." Eberon pulled me from the distraction of walking down the main path as he handed me a warm bag that smelled sweet.

Blinking down at it, I saw what I'd first thought was a bag was actually made from the largest maple leaf I had ever seen. I untucked a corner, and the steam hit my face.

"Careful, that's still hot." Eberon fanned it with his hand, and Schula reached over to pull out a nut I had never seen before.

"What is that?" I pulled one out for myself. It smelled like syrup and honey.

"Pecans, a tree nut." Schula popped it in her mouth and smiled. "Good choice, Eb. Now to Thain's place?"

Cupping the treasure deep in my palm, I studied the shape and smell. While the mountains were abundant with walnuts, any other nuts came from foreign traders through Sulls. There was no way Bryn could have afforded something like that. And here, in this strange city of fae creatures, it was a common street food.

Thain led the way, and I put the pecan on my tongue. The texture was like a walnut, but the flavor was sweet and smoky. I could get addicted to these. I savored it as long as I could, but when the flavor had all melted off, I chewed and grabbed another.

The streets wound around the trees and pools of water. Bridges of braided roots grew over the ponds, jumping playfully in no discernible pattern. We took several of these bridges as well as a few paths through thickets of small white flowers. I couldn't tell how much time was passing, if I was eating up everything before me in an instant or if I was dwelling on each plant, each face, for so long that our destination was hours away. I noticed when there were only two nuts left in the pouch, and I put it in my pocket. Those were to be savored later.

Thain slowed down at a blue fence and held the gate for us all to enter. The front garden was small but crafted into a world of roses and blue vines. The house behind it was large, with a blue door to match the fence. The windows and balconies climbed three floors off the ground, and gnarled oak trees hugged it on either side. Puko took off for the branches above, startling me when I had all but forgotten his presence.

"Wairen." Thain turned to the open door to greet a fae that appeared to be made entirely of birch bark. "It's good to see you again."

The person with the tree-like appearance nodded deferentially. "And a pleasure for your safe return."

"It's good to see you looking well," Schula greeted, and Wairen offered a charmingly awkward smile, like the toothy grin of a toddler still figuring out the world.

"We have a guest," Thain said, moving to the side so Wairen could have a clearer look at me. Lifting a hand enough to offer a small wave, I forced a smile to cover my nerves.

"A guest," Wairen said, mimicking my wave with awkward hands. "Delightful, a guest. Are there things? I will take the things."

Wairen wore not one stitch of clothing, but upon closer inspection there were no anatomical features to identify them as anything but a living tree. Their smooth, bark-like body held only a general shape. "I'm grateful for your hospitality." The words came automatically, an echo of many, *many* lessons by Mila.

"Thanks, old friend." Thain turned to Wairen, handing over my sack. "We are expected in the throne room soon."

"Certainly." Wairen nodded. "Important business."

Thain brought us inside to a lush receiving room of brocade chairs around a roaring fireplace, carved wood detailed with twisting plants. I noticed a collection of liquor bottles lining the mantle; Thain and Bryn had a hobby in common.

"Welcome to my home." Thain gestured toward the stairs. "You have free run of the place. My room is the only one on the third floor. On the second floor, you will find a bedroom with a red door. The kitchen is through that archway if you're hungry, and Wairen is always here if you can't find me."

The tree-like fae in question made their way up the stairs, my things in tow. Once Wairen disappeared into the second-floor hallway, I turned back to Thain.

"Is Wairen . . ." Clearing my throat, and my thoughts, I didn't know how to ask. "Are there servants in Thanantholl?"

Schula snorted. "*No*. Wairen is a part of this place. They like to keep the tree, and by extension the house, tidy."

Eberon hummed, eyes drifting up the stairs. "Don't ask them for the work of servants. They don't eat food, so their cooking is atrocious, but caring for their tree and the grove around it is a basic desire for most dryads. I think Thain meant that if you need to know where something is that Wairen would be able to tell you."

"Only the king has servants, keepers of the palace," Thain added. "Wairen has lived here for a long time. Their tree is at the back of the house, and as they find pleasure in keeping this place free of pest or disease, I have always kept their tree safe in turn."

The stress fell off me, and my shoulders relaxed. There was no way I would ever feel comfortable with another person doing things for me like that. "All right, understood."

Mostly, at least. There were still questions about what a dryad was and why they cared for a tree when they appeared to be part tree themselves, but now I wanted nothing more than to find a way to wash my face free of the grime of the road.

"You are welcome at my apartment or Eb's house, but Thain's will be the quietest, and we thought you'd prefer it." Schula stretched her arms, allowing herself to fall back onto the shoulder of a bemused Eberon as she yawned. "We should go."

"Am I perhaps a piece of furniture now?" he asked.

Schula didn't have an answer, only a nonsensical "Mm-hmm," as she cracked her neck and stood up straight again.

"Right." Eberon turned to me. "Our first duty is to the throne. We need to report in, but I'll send some things over for you to try on while we're gone. We'll be back before sunset, and I'm treating you to a dinner worthy of Thanantholl."

"I understand. I'll be fine here, go do what you need to do."

Schula wiggled her fingers in a silly wave, looping her arm with Eberon's and pulling him out the door. Thain took a few steps but paused in the doorway. He looked over his shoulder at me, one hand on the doorframe, the light coming in from the street behind him illuminating his outline.

Swallowing down the overwhelming sensation of just how solid he was—in size and in temperament—I stilled at the bottom of the stairs.

"I hope you can consider this your home for now. We're glad to have you with us. I'm glad you came." Thain gave a rare smile before slipping out the front door.

I watched them through the bay window, making their way down the street and out of sight. After they were gone, I watched the people of Thanantholl.

Thain obviously lived on a less traveled road, because few crossed the path of the window for me to see. Sharp eyes and pointed ears went about the day at ease. Things that might once have given me nightmares now walked only feet away, and I could only be glad they weren't the wraith.

"Would you like to see your room, Wren?" Wairen creaked down the stairs. "I am particularly proud of the plants in this room."

"Yes, please. Wait, do you grow plants inside the house?" Curiosity had me drifting up the stairs after Wairen.

"Yes, very satisfying. Very pretty." Their words were short but pleased as we made our way to the top of the stairs.

Plants in the house. What next?

ELEVEN
THANANTHOLL

The second floor was not what I'd expected. The curved hallway was wide and lined with carpet. I stopped to take my filthy boots off before walking down the hall in my stockings. Paintings of fae, many of whom looked like Thain, lined the walls. Each door was a different color, and near the far end I found a bright red door, the frame painted with small blue flowers. My fingertips brushed the painted surface, wondering how they got it so vibrant.

Wairen opened the door, and I found a room nearly the size of my cabin. On a platform in one corner was a plush red-and-white canopy bed. Next to that was a beautiful carved wardrobe large enough to climb into. The ceiling was painted to look like a bed of roses. A small table between two red velvet armchairs held my sack of belongings, and my second axe was propped against the wall. I took the good axe off my belt and put it with the other.

And, as Wairen had promised, there were plants. There were flowers everywhere in decorative pots, many of them serving no purpose but ornamentation, though there was a small white flower that would make a relaxing tea under the window. A vanity with a matching red stool was near the double doors that had been left open to show a balcony with wooden rails covered in ivy and a bench formed from one of the oak branches that dipped down onto it.

"Wairen, this place is beautiful," I breathed.

They puffed out their chest. "It is. I will leave you now, and I will knock when I come to water the plants."

After waiving Wairen off, I stepped into the room toward the balcony. This place was beyond my imagination. The outpost had been extravagant, but this was downright overwhelming.

Caw.

Puko landed gently on the ivy-covered railing and began preening his wing. Stepping outside, I pulled a lungful of fresh air through me and stroked the feathers on his head.

"I suppose this is where we're staying for a while. Try not to be a nuisance."

Puko croaked at me then made several irritated clicks before returning to his grooming. I left him to it and explored more of the inside. A wide door by the wardrobe opened to a bathroom. If the bath at the outpost had been a dream, this one was a heaven.

The room was made of carved stone. The bath was sunk right in the floor, and the water nearly filled it to the brim. Steps brought you down into the steaming water, and trays lined the edge with soaps and lotions. Unlike the concealed pipe at the outpost that poured water into the bath, the water here fell from the mouth of a brass unicorn that kneeled over the far corner of the tub. A nozzle to the side of it turned the water on and off. The south wall held shelves of soft towels, and the north wall was one giant mirror.

This place was like the public bathhouse in Sulls I'd gone to once as a treat. Back then, I'd used the towels to hide my back and stayed unnoticed in the far corner, but this room was empty except for me, and I intended to enjoy it to the fullest.

I shut the door behind me and stripped immediately. I barely had my last stocking off before I reached the steps that took me into the blissful water. In a few short days, I had become dependent on a hot bath, which I had rarely even had until I'd met the fae.

I was content to soak for what must have been an hour before cleaning myself. I was scrubbing my hair when a gentle knock came through the door.

"Do not be alarmed," Wairen said.

"Is something wrong?" I asked, completely unprepared for the door to the bathroom to open. I spun, hiding my back as the dryad leaned through the doorway.

"You have received a gift. I am laying some clothing out on your bed and will be gone in a moment," Wairen said.

Sinking into the water, I was unsure of how to respond. Had they seen anything? There was no reaction if they had. I had spun around before the door fully opened, right? What had they said? *A gift?*

"Thank you," I said, and Wairen appeared pleased as they closed the door once more.

I took plenty of time cleaning myself so Wairen would be gone before I climbed out of the bath. That had been a close call—too close. Wrapped in a large red towel, I peeked through the bathroom door to make sure I would be alone.

Four dresses had been laid out as well as underthings. Matching slippers sat on the floor next to where I'd left my dusty boots, and they all looked like they would fit. Each piece was made from materials I had never felt before, and on top of one of the dresses was a note.

A few items to welcome you to our city.
—Eb

A smile touched my lips as I let my fingertips run down the cool fabric of a sleeve. A gift. A *gift.* I swallowed down the feeling that I didn't deserve it. I would make sure to thank Eberon for these beautiful things and to wear them well. I had worn simple dresses before. They'd helped me blend into the larger settlements and cities, but they were never required. These dresses, though, these were different. The fabrics were light and expensive looking, the colors vibrant. I was able to try them all on, but how to fasten them I wasn't sure. More lacing and ties similar to the shirt Schula had put me in for training, but different enough that I didn't know what I was doing. Two of them I could see right from the start would be far too low at the back and reveal my magic seal. Another was too low in the front, and while I wasn't usually so shy about my clothing, I wasn't ready to be so bold in an unfamiliar city. Perhaps if I had the same plump curves that Schula had, but I didn't.

That left me with one dress. A deep purple one that covered me high on the back, gathered across my chest while still covering it, and swept to my ankles. The sleeves covered me to my elbows, clinging tightly to my arms. There was still the matter of tying the lacing at the sides, but for now I was at least covered.

I walked around my room several times. The dress swayed around my legs, leaving me with the feeling of nakedness. With breeches, my legs never directly touched each other, so the dress would take getting used to. I'd need to find more of the clothes Schula wore most days, but these would come in handy if such dress was expected in Thanantholl.

I went out to the balcony to find Puko gorging himself on a bowl of dried cherries that Wairen must have left. I sat on the oak bench, watching him. The fae below were easier to watch from outside. I wasn't directly over the street, but I could still see it. I didn't know how long I sat there watching and thinking and braiding my hair. When I spotted Thain, I smiled and went back inside.

I could hear him come in downstairs as I walked through the hallway. When I reached the top of the stairs, I saw him talking to Wairen, who was moving through the arched doorway to the kitchen, then Thain looked up and stilled.

Heat rose high on my cheeks as those two silver points of attention fixed on me. I knew it, these garments were still too fine, and I was still too unfamiliar to wear them well. But they were a gift from Eberon, and that meant a lot to me. I would simply have to adapt, because this was my chance to find a place where I could truly belong without constant judgment.

Thain blinked when I cleared my throat. "I'm not sure how these laces are tied, could I ask for help?"

"Of course." He moved up the stairs with that annoyingly silent walk of his, his eyes moving down to the fabric I had tried to gather where the laces would hold it in place. His hands, calloused and brutal as they were, gently moved my fingers out of the way as he pulled the laces in place.

"Is all the clothing from Thanantholl so complicated?" I asked.

He shrugged. "Eberon's taste, but you'll see more like it. Tomorrow, we'll find you clothing that *you* are comfortable in. Turn."

I showed him my other side, and he repeated the process. Closing my eyes, the campfire scents of Thain seeped into my breaths as he finished and we stepped apart. "Thank you. I don't know that I've said it enough lately, but I have a lot to thank you for."

"Anyone would have done the same."

Maybe, but I still had my doubts. Too many times had I seen the opposite in humans. If I was being honest, my stomach still twisted in knots at the thought of trying to integrate with such a huge city of people. But compared to what I'd left behind, *who* I'd left behind, it would be too painful to turn back now.

Thain's attention shifted a second before I heard a knock at the door. "Eberon."

He strode down the stairs, but Eberon let himself in before Thain could reach the door.

"Wren, that suits you well." A smile spread across the golden fae's lips. Eberon had changed into much nicer clothing than what he'd traveled in, and that was saying something. Golds and oranges complemented his neat red hair, and his leather boots were well polished. There wasn't one part of him that wasn't embellished with added ornamentation, and somehow it fit him perfectly.

I walked carefully down the stairs, not tripping over the slippers or dress. I tried to walk with a sway, like Schula did. I felt ridiculous, so I stopped.

"I need to get changed. I'll be right back." Thain nodded to us as he went upstairs.

"I hope you're hungry, we have a table at the River's Edge." Eberon swept to the fireplace and took a decanter from the mantle. "If you liked the pecans from earlier, you'll be in for a real treat. The food there is the best Thananthioll has to offer."

A knock at the door drew me away. I could see Schula through the window, and I let her in. She glided through the door in a silver corset and a full black skirt that looked to delight her just by the wearing of it.

"You look amazing," I said.

"You look absolutely charming! If I wasn't worried about Eberon getting a bigger head, I'd tell him he did a good job." Schula beamed at Eb, who rolled his eyes. "Where is Thain?" she asked.

"Getting dressed." Eberon had poured himself a glass from the decanter and was leaning back in one of the armchairs by the hearth.

"I see you haven't been here for ten minutes and you're already into my brandy." Thain came downstairs wearing stunning blacks, blues, and silvers. His usually tousled hair had been tamed into a ponytail.

"A testament to your good taste in drink." Eberon flashed a sharp smile before draining the glass. "Shall we go then?"

Thain grunted, and Schula looped her arm in mine as we all followed Eberon out the door. As the sun began to dip low, fireflies sparkled like stars fallen on Thanantholl. They were on everything, adding a glow to every surface still enough to land on.

We walked near a grotto, open on one end, though how far back the cave went I couldn't see. We passed close enough in front of it that I noted the glass ballroom floor and orchestra pit just begging for a party. Servants bustled around with decorations and brooms.

"The palace is in there, beyond the opening." Schula watched me as I took in the scene. "King Baeleon is fond of dancing. I'm sure you'll find out for yourself soon enough."

"There's the River's Edge up ahead." Thain pointed to a bend in a small arm of gently flowing water. Tables dripping in white decorations were illuminated by candles. An overhang away from the water held more tables, and a building beyond that smoked from three chimneys where the kitchen must be. We entered the yard through a gate and were escorted to a table by the water by a fae who smelled of lilacs and seemed to already know my companions. Or at least, she exchanged pleasantries with Schula and greeted the rest of us as she brought us to the table.

Sitting down, I nearly couldn't see Eberon across from me for the large pot of chrysanthemums in the middle of table. The seats were polished wood and made for comfort with linen cushions. I watched as a firefly landed on one of the flowers, crawling into the petals as it glowed.

A short fae with hair that moved like she was underwater despite the dry air around us drifted toward the table. Her aqua skin was covered in bumps.

"Well, if it isn't my favorite triquetram, back from the border." She leaned in closer to me and sniffed, her eyes widened. "And who is this?"

I blinked and leaned away at the odd interaction. Was it normal to smell people here?

"This is Wren," Thain said, seemingly undisturbed by the stranger smelling me. "You'll hear soon enough what the king wants everyone to know."

She tilted her head, more of her hair swishing to the side in that underwater manner. Her mouth popped open as she came to some realization. "How old are you?" she whispered at me.

"Twenty-five." I was as quiet as I could be, but a few heads turned to us from neighboring tables anyway.

"Not the time, Marila," Thain said, soft and firm.

Marila was nearly bouncing on her toes now, suppressing a grin and clearing her throat. "I understand. Ahem, the special tonight is duck or salmon. Both pair well with the house sweet red wine or, if you prefer, our fresh barrel of cider."

Schula ordered one of each special for the two of us so I could try them both before choosing. She said she would like either. Across the water, we watched the sun dip below the treetops, setting the city ablaze in pinks and reds. I drank my cider and let the conversations around me buzz through the background. There was too much to see to distract myself with chatter. Maple leaves still fell, and crickets came out to serenade Thanantholl.

The food came and went. Each plate before me was better than the last. Schula had to cut the duck and salmon in half in the end as I couldn't decide on one. The cider had gone to my head by the time we were finished eating.

"Wren, you look flushed, are you all right?" Thain slipped cool fingers onto my forehead and frowned.

"I think the cider is getting the best of me." I brushed his hand away. "I'll be fine if I stop now."

They brought me a glass of water, and once I had finished it, Thain took my arm to walk me home. Schula and Eberon stayed and said their goodnight to us there at the table.

Eyes darted to me as we passed groups of fae, but it was starting to get too dark for it to bother me. The path to Thain's house was a twist of roads and bridges I wouldn't be able to follow again without help. The cool night helped sober me up, but I still focused on my steps in the foreign slippers so I wouldn't fall. After a long silence, I couldn't take it anymore, and I spoke.

"I'm sorry if you left early because of me."

"No, if anything I should be thanking you. I can't stay out celebrating nearly as long as Eberon and Schula can." Thain gave me a half smile. "Even just the three of us wears on me after a time."

"Can I ask you about a word I heard again earlier tonight?" We walked under a lattice of roses, and he led us down a new road.

"That depends on what it was, but ask away." His large hand was a steady warmth on my back as we walked. If I stumbled, he was right there. It was comforting.

"What exactly *is* a triquetram?" Our server had called them that. "When we met, you told me it was your team."

Thain hummed a noncommittal sound. He turned us onto the street where I finally saw his house. "The magic of the Wyldes comes in threes. That is even true for those of us born with magic, the fae. Somewhere out there, you have two . . ." He frowned. "Two matches. Two other people with magic that can match, oppose, and balance your own all at once. That is your triquetram, and some go their whole lives never finding any of their set."

"That's kind of sad." I said. "But Schula and Eberon are your triquetram?"

He took a moment to answer. A sadness crossed his face, but it was gone when we reached the yard.

"Eberon is. Schula hasn't found any of hers yet, and she travels with us as our third." Wairen opened the door as we reached it. "And with that, I think you should get some sleep."

We said our goodbyes at the foot of the stairs. By the time I reached the top, I looked down to see Thain in an armchair with his decanter of brandy. I went to my room to find a nightdress laid out on the bed. I left my purple dress on the floor where it fell and climbed into bed with the cotton dress pulled down to my knees.

I would have stayed up into the late hours to think, but the cider brought me to sleep before I could fight it.

TWELVE
PEARL STREET

Puko cawed in my ear. A startling wake-up call, especially since it took me a moment to recognize the room. It had been so long since the outpost that the softness of my bed had been a problem to sleep on. I had thrown the linens on the floor at some point and curled up on my side near the edge of the mattress. The pillows I had thrown against the wall in my sleep.

All I could see when I opened my eyes were the long black tail feathers of an annoying bird. He pecked my nose and flapped away out the balcony window. Groaning, I stretched out my stiff back and got ready for the day.

I studied the hallway as I walked along. I had walked on rugs but never carpet before coming here. I ran my fingers over the ornately carved frames that held paintings of strange fae. The other doors, like my own, were a solid color, but the doorframes were all painted with wildflowers. Every other lantern in the hall was lit. Just enough light to mix with the rising sun and make it bright enough to see where you were going. By the time I had reached the end of the hall and the top of the stairs, my stomach growled. So downstairs I went.

The sun didn't reach quite this far down yet, and the great fireplace had to be lit for both warmth and light. I heard birds outside, and the rustling of leaves in the wind. Activity from the kitchen drew my interest.

"Wren, please come have some breakfast," a light voice sang through the great room from the doorway opposite me. The voice wasn't one I knew, but I also heard the unmistakable grunt of Thain when he didn't wait for his tea to cool. If Thain was there, it was probably a friend. Though, I wasn't sure how to feel that they were already calling me by name.

The kitchen was large. One end of the room held the cookstove and shelves of storage. A carved lattice of white wood divided the working end from the rest of the room, which held a table under a window to the garden. Thain gestured me to sit with him, and I did. Bowls of fruit and strange oatcakes were spread before me.

"Sleep well?" Thain put an oatcake on the plate in front of me.

"Yes, thank you," I said, inhaling the aroma from the warm pastry.

"Hmm." Thain frowned and drank his tea, looking directly at what must have been tired circles beneath my eyes.

"Well," I admitted, "the bed is a little soft after all those nights on the road. I'll get used to it." Softer than sleeping on the road. Softer than my hay bed from home.

Thain laughed, that low, feral joy of his that used to frighten me. "After weeks on the road, a bed can be too much."

"You are welcome to sleep out under my tree."

I had nearly forgotten the other voice in the room when I turned to see another tree person. She could have been Wairen's sister. Pale and tall and standing up straight. A birch fae. If she'd stood still, I would have thought she was growing through the kitchen floor.

"No, thank you." I watched her move in that same stiff way Wairen did; perhaps it was a dryad trait. "I didn't know there were more people in the house. It's nice to meet you."

"Yes, it is nice to meet you again." The birch fae nodded her head and moved toward the window that looked out into the yard.

"That *is* Wairen," Thain said. "The tree sprites don't understand male and female the way we do. What does a tree care for 'that sort of nonsense,' as Wairen puts it. I believe they think you will be more comfortable around someone more female in appearance."

"Oh." I stared after Wairen, who was now watching something out the window.

"Wairen is a wealth of knowledge and would likely be better company than me."

"I'll keep that in mind." I turned to my plate and tasted the warm oatcake. Like everything else in the Autumn Lands, it was a new wonder to experience. I bit into it, the softness surprising me as a drizzle of honey hit my tongue.

"The king wants to meet you this afternoon." Thain drained his tea and sat back in his chair. "As for this morning, we're going to find you some clothes."

"I couldn't, I don't have enough money. Besides, Eberon already gave me so many things."

"Clothes you feel comfortable wearing," Thain clarified. "Something you chose for yourself."

Nearly choking on my tea, I cleared my throat. "For someone of so few words, you are shamelessly observant."

The barest hint of amusement crinkled around the corners of his eyes.

Bryn had been a jovial man. He could not get enough of a good story, he knew no strangers, and he was quick to offer help. Observant, however, he was not. Mila was the most practical person I knew: if it wasn't essential, it wasn't important. But Thain, who I could still barely get a read on, was forever pointing out the smallest things.

I wonder if anyone pays as close attention to Thain as he does to the rest of us?

I finished my cake and ate another while watching the breeze tickle the garden. In the mountains, we wore loose breeches to the knees and plainly cut tunics with little shape to them. Even the dresses were simple and formless, in a freeing way that allowed movement. From what I had seen of the city so far, I was in for something very different. I traced the delicate lip of my cup with a finger as I ate the last few bites of oatcake. When I was done, I thanked Wairen and headed toward the door.

Thain was dressed simply in black, standing by the window as he watched the street outside. He wore the same sort of thing he did while traveling through the mountains, and he looked more ready for an adventure than a trip to the market. I held back a smile and walked up to him.

He opened the door for me, and we walked into a haze of falling leaves. Smoke wafted overhead, carrying the smells of morning baking and burning sandalwood. Thain took us not too far from his home to the busiest street I had seen so far.

Fountains and benches lazed under the trees. Shops of every sort welcomed the heavy flow of traffic through their doors, and market carts shouted for nearby business.

My mouth hung open in awe. How had we been so close to such a market without all that noise bothering us? Fae of feathers, fur, and a rainbow of hues walked around us on the crowded cobblestones.

Several curious onlookers paused or slowed down to openly stare at me, but I had become skilled in avoiding eye contact, and thankfully none approached us.

Thain guided me to the side of the street. We walked where there was slightly less of a bustling crowd, and I turned my attention back to the amazing shops around us.

Almost all of them had glass windows and held wonders inside. I could get lost forever in the depths of what I learned was called Pearl Street. I stopped to watch a carver working on the most beautiful stone statues in the window of a dark green shop. Flakes and dust from the red stone he carved covered the floor and his apron.

"If you'd like to watch, we can come back later. Schula is expecting us, but I'm sure she wouldn't mind coming back here," Thain offered.

"Schula?" I asked.

He shrugged. "If you wish, I could try to advise you on clothing, but Schula has the more discerning eye."

"No, I would love her help." I took one last look in the shop window as we continued on the path we had been on. "I'm sorry, it's all a bit distracting."

"Have you ever seen such a skilled carver before?" Thain asked. "Thanantholl is famous for our craftsmen."

I thought of Bryn and my little carved bowl back at Thain's house. Self-taught and always trying new things with his carvings, each thing he made was different from the last. "I like to think so."

Suddenly, I didn't want to watch the carver anymore. We walked on in silence, and I tried to force my mood back to pleasant. I didn't want to be the dark cloud hanging over this happy market. A happy market I imagined myself walking through on lazy afternoons. Maybe one where I could be a familiar face with my favorite shopkeepers, just as Bryn had been. My association with him had never gained me the same warm greetings and secretive samples of new items, but I'd watched every one of them all the same.

Here. I wanted that here.

We resumed watching the shops ahead until I spied a familiar silhouette.

"I think I see Schula." My eyes had drifted toward a large shop with bright green shutters. Each window had a little wooden box under it where yellow flowers dripped down, reaching for the ground with buttery petals. A still white figure stood outside, eyes roaming the streets around her.

"You're right." Thain followed my gaze.

Schula spotted us before we reached her. She gave us a small smile and pushed off the building she was leaning on to meet us halfway there.

"Hello, Wren. Are you ready to do some shopping?" she asked, taking my hands.

"I think so. I don't have a lot of coin, and I don't know if the fae will accept human currency, but I have some bronze pieces and two silver coins that could be melted down." I reached for the pouch in my pocket. Schula swatted my hand off course and wagged a finger at me.

"No, no, no, that's not how this works." She slung an arm around my neck and gestured to the store behind her. "You see, I'm to dress you properly and make sure you're ready for your debut tonight, and it's all on the king's bill."

"How?" Thain asked, crossing his arms.

My eyes nearly popped out of my head. The clothing in the windows behind her was impressive. Tiny embroidered details and gold finishing threatened to give me a heart attack. "I can't accept something like that!"

Schula pulled her lips between her teeth for a moment, following my gaze to the window of clothes. "Well, I'm persuasive. And he likes me. Or he likes that I irk my father. It doesn't matter; just know we have the king's tab to fill."

"Schula," I started, "I really can't, this is too much."

She gave a dramatic sigh. "I'll just go back and tell King Baeleon you refused his hospitality, shall I?"

My back stiffened. "No, no, that does sound worse." I knew I was being backed into a corner, but I wasn't about to offend a king. "We can pick something out. I'm sorry, I'll go in."

Schula clapped triumphantly. "Good, let's go. Come on, Thain, you can carry our bags."

He raised an eyebrow.

"Well, I can't come to my favorite shop and not get a thing or two myself, can I?" Schula patted Thain on his giant muscled shoulders. "Come along now, Baeleon's orders."

And with that, I was pulled inside the bright storefront.

THIRTEEN
DRESS TO IMPRESS

White linen was draped over every window and chair, stark against the dark wood of the building. Tree branches sprouted from the floor, and on them hung displays of fabrics. Between the branches stood wooden dress forms, clothed in what must have been Autumn Court fashions.

Just like Schula wore, there were many loose tunics that tied at the sides and tight leggings that extended all the way to the ankle, buttoning or lacing against the leg. I looked down at my breeches. They stopped at the top of my calf, then I put on my tall wool stockings and the boots that came to my knees. Schula's boots were shorter. So were Thain's.

"Welcome. What brings you to my humble shop, Master Thain and company?" A tall fae with the nose of a deer and small budding antlers glided over to us. Her nose twitched like an animal scenting the air around her.

"We're here for this one." Schula pulled me forward. "How soon could we have something ready to meet Baeleon? Nothing terribly formal, but we need it today."

The tailor's eyes narrowed to me. She seemed to be measuring me with her eyes. "I have many pieces that would fit her with little altering. Yes, I think I have options for you, dear. *Maribell*!"

A short, panicked girl with black down-feather hair rushed from behind a table of fabric in the back of the store.

"Yes, mistress." She halted by the doe fae's side.

"Settle this party in the large room and bring me the smaller-sized collection we just finished."

"Which pieces, ma'am?" The small fae squeaked at the sharp look from her mistress. "Right, yes, the new collection. *All* of it. Right away. Please follow me."

"Hello, Maribell." Schula smiled at the assistant. "Do you remember me?"

"Of course, Lady Schula." The petite tailor smiled once we were out of sight of her mistress. "You go through tunics like a growing young male. I'm glad to see you well."

"She wouldn't go through that many if she would wear things more than once," Thain added, earning an icy glare.

Maribell did what she could to contain her smile, but it still slipped through the cracks. I liked her immediately.

"Here is the large room. Can I send in anything while I gather your clothes? Tea, perhaps?" Maribel beamed up at Schula.

"No, thank you," she said. "Good luck with Mistress Rhisa."

Maribell nodded and scurried away. Thain, Schula, and I took a seat on the white chairs in the room. A section in the corner provided a spacious curtained changing area behind a large screen, and several mirrors hung at angles against one wall.

"The tailor seems harsh," I whispered.

"Mistress Rhisa has always been that way. But she makes the most comfortable things." Schula smoothed her tunic with a hand. "Maribell at least makes a very good wage here, even if she has to put up with Rhisa's eccentricities. Don't worry about Maribell. She could open her own shop at any time, but she chooses to stay here to learn from the best."

I'd noticed the differences in some of the fae, but this was the first time I was meeting any of the more animal-looking ones in person. "Are the shop workers here different kinds of fae from you two?" I asked.

"Yes and no," answered Thain. "But it's taken centuries to get us all away from one another's throats. Now it's considered in bad taste to point out who is one kind of fae and who isn't."

"Not that it doesn't happen anyway," Schula grumbled.

I wasn't given much time to think about the social structure of the fae types before Maribell burst back into the room with armfuls of clothing.

She shifted her stack around until her hands were free enough to clap twice. My jaw dropped as branches sprouted from the walls and Maribell began hanging clothing up. Three times she came in and brought clothing to us. On her last trip in, she was followed by the doe fae.

"Mistress Rhisa will now guide you through the fitting," Maribell announced, but she stayed in a nearby corner, ready to help.

Mistress Rhisa had gentle hands, despite her demeanor. The fine lines of her face reminded me of all the places that wrinkled when Mila was concentrating on something, though Rhisa had far smoother skin otherwise.

"Let's see what we're working with, dear," Rhisa announced, tugging my wrist and pulling me across to the changing space. Within minutes, she had piled cloth across a branch by the screen and pulled me behind it. "Off with the old, on with the better."

"Wait." I clutched at my clothes. "I can do this on my own, please!"

My marks, she would expose my marks. I had been a fool to get this comfortable, this complacent until I understood more about what this seal meant here.

"Shy." She tsked and shook her head, bony fingers still making their way to the laces on my clothes.

"Mistress!" The curtain slid open just enough for a white shape to slip through. "I will assist as well. I just remembered I wanted to speak with you about a new coat."

All the breath fell out of me, and the tension with it. Schula placed herself firmly at my back, even as she began working at my laces as well. Her eyes didn't leave Mistress Rhisa as she described the desire for an embroidered coat that would match some dress she'd had made recently. Even though she didn't meet my eyes, a cool hand cupped one of my shoulders and gave it a gentle squeeze.

What followed next was a masterful whirlwind of being posed, stripped, and dressed again. Satins and silks draped my bony frame, all of them cinched to my waist with more ties like those on Schula's tunics.

Mistress Rhisa was a master of her craft. I might not have known much about tailoring beyond repairing the breeches and tunics of the mountain people, but I could see her expert eye catch at every bit of her work that didn't sit precisely where she wanted it to. "Too short. Too loose. Wrong color. Not with *those* freckles—Stars, no. That color does you no favors. Perhaps buttons. Longer skirts."

"She has a preference for pants over dresses I think, mistress," Schula added.

"Noted," was Rhisa's short reply as she practically ripped a shawl from me and slid a tunic over my head.

"Don't I need something, I don't know, formal? To meet a king?" I sputtered through the silk being shoved over me.

"Yes, a formal pant. That's what she said," Rhisa quipped. "Elbows in."

"But usually dresses are—" I closed my mouth as this new tunic was torn from me and a pair of brown pants shoved over my feet.

"Is that a human trait? Dresses are formal?" Schula asked.

"What nonsense." Rhisa snorted.

"Um, I guess so?" I helped slip the high waist of the pants over my hips. "I've rarely worn a dress before yesterday, and never one so nice."

"The formality of what you wear is dictated by the cloth it is made of and what embellishments adorn it. In Thanantholl, a silk tunic is more formal than a cotton dress," Schula explained. "Here you wear what makes you comfortable, what you like."

"There, that is presentable enough." Mistress Rhisa tugged my arm and pulled me from behind the screen. "This one, I am happy with. I could have it ready within the hour."

I stumbled behind the tailor and stopped abruptly. Thain still lounged on the seat, and Schula came around me to join him as she flopped onto the cushions. I stood up straight, and Schula whistled. Thain simply stared in that unblinking way of his.

"Masterfully done, mistress." Schula applauded and twirled a finger in demand that I turn around to show off all sides of the clothing. "I would never have guessed it wasn't custom-made for her."

"You should go to the wall of mirrors, dear, though I'm sure this is exactly what you want." Rhisa's nose turned up as she took a spot on the wall. Maribell gathered rejected garments and scurried away with them.

The mirrors showed me a new person. The cream-colored satin held a sheen that made my skin glow. It bloused at my breasts, giving an illusion of fullness that I didn't quite have on my own. My waist, already narrow, was tied with golden cords that wrapped around me twice. The full sleeves gathered at my wrists with more gold, and the shirt fell to the middle of my thighs. The black pants were of a fine leather, the thin belly skin of some creature I didn't know. The outer seam split at my knees and laced with a cream ribbon that glued the whole thing to my form. I stood in my bare feet, my stockings and boots gone.

"What do *you* think?" Schula asked.

"I love it." And I meant it, but I cringed at the price of specially tailored clothes. "How much?"

"Don't worry about it," Schula said. "Baeleon loves to spoil his guests. Don't take this from him."

"We'll take it," Thain announced. "And three more like it, in whatever colors you see fit, mistress. Cotton or linen. I'll pay your courier well for the trouble."

Schula leaned back and shot a peculiar look at Thain before a slow smile spread across her lips.

"Don't you get in on this too," I began.

"Very good!" Rhisa seemed pleased with herself, and more than ready to stop my protests before she could lose any business. "We will have them by the end of the week. To your address, Master Thain?"

The dark fae nodded and stood. I slipped behind the screen to put my own clothes back on and left the new outfit on an empty branch.

"Thank you for visiting the Dancing Willow." Rhisa swept her limbs into a delicate bow, and Maribell saw us onto the street.

"Thank you for your patronage!" Maribell called before gently shutting the door behind us.

"Well, that was something." Schula patted my back. "Why don't we look around for a while before your clothing is ready?"

Thain stretched his right arm and rolled his neck. "It's too crowded here."

"Busybodies," Schula stated. "And none of them will keep me from finding out what smells so good in that soapery."

She had no problem walking away, giving us little choice but to follow. Eyes raked across us as though there were something here to be gawked at. Me. A performer in a band of players. The shops around the Dancing Willow swept away my annoyance quickly, though. Windows full of finely crafted items surrounded me. I let out a sigh and stepped forward. How could I be mad when I was as curious about Thanantholl as it was about me?

"What's that place?" I pointed to a low yellow building with a fat, smoky chimney.

"A tea parlor. You can have a cup and sit down to enjoy it," Schula said. "Or browse the shelves and buy some to take home."

"Can we look in there?" I asked. The only tea I ever drank was made from native mountain plants. Usually ones I had gathered myself. Even our stores on the road had been gathered from the mountains before we'd left the outpost, and I was eager to try more flavors of the fae city.

"Of course." Thain led us through the doors and into a world of scents. Fat jars lined the walls, filled with dried leaves and flowers. I stopped to smell each one, and Schula ordered us all a pot of tea sweetened with honey. Thain sat at a table and waited for Schula and me to finish browsing. We enjoyed our tea, and Schula traded me a little bit of human money for a shiny silver fae coin. She said it was a new oddity to add to her collection of world travels. The tree sprite that worked the counter somehow completed every transaction without saying a word, and we eventually walked out, me with a bag of teas I had never seen before.

Pearl Street continued to ensnare me. It showed me a side of the fae that would have enchanted anyone. Even the hardened people of the mountains. Delicacies and drinks could be discovered on every corner. The shops were full of mesmerizing goods, and the fae that crafted them were overjoyed to show me how they were made. There were spices to smell, books in foreign tongues to read, and art to see.

We went into a narrow shop where Schula bought me a pair of sensible black boots like hers. They came only a handbreadth above my ankle, a completely different feel from my tall mountain boots. We watched a sculptor in his window as he traced the delicate lines of a swooping bird out of clay. A metalsmith displayed a silver set of woodcarving gouges, and I clutched my tunic over my heart. I wished Bryn could have seen them: they were so beautiful and sharp, and he could have carved wonders with them. Then out of nowhere, the tears fell. It distressed Thain, Schula, the shopkeeper, and myself greatly until I could sort myself out and explain.

Finally, Thain bought us all a round of bread, stuffed like a pocket with meat and sauce. We sat on the edge of a fountain to eat.

"Once we're done here, we should pick up your new clothes and go," Thain said.

"I need to change too." Schula looked down at her linen tunic. "I don't suppose this is up to Baeleon's standards."

"No, you go on ahead. Wren and I can meet you and Eberon at the grotto." Thain took a large bite of his lunch, fangs easily tearing through the meat.

Schula glanced at me, her face impassive, but her hand reaching out to pat my back told me everything I needed to know about where her mind was. "You're right. Baeleon is sharp, I'll have to mind that when I dress. Maybe a few extra jewels, to distract."

Thain's brow knit, looking at Schula. But my eyes blew wide, my mind racing through the clothes I now had available to wear. Suddenly, I was beyond thankful for Schula's help in the dressing room, because not only had she helped me hide the mark from the tailors, she'd ensured I had things that would cover them. Especially from a king, who'd likely had a hand in this dispute with the witches.

"Thank you both for today," I said. "I promise to pay you back when I get settled."

"Enough of that." Schula stood and stretched. "I'll see you later, don't let him get you riled up. There is no reason to be nervous, the court will be very surprised to meet you. Pleased, but surprised."

"That's an understatement," Thain mumbled.

Wonderful. The center of attention. Just where I wanted to be.

"All right." I sighed. "Let's go."

FOURTEEN
A PALACE OF WONDERS AND FEARS

I sat at my vanity while Wairen watched me braid my hair. They had taken interest in the task, and while I had never had an audience before, I found I didn't mind the dryad's presence. If anything, it was a blessing that Puko had taken to Wairen's company, or perhaps the other way around, because while his head feathers were being stroked by the tree fae, the silly bird wouldn't be getting in my way.

What I could have done without at that moment was the burning sensation on my back as I sat rigid, trusting the garment I now wore to protect my secret. The problem wasn't that any magic within me was sealed but that witches had sealed it. A witch had sealed it before I was found, and Mila had resealed it during our failed attempt to undo it when I was a child. And though Thain was in the room with me now, relaxed and unreadable as ever, I still couldn't shake the tone in which he'd spoken of the witches.

It had been foolish to allow myself to forget even for a moment that I carried these marks on my back.

Thain leaned against the wall, going over what I was expected to know in the presence of a king. His lifetime of court etiquette shoved into an hour of mind-numbing lecture.

"It figures the first time you have something to speak at length on, it's a subject of as little interest as possible." My fingers worked swiftly, tucking the last bits of hair into place on my left side.

Even in the mirror, I saw the lines of his mouth slant up to one side.

"And since you'll be the youngest in almost every situation you find yourself in, you'll want to make sure you bow exactly as low as the person you are introduced to." Thain scratched his chin.

"Unless it's royalty, in which case I make sure to bow lower," I added.

"The other courts have other rules, but we'll bother with them when the time comes. For tonight, I think you're ready." Thain nodded.

"As ready as I can be." My calloused right hand twitched. "I don't suppose an axe at my hip is proper court attire?"

"We'll all be right there with you." Thain cleared his throat. "Besides, Baeleon is easy to please. You'll be the most interesting thing in the room, and he lives to be entertained."

"I wish I wasn't." I sighed and stood. Wairen now turned their attention fully to the raven.

"Would you rather be looked down upon by the humans again?" Thain asked.

"No," I murmured.

"I know it's hard for you to believe there are people out there who want to meet you, but I promise there are." Thain looked handsome in his court attire, but he was obviously uncomfortable outside his road-worn tunics. I glanced in the mirror. The person looking back at me was unrecognizable. A few days of food and people willing to talk to me had done quite a bit to the lines of my face. If only the shadows of grief didn't cling so hard, I wouldn't even know it was me standing there in fine clothes about to enter such a grand place as a palace.

Thain pushed his weight off the wall and offered me his hand. "I promised you a welcome. Let's go have it, then." Thain kept a steady pace. I was glad for the Autumn Court clothing, because fewer eyes lingered now that I didn't look so out of place. We crossed several bridges, and a wet maple leaf managed to fall right on my forehead while we were walking, but otherwise we had a silent trip to the grotto.

"Looks like we're the last to show up." Thain nodded toward a bench where Schula sat and Eberon paced in front of her. When the golden fae spotted us, he stopped in his tracks then stomped toward Thain.

"About time you showed up! You can't just waltz in to the king's own parlor whenever you feel like it." Eberon ran both hands through his fiery locks, messing up someone's hard work putting them in order. "Do you know how hard it was to quell his impatience? To get him to wait until tonight? The court is in an uproar in there right now, waiting to see her."

"We arrived when we arrived, and Baeleon will not die for not having a new bauble to display," Thain said quietly. Eberon's mouth snapped shut, and a fierce blast of warmth hit me as his fist ignited then extinguished like a candle.

"You're right." He resumed pacing and fidgeting with the obsidian ring on his thumb. "I'm sorry. Wren, I'm sorry."

"We aren't even late," Schula chided. "If it would make you feel better, Eb, we can go inside and wait where the staff can fret over us."

"You said the palace was inside the grotto?" I nudged the subject away from the courtiers and to where I was about to be paraded. The grotto opened up only yards from us. A cavern mouth that was surprisingly clean and polished. A lazy arm of water swept through it, and the only access further in was a golden bridge. The ballroom floor and decorations lay just beyond the bridge, and even now several guests were being entertained there.

"Beyond the mouth of the cavern there, around the bend." Eberon stopped his pacing and approached me, straightening my shirt and inspecting me.

"She's fine, Eberon," Thain snapped, moving Eberon's hand from fussing at a piece of thread on my shoulder.

"Let's just go inside if you're going to mother hen us." Schula stood and brushed off her brown leggings. She wore a yellow shirt in a similar style to mine, and her long white hair was loose, with bits of silver somehow fastened in a scattered pattern of round charms.

"Right, sorry." Eberon cleared his throat. "Yes, let's go."

The air in Thanantholl always had a slight crispness to it. It was the land of a never-ending season, after all. The grotto, however, breathed a chill into my skin as we crossed the gilded bridge. It was wide enough to trot six horses at once. The embellished stones underfoot were carved to look like a bed of leaves.

The water under us carried leaves away silently. On the other side of the bridge, the floor came into view.

Past the dance floor and around a bend, the slick cave wall opened to a breathtaking façade. Shiny white stone, cut into gold-embellished bricks, walled the back of the cave off. A door two stories tall was left half open and heavily guarded. The white wall held balconies, windows, and columns. Red and gold banners hung from several places, displaying a maple leaf and a crown.

"This is the Autumn Palace," Eberon said. "The wall is ten feet thick. This is the only way in or out. The remainder of the interior is carved from within the cave and surrounded by the cliffs around Thanantholl."

"I've only seen one palace, when I went to Sulls. It's where the sultana lives. This . . . this is beautiful. It makes the jewel of the plains, Sulls, look like one of the mountain villages." A calming breath was almost not enough as the magic in me danced and cried to leap out of me. The urge was so strong it was painful. Schula looked at me sideways, a knowing sadness in her eyes.

"I felt the same way when I first came here." Schula put a hand on my back, rubbing along the seal under my clothes, soothing it. I sighed in relief.

"The king resides here," Eberon explained. "But there is one room large enough to hold the Autumn Throne and host an event. That is the part of the palace we will see today."

As we came closer to the door, Eberon walked ahead and spoke to one of the guards. After a brief exchange, we were waved inside.

"It seems dangerous to have only one exit," I said as we walked down the polished halls.

Thain thought for a moment. "We haven't had war between the courts in centuries. Disputes? Constantly. But most war here happens in the Unclaimed Wyldes."

Eberon added, "Most wouldn't dare attack a king in his own city. The magics of the Wyldes have a way of working with those who care for the land. Even the very rocks can surprise you, if they like you."

Now, that's a frightening concept.

"That's the throne room, at the end of the hall." Schula pointed to a set of golden doors with mother-of-pearl inlays that looked like willow trees.

"Just breathe, we're here with you," Thain whispered in my ear as we approached. A pair of guards crossed an arm over their chest in unison, fists hitting their left shoulder. Then they swung the doors open.

"Hells take me," I hissed, and Schula's hand firmly guided me in the room.

"Announcing the triquetram of Lord Thainalan the Ravager, Lord Eberon, and Lady Schula!" I hadn't seen the herald, and I nearly jumped out of my skin as he shouted. "Accompanying the youth Wren of the Southern Mountains!"

You could hear a pin drop in the cavernous hall. That, and probably my heart racing and echoing off the walls.

"Come in, friends. Please, join me." At the end of the long room stood an ancient-looking throne. The round dais held only the throne and two guards; below it was a lower dais that surrounded the first. The floor below that was more polished stone. Red carpet made a path from the door to the dais, which was the only portion of the floor not covered in a huge mob of fae socialites in extravagant clothes and jewels.

I nearly fainted.

Eberon tugged my elbow forward. "Welcome to the Autumn Palace."

FIFTEEN
THE AUTUMN THRONE

Fae of every color lined the room on the floor level. Whispers spread like wildfire from lips to ears. Many of the fae were dressed much like Schula and I, which eased my tension, but others were in wild outfits like something from a strange dream. Tapestries dotted the walls, and chandeliers sparkled overhead like stars. But nothing I saw in the room commanded more attention than the fae sitting on the golden throne.

Blond, tan skin, tall and muscled. He looked to be perhaps forty or so by human years. How old a fae had to be to look like that, when Thain still looked barely twenty-five, sent my head spinning. His presence shifted the air around him, a golden light of power so strong that I had to leash my terror. His aura was palpable. I had thought Thain was the most powerful fae I would ever encounter. Thain was still a child compared to him. The king wore red and orange brocade with golden maple leaves embroidered all over. His crown was a golden laurel, and a ruby in the shape of a maple leaf shone on his ring finger. An obsidian band sat on each thumb.

Thain, Eberon, and Schula stepped forward and stopped in front of the lower dais. Thain gave me a look that had me join them, and together we bowed. I took the opportunity to wipe my palms on my tunic.

"Thank you for meeting with us, Sire." Eberon spoke low, but loud enough for the nearby fae to hear.

"If your story rings true, it will be me who owes thanks. Rise." The fae's blue eyes flickered to me, then back to Eberon. "Come, come sit. I want to hear everything."

Thain gently touched my arm and led me to the lower dais, where four chairs had been prepared. Gold and opulent and topped with a crown of jeweled scrollwork, the chairs held plush brown cushions that made them softer than they first appeared. We each took a seat, and I was more than aware of the crowded room, all eyes on the dais. Eberon sat nearest to the king, and I sat between Thain and Schula, all of us to the left of the throne.

"What is wrong with her?" King Baeleon asked.

My throat tightened, and I clenched my jaw. *He knows? How?*

"I think the issue here is the crowded room." Eberon inclined his head toward me as he addressed Baeleon. "She grew up among very few people; the crowd is a bit much."

All the air left my body. *He doesn't know. How would he know? Breathe, before you give yourself away.*

"The crowd? That, I can do something about." The king clapped once, and an orchestra that I hadn't noticed in the back corner began to play a light tune. It was merry and fluttered high and low like leaves on the wind. The roomful of fae dropped their eyes from me and began dancing. Servers with gold trays burst from the side doors and brought delicacies and drinks around the room, starting with the king, of course.

"There! Now, I have many questions for you." Baeleon smiled, dimples warming his face. He seemed likable, for a fae who could probably do incredible things beyond my imagining on a whim. But there was still a hard edge in his eyes that kept me at the front of my seat, ready to flee. A primal instinct, I was sure. You probably didn't keep a fae throne this long by being soft.

"What would you like to know, Sire?" I tried to copy Eberon's words and movements, and he gave me an encouraging smile.

"Eberon, the fiend, wouldn't tell me much." The king leaned back and crossed his outstretched ankles. "I'm told they found you in the mountains south of the Wyldes, but that's about it."

"Yes, I lived between a few small villages and homesteads. I was raised by a woodcutter named Bryn. We lived in a cabin he built himself, and cut and dried lumber for coin." A pang shot my heart. It was dulling with time, but it was still there.

"And you've never seen a fae, or anything else of the Wyldes before now?" the king asked.

"No, Sire. Thain was the first. The people of the mountains still have stories of the fae, but I never expected to see one in my lifetime." I folded my hands in my lap and blushed as Baeleon laughed heartily.

The room around us, still dancing, laughed along with their king. My eyes flicked to Schula, who had an expression that read, *Just go along with it*, and Thain, who looked more grimly resolved to be in this room than anything else.

"Well, now you've seen a great deal more than one of us." Baeleon's laughter boomed. "So, you grew up as a human. Did you know you were something from the Wyldes before Thainalan found you?"

"Yes, Sire." My back itched, and I hoped he couldn't sense what was on me. "I have always known, everyone around me knew."

"And you have no knowledge of your parentage?" He took a glass of wine from a servant, who then offered the tray to the rest of us.

"None." A hand was placed over mine, and I looked over to see Schula giving me an encouraging smile. "As far as I know, I am half human. I have no glamour, and my appearance is completely human."

"And your ears?" He tilted his head. I could feel Thain stiffen beside me. I'd put my hair in two thick braids that covered my tips easily, but for the king of my friends and saviors, I would reveal my shame.

"My ears may have been the only hint to my lineage, Sire, but they reveal no secrets now." With fingers numb not from the cool autumn day but from the swirling anxiety of the moment, I began to unravel my braids. Schula leaned over, helping me gather my hair to the back of my head and block the view from the room as much as she could, but it was too late for that. Several gasps behind me told me that the dancing courtiers hadn't completely given up eavesdropping, and I knew just how sharp their sight was to see what I kept under those braids. When I was done, I tucked the hair behind my ears long enough for the king to take a look.

"Who?" The king leaned forward and slammed a fist on his throne, shattering the wineglass in his other hand as servants scurried to clean up. "Who would do such a thing?"

The scene must have been familiar to the courtiers, because the only one in the whole room who flinched was me. With a deep breath, Schula and I began to re-braid.

"I'm afraid I don't know. I was found in the woods this way," I managed, shaking from the power behind the king's fury but keeping my voice level.

"Are you certain it wasn't the humans who found you?" he growled.

My fingers curled into fists in my lap, steadying my heart against the slander to my father. "I would stake my life on it. The one to find me was the one to raise me until the day he died to protect me." Baeleon didn't look convinced. Eyes around the room, advisers at the edge of the dais, and even attendants carrying food and drink all seemed to be waiting for an indication of who to side with. Their king, surely, but Bryn had *not* harmed me. Not once, not ever.

"My king, the human who found and raised her died saving her life from raiders," Thain said quietly. "I witnessed it myself."

Baeleon eased into his throne again, nodding slowly with approval though still wearing the sour emotion on his face.

"My condolences," Baeleon said, taking a new glass of wine from a footman. Some in the room behind me cooed their sympathy.

"Thank you." My breath shook slightly, but my heart calmed enough to smile for the king. A show, this was all a show to entertain and to please. The feeling of being on display was not new to me, but their reactions were wildly different than what I was used to.

"I understand you are hosted by Thainalan. If you wish, I could give you finer rooms in the palace. You would be well cared for while you settle into the Wyldes," the king offered.

I hesitated, and he seemed to pick up on it.

"Of course, you may stay where you wish." He inclined his head toward Thain. "The offer, however, will remain open if you ever grow tired of his dreary moods."

"Thank you, Sire," I said. I wondered how Thain felt about being called *dreary*, but I could see how the king, who surrounded himself with courtiers and music, would think that. But unlike the king, a quiet house with Thain and Wairen was most definitely my preference.

"What a strange situation," Baeleon murmured. "My court finds a youngling who survived the disease, but in turn we must find the youngling a place."

Shifting on my seat, I looked to Eberon and Schula for any indication of what I was supposed to do here. Was this uncomfortable pause supposed to be filled? By me? Or was Baeleon thinking out loud?

An aged fae, something very tree-like but with the mannerisms I'd grown used to with Eberon, cleared his throat at the bottom of the dais. I'd nearly missed seeing him entirely, but he was on the king's other side. "Perhaps a council to discuss the matter, Sire?"

Baeleon waved him off. "Bah, my council takes much of my time as it is. And, as much as I detest saying it, this matter is for more than my own attention." The king's eyes slid around the room, pausing on a few people scattered about. Not that I could tell which ones, the room was so constantly moving and there were so many people.

"Tell me." He turned back to me, and I jumped in my seat. "Have the courts of these lands been explained to you?"

"Yes, some. We traveled through the Summer Lands, and I know there are two more I have not seen."

Baeleon inclined his head. "I happen to have ambassadors from each of the other courts here as we speak. There's always someone crawling through these halls when the doors are open. I met with some of them last night, as a matter of fact." He waved over a servant with a tray of dried fruits. "Circumstances being what they are, all four courts have agreed to a year's time in which you are free to roam the Wyldes, a citizen of all of them until you choose one for yourself. You have all the privileges and protections that each court provides while in their borders."

"But they haven't even met me," I said, then snapped my mouth shut. This open acceptance had to be a trick of some kind. Eberon looked more amused than anything else, Schula seemed pleased, and Thain just added a nod.

"Thank you for your generosity." Eberon gave a small bow in his chair. I took his lead and bowed my head too. "I believe what Wren means is she is still learning of the fae generosity after so long among humans without it."

I nodded vigorously, latching onto Eberon's explanation, and the king laughed.

"It is well, young one. You will see soon enough how different from those human animals we are." The king took a long drink from his wine, and I couldn't help but feel a small pang of annoyance that he would disregard half of my lineage so easily. He finished his glass, and as another was poured, he addressed our party.

"You three." Baeleon swept the hand holding his wineglass at the triquetram around me. "You, of course, are tasked with traveling her through the Wyldes."

"Of course, Sire." Thain gave a rare smile, and Schula bowed her head. "We are honored to guard her and guide her."

"And Thainalan, if she has magic, you are to assist her in managing her powers. What may not have surfaced in the human realms will surely spring forth here." Baeleon leaned forward, to my horror, and took a deep breath through his nose in my direction. "Ah, and unless I grow feeble in my old age, I'd say she has quite a bit of it under the surface."

Oh no. Oh no no no. My back *burned,* and I clenched my fists so tightly that my nails drew blood in my palms. If he looked deep enough, he'd find magic all right. But would the seal restraining it turn this evening of spectacle and merriment into something far worse?

"Yes, Majesty." Thain bowed again.

"Now, with that business out of the way, I'm sure you know of our dire situation." Baeleon gave me a pained look. "Many of our younger people are dead."

"Yes, Sire. I've been informed," I said, mouth dry.

"Very well, then, I would like to know your age and birthday, if I may," he said, and many of the courtesans danced just a bit closer to the dais, all the better to eavesdrop.

"I am twenty-five years old." The number felt so small, so insignificant in the room, and yet I heard a number of pitiful murmurs. "And since I was found as a baby, I'm not sure of my precise birthday. But I was only a few days old when I was found around harvest season, weeks at best, so Bryn and I always celebrated my birthday on the autumn equinox. It's close to when I should have been born."

"The *equinox*!" the king exclaimed, slamming his hands against the arms of his throne, causing me to jump and the music falter for a moment as he splashed wine onto the floor but didn't shatter the glass this time. "A glorious day! Did you know of this, Eberon?"

"No, I didn't, Sire." Eberon gave me a grin. "A good day indeed. Wren, it's the first day of power for our court. I'm only sorry we missed celebrating with you."

"I can promise next year will be the most exciting birthday you've ever had. You'll have to see the festivities in Thanantholl." Schula smiled. "That is, if you want to, of course."

My eyes rounded, and everything in me tried to relay without words that, no, I most certainly did *not* want the most exciting birthday I'd ever had, shaking my head in small but significant motions. Schula simply covered her smile with a wineglass.

"To have a birthday on the equinox is quite a celebration around here." The king gave me a wink. "The finest day of the finest season. And almost always a sure sign that you belong with the Autumn Court. Are you certain you don't have a particular pull to this place?"

"I would love to see Thanantholl on the equinox." I smiled, resigning myself to his invitation. "I'll be sure to be here for it, Sire. All of the Wyldes has felt so alive to me, I'm afraid I wouldn't be able to tell the difference yet."

"The human blood meddling, I'm sure." He waved me off, taking a swig from his glass. "You'll find yourself in the Wyldes, now that you're in them. Give it time. Now, with that business out of the way, let's become more casually acquainted. What do you think of the food here? I'm told Eberon took you to the River's Edge."

We talked for an hour about things to see in Thanantholl, the food, the craftsmanship, the architecture. Baeleon gushed about everything the Autumn Lands had to offer. Servants came and went with food, and after a time, the orchestra took a break and several important fae came forward to introduce themselves.

Nymphs, sprites, wisps, fae of every kind came to greet their king and steal glances at me. Some were beautiful. Some were frightening. All were strange to me. I had barely gotten used to Thain, Eberon, and Schula. I wasn't ready for a parade of every person in the palace. Yet here they were.

Another hour dragged on, and then another. Between all the wine and the amount of time the king had held me hostage with his parade of lords, I was squirming for the privies. Schula was too, or she sensed my emergency and came to my rescue.

"Sire, may I excuse myself to the washroom?" She stood gracefully, and the king nodded before returning to the newest lord to approach the lower dais. "Thank you. Oh, and Wren, would you like to know where they are? I can show you."

I latched on to her, barely remembering to bow, and we left the room. Fae left and right tried to pause us for a chat, but Schula expertly avoided each one. The twisting golden halls of the palace echoed our footsteps as we turned further in.

My muscles relaxed with every step away from the noise of the great hall. I nearly sighed with relief when we turned in to an empty hall.

"Forgive Baeleon. His social appetite hasn't been sated no matter how many centuries he indulges it." Schula smiled. "I know it's not your favorite thing, but we all appreciate it. I'm afraid your name is going to ripple through the Wyldes now, though."

"I was ready for that," I said. I sighed. "Thank you, I don't think I can stand it anymore."

Her eyes softened, and a cool hand rested on my arm. "Any time."

Schula was such a comfort. I didn't understand the dynamic of many kinds of family members, but I liked to think we were already getting along well. If anything, I wished to find a way to repay her kindness, but that wasn't the only thing on my mind. "Um, you weren't lying about the privies, were you?"

Schula gave a light laugh, like snow dancing in the sky. "No, I wasn't. We're almost there."

SIXTEEN
SMALL TRUTHS

The washrooms, like everything else in the palace, were polished and grand. The room next to them was a large bath, open for anyone to use. I peeked in while Schula took a turn at her business, and it might as well have been a pond for as big as it was. Fragrant steam misted the room, adding an air of mystery to the dark corners where I couldn't see. Small trays of candles floated on the water's surface, flickering and dancing with each ripple.

I will never get used to how these people view the ritual of taking a hot bath, but I think I'm starting to agree with them.

"Welcome to the bath, may I get you a towel?" A water nymph stood in attendance near the doorway.

"Oh, no, I was just looking. Sorry, I'll go," I muttered and began backing away.

"Wait." A commanding voice echoed off the polished stone room. "I smell something interesting. Please, come closer."

I looked to the attendant, who seemed cautious but nodded me in. My footsteps rattled around the room as I skirted the pool and went to a flickering corner of candles. The smell of damp wood, the one after a summer rain on the forest floor, perfumed the air. The sole bather in the grand bath was a pink woman, with black hair no longer than the boys' of the mountains. Her eyes were solid white, and she didn't follow my movements with them.

"What can I do for you, lady?" I hoped I wasn't calling her the wrong title, though other than the king there seemed to be only lords and ladies here.

"Ahh. The reason I was called to counsel with the Autumn King and the other two dignitaries last night. The youngling." She tilted her head back against the side of the bath, stretching her arms out with no concern about her nakedness. She gave off a dangerous aura, not unlike Thain when I'd first met him. Something feral. Maybe something a little bit like the wraith. "Not so young right now, though, are you? I wonder if I could taste your sire on you." The way she grinned at her own words made me nervous.

"Wren, there you are." Schula had found me in the bath. She stood in the doorway, arms crossed.

"Wren, is it?" The strange fae's lips curled upward, and she licked them. "Wren."

Schula froze when she spotted the fae in the bath, then she nodded to her. "Krissaph, if you'll excuse us."

"Ah, the frigid bitch is here. Run along, little Wren, I'm sure we'll meet again when it is my king's turn to entice you." She stretched again, chuckling to herself.

I didn't need to be told twice. Schula let me out before her, and the water nymph bowed us out.

"What were you doing?" Schula hissed at me.

"I was just looking at the bath!" I said. "I didn't know anyone was in there."

"It wasn't your fault." Schula sighed, raking her fingers through her hair. "I'll take you to a bathhouse later, a nice one without Spring Court rubbish in it."

"She was Spring Court? What was that talk about her king?" I looked over my shoulder. "I thought the Spring Court would be different."

"Warmer? Pleasant?" Schula began walking us back to the throne room. "Krissaph is a succubus, one of the unseelie fae."

"Unseelie?" The word tickled at the back of my mind; I'd heard it before. Possibly from Mila.

"No matter what kind of fae creature you are, from sylph to fae to wraith, you can be classified into one of two categories." Schula grimaced.

"The seelie are mostly what you've encountered so far. Fae who are essentially considered of a good nature. Well, by the standards of the Wyldes. We don't have the same morals as the humans, but for the most part, we could get along.

"The unseelie, though, are all made of something just a little darker. Always something greedy about them, but they all want different things. Let's say Eberon was made to be sociable, and Thain was made to be contemplative. I would say the unseelie were made to be wrathful or envious. Enough so that their baser instincts could be to take something or harm someone. That wraith you encountered in the mountains with Thain, that was something unseelie."

"That's right, Mila told me once." I gestured to my back and whispered, "The witch."

"Anyway, don't listen to Krissaph, but if you run into her again just—" Schula cursed. "Of course you will. Wren, she's an ambassador from the Spring Court. Just try to stay out of her way as best as you can."

I grimaced. "Do all of the courts have unseelie fae in them?"

"Everywhere in the Wyldes," she said. "Some can actually be pleasant. Born unseelie but who keep a firm grasp on their behaviors to blend into society better. Most of the unseelie, if they belong to any court, are in Winter."

"Oh." We stopped talking as we rounded a corner to the main hall of the palace.

"Well, that's a conversation for another time." She put on a smile and took my arm. "Are you ready to endure our beloved king a little longer?"

"I just wish it wasn't all so false," I grumbled.

Schula's brows pushed together. "What do you mean?"

"All the honeyed words, the sympathetic gasps. I feel as though I'm a player on a stage," I clarified.

Schula softened. "The fae are rarely so false with their reactions. This is a people of displayed emotions. A people who were all touched by terrible loss just a few decades ago. All of them are genuine, including King Baeleon."

It stunned me to silence.

"So, ready?" she asked, beaming at me.

A deep breath steadied me, and another prepared me for the room.

"As ready as I can be." I put on a smile myself, and we were saluted into the throne room to fend off more courtiers.

The celebration went on for hours. The king kept us near him, but I felt more like a trophy to display than a guest. He didn't ask me many more questions, the odd one here or there when he wanted to know what kind of wine I liked or if I preferred the architecture of Thanantholl to my home. Nothing of much consequence, though. But plenty of the other fae took an interest and paid their respects to Baeleon before approaching me.

Thain grew unsettled as the party went on, probably annoyed that he was here for so long. He even glared at a visiting lord who had only stopped to greet me. Schula shot him a look, but I didn't blame him. I was getting restless too. As thankful as I was for the new clothing, I was ready to yank off the silky attire the moment I got to my bedroom. I worried with every movement that I would ruin it somehow.

It was late before Baeleon let us leave. With the constant flow of food and drinks, none of us were hungry. All I wanted to do was go to bed.

Stumbling home, Schula said her goodbyes and turned down her road. Eberon was still at the party, enjoying himself, or so he claimed. The socialite. That left me to stumble after Thain, trying not to yawn too loudly as he wound through the sleepy streets back to the house.

The night air was cold, but not so much that it bit and nipped like a winter's night. The road was paved with wet leaves that had fallen during the day, waiting for a good rain to sweep them to the sides and away into the waters that veined Thanantholl. And tired as I was, the sensation of being alone in the quiet with Thain felt good. Comfortable in a way that I didn't feel with anyone else. Maybe Mila, but she would find a way to insert lessons if the silence went on for too long. And Bryn couldn't let any silence fall without digging up an amusing story I'd already heard a dozen times over, but he loved to tell them, and I loved to listen. With Thain, the quiet peace that was usually mine to bring to the room was both of ours, and I found it more than pleasant to share it with someone else.

We arrived at his tree-twined home with nothing to welcome us but the rustling of breeze-addled leaves. Thain opened the door, having me walk into the warmth first.

"Are you going to make it up the stairs?" Thain teased.

Too tired to engage in the banter, I gave him a rude gesture, and he laughed at me as we climbed the staircase, parting as I found my way down the second-floor hall while he continued up to his third-floor quarters.

The room was dark and quiet. The curtain was pulled back enough at the balcony that I could see Puko had found himself a comfortable bed in the ivy-covered railing, so I turned my full attention to drawing a hot bath. I left my underthings on the floor and sank into the water with a sigh. I was drained from the party, which is what it must have been. If *that* was a party, I was completely on Thain's side about avoiding them in the future. Eberon ate it all up, not that it surprised me. Schula had told me she liked dressing up and didn't mind the small talk, though she didn't go looking for it either. My idea of a party was dancing with no more than three witches from around the mountains on midsummer night, and none of *them* cared who my parents were. They simply traveled at Mila's invitation and celebrated the night together. Especially Gilly, when Bryn would let her into the cabinet of spirits he kept for special occasions. But none of them held anything against me that was so far out of my control as my blood.

The bath did wonders for me, and combing my hair out was soothing. I braided it like I always did and put on my old clothes. I went onto the balcony to do some stretches and found Puko gorging himself on a plate of walnuts.

"I'm not entirely sure you've had the healthiest diet for a bird. What would Mila think?" I looked at him. He eyed me and cawed.

"Suit yourself." I sat and stretched for my toes. The night air was cool and had turned misty. It would probably rain overnight, but it seemed to rain a lot in Thanantholl. A branch of water across the road from Thain's home pattered along quietly, taking with it fallen rose petals and bright ruby leaves.

"How long do you suppose we'll be here? In Thanantholl," I asked the bird. He continued to crunch at his dinner. "It sounds as though we'll be traveling again at some point."

I moved on to another stretch, my arms this time. It was peaceful here, and beautiful. I hated to admit it, but the Wyldes felt right. Something in my bones knew I belonged here. Tomorrow, I would have to make an honest effort to learn about the fae. About my people.

I stretched for a little longer than I would have liked, but not as long as Schula would have made me. The moon was going to be full soon, and the night air glowed silver. By the time I was done stretching, Puko was done eating. I took his plate inside to my table and lay down in my tunic. I was exhausted, sure that the moment my head hit the pillow I'd be able to fall asleep.

I didn't.

I couldn't stop thinking about the palace. The fae that had stared at me. The king's heavy presence. Lady Krissaph's words. I turned on my side, and the wraith came to mind. I shoved it away and sat up. Sleep was useless. Maybe some time by the warm hearth would do me good. I shoved my legs back in my breeches and stockings—not my nice new things but something that didn't take me several minutes to figure out how to lace—and crept downstairs.

The fire was inviting. Its warmth reached me from the top of the stairs, and I sank into it as I descended the staircase. When I neared the fireplace, I nearly jumped out of my skin. The chair that faced away from the stairs wasn't empty.

"You're up late." Thain was sitting forward, elbows on his knees and a glass of amber liquid in one hand. He had discarded his doublet and rolled up the sleeves of his fine shirt.

Closing my eyes, I sighed out all the tension. Jumpy, I was just jumpy about my seal. These worries were building and making things worse, but I still didn't know what to do about them. Other than finding a way to finally open it up and face what was inside.

Nope.

"I couldn't sleep." I sat in the chair on the other side of the fire. "You're up late as well."

"I suppose I have a lot on my mind," he said after a while. "What seems to be keeping you up?"

"Several things." I sank back into the chair. "I'm still coming to terms with what I am. I mean, I've always known, but I didn't realize until coming here what it really meant."

"Ah." He set his glass aside and sat back. "It's a lot to take in, I'm sure."

The only thing I could do was hold my tongue. If learning more about the fae was the only problem on my mind, this wouldn't be so much of a struggle. But the more I learned that my involvement with Mila—with a witch—might be a problem, the more stress seemed to pile on top of me. The Wyldes were not a place where I would be ostracized for being part fae, a blessing I never thought I'd have, but I couldn't help feeling as though I'd lose it all if they found out I was raised with a witch.

"Are you all right after the event tonight?" he asked, his voice low like a fire that was settling down once the logs were dried and the bark was black. There had always been something smoky about the way I perceived Thain, even his hair that never quite lost the campfire scent to it.

"It was a spectacle," I said, and Thain's low, rumbling laugh sent a warm comfort through me.

"You don't like it any more than I do," I prodded, face warming but a smile on my lips as I picked at the hem of my sleeve.

"That I don't," he agreed. He reached out, brushing a stray bit of hair off my forehead, the roughness of his fingertips light on my skin.

"So, I'll be asked to travel to all the courts?" I voiced my newest concern. "Why can't I just stay here, in Thanantholl?"

Thain sighed, looking out the window where the moon lit up the city around us. "Baeleon speaks for the land, just as the other courts speak for theirs. I'll not pretend to understand what politics brought them to this decision, but I also wouldn't hold you back from your greatest chance at finding the best place for you."

Tracing the lines of him with my eyes, every part of his face the moonlight touched, my stomach twisted to think the most kindred spirit I'd found might not be part of that "best place."

"What's to stop me from simply announcing that the Autumn Lands feel the most like home?" I asked.

"You'll find a place that draws you to it," Thain said. "You'll know what feels right when you're there."

"But what if I don't? What if the parts of me that aren't fae prevent me from having the full feelings the rest of you do?" I swallowed. "I'm tired of being told I'll feel a certain way. This was supposed to be my chance to find something for myself that wasn't defined by how everyone around me felt about my presence. I don't know enough. I don't have enough information about this place, and I don't truly know what it means to live a life here. Not yet, anyway."

The quiet of the house stretched between us, Thain swirling his glass.

"Tomorrow," Thain said, interrupting my thoughts, "we can go to the library if you'd like to learn more about our history."

"Aren't you old enough to have lived most of the history?" I asked, provoking a laugh from him. His fangs glinted in the flickering light.

"Why don't we leave it to the scholars who are better suited to it." He reached back and untied his ponytail, scratching his head and letting his hair fall freely.

He emptied his glass, setting it on a side table as the fire glinted off the black band on his thumb.

"Can I ask about your ring?" I asked, and he glanced down at his hand. "I saw you and Eberon wearing those black rings on your thumbs. I saw the king wearing them too. Do they mean something?"

"Mmm." He looked down to his right hand and played with the obsidian band on it. "This ring means I've found and lost a member of my triquetram."

"I'm so sorry, I shouldn't have asked," I whispered. "So, the king then? Did he . . . ?"

"Yes, both of his. Baeleon is old, though, it's to be expected eventually." Thain stopped fidgeting with his ring and pulled the bottle from the mantle to pour another drink. "Have you had any experiences with your magic showing up? Any events at all?"

Chewing on my lower lip, I mulled over my answer. Of course there'd been an event, a huge one that had shaped my whole perspective on magic. Namely that I didn't want it. But the king had asked him just today to guide me on my magic, something that terrified me to no end. What if he found out what a danger I could be and didn't want me in his home anymore?

"When I was a child," I began but stopped. My fingers dug into the arms of the chair.

"Go on," he urged softly.

"I set fire to a house by accident," I admitted. Suddenly, I was keenly aware of my beating heart. The heat that consumed my palms, the stiffness of my back. He didn't have to know how bad it had been. Thain never needed to know, because it might change things between us, and I couldn't handle that. "Thank you for talking with me, Thain. I think I'm ready to go to bed now."

My heart was pounding. I had to get out of there.

"Wren?" Thain called, but it was too late. I had already leaped from my chair and was on the stairs before he set his glass down and stood up. I glanced back to see him standing, staring up at me, but he didn't give chase.

I topped the stairs and ran down the hall to my room, not looking back. *Coward*, I chided. *You are a lying, hiding coward.*

SEVENTEEN
VAST KNOWLEDGE

Thain didn't mention the previous night at breakfast. He didn't mention it while we walked through the city, or when we entered the palace and went down the long, torchlit hallways that led to the library. By nature it wasn't unusual for him to not talk much, but I couldn't stop thinking about how he'd looked by the fire as I went up the stairs and away from him.

Guilt sat like a stone in my belly, but so did the terror of facing my magic. I could feel it struggling against the seal, and it only grew stronger as I stayed here. The distraction was particularly fierce today, and I nearly ran into Thain as he stopped at the doors.

"This is the Library of Autumn. The other courts have their own equivalent." He stood aside to show me the elaborately carved wooden doors, a cold metal handle shaped like vines protruding from each.

"That handle is iron, to remind us of the sacrifices it takes to carry the burdens of truth." He pointed to the left handle first, then the right. "This one is silver, to remind us of the riches those truths can bring us."

"Does it matter which one we open?" I asked, my words bouncing off the stone floors.

"Every choice in the Wyldes matters." There was an intensity to his words, his gaze, that wasn't out of place for the impassive Thain but was still not quite expected.

My first thought was to suffer with the iron handle, even though it wouldn't hurt me to do so. My hand lifted toward it first, but something stopped me. It made sense to suffer for the reward, but I wasn't the one doing the suffering of research. I was here only for the riches of knowledge. I placed my hand on the silver handle and let us in.

Once my eyes adjusted to the candlelight, before me I saw a room of books, scrolls, and shuffling scribes. The shelves stood in the middle of the room so the walls would be free to hold a massive mural.

Thain strode through the library and straight to the desk of a dusty gray creature. With an upper half something like a human and the ears and lower half of something goat-like, he sat, hunched over a half-written scroll, drinking deeply from a wine bottle.

"I told you, Memna will bring the documents when they are *ready.* Not a moment sooner." He stroked his beard and continued scrawling.

Thain didn't make a sound, he just waited patiently for the scribe to look up from his papers. It didn't take more than a moment for him to finish the line he was working on and set his charcoal stick down.

"Lord Thainalan!" The creature shot up, nearly knocking his wine bottle on the floor. "What brings you to the library, business for the king?"

"Not specifically. I'm here for this one." Thain nodded toward me. "This is Wren."

As if that was enough of an introduction. But before I opened my mouth to clarify, the librarian's goat ears twitched, and he crinkled his nose.

"Wren, where have I heard that today? Wren! The found faeling?"

I muttered under my breath, "I'm not a child."

"The very one," Thain answered, folding his arms over his chest and leaning his hip against the desk. The librarian looked downright giddy as he clapped his hands together. "Splendid! Wonderful to meet you. I would be delighted to share my knowledge." He scooted off his chair and approached me slowly, crossing an arm over his chest in the palace salute. "My name is Cosimo, the caretaker of lore here at the palace. I would be happy to give you a brief history of the Wyldes."

"Hello, Cosimo." I mimicked the Autumn greeting.

"I'll wait here. I have something I need to look into." Thain waved over a clerk, who scurried over with her arms full of documents.. "Cosimo is a satyr of abundant knowledge; he can answer your questions, and I'll be here when you're done."

"All right," I began, but already Cosimo was practically bouncing next to me.

"This way, Miss Wren!" Cosimo's hooves clicked on the stone floor as he led me to a far wall. Candles flickered from every angle, and I was mesmerized by an ancient mural that stretched from one corner of the library wall to the other.

"We'll start here, one of my favorite pieces. This is the tale of beginnings." Cosimo pointed to the first part of the mural, a collection of stars. Cosimo's soft voice lilted through the story. "One day, two of the stars descended, creating the Mother and Father to all fae kind. They called themselves Titan and Oba. From them sprang all life in the Wyldes."

I leaned in to inspect the two figures, depicted with a shining light around their bodies. The next images were of a ferocious war. I grimaced, wondering what would lead to that so quickly in the mural.

"With their work completed, Titan and Oba returned to the stars, leaving their creations with only a few rules. Those rules guide how our magic functions. As I'm sure you've learned by now, we cannot lie, we cannot go against our word, and our magic is deeply connected to our emotions. What magic have you been blessed with?" Cosimo asked.

Grimacing, I kept myself facing the mural. "Nothing yet, maybe nothing at all as I'm only half fae."

Cosimo tutted with sympathy, looking as though he wanted to talk about it.

"The stars." I changed the subject, pointing to the next bit of the mural. "They left?"

Cosimo's attention moved back to the wall, and I sighed. "Indeed, they did. With the stars returned to the sky, none were left standing above the creatures they had created. A bloody war broke out as the fae fought to establish rulership over one another." We walked further to find a circle of creatures somewhere in the Wyldes. "After what we've come to call the Five-Hundred-Year War, a conference was held. Representatives of each faction came forward to end the fighting and attempt peace."

"Five *hundred* years?" I gasped.

"And another year for the conference." Cosimo moved along. "I'll skip the failed attempts, but suffice to say the end result was the four courts we have today. Moving down here, we see the establishment of boundaries, and first contact with humans."

"The fae were here that long before humans?" I asked, not that it surprised me terribly.

"Oh my, yes, and longer than I've gone into explaining, but here you see first contact." Cosimo pointed as he spoke. "Ancient humans were seen as little better than cattle. No magic, short-lived, and they breed like flies. Wars happened, human numbers against fae magic. Messy business. In the end, a healthy fear of the fae was established simply to keep them out of the rich lands of the Wyldes."

"I had no idea there were wars, that the humans could even fight back enough to be worth the effort." I traced the tile border of stars around the mural.

"You aren't the first to voice their surprise." Cosimo chuckled. "Moving on, here we see the crowning of King Baeleon . . ."

I was taken down the wall through coronation and war. The fae had not been a peaceful people until very recently. Entire races had died out. A particularly terrible war had Cosimo stopping to sigh.

"The War of the Wyldes." He rubbed his temples. "An opposition to the long-established courts. Some races choose to live in the Unclaimed Wyldes rather than under the banner of one of the courts."

"Aren't there still fae creatures living in the Unclaimed Wyldes?" I asked.

"Yes, some. Not nearly the numbers there were before this war." He stroked his beard. "This was the last time the four courts truly worked together. Countless lives were lost, sadly. The four courts won, barely. Unseelie horrors . . . Er, do you know about the seelie and unseelie?"

"Yes, I've been told a little about that," I said.

"Right, good. Many unseelie horrors were wiped out, but of course not completely. The dragons were wiped from these lands, or at least none have been seen since, but the devils can sleep for centuries in hiding, so who really knows? The elves were nearly decimated. Heh, now there was a faction that left cursing our names. They were banished, and our kind doesn't live well outside the magic of the Wyldes. I think they numbered only five males anyway, so even if they live there remain only five. An entire breed of dryad was nearly wiped off the map, but the few who had remained loyal to the courts have really brought their species back to thriving. The selkies were banished, though a few weakened descendants still lurk along the coasts to prey on humans from what I've heard."

The mural spared no gory detail as a dragon was gutted with spears. A dark blue fae was depicted ripping off something's head. I shuddered, sneaking a glance to the middle of the room where Thain sat by Cosimo's desk. Moving down, I saw several figures that froze me in place. They looked human, or they were depicted with the round ears that humans had been shown with earlier. But these figures wore draped clothing in dark colors, and their lifted hands glowed with a color I knew all too well: a bright purple fire. These were witches, and they were being slaughtered with the rest of the creatures in the mural. An arrow shot through one of them, and purple fire consumed a fae warrior opposite the witches. Was this what had made Thain say those things back at the outpost?

"How awful," I whispered.

"What I'm truly glad to see gone are the upir." Cosimo scrunched up his face, oblivious to my distress. "An ugly breed of creature. Crafty things, though, so a couple may have survived, but none have been seen."

Blinking away any signs that I held a connection to those images of the witches in battle, I followed his eyes to an unsightly woman in black, ripping the heart from a fae with a wide smile on her lips. Cosimo cleared his throat, bringing my attention back to him, and we began to walk again.

"Moving on, we have the coronation of the queen of the Spring Court after her father was slain." He tutted, shaking his head. "An ugly business that was. Very messy, and rare that the throne went to a direct descendant of the previous ruler. Oh well, King Diamid is now crowned ruler of the Spring Court, so I suppose it didn't matter for long."

My brows drew together, trying to piece together what that was supposed to mean and if Baeleon's eccentricities were a part of his station more than his nature. And why would it be rare to have the ruler's child inherit the throne? What was that about?

Cosimo continued his stories, following a theme of bloody wars and toppling of royals interchangeably. Both, it would seem, happened often. The end of the mural, which now began to reach around the corner of the wall, was a fresher addition depicting the plague that had wiped out so many young fae. It was a very sobering end.

By the time we'd circled the room and Cosimo walked us back to his desk, we found Thain reading from a crumbling tome.

"Finished?" he asked, closing the book.

"Indeed. A brief history, but it should suffice." Cosimo bowed. "If you ever wish to dive deeper into the subject, I have abundant resources that could assist."

"I appreciate your time today. We'll be leaving then." Without another word, the dark fae strode for the door once again.

"Bye, Cosimo." I offered a wave. The odd little scholar's delight in history was infectious.

Thain led us out of the palace and through the streets. My eyes took a moment to adjust to the light.

"What were you reading?" I was curious what would interest the quiet warrior enough to look into.

"A history of witches," he said flatly.

I stopped in my tracks, my heart pounding. "Why?"

Thain's answer came softly, firmly. "You know why."

My heart rose to the base of my throat, choking, suffocating. Thain knew. He *knew*. How did he know? Thain didn't stop for me, if he even realized his words had halted me on the spot.

"What were you looking for?" Voice strained, I followed at a healthy distance.

"You know what I was looking for, Wren." He kept walking. "You don't want to have this conversation here; let's go home."

It was true, I didn't. I followed in silence, over the bridges and around the trees, wondering if I would need to take King Baeleon up on his offer of palace rooms or if this had already been revealed to the strange king.

Other citizens gave Thain a wide berth in the streets. All I could do was stumble after him, trying to keep up. My stomach turned into one big knot when we reached his quiet little street. The once welcoming door now looked ominous.

Thain still didn't look at me as he yanked the door open, bringing us inside. He shut the door and turned to me. "Do you want to explain?"

"Explain what?" I swallowed my nerves at his anger and scowled at him, holding my own.

"Why you have the markings of a witch on your back. Wairen saw them the other night." A ripple in his appearance flashed claws and muscles that hadn't been there before but that I'd seen at the edges of every fight he was in. His glamour slipped. Hells, he was suffocating me with the thick air around him, hungry and feral and in an agitated state I'd never seen him in before—angry.

He wanted to be angry about it? I'd had twenty-five years to be angry about it, and I had no problems letting him know it.

"It's not as though I asked for it." Clenching my fists at my sides, I lifted my chin at him. "They were there when I was found. It's another thing that was done to me before I could even speak my first words. It's something I desperately want to rid myself of, and at the same time I'm terrified to let out!"

We had both exploded. A crack in the perfect quiet I had come to know between us. I didn't want this. I didn't want any of this. Hiding it all had been bound to come out in a messy way; I had been a fool to think it wouldn't. And he had been crystal clear that there was some problem between the fae and the witches.

"Thain—"

"But you've been hiding it." His soft words lashed out. "You are a part of this land, Wren, whether you will admit it or not."

Every word I'd said to him surfaced, each moment in which I'd carefully chosen to speak in a way that didn't wholly include myself in the Wyldes. I'd been working on it, to be sure, but at the beginning . . . "That's not fair."

"Do you know what it means for me to have brought witching magic inside the city?" he asked.

"I'm not a witch," I argued. "The only thing these marks do is close off another terrible accident that I can't control. Just because they are on me doesn't mean I can do any magic with them."

"I brought you here." His voice cracked, and I realized it wasn't anger. "I asked you to let me help you."

"Thain—"

"I brought you to my city, my king. My *home*. And with you here, I . . ." He turned away, and I couldn't see his expression anymore, but I knew it for what it was now. Betrayal. He felt as though I'd betrayed him.

"They can't come off," I said. "Something awful could happen, and I won't let it happen here."

"You had every opportunity to tell me." He ran a hand through his hair. "I wanted to help you, remove you from that place and bring you to the Wyldes with the rest of our people. All you had to do was tell me what I was dealing with so I could fix it."

Anger scalded my bones and roared out of me in a flood. A dam that broke, releasing every piece of hate that had been piled on me with every stare, every whisper, every snide comment and spoken threat.

"I am *not* something to be fixed." My voice carried steadily through the room as I glared at him, shoulders squared. "No part of me is something to be fixed."

"And you don't think you risk anyone around you?" he demanded. "I've seen what the magics from their kind can do. I've watched skin boil off the living, I've watched purple fire swallow people whole, and I've watched blight poison the eyes of their enemies until there was nothing left but black rot. Their enemies, *my people*."

I paused. Thain was old, and he'd seen a lot. There was no disputing his words, but I couldn't reconcile them with the witches I'd known all my life either.

"Do you even know what the marks are for?" His voice was so soft now, the fight completely gone from it.

"Yes, my magic has been sealed shut. Yes, by a witch." I was already backed against the door, the firmness of it grounding me.

"You've known you have magic." He flexed his hands open and closed.

"I never denied having it."

"Why is it sealed?" he asked.

"I told you; it was sealed when I was found in the woods," I said evenly.

"My friend, *a witch*, tried to unseal it when I was ten. It didn't go well. She had to seal it up again."

"So you've been building it up all this time? No release?" he hissed. "That witch was a fool."

"That witch saved my life," I snapped. "And what do you know of it? I can't even tell you who my parents were. For all you know, I'm not even your kind of fae. What if I'm half nymph or sprite or whatever? I can't glamour. Maybe I should just go work for a shopkeeper who screams at her assistants like servants."

I knew it was unfair to bring up Mistress Rhisa, I knew I wasn't being reasonable. But in that moment, neither of us was, and my only thought was to let it all out.

"This has nothing to do with you being half human. Whatever you are is no sprite—not that it would matter if you were—and the fact that you've been in control of yourself is a wonder. This is about you hiding something so important when I could have helped you before you brought it into Thanantholl."

"I didn't ask you to!" I snapped, tears now fighting to form. My back tensed, a flash of cool air whispering past my ear. "I didn't ask you to help me. I'm not something to be fixed, or found, or paraded in front of a throne room. You of all people should know how that feels."

"You know nothing of my responsibilities." He took a small step forward. "You're as much a part of the Wyldes as any of us, and still you recoil from us, from me, like we're some kind of monsters. You forget, Wren, that you're half monster yourself."

Hands slammed on either side of me, his claws digging lightly into the wood. His face was only inches from mine, and I could feel his hot breath fanning my face. He was furious. I was furious. Snarling and glaring and no more than a heartbeat from letting out more of the anger that swirled inside at everything and everyone who had done something to me or thought something about me that took away yet another decision from me. It felt like everything was boiling over outside of our control.

"Thain?" Schula's voice cut through the door at my back. My heart thundered, but I couldn't tear my eyes from Thain. He took a step back and visibly heaved with the effort to contain himself. A brisk wind blew through the room, flickering the fire and scattering papers.

"I'm coming in!" Schula swung the door into my back, not knowing I was right there, and she half caught me as I stumbled. Those cool hands on my arms made me realize how warm I was. My back was burning. My seal was burning. And in my eyes, hot tears were burning through all my rage.

"What's going on here?" She stepped into the room between me and Thain. Her nose twitched, and she spun around. "We're leaving."

"*You knew*," Thain growled.

Schula froze, her eyes darting to me, then to Thain.

"When?" he asked, his eyes losing focus as he searched his memories. "The outpost, the bird in the bath."

"We're *leaving*." Schula lowered her voice. "I'll see you again when you can control yourself."

Pulling me outside with her, she closed the door behind us and hurried out the front gate. A terrible roar shook the house behind me. I could feel it through the flagstones underfoot as birds fled the tree overhead. Schula kept an arm around me the whole time as she wound us though unfamiliar streets and over new bridges. A caw overhead told me Puko was following.

I sobbed, my shoulders shaking. Schula didn't say a word as she handed me a handkerchief. For now, that was no longer my home.

EIGHTEEN
A NEW HEARTH TO COME HOME TO

Schula's small apartment over a bakery was comfortable in a different way from Thain's house. Unlike his home, there were no decorations. There were, however, many windows and more clothing than I had ever seen in one place. The furniture was all well-used, either secondhand or worn with age. A huge bed sat in one corner while the kitchen and a table took up half the space. She had shelves of books, and a small copper stove in the center of the room provided heat.

Schula pulled me into her apartment and opened a window, where Puko landed and began preening himself. She stuck a log in the stove and practically dragged me into the bathroom. The white walls held a mirror and a shelf of soaps and towels. The bath was wooden, like the one from the outpost. In it were two benches.

Without a word, Schula started the water and undressed, then helped me do the same. She helped me onto a bench and began scrubbing my back. I eventually snapped out of my stupor and took the soap, cleaning the rest of my body by myself. Once we were both clean, she sat with me in the warm water and held me.

"You're staying as long as you want. I can sleep on the floor, or we can share the bed. Stars know it's more than big enough. I'm going to get your things from Thain's house. Have you eaten lunch yet?" I shook my head. "I'll bring that too. You can stay in the bath, or you can lie down on the bed. I have books if you want to look through my shelves, and if you get cold there's a stack of wood for the fire. Wren, look at me. Will you be all right if I leave you for a little bit?"

Nodding was all I managed by way of an answer. She hugged me and got out of the tub. I sniffed and looked at her for the first time without clothes. Really looked at her. The snow-white skin of her back was covered in scars. I didn't ask about them, just like she never asked me anything unless she had to.

"There are plenty of clothes in the wardrobe by my bed," she said, pulling on a fresh outfit. "Take something. I'll be back as quickly as I can."

"I messed up," I managed.

Schula came over to the edge of the tub and pulled me in tight. My forehead sank to her shoulder as she stroked my back.

"Maybe, maybe not. It sounds like you both said some regrettable things, but that happens. I've done it, Eb has done it. We can't change what was done, but we can get you in better shape and then deal with the rest later. Okay?"

"Okay," I said. "I'm getting you wet again."

"Shh. I don't care, this is important. You are important." She pulled back from me. "I'll be back soon."

She left the room. The front door closed, and a lock clicked a moment later. The water welcomed me as I slid down the bench until the hot bath reached my chin. I stayed for a while, but I'd had enough of hot baths for the moment, and when I was sure of my legs, I got out.

The air was still warm when I left the water. I found a comb for my hair and wrapped myself in a towel. Schula had drawn all the curtains for me, and I could hear Puko's protests outside the big window by the door.

Her wardrobe was full of either comfortable white clothes or vibrant, colorful finery. I took a cotton shift and leggings that buttoned down the side of my calf. Once I was dressed, I opened the curtains again and let Puko in through the window. He ruffled his feathers indignantly but otherwise seemed fine.

Schula's bookshelf was full of interesting things. Not just books but maps and drawings as well. I found an illustrated guide to plants of the Winter Lands and decided it was something I could read through without upsetting myself. I put another log in the stove and curled up on the floor with the book. I felt the slight whisper of a winter chill before I heard footsteps outside.

"It's me." Schula swung the door open with a foot, carrying my sack of belongings over her shoulder. Puko gave her a caw of acknowledgement and went back to preening.

"There is someone you might like to meet. She's bringing up some food." Schula set my things on the bed and took off her boots.

"Thank you, Schula." I stretched and stood just as a knock on the door startled me. Puko flapped away as Schula went to answer it.

"Mama Flori, thank you." Schula opened the door to reveal a wrinkled gray figure. She had features like a mole, and her dress was covered in flour.

"Of course, love. Now, you promised me a cute little fae? I'm so glad you aren't all alone up here anymore." The woman handed two leaf-wrapped packages to Schula and waddled through the doorway.

"Wren, this is Mama Flori. She runs the shop downstairs and rents me these rooms." Schula gave me an encouraging smile, but meeting more fae was the last thing I wanted right now.

"Hello, Mama Flori." I stood straight while the old sprite circled me, clicking her tongue.

"Thin, too thin. Wren, was it?" She stopped in front of me, and I had to bend to meet her as she gripped me in the most ferocious hug I had been trapped in since Bryn died. "I can fix you right up, love. Don't you worry. If you need anything at all, you come downstairs and talk to Mama Flori and her boys, you hear me?"

"Yes, ma'am," I found myself agreeing. Her breath was awful, and her arms were like tree trunks, but she was maybe the warmest person I had ever met.

"Where does this one come from?" she whispered none too quietly to Schula while still hugging me.

"We found her in the mountains south of the Wyldes." Schula hid a smile behind her hand. "Wren here is half human. Her home was attacked by raiders. She's here with me now."

"Oh, you poor thing!" Mama Flori wailed and squeezed into me a little harder before holding me at arm's reach. "Schula, you need to feed her!"

"We've *been* feeding her, Mama Flori." Schula came over with the two packets of food. "In fact, you just brought us lunch, remember?"

"Lunch! Yes. Come here, love. Sit down and have some food." I was half carried to Schula's table and plopped in a seat. Mama Flori took one of the packets from Schula and unwrapped it in front of me to reveal a small pie, oozing with gravy from the slits in the top.

"Mama Flori is famous for her pies." Schula brought over a glass of cider for me and took a seat. "What's in today's, Flori?"

"Mushroom and chestnut with venison." The mole sprite fussed over me as I took the first bite, and my eyes widened. It hit my tongue the same way those pecans had the first day I'd arrived in Thanantholl. This was familiar in small ways that reminded me of home. Most of what we had eaten came from the forest, and this pie was the forest wrapped in a buttery crust.

"This is delicious," I managed to say after I swallowed. The steam now pouring from the inside of the pie tickled my face.

"Oh, love." Mama Flori patted my back and continued to hover as I ate the whole thing. A bemused Schula sat across from me, slowly eating her own lunch undisturbed.

"Mama Flori, thank you for coming by. I hope you don't mind adding a tenant for a while, but does she pass your standards?"

"Stars, yes!" she wailed. "Wren, love, you stay as long as you want. If you need me, I'm downstairs. I'll always have time for my lovies. You promise me you'll come see Mama Flori?"

"I promise." I smiled. After a little more fussing, Mama Flori finally left, and Schula closed the door behind her.

"So, what do you think of our landlady?" She grinned.

"She's something else," I said. "I don't know how to put it, I've never been . . ."

"Mothered?" she offered, and I nodded. "Neither had I, until coming here. Mama Flori has made my life here a thousand times better than the life I left back home."

"Mothered." I tasted the word in my mouth. Of course I hadn't been mothered, all I'd had was Bryn. Even Mila and her coven, the only women in my life before now, had been like stern aunts. Never had I been mothered, and it was precisely what I needed today.

"I hope she didn't bother you too much. I bought lunch downstairs, but she insisted on meeting you." Schula took the leaves and cups into the kitchen.

"No, she was great." I stood and scooted the chairs back into the table. "I didn't think I wanted to see anyone for a while, but I'm glad she came up. What do we do now?"

"Now, we put your things away. I have shelf space, just let me clear it off. Then, we do whatever you want to do. That can be books, or a walk, or just talking." She went to her bookshelf, picking up the plants of the Winter Lands book on her way. "Are you still reading this one?"

"Oh, no. I just wanted something to look at. Something peaceful, like plants." I went over to the bed and began unpacking my things. "Um, how did it go? With Thain?"

"Thain will be fine. He's mad at me too, but he won't tell the king." Schula began rearranging her shelves. "Speaking of Baeleon, he's summoned Thain for something. This happens sometimes; when Eb and I aren't with him, it means he's getting a special Thain-only task. For the best, I think, because he needs to cool down and reflect on how he handled himself. He's going to come back and be ashamed, you'll see."

"I should probably tell you what happened," I mumbled, fidgeting with the wooden cup Bryn had carved for me.

"I would like to know, in due time. Right now, I think we all need to calm down and take it slow. Maybe tomorrow, unless you really want to tell me. First, I'd like to hear about all these wooden things you've brought along. Wairen had already packed most of your belongings by the time I got there, but I did get to see some carvings." Schula set a stack of books by her feet while she made room on another shelf for them.

I hadn't talked to anyone about Bryn or my life in such detail. Just enough to know what had happened. Schula was quickly becoming my rock in this storm of the Wyldes. I just hoped that someday I could repay her kindness.

"All right, I'll tell you all about them."

We never finished unpacking. The afternoon and evening flew by with my stories of the mountains. Schula told me a few of her own. She never admitted it, but I thought she was born somewhere in the Winter Lands. Not that it wasn't an obvious conclusion to draw from her appearance, it was just never outright said.

We had laid ourselves on the bed around my things and fallen asleep sometime before dawn, and it was midday before I opened my eyes again.

"Nice to see you still in the land of the living." Schula smiled at me from the floor, where she had curled up with a bear pelt and a book next to the woodstove. The day was crisp, and we'd let the heat flicker out overnight.

"I haven't slept that well in days." I smiled and dug in my sack for the wool blanket from my bed in the mountains and joined her on the floor. "So, what will we do today?"

"Today we meet Eberon. Thain will have talked to his triquetram before leaving, even on a mission from His Majesty. We can decide what needs to be done from there." Schula stretched under her fur and closed her book. "First things first, though, have you been keeping up with our exercises?"

"Some," I admitted. "Not as well as I could have been."

"We've all had a lot going on. Would you like to start them again? A morning routine, perhaps? Tomorrow?" she prodded.

"Sure, I do still want to learn." I yawned.

We sat in comfortable silence for a while. Eventually, she got up and brought over a bowl of dried plums, which we shared pieces of with Puko. The room warmed up, and we left our blankets on the floor while we cleaned ourselves up.

"We should talk about yesterday," I said, combing my hair at the table.

"Probably." Schula was lacing her pants. "If you're ready. I gather it was about your magic?"

"Yes," I said. "Wairen saw my back the other night."

"Oh." Schula looked up at me. "And naturally told Thain."

"Right." I fidgeted. "Is . . . I mean, how bad will this be?"

"Ah, how do I put this?" She shoved her boots on her feet. "The witches were in a vicious conflict with the courts a long time ago. These days, they keep humans out of our land and the fae out of theirs. The wicked fae, anyway. But once upon a time, our kinds were friends."

"What changed?" I asked. "What turned an alliance with a group of the most peaceful people I know into a war?"

Schula smiled sadly. "It wasn't only the witches but anyone who disputed the drawing of lines for the courts. It all boiled down to claiming ownership of land."

"The Mother has no borders." I murmured a line I had heard so many times in the quiet of a hut filled with drying herbs and crackling fire.

Schula shrugged. "Sounds about right, from the stance they took. But our kind will clash to ruin without borders. The courts remain apart, and though some travel and visiting can happen, our natures won't allow us to thrive in the heart of another season's magic. A Spring fae might feel all right in Summer, but the Autumn Court would forever be like living with an itch that won't go away. A winter fae might weather their days in the Autumn Lands, though the warmer days might be uncomfortable. And if the courts didn't separate from the Unclaimed Wyldes, these lands would have fallen into desperate chaos long ago."

"And the witches would never feel the need for any of that," I said slowly.

"The fallout from the dispute was terrible, or so I've heard, and the fracture left the witches chased from the Wyldes for good. There has never been proof that they would retaliate or even bear ill will toward these lands and people, but any who lived through a conflict with that kind of magic will carry the scars from those days. My partners were both alive when it happened, and I can't imagine what they saw back then to shape their views of witchkind. Some even think the witches had something to do with the plague, though no one has any proof."

Letting out a slow breath, I fidgeted with the end of a braid. "And what do you think of it all?"

She looked tired, aged, when she answered. "I think the fae can be joyous, busy, lovely people, but I also think some of us can be cruel, judgmental, and stubborn. I can't hate the witches for living their lives the way they did, and I don't have enough experience with them to say who was right and who wasn't. But if you're worried that any of this colors the way I see you, don't be. You've only been with us for a short time, and already I consider you a friend I wouldn't want to lose. As for the rest of our kind . . . It would take an incredible effort on the part of the witches, because I don't believe we would ever reach out our hands first to reestablish any kind of relationship with them."

"That's no way to fix the rift." I frowned.

"It's not, but old fae are set in their ways." Schula shrugged. "I wouldn't think Thain would be that set in stone about anything, given his nature, but he has lived much longer than most fae I know. He can be hard to read, and he had personal experience in that war."

"If he isn't mad about the witch seal itself, he must be mad about something else," I said. "He made it sound like it was about how closed off I've been. The fact that I'm still keeping secrets."

"And it's no business of his that you are. He has plenty of his own," she told me.

"I wasn't trying to make him mad." I watched Schula come over to me.

"Someone else losing their temper is never your fault. If you haven't noticed, Thain is more beast than the rest of us. When he gets back, he'll come running with his tail between his legs, begging forgiveness. I think he's just been trying really hard to help you. He was excited to report to me and Eb about the lost fae he found. An excited Thain isn't something you see often." She smiled and squeezed my shoulders. "Now, get up. We've got a fire fae to bother."

I couldn't help but smile as she pulled me out the front door. Puko landed on my shoulder and eyed me, making Schula laugh. Downstairs, we ran into Mama Flori. She demanded we stop and talk to her, and then she sent us on our way with a loaf of cinnamon bread and a packet of breadcrumbs for Puko.

My stomach was a pit of nerves. I hoped Thain had talked to Eberon before leaving Thanantholl. I also hoped, despite our argument, that he was all right.

NINETEEN
EBERON'S HOME

Schula took us down the winding lanes of the city as a misty fog rolled through it. The smell of damp leaves burned into your nose, and smoke from chimneys drifted overhead, sprinkling hints of ash from above. Schula had lent me a light coat and told me it was the heaviest piece of clothing anyone could need in the Autumn Lands. I smiled into it. It smelled like her. Like standing on the top of a mountain, fresh snow and crisp air as far as you could see, and nothing else. It was a wonder to live where I would never be hot in the summer or freeze with the snows. Schula told me it rarely even frosted here, and the food that I'd fought to hoard in my cabin for winter grew bountifully here every day.

A twisting bridge of oak tree roots carried us to a long street of townhomes. Puko was content to stay on my shoulder as long as I kept feeding him the crumbs Mama Flori had given us. His weight was a comfort. Schula's presence was a comfort. Hopefully seeing Eberon would also be a comfort.

"Eberon lives on this street?" I asked.

"His family does," the white fae said. "His mother in particular is . . ." Schula swirled a hand in the air, grasping for a word and finally landing on, "Eccentric. But loyal to Baeleon since the beginning. I think you'll learn a lot about Eb just by seeing how he lives."

"Will he be mad at me too?" I wondered out loud.

"No, not Eb." She held the warm loaf of cinnamon bread close to her. "You'll see."

The street wound around homes and yards. Fae of all kinds hurried about on business of their own. I was still trying to understand the buildings of Thanantholl, but from what I could see these were homes for the rich.

Around the bend, under an ancient chestnut tree, sat a fat house with dozens of windows and a garden of mums. Schula took us through the front gate and up to a bold red door.

"Puko, you might not like it here," I told him. "Lots of people, and we're out of breadcrumbs."

He ruffled his feathers indignantly and took off. Schula knocked on the door, only to have it swing open as she was doing it.

"There you are, I was about to come drag you out of bed," Eberon huffed. "Wren, it's nice to see you. Come in, don't mind the parlor. Mother is planning another party, and her friends are all helping."

"You come pull me out of bed and I'll freeze over your perfect hair." Schula stuck her nose in the air and followed him inside.

"Clever," he said flatly. "We can use the study, follow me." The inside of the house was much like Thain's. The walls were covered in portraits, plush rugs coated the floors, and none of the walls were flat. Everything held an organic shape matching the curve of the trees outside. The tables in the hallway, the hearth in the parlor, even the paintings on the walls were made to go around curves.

Eberon took us a little way into his home and down a hall. I saw the gaggle of women fussing in one of the rooms and was glad we were bypassing them. I picked out Eberon's mother right away. Tall and golden, shining brightly with the same shock of red in her eyes as her son. Her hair was nearly alive with fire, and she wore golden cuffs on her delicately pointed ears. Another beauty in a land of wonder. I tugged at one of my earlobes and let my hand drop away.

The study Eberon took us to was small compared to the rest of the house, but still more than enough room for the three of us. A desk sat under a large window, and Eberon sat behind it. There were armchairs for Schula and me to sit in. The walls held shelves, and somehow more portraits.

"All right, I suppose you have things to say." Eberon looked at Schula.

"I do. You need to help him control his temper or find releases for it." Schula scowled. "He's your damned triquetram, act like it."

"That's between me and Thain." Eberon sniffed.

"You brought me into it when you invited me to be your third," Schula hissed, baring her teeth. "And you brought Wren into this when she was made to feel attacked in what should have been her home."

Eberon paled. "Wren was there for it?"

"What the Stars did you think this was about?" Schula glared.

"Wairen told me he lost his temper, they didn't say . . ." Eberon cleared his throat. "They didn't have time to explain in detail as Baeleon's summons was urgent. I will address the problem, but right now we have more pressing matters."

"What did the king send him out for?" Schula asked, her anger on pause.

"More worry about the wards. Galavan is dead." Eberon rubbed his temples, propping his elbows on the desk. "That alone speaks volumes of the problems we have to deal with."

The name sat at the edge of my mind, almost within reach. I'd heard it somewhere before.

"Dead?" Schula whispered. "How? He's a thousand years old."

"If I had to guess, I'd say his arrogance did him in, but I don't know for sure. That's what Thain is doing, looking into it." Eberon grimaced.

The fight that Schula carried in her shoulders had left her. Rounding the desk, she rubbed a hand on Eberon's shoulder, and he lifted his right hand to cover hers.

"He'll be all right," Schula said. "He's Thain."

"I know he will," Eberon murmured, then huffed a sound of hollow amusement. "You'd think this would be easier by now. I wish Baeleon would send me with him, but—"

"But he's Thain," Schula finished. "The king calls, and Thain answers. I know."

The moment suddenly felt so intimate, like I was looking through a window at another piece of this world that I knew too little about: what the bond between them was, the ways in which these lands put Thain to use, and where any of them stood before the king.

"The patrol from the Spring Court," I said once I remembered the name. "Is that who we're talking about?"

"Yes." Eberon looked at me. "But it wasn't the whole patrol, it was just Galavan."

"What could have killed him?" Schula asked, dropping her hand from Eberon's shoulder and crossing her arms.

"Whatever it was, we can only hope Thain finds and kills it." Eberon sighed. "In the meantime, since we were the last patrol there before the incident, we will be going to the Spring Court."

"Are we under some kind of suspicion?" Schula frowned.

"Stars, no." Eberon snorted. "At least, no more than anyone else. But we're to pay our condolences for His Majesty. He chose us because we were the last patrol to see Galavan alive, and because we already have business to travel the Wyldes."

Two sets of eyes fixed on me. "Me? I'm going?"

"Yes, you." Schula tilted her head. "Not bad, Baeleon, not bad. Send a reliable triquetram, or at least part of it, to show respect, and give the Spring Court the first chance to impress Wren."

"Precisely," Eberon said. "And if we happen to learn anything while we're there . . ."

"Fair enough. When do we go?" Schula asked.

"Tomorrow or as early as possible." Eberon pulled a sealed letter from his vest. "And we're to deliver this, as well as use a hefty purse to arrange a gift when we get there. Something showy, befitting of our king, but otherwise left to our discretion."

"Wren, I know you're still settling into things, but are you up for a trip?" Schula squeezed my hand.

I took a deep breath. "Yes. I mean, I need to visit the other courts eventually, right?"

"Right," Schula agreed.

"Thank you." Eberon smiled from behind his desk, shoulders relaxing. "Aside from our somber business, you'll enjoy the Spring Lands. King

Diamid is quite jovial, and his court aims to please. Now, with that business out of the way, is that bread from Mama Flori?"

Schula laughed and placed the cinnamon bread on the desk. Eberon sent for tea and plates, and we discussed our travel plans. I still worried about Thain. I hoped whatever had killed Galavan didn't come after him too. I didn't want the last words between us to be an argument.

Not too far into the afternoon, our plans were decided. In the morning, we would leave Thanantholl behind.

I had never ridden in a carriage before. Eberon tried to tell me it was nothing fancy, but to me every carriage was fancy. In Sulls, carriages and horses were for rich merchants with guards that would yell at you to get out of the way. But this wasn't Sulls, this wasn't even a human city, it was the Wyldes. To be honest, walls between me and the watchful fae of the roads would be a blessing. I was going to be ogled in the Spring Court; I didn't doubt that. But a rest from it before I got there would be refreshing.

The three of us were preparing to leave from Eberon's home. The yard out back housed the horses and carriage we'd be taking through the Wyldes.

Schula spoke to the stablehand that held the reins of our horse. A horse with a shiny black coat, bred by Eberon's family for strength and endurance, apparently. Puko sat on top of the carriage, keeping an eye on the new beast. Eberon set his travel bag in the carriage where I was already seated. I remembered Thain telling me how he didn't need to travel with anything, he just lived off the land. When I asked Eberon about it, he sniffed and told me we were going to travel as dignitaries from another court, not animals in the woods. We would need whatever items necessary to appear ready for society.

"Do you have enough clothes?" Eberon asked me.

"Yes, Schula brought me the rest of our order from Mistress Rhisa. I'm just traveling in my old clothes so my new things don't get dirty."

"Very good," he said absently. It was clear his mind was on the mission. Whatever I had thought about Eberon, he was dutiful and thorough.

"Are we almost ready?" Schula stuck her head through the window.

"Is Boxfield hitched?" Eberon asked, and Schula nodded. "Then yes. I'll drive the first stretch, why don't you catch Wren up on the Spring Court."

"Can do." Schula reached overhead and lifted herself up into the carriage through the window rather than coming around to the side with the door. Eberon scowled, Schula laughed. The golden fae huffed and walked away, closing the door behind him.

"I'm a little nervous," I told Schula once Eberon had settled on the driver's bench.

"Were you nervous coming to Thanantholl?" she asked.

"I guess I was," I admitted.

"And have you enjoyed it?"

"Yes." I gave her a half grin. "I know I don't really have anything to be nervous about, but all the staring and the whispers."

"You're going to be the center of attention for a while. On the bright side, I can introduce you to two fae even younger than you," she said.

"Really?" I perked up, playing with the ends of my braids.

"You know we've had eleven children since the plague, right?" I nodded. "Two of those little miracles are twins. Not only twins, but the Spring Court king's own grandchildren."

"He must feel blessed."

"Trust me, the whole court dotes on them. Two little mischief-makers, six years old, and they already know how to torment their poor tutor." Schula cackled. "And they'll most certainly outshine you after a couple days, once the news of you has made its rounds."

"I don't know what to do with children." I hesitated. "It's not like the village women would let a half fae play with their babies."

"Oh, you don't do anything with Alban and Arran; they do things with you." Schula sat back as the carriage began moving. "On that note, check under your pillows for bugs or other tricks before bed each night. But the twins aside, I'll tell you about the Spring Court if you like."

"Yes, please." I sat forward. "Tell me what I'm getting into."

Schula hummed, amused. "The high city of the Spring Court is called Dwellonmar, and it isn't in a valley but in the hills. Not a flat road in the whole place, but I'm sure you can handle that, being from the mountains. Remember, Eberon and I have the somber task of representing our court through the memorial, but your job is to be introduced to the Spring Court. You'll likely have a handler of some kind to show you around and attempt to charm you."

"Delightful." I changed the subject. "What is a fae funeral like?"

"Short, as far as ceremonies go around here. The head of his family will say a few words over the body, which will be prepared for display with flowers and candles on an altar. Then other fae will be given the chance to walk up and see the body. Say any last words or leave a flower. Then we burn our dead. That's it. The real celebration of life will be the memorial feast."

"We burn our dead in the mountains, but only because the ground is too hard to bury them most of the time," I said. "At the base of the mountains and in the plains, humans bury their dead and leave carved stones as a monument. Funerals are performed by local leaders, and they can take all day to sit through. Lots of crying, and speeches, and people talking."

"Sounds like a bunch of fluff." Schula snorted. "A service for the living rather than a goodbye for the dead."

"I guess it is like that." I watched out the carriage window.

"Did you get to hold a service for Bryn?" Schula asked softly.

"No." I didn't look at her, still ashamed that I'd been too afraid to see his body. "He was well loved, I'm sure the villagers did. Not that it would have mattered, as I wouldn't have been welcome anyway."

She squeezed my shoulder and left me alone. Schula could read me like an open book, and I would be forever thankful for that. We rode in silence for a long time, watching the leaves out the window and thinking.

The strange thing was that I wasn't thinking of the Spring Court ahead of me, or even of Bryn. I was dwelling on Thain's words. Even said in anger, maybe they were true. Maybe I had closed myself off from the very people I wanted to be a part of.

TWENTY
SPRING AND INTEREST

CAW!

My eyes opened to a black blob sitting in the window.

"Be quiet, Puko." I groaned and pulled the blanket over my head. We had already been traveling for days, and sleeping in the carriage was getting quite old. I could appreciate the fact that we would arrive sooner than if we had walked, and I certainly appreciated it while we slipped through the Unclaimed Wyldes, but my backside was sore, and if I had to hear one more lecture from Eberon or play one more game of dice to pass the time, I was going to scream. And the worst part of the entire trip was that I wasn't bursting with excitement at every new sight and sound and food and story because I was so wholly consumed by the fight I'd had with Thain.

And I hated it. And I regretted it. And I couldn't do a damn thing about it because we were traveling to opposite ends of the Wyldes.

"Have you had a good look around? We're in the Spring Lands now," Schula said from the bench opposite me. She wore a butter-yellow dress, a new fashion from the Spring Lands, apparently. Eberon and I had already changed as well, knowing we would arrive today. Now that we were finally here, I pulled Puko inside to sit on the bench next to me so I could watch the view.

I stared out the window. Rolling green hills and trees in bloom dotted the countryside. The road was well traveled, and I could tell it had rained recently from the muddy tracks and prints. A few fae, on foot or horseback, waved at Eberon as we passed. "It really does look like spring, even though it's nearly winter."

Schula laughed. "Well, yes. That's how it works over here."

"So, what is our first stop in Dwellonmar?" I asked.

"The palace. We're expected, after all. He will give us some kind of accommodations, and then we will be free to leave and buy an appropriate gift. I will warn you, though, we'll be eating dinner with the court."

"Lovely." I sighed.

"It won't be too bad. We won't be the center of attention or anything. The dinner will be toned down, what with the recent events," Schula said. "Here, I think we're coming up on Dwellonmar now."

We both gazed out the window to the hilltop ahead of us. The traffic on the road had certainly picked up since I'd last looked out. Wind swept through the grass as we crested the top. A caw overhead told me Puko was still with us.

"Oh my," I breathed. The morning sun rose behind the hills of pink blossoms. The city was surrounded by hawthorns, woven together like a wicker fence. Thorns as long as knives grew between the trees. Dwellonmar was a fortress, a protected grove of flowers and springtime. Where Thanantholl was protected by cliff walls, Dwellonmar was concealed by the growing arms of the Wyldes itself.

"It does make an impression," Schula said flatly. "The inside is much better, or at least much prettier. We're nearly at the gates; they'll want to look in the carriage to know who's coming in."

"How do they know who is Spring and who isn't?" I asked.

"They just know. Once you're part of a court, you instantly know who's on your side." Schula sat back and straightened her leggings. "Part of the magic of the Wyldes."

"Oh." I watched out the window as we slowed, joining the line waiting for entry to Dwellonmar.

"You know, if we unsealed you, I'd bet you could sense a lot more of these things too," Schula whispered.

I gave her a look, and she shrugged. "Not that you have to, I'm just giving you information."

"Yeah, I know." I sighed. "I just wish you weren't right."

"Next!" a guard called from up ahead.

"Ugh, here we go." Schula sighed, and the carriage pulled forward for inspection.

Past the gates, I finally caught a glimpse of the city. It was all hills and trees in pink bloom so thick the falling petals looked like snow. The buildings were bricks, not like the smooth clay surfaces in Thanantholl. The roof tiles were shiny copper, but some had aged to green. Decoration was everywhere, from flower garlands strung over doorways to fountains tucked in every corner.

"It's beautiful, and it really is an eternal spring here." I watched a group of sprites cleaning laundry in a large fountain. One splashed another when she wasn't looking, and the whole fountain laughed about it. Someone nearby was playing a stringed instrument.

"That it is. It can get old, though, constant cheer and dancing and nonsense. I honestly don't know how they get anything done around here," Schula drawled.

"Don't say that out loud," Eberon warned from the driver's bench.

"Sorry, sorry." Schula waved a hand. "Lazy spring days aside, if this is where you belong, of course we are behind you all the way."

"I've actually been worried about that." I left my window to scoot closer to Schula. "What if I don't feel that magic with any of the courts? I won't belong anywhere."

"All fae belong somewhere, even half fae. It's possible you won't feel that pull very strongly with your magic all sealed up like that. But let's say you don't feel it at all; you'll always have a place with me, you know. If you don't feel it, you have the freedom to go wherever you want."

"I suppose so." I watched out the window as we wound up the hills. At the top was a large structure of pillars and steps. "What is that?"

Schula looked out her own window. "That is the palace, the Steps of Spring, they call it. There are one hundred steps leading up to an enclave of trees and marble. The inside is a maze. Try not to wander it if you can help it."

"Is it that bad?" I watched it disappear behind the next hill.

"Yes." She scrunched up her nose. "I've heard plenty of tales. And the Spring Court has a particularly mischievous batch of unseelie that are ready to tempt lost fae. Just stay with me or Eberon."

"I don't think that will be a problem." I pulled my head back from the window, and we rode up and down and up again.

Schula sighed. "I guess it's time." A soft white glow covered her as she slowly changed. Her skin flushed to a light rosy pink and her eyes darkened to a firmer blue, no longer the usual eerie ice. Her sharp features softened, her long fingers shortened.

"Is that what glamour does to a fae? You look more . . ."

"Human?" she finished for me. "Some part of us, whatever part we used to deceive and hide amongst humans, remains in our glamour. I still have my ears, my teeth are still sharp, but this is what glamour is. And for whatever reason, the Spring Court favors it in formal settings."

"You look beautiful either way," I said, and a tinge of pink touched her face as her smile warmed.

"Thank you. It looks like we're almost there." She averted her eyes and looked out the window, so I did the same.

The carriage pulled up near the Steps of Spring, and we were helped out by two attendants.

"Welcome! Welcome, it's been too long. Please, come this way, I'm sure you're all in need of rest. The footmen will attend to your bags and your horse." A tall fae with a dark complexion and long pink braids bowed to us. He wore a waistcoat and loose pants, similar to Eberon's attire for Dwellonmar. But his was a sage green that matched his eyes. The lines around his mouth revealed a lifetime of smiling, and the mirth in his voice added a warm joy to the timbre of it. As he helped Schula down from the carriage, he pulled her into a tight hug.

"It's so good to see you, Caldon." Schula squeezed him before pulling back to arm's length and adding firmly, "I sincerely hope there is lunch in my room."

Eberon's head whipped toward Schula at her words, his eyes wide. My heart skipped a beat too. I'd thought they were here on a diplomatic mission; was this going to cause trouble? But Caldon just laughed, a light sound like bells in the wind.

"I wouldn't dream of starving you, my dear. A hungry Schula is a dangerous one." The smile was genuine, and for all my fear of the unknown fae, I liked this one just a little more for it. "If you'll all follow me, I'll take you to your rooms to freshen up before His Majesty calls for you."

When his attention shifted off Schula, it landed on me. Everything about him was still warm and welcoming, but the light of curiosity in his eyes was new. "And this is the one we've heard so much about?"

"Wren, this is Caldon of the Spring Court. The most gentlemanly scoundrel I know," Schula said in introduction.

Caldon, to his credit, laughed it off. "You wound me terribly." He placed a hand over his heart then turned to me with a bow. "A pleasure to meet you."

"And, Caldon, this is Wren," Schula offered.

"Nice to meet you as well." I mimicked his greeting, already reflecting on how many times I was going to need to bow in this place with a sigh.

"Your attendance is greatly appreciated," Eberon added. "Please let us know if our party can compensate you in any way."

"Nonsense, Lord Eberon, your company will be more than enough." Caldon inclined his head. "Just repay me with one of your enchanting tales later. If the rumors are true, I hear you're a delight in a conversation."

Eberon looked to be what I could only describe as flustered. Whatever narrative of dignity and diplomacy he had prepared in his head, Caldon had just dashed it to pieces.

We were led up the steps to a doorway. All the steps. All one hundred steps. My thighs burned by the time we made it to the top, but I wouldn't let the others see my fatigue. Once through the marble columns, we appeared to be in a tunnel of ivy.

"Don't let the ivy play tricks on you," Caldon said. "I've prepared you rooms from which it should be easy to navigate to the bath and to the great hall."

We wound through the halls, every twist and turn changing from a wall of ivy to pillars of marble, from stone fountains to sunlit grottoes. I never would have guessed from the outside how big it was in here. I'd lost track of the way long ago, but Schula and Eberon trusted Caldon not to get us lost, so I would too.

We rounded a column and were taken down a hall of ivy with an oak door somehow firmly ingrained in the wall. Caldon opened the door to reveal a small common area with a table. Three doors led off the common room, and more importantly, on the table in the center of the room was a feast. Bowls of fruit and trays of pastry were decorated with flowers tucked in between.

"It will do." Schula clicked her tongue, and Caldon let out a full-bellied laugh.

"I'm very glad it meets your standards." He stepped back outside and pointed down the hallway beyond our door. "From that corner, the large hallway with the lion fountain in it, turn left and left again for the baths. If you turn right, you will head straight for the great hall."

What in the Mother's name is a lion?

"You accommodate us, Lord Caldon." Eberon bowed. "Thank you for the hospitality."

"My pleasure." Caldon eyed Schula with a sly grin. "If you need me, any of the attendants can fetch me at once. For now, I'll let you settle in."

Schula shook her head with a smile.

Then his eyes slid to me, pinning me in place. "If *any* of you need me."

Something in me numbed and heated and stilled all at once. What was that expression? What did that mean?

"Thank you," I said, realizing I'd hardly spoken since we'd met. He winked at me and left.

The door barely closed before Eberon rounded on Schula. "Explain."

"Oh, simmer your embers." Schula sat down at the table. "I've known Caldon longer than I've known you. Now, I dare you to stop me from eating half this table right now."

Stomach growling, I sat down with her and looked up at Eberon.

"Fine." He threw up his hands. "But please notify me next time you're ready to stop my heart. We are still dignitaries here. King Baeleon entrusted this task to us."

"Deal." Schula grabbed a plum from a bowl and took a large bite, which signaled Eberon to sit and me to take a round crust stuffed with something red. We were finally in the Spring Court, and I was ready to see what they had to offer.

TWENTY-ONE
CALDON

The summons came within the hour in the form of a satyr in royal colors. Fed, dressed, and faces washed, Schula, Eberon, and I walked down the main hall to meet the king. Fae flowed into the hall from every corner. They seemed to be there on business, but not in any hurry to do it. One tree nymph sauntered down the hall with a basket of flowers. She stopped to place one in my hair before twirling and wandering off again.

The difference between Thanantholl and Dwellonmar ran deeper than its architecture. The pace in the hallway was a stroll. No one was too bothered to stop and exchange greetings; nothing was carried out with urgency. Things would happen when they happened, and no sooner than that.

The green that engulfed the ceiling gave the whole palace an earthy scent, with hints of tea and lots of florals. Something about it made me want to take a nap (although the more likely reason was that I hadn't seen a mattress in days).

"Finally," Eberon huffed as we reached a grand doorway. He gave our names to the little herald standing by the guards, and we were promptly led through the door.

"Lord Eberon and Lady Schula." They walked forward to bow before a bearded copper fae on the throne at the back of the hall. He wasn't on a dais like King Baeleon, rather he was surrounded by fae lounging on cushions on the floor.

Diamid was big. His frame was fleshed out with more meat on his bones than some of the others around him, reminding me of Bryn. He even had a beard and eyes that crinkled when he smiled, but that was where the similarities ended. The Spring Court's king had a long beard of pale green, possibly hinting at whatever was under his glamour. And it was braided, tiny intricate patterns that looped and draped down the front of him, with more over his shoulders from his long, straight hair. He wore fine, yellow clothes and polished stone jewelry everywhere I could see. Around him, his family dressed much the same.

Wooden stringed instruments played from all four corners of the room in unison, and several sprites danced from wall to wall and back again.

"The youth, Wren, of the Southern Mountains!" The herald announced me just as they had Eberon and Schula, so I followed suit and bowed to the king.

"Stand!" King Diamid commanded in a light, mirthful voice. His court was all smiles, and I noticed two identical pairs of green eyes watching me from cushions near the foot of the throne. I smiled, and they looked at each other with mischievous grins. The twins.

"Come, sit or stand or dance if you will." The king sat up straight in his throne. "We have things to discuss, yes?"

He gave two quick claps, and the music stopped. The court scurried to remove the cushions from the floor. Three chairs were brought near the throne for us, and the courtiers took up positions around the walls, chatting among themselves, while some still danced. I didn't see where the twins had disappeared to in the commotion.

"Thank you for seeing us on such short notice, Majesty." Eberon bowed and took a seat. "Our deepest condolences to your court, and a letter from His Majesty King Baeleon."

Eberon handed the sealed letter from his breast pocket to a guard, who looked it over before handing it to his king. Diamid broke the seal and read it right there.

"Ah, Baeleon never did mince his words. A nice sentiment, though." He put the letter in his own pocket. "A sad business, Galavan's passing. His triquetram is understandably shaken up about it, as is all Dwellonmar."

A pang shot through my heart. Galavan had managed to find all his triquetram, and now their bond was broken. Two more fae would wear those cold black rings. Maybe I didn't know what it truly meant yet, but my grief for Bryn was so very heavy, and I could only imagine the same rested on their shoulders now.

"We will attend the ceremony, of course, to pay respects," Eberon said. "I understand it will be tonight?"

"Yes. We feast here after the family speaks, then when you are ready, the farewells can be done at the top of the steps on the north side."

"Quite an honor," Schula whispered. "Your Majesty is too kind."

"Galavan will be missed." Diamid sighed. "But the mourning is for later; for now, I would like to show Wren here some of my fair city."

Eyes shifted to me. "Thank you, Majesty."

"Caldon will attend you through the streets, give you a small taste of Dwellonmar, and I hope you will stay as long as you wish. I insist at the very least that you are here for the spring equinox."

"I may come and go before then, but I will do my best to be here for such a special time." Eberon had coached me on what to say if this particular offer came about. It seemed to please the king.

"Well said, young one, well said." He sat back in his chair. "I have much to prepare before sunset, but Caldon will take care of your every need. Will you join me tomorrow for lunch? We are having a picnic; Caldon can lead you to it."

"Yes, Majesty." I gave a small bow from my chair. "Thank you."

"Very good." He smiled, pleased. "Caldon! Caldon, escort our guests."

The fae in question had been talking to a group lounging near some of the musicians. He looked up when his name was called and grinned when he spotted us. Leaning down to excuse himself, he made his way over to the king's area.

"I am at your service." Caldon placed a hand on his heart before his king, then turned to offer me a hand up. I looked at Schula and Eberon, who nodded.

"Thank you," I told him as he assisted me to my feet.

"My pleasure, lovely one." Caldon's words were a warm whisper, not for the attention of others around us. My eyes shot to Schula, but she was already occupied. Eberon had stood to extend a hand for her in the same courtesy, and she was straightening her clothing.

"Take the youth to see the city of gardens and take the ambassadors wherever they wish to go," the king told Caldon, who nodded.

"Thank you, King Diamid." Eberon and Schula bowed; I did the same. "We will see you tonight."

"Take good care of them." The king nodded and clapped, resuming the music and merriment.

Everything felt so loud, so boisterous, in a moment where I was still hot from nerves and stiff from anxiety. It was a relief when Caldon gestured for us to follow him out of the great hall, and the attendants at the doors allowed them to close behind us with a muffled thud.

All the air flew out of me, then came back in with a slow pull. The grounding presence of all the greenery and the smaller space with fewer people in it was a blessing.

Caldon lead us through the twisting path to the front double doors, where the sunlight beamed down on the warm steps outside. Fae lounged on them, some braiding hair and others indulging in a moment of rest or having soft conversations. The city rolled below, buildings and trees competing with one another to sprout in every pocket where there wasn't a patch of flowers.

"I was thinking of taking Wren to the Fountain of Faith first, unless there are objections?" He looked at me with his big, lazy eyes, smiling. Always smiling, it seemed. I remembered how Thain rarely smiled. I wasn't sure what to make of Caldon, but he reminded me of someone.

"Wren, Eb and I have business at the markets." Schula grabbed my hand and squeezed. "You're in great hands with Caldon, and it's his job to show you Dwellonmar. Go with him."

"Are you sure?" I did want to see the city, but I hadn't been away from at least one of the three who'd found me since I'd arrived in the Wyldes.

"Absolutely," Eberon said. "Besides, we have boring errands, you go have fun. It isn't your job to do the king's shopping."

"All right." I squeezed Schula's hand back and let go. "I'll see you tonight?"

"Of course." She smiled and nodded at Caldon. "She comes back in one piece, or I send you home tonight in pieces yourself."

"Duly noted, Lady," Caldon mused. "Shall we, Wren?"

He offered me an arm, something I had seen a lot of the Spring Court do. I looped my arm through his as I had seen done, and we started down the steps.

"Tonight, then." Caldon bowed his head to the others, and they went another way. I was well and truly at Caldon's mercy, and my stomach wasn't quite sure how to take that.

Caldon hadn't relinquished my arm since he'd taken it on the steps. We certainly drew eyes, but the fae in the Spring Lands had a different feel to them. Instead of socialites, tradesmen, and partygoers, I felt lazy days on a warm hillside or dancing in a mountain spring. I received more than just stares, I received smiles, and whispers, and several times flowers. Caldon seemed to know everyone by name.

"The Fountain of Faith was built for the coronation of our first king, Vrahn," he said as we approached a large courtyard. "There really isn't any history behind it other than that, but it's a popular spot for an outing."

"Will it be crowded, then? Maybe we should come back another time." The crowds were definitely wearing on me.

"No, now is as good a time as any to see it with few others around. Many are preparing for tonight." We rounded a corner, and at the end of the path I could see it. "Besides, we're here."

I walked ahead, staring at the fountain. Carved from some sort of black stone, streaks of white crystal ran through it in thin dashed lines that crossed over one another to make hundreds of eight-pointed stars no bigger than my thumb. The sun peeking through the exposed parts above splashed against the cut crystals in a glittering display. It looked like someone had cut a piece of the night sky and brought it down to be touched by mortal hands. In the pool below, in the center of the swirling stars, was a spray of water that glinted as drops fell all around the sculpture. "It's lovely."

"Yes, it is lovely. But more importantly, my favorite sweet shop is on this corner. Wait here." He left me in the shade of an olive tree and swept away to a store nearby. I was content to watch the fountain. No one was bothering me, and it was mesmerizing. Eventually, Caldon came back with a small paper box.

"Candied cherries, you must try them." He opened the box to reveal a pile of shining cherries, like a fortune of rubies coated in syrup. "Please, ladies first."

"Thank you." I gingerly took one and popped it into my mouth. It barely hit my teeth when it burst open, flooding me with warm cherry and honey and I didn't know what else.

"Delicious, right?" He took one for himself and snapped the box shut. "But there will be more of that later. Let's see . . . What else can I enchant you with in Dwellonmar?"

"Enchant me?" I looked at him sharply.

"Well, yes. I'll follow my king's orders, but I consider escorting a lovely lady a definite perk to the job. Ah, and that tells me just where to go. Come on!"

He offered an arm again, and I hesitated a moment before taking it. He talked too fast, and his words were too smooth. I'd watched his kind among the humans too. The handsome young men who would say sweet words to get you in their beds. But never had those tricks been used on me, and it flustered me to have that sort of attention. Some part of me didn't care, though, and I smiled despite everything, looping my arm through his.

"Where exactly are we going?" I asked.

"Somewhere!" He grinned, and we took off. Smiles and waves followed us as he twisted and turned me through the streets. Spices hit my nose, and more fresh flowers, and smoke. I giggled as we turned in to the open market to see colorful tents and stands all around us.

"I can't let you leave Dwellonmar without buying you something to wear." He led me through a row of fabrics outside a large building. "Let's see, fawn skin, chestnut freckles, smoky eyes. This one!"

He pulled out a pale peach dress. The style was light as a breeze and similar to many I had seen throughout the city already. My arms would be left bare, but the fabric would flow down my body to the floor. "Would you honor the Spring Court by trying on a piece of our craftsmanship?" he asked.

His soft hands brushed a stray lock of hair from my face, and heat rushed to the surface. I couldn't say no.

"Of course." I had barely uttered the words when an attendant from the shop pulled me into a dressing closet. We tucked my leggings into my boots, and she stuck a bluebell in my braids before practically pushing me out the door to Caldon.

"Beautiful!" He beamed. "Wren, will you accept this as a token of goodwill from my people?"

"I, I guess, but—"

"No buts, this is me doing my job. I've shown you a landmark, our markets, our fashion . . . Let me think. Oh, the lake." He paid the attendant and asked for the dress to be sent to my room at the palace. Then we were off again.

Caldon's constant smile and childish nature pulled me all over Dwellonmar. I felt the touch of spring wherever we went.

We sat by a lake and listened to minstrels in a square. We saw art and watched a painter at work. Caldon seemed to know the moment I needed to rest and when I needed to stand in the shade. When he was finally done with me, we walked back to the palace, and he took me straight to my door.

"I'll come for you tomorrow just before midday," he promised.

"Tomorrow?" I asked. "Right, the picnic. I'll see you then."

He nodded, and I slid into the room. Eberon and Schula were nowhere in sight, so I went to lie on my bed for what time I had left until the ceremony. On the neatly laid linens, I found my new dress, a box of candied cherries, and a silver necklace with a smoky quartz set into it.

For your eyes. Never forget the adventures you've seen.
—Caldon

And in that moment, when my heart thudded and my breath caught, I knew I was in trouble.

TWENTY-TWO

SMOKE AND QUARTZ

We attended the ceremony as a group of three, Eberon in his Spring Court attire, Schula and I in our Autumn things. I was saving my new dress for the picnic tomorrow, partly because the king would probably like to see it, partly because Caldon would be there. I hadn't taken off my necklace since I'd first laid eyes on it.

"Stars, there are so many fae here," Schula said, a somber expression creasing her face.

"I would expect no less." Eberon shuffled down the hall in front of us, ensuring we weren't getting lost in the maze.

"You were getting a gift from the king this afternoon, right?" I asked Schula.

"Right." She nodded.

"What did you end up getting?" I prodded.

"You'll see. It's very Baeleon. He'll be pleased." She pushed me forward. "Let's try to get a seat high on the steps, shall we?"

"Here, this will work." Eberon pulled us through a doorway into the light of the setting sun. The top platform that jutted out into the staircase like a balcony was roped off. On a slab lay a gorgeous male that must have been Galavan. He had been tall, with silver hair and a square jaw. He was surrounded by flowers, and his abdomen was covered in roses.

"A belly wound?" Schula whispered, then turned to me. "We don't usually conceal any of the body."

"What could have done that?" I asked.

"Not much." Eberon grimaced. "This is a discussion for our rooms; let's just watch the ceremony."

All kinds of people crowded the stairs to watch. The king himself was on the other side of the body from us, surrounded by Spring guards and mourners. As the sun kissed the city walls in the distance, a fae approached Galavan's body. She was as beautiful as he had been, tall and dark with silver hair. She carried a plain, unadorned staff, and when she tapped it on the steps, a silence fell over Dwellonmar.

"My cousin will be missed," she said, addressing the crowd. She stared for a long while, then stepped to the body and stroked his cheek with her free hand.

"Galavan, we went on many hunts together. I wish we had many more. But the Stars put us here as they see fit, and they take us away as well. You were a strong leader. You are loved. You are missed. Goodbye, Galavan."

She stood back from the body and produced two obsidian rings. She looked to the king's side and nodded two fae forward. Lean, muscled males. Warriors.

They somberly stepped forward, and the fae placed the rings on their thumbs. She bowed her head to them and whispered something. Then she retreated into the crowd and sat down.

"That was it?" I whispered. Schula nodded, not letting her eyes drift from the body.

The two males spoke, just as quickly as the female had. After them, the king said a few words, and so did many from his court. All of them said words of goodbye to Galavan, not for each other. Once the king and court were done, they retreated inside, and a line formed quickly for people to say their own goodbyes. There was still gray light in the sky, and a few candles had been lit around Galavan for the mourners, but that was it.

"Come on, let's get inside," Eberon said.

"Don't we need to say words too?" I asked as he helped me stand.

"We will later, this line will take a while," Schula said. "But you hadn't even met Galavan, so you can stay at the table. Let's see what sort of food the Spring Court provides on such an occasion. We'll step out when it's time."

We headed back to the great hall, which had been completely transformed. The ivy-covered walls were now roses from floor to ceiling. Low tables and cushions lined the floors, and attendants in white escorted guests to their seats in order of rank. It didn't take long for us to be seated close, but not too close, to the high table.

"Lord, Lady, Miss." Our attendant, a small red nymph, bowed and left us to our seats. The table was already laden with bowls of Spring fruits and vegetables.

"Stars, I'm hungry. It's been a long day since lunch." Schula took her seat and scooped a large helping of carrots onto her plate.

"Lavanah did a wonderful job," Eberon commented, taking his own seat.

"Was that his cousin?" I asked.

"Yes," Schula said around a mouthful of carrots. "Our tribute should be here soon. It will brighten her eyes just a bit. Don't you think, Eb?"

"I hope so." He served himself and me some kind of egg dish, then reached for a bowl of plums. "I'm more curious about what Thain has found on the border."

"You miss him." Schula watched Eberon's hands as he moved. No, his ring.

"That is irrelevant to this mission." Eberon did his best to even his tone as he began inspecting the food.

"Your emotional stability and well-being *is* relevant to this mission." Schula stared at him.

"These plums are delicious." I tried to break the tension.

"Right? They're my favorite." Across from me at the table, an old willow sprite and the twin princes were being seated. One of them stared at me, pointing to the bowl of plums.

"Good evening, Highness, Highness, and Master Draedon." Eberon bowed his head from his seated position. The princes cordially stood and bowed, then plopped into their seats, grabbing for every bit of food within reach.

"Their young highnesses are supposed to practice dinner etiquette." The sprite looked tired beyond his years, however many years that was. His soft purple clothing and pale blue beard caused his bright yellow eyes to stand out. The twins looked at each other then at their tutor.

"Sorry, Master Draedon."

"Sorry, we'll practice harder."

"It's quite all right, boys, but you should introduce yourselves." The old sprite smiled and took a seat himself.

"I'm Prince Arran." The one on the left bowed his head.

"I'm Prince Alban." The one on the right bowed as well.

"Prince Arran, Prince Alban, allow me to introduce our party. I am Lord Eberon of the Autumn Court, and this is Lady Schula of the same." Eberon bowed his head, Schula followed suit. "This is the recently found youth, Miss Wren of the Southern Mountains."

"A pleasure," the boys said in unison.

"So, Miss Wren, I'm sure you've had a number of us who want to talk to you, but can an old scholar ask a few questions about the current state of humans?" The sprite was directly across from me, between the twins.

I was surprised that any of the fae would take an interest in humans at all, but the charming old willow was very earnest, and I was more than glad to give him what answers I knew. It didn't take long at all for me to fall into the conversation. It was almost like talking to Mila, someone with a teacher's nature. The hall filled, and the food emptied, was refilled, and emptied again. The princes did their very best to behave and entertain the guests around them. Alban seemed to be having a better time with Schula than Arran was with Eberon, but otherwise they both did splendidly.

"Ah, here we go." Eberon drew me from my discussion of the current state of Sulls' military when the doorway was cleared to make room for a large troupe of fae in colorful green costumes.

"You had better introduce them; King Diamid is already looking your way." Schula smiled, the twins wide-eyed at the players pouring through the door.

"Right." Eberon stood. "Sire?" Eberon said over the crowd, and the king nodded to him with a smile. "Galavan's passing is felt even as far as the Autumn Lands. At my king's request, a tribute to the fallen warrior has been prepared. In true Autumn Court fashion, as you all know of King Baeleon, my only requirements were something fitting and something dazzling."

A small round of laughter and clapping echoed through the room. The king smiled and nodded once more. The princes were about to bounce out of their seats.

"Galavan was known by the Autumn Court for two things: his love of the hunt and his love of a party. I could think of no more fitting tribute than a show of acrobats depicting one of his most famous hunts. Today is a solemn day, but let us not forget whom we mourn." Eberon bowed to another round of applause, and the king clapped for his musicians to begin playing.

The players quickly took up positions between the tables and played out the hunt of some great stag, a player in an elaborate mask. Some in the room teared up. I searched for Lavanah at the high table. A single tear rolled down her cheek, but a small turn at the corner of her lips told me it was the perfect gift. Of course it was; Eberon had had a hand in it.

"Marvelous." Master Draedon clapped softly and smiled at our party. "And none here will soon forget it is most definitely from King Baeleon."

"Naturally." Eberon smiled and bowed his head.

The princes were thoroughly distracted by the players, and I was eager to continue my discussion with the tutor. Schula and Eberon took the opportunity to slip out of the hall and pay their respects to the body. The candles grew low, and one by one fae either left for their rooms or fell asleep right at the tables. Master Draedon excused himself and led his young charges to bed. Schula and Eberon weren't back by the time our company had left, and I found myself drifting off over my glass of wine.

"Wren?" Caldon's soft voice tickled my ear. "I can't have our important guest found sleeping on a table. Let me escort you to your room."

"Caldon." I sat up straight, rubbing the sleep from my eyes. "I was just waiting for Schula and Eberon to return."

"I would be happy to let them know where you went if you like." He offered a hand, and I took it.

"Well, I don't want to fall asleep on my plate at my first visit to the

Spring Court." Either the wine, the heat from Caldon, or my own shyness around the opposite sex brought a flush of heat to my cheeks. Caldon didn't mention it. He simply took my hand and led me from the hall.

"That Eberon is a clever one; Galavan would have loved the players."

"He seems so competent with these important court situations. That's probably why King Baeleon sent him here." I repressed a yawn.

"You don't become a king without having your wits about you. And Baeleon has been king for a long time." Caldon's warmth was about to smother me. That was, if my own heart didn't crush my ribs first. He had laid a hand on my arm as he walked with me, keeping me steady from the treacherous wine tripping my feet.

"King Diamid seems very fit to his crown as well," I said. Caldon beamed at the compliment to his own king.

"And how have you found life among the fae so far?" he asked.

I heard it for what it was: *How have you found life in the Spring Lands so far?*

"I am learning every day. It's certainly different from my life before." We reached a fountain against a wall depicting a strange creature covered in what looked to be a head of hair but with the face of a cat, mouth agape and spilling water into a bowl below. I'd seen it earlier, and from the directions we had been given on arrival, I recognized it as the lion fountain where we would turn toward the quarters we had been given for our stay.

"I'm glad to hear it." Caldon stopped me at the door. "Rest well, Wren. I'll see you tomorrow."

"Thank you, Caldon." I opened my door and steadied myself on the frame.

He leaned forward, his face inches from mine. It sobered me up as his eyes crinkled in amusement at my face. He reached forward and lifted the smoky quartz from my neck, kissing it gently before letting it fall back onto my skin.

"Good night, Wren." He nodded and turned back down the hall. "You know, I think gray is quickly becoming my new favorite color."

He rounded the corner, and I grabbed the smoky quartz at my neck.

Oh no.
Oh no no no.
I was not ready for this.

TWENTY-THREE
A PICNIC

Something felt off when I woke up. I opened my eyes to a simple room of greens and yellows. My bed was warm, I had a water pitcher and a towel, my things were set on a chair, and in the mirror on the wall I could see my reflection. Nothing was wrong, and yet something was off.

"Puko." I shot up in bed, my head swirling from last night's wine. I hadn't seen Puko since we'd entered the city. He always came and went as he pleased, but he usually woke me up each day. Maybe he didn't like the Spring Lands, or maybe he couldn't get to me inside the palace. I didn't like it, but I decided to give him a couple days and see if I could find him outside.

I reached up to touch my hair and decided I needed a bath. I began gathering my things when a soft knock at my door startled me.

"Yes?" I shoved my fresh underthings into the towel in my arms.

"It's me." Schula's voice came through the door. "Are you going to take a bath? I was thinking about going soon."

I opened the door to find her with an armful of clothes and a comb in her other hand. "I was about to go myself."

"Shall we then?" She eyed my armload and offered me her arm like the people from the Spring Court did. I shook my head and took her offer, lacing my arm through hers.

"Should we tell Eberon where we're going?" I asked as we passed through the common room.

"I already told him I was going, I'm sure he'll figure it out." We closed the door softly behind us and turned toward the main corridor. Schula took us to the lion fountain and turned two lefts toward the baths. Few other bleary-eyed fae were up, and when we reached the baths they were nearly empty.

Hot pools of water steamed and fogged the room. Ivy grew everywhere, but the ceiling was made of glass, and sunshine lit up the room. The sky was bright and cloudless overhead.

"I can't believe how addicted to a hot bath I've become." I tossed my clothes in a basket by the wall and made for the washing area.

"I can't believe you took cold baths before now." Schula took more time folding her clothes, but she soon joined me.

Schula scrubbed my back while I kept it facing the wall. I helped her wash her back in turn, and we finished quickly so as to get into the hot pools as soon as we could.

Schula sank in, melting off her glamour and returning to the icy-white fae I knew.

"So," she began, innocence dripping from her words, "you spent the afternoon with Caldon?"

Sinking down into the water next to her, my back against the side of the pool, I eyed her. "Isn't that what I'm supposed to be doing here?"

A wide grin spread across her lips. "What do you think of him?"

"Isn't my job to reflect on Dwellonmar and not Caldon?" I asked.

She flicked water toward me. "You know what I mean! Don't be stingy, tell me everything."

"Hey!" I put an arm up, shielding my face from the assault. "Schula, are you telling me you're a gossip now?"

She snorted. "That's not new, ask Eb. Come on, tell me."

Sighing, I rested my head against the stone edge of the pool. "Well, he has a lot of energy for prancing about the city, that's for sure. He is thoughtful, and suspiciously kind."

And that was probably what gave me the most pause. Kindness. When to accept it, and when to be suspicious of it. The way I'd interacted with kindness before could not be the way I interacted with it now, but there was still something about Caldon that was too much.

"I don't know what to make of him," I finished.

A long, white arm dragged through the water, sending ripples through an otherwise empty pool as Schula hummed, calculating a response. "Caldon's charming, and King Diamid knows that. As a dignitary, he's good at lowering one's defenses around him and by extension the Spring Court. His job here is indeed to lure you to Dwellonmar, but I'm also sure he's enjoying it." She turned her head to me. "I don't know what it's like to go through what you've been through, but I'll wager you haven't been sought after by many in a romantic way."

"No." I closed my eyes. "No one of sense wants to be with a half fae."

"Well, I think Caldon does." Schula scooted closer to me on the bench. "I've never met anyone who enjoys the company of the opposite sex as much as he does. I'm not saying you could expect anything permanent or lasting from him, but if you want to see him, it is an option."

"It sounds like you know him well." Peeling one eye open, I watched Schula's reaction.

"You could say that," she admitted with a sly grin. "Our situations may not be the same, but similarly I grew up restricted in some ways. When I left home, I wandered a lot. Not only was I not sure where I could possibly find a home, I didn't know enough about myself or what I wanted. I met Caldon here in Dwellonmar, and it was rather perspective-shifting."

There were so many more pieces to Schula than I had realized before. So open and comfortable with herself, I had thought she was an entirely new species of person when we'd first met. Whatever she had been through was probably why she'd seen through me at first sight. For her kindness in my darkest days, I would forever be thankful to her.

"And if I don't want to develop feelings of any kind?" I asked.

Schula heaved a dramatic sigh, throwing an arm over her forehead. "How utterly dull!" She let her arm fall, then dropped her expression for an easy smile. "It's your decision. Don't ever think I'm pushing you into something you don't want to do. I only ask because Caldon asked for my blessing."

My head jerked back. "He did? Why?"

She shrugged. "His way of being a gentleman, I think. He doesn't court a fae who would take a lover for life, but he does consider all parties around him before he makes a move. Maybe he asked because he and I had a past, but there's nothing there now. Mostly, I wanted to see where your thoughts drifted, but I'm a busybody after all."

That almost pulled a laugh out of me. "You are, aren't you?"

She closed her eyes and shrugged. "So the Stars created me with the virtue of curiosity."

It was my turn to flick water at her as she cackled. "Isn't it, I don't know, shameful?"

I had caught teenagers in the mountains tumbling naked in the woods. You didn't bed a girl you didn't want to marry, or at least you didn't get caught doing it. Not when you were human.

"This isn't the land of men, Wren." She looked at me with those pale, gentle eyes. "It's rare to find someone who would choose to mate for life. There is a bonding ceremony, like a human marriage, but our population survives on lovers. When you're talking hundreds or thousands of years of life, a mate is a difficult commitment to swallow. Taking a lover is perfectly acceptable here. It's good for the soul, anyway."

Mulling it over, I recognized that I was still trying to shift my perspective to an entirely different culture. "That makes sense. But, it's still not for me. Not right now."

"Look, all I'm saying is follow your heart. You aren't with the humans anymore. This is what the fae do: we live, we love, we cry, we fight. Why live life bottling yourself up when you might experience something instead?"

Bottling myself up. Was that what I'd been doing? I *had* kept myself closed off. It was a way to protect myself. But here, everything was so frustratingly different. It would come down to taking Wren of the Southern Mountains and Wren of the Wyldes and separating them.

"I'll try to open up more," I said.

"You don't have to open up if you aren't ready." She reached out and took my hand, giving it a squeeze. "Just remember, you have all the same options as the rest of us here."

"I'll keep that in mind," I said.

With that lull in conversation, we agreed to get out of the water before more people woke up and came to clean themselves. Schula went looking for her comb while I was drying my hair.

Caldon. Could I do it? Could I take a lover just like that? The witches did it; they wouldn't take a husband, but they took lovers to make children. Even Bryn would go out at night to tumble some woman or other when we made our trips to Sulls.

Is that what the necklace means? Is it some kind of signal from Caldon? I needed to clear things up with him, just to be certain. Besides, if I was interested in anyone, it was . . .

I pushed the thoughts away for now. First things first, I was expected to see the king at lunch, and I needed to get ready for that. The Mother Herself could see my nerves rattling over it.

"Wren, you know I care about you, right?" Schula asked, drawing me from my thoughts.

I offered a quick smile between detangling knots. "Yes, I care for you too, Schula."

She grinned. "Wonderful, because after this we're stretching!"

Caldon came for me just before midday, as he'd said he would. Schula and Eberon hadn't specifically been invited to the picnic. They could have come anyway, but Eberon insisted he and Schula had things to discuss. Schula, the fiend, saw me off with a wink.

Meeting a king was stressful enough on a regular day, but the amount of time I spent struggling over wearing my new necklace nearly caused me to be late. In the end, I wore it for the simple truth that I'd never owned jewelry like it before, and I wanted to look as much like the rest of the court as I could. In Sulls, the wealthy could afford rare gems set in gold or silver. Those with a little extra to spend could afford copper or bronze trinkets, possibly with polished stones. The rest of us made colorful baubles from dyed strings and clay beads. The quartz I settled around my neck was the finest craftsmanship I'd ever seen up close, let alone owned for myself. And when Caldon arrived at my door to escort me, it was obvious he noticed.

Thankfully, he didn't say anything, but that meant my question regarding the meaning behind it remained unanswered.

The conversation was light as Caldon led me through the twists and turns of the hallways. Even so, I couldn't remember a word either of us said, too aware of my breathing, my heartbeat, and my warm palms. *Lovers*. The word thundered in my head. Something I'd never thought of for myself. Ever. There was something about it that was so attainable here, and my mind marveled at the concept that I would be allowed to reach for it. But there was also something distinctly wrong when my mind tried to paint a picture of me and Caldon together in that way.

Something deep blue like the night sky peeking between the silver stars crawled into the edges of my mind. Not quite coming into view, but not quite gone, either.

"Wren?" Caldon stopped.

"Hmm?" He had said something. What was it?

"I said we're here." Caldon gestured to an open doorway before us.

"Right, yes." Resisting the urge to fidget with my clothes or double-check my braids, I managed to follow Caldon as he escorted me into an open glen. The sky overhead was unbroken, and if I didn't know any better, I would have guessed we were outside the palace altogether. The ground was dirt and grass, sloping gently up to a hill. The king sat atop a grand blanket and cushions. Settled around him were several fae, including the princes and Master Draedon. The walls, however, remained all around us at a distance. Far enough to give the illusion of open meadow, close enough to remind me that I was still within the Spring Court's domain.

"His Majesty requests you join his family," Caldon said softly. "On his left is Prince Alban, Prince Arran, and Master Draedon, whom you met last night. To his right is Princess Vray, the twins' mother, and their father, Lord Norfeld."

"Thank you," I whispered. We approached the top of the hill, and King Diamid waved us forward.

"Sit! Join us, Wren." He had an air of command despite looking little older than me. His daughter and her mate were smiling as well, and Master Draedon nodded at us.

"Thank you, Majesty." I bowed and took the indicated seat. Caldon bowed and left.

"Such grim circumstances for our first meeting," Diamid said, plucking a grape from a bowl in front of him. "A beautiful sendoff, though. That party you arrived with know Baeleon's tastes well."

"Father, maybe we should speak of lighter things?" Princess Vray nodded toward me. Her droopy eyes and full lower lip gave her a dreamy, melancholic appearance. "It's nice to meet you, Wren. Caldon tells us you are enjoying the Spring Lands?"

"I am." A twinge of burning at my back itched, but I ignored it. "Dwellonmar is a lovely place, and the slopes of your roads remind me of growing up on a mountainside."

"Surely not as steep as all that." Lord Norfeld laughed, his pinched nose the most prominent thing about him before I noticed he had been the one to give the princes the shape of their mouths.

"A *mountain*?" Arran perked up from his tart.

"Like the Winter's Teeth?" Alban hissed.

"Gracious, no, not there." King Diamid patted the princes on their heads and laughed, filling the glen. "Tell me about your home in the mountains, Wren."

"Well, I lived in a log cabin built by my father—the man who found me, that is—he was a woodsman, a woodcutter for the surrounding villages." I wiggled a little in place as the itch on my back didn't relent.

"Wasn't it cold?" Vray asked, her words promising more interest than her expression as she turned her eyes toward a floral decoration on the table, picking up two white blossoms to begin twining their stems together.

"Sometimes, not all year," I answered. "I lived through each season as it came. I could never have imagined the Autumn Lands and Spring Lands as I know them now."

"How can you live through all the seasons changing all the time?" Arran asked skeptically.

"Hush, Arran," Princess Vray told him absently. "Even princes have to let their guests talk. We invited Wren here, after all."

"Sorry, Miss Wren." Arran shied away behind Master Draedon, playing with a willow blossom in his teacher's hair.

"Please, I'm honored by the invitation." I bowed my head and channeled my inner Eberon. "Feel free to ask me anything."

"Did you have a tutor?" Alban asked. The king chuckled and plucked another grape.

"No, no tutor. Well, a woman did teach me to read and write and things, but I'm sure I'm not very learned," I answered.

"A woman, not your guardian?" The king turned to me. "Did the humans treat you well?"

Tedious. This was another tedious parade, though I could be thankful it wasn't in front of all those extra pairs of eyes as Baeleon had done. I swallowed a sigh.

"For the most part no. The humans are . . . The unknown scares them." I gripped my hands in the grass around me, trying to ignore my itching back. "There were a small few around me, though, who treated me well."

"And were you afraid at your first fae encounter?" Vray tilted her head, finally looking up from the flowers.

"Truthfully, yes. But any fears I had are disappearing as I meet more fae and see more of the Wyldes."

"But you are half fae yourself," Lord Norfeld said.

"True, and that scared me as well. I didn't know what might happen to me, or if I would watch those around me grow old while I stayed the same. I had no one to tell me what to expect."

"How dreadful." Vray lowered her head back to the flowers.

"What powers have surfaced for you?" Diamid asked. "Nothing too troublesome in your human home, I hope."

A sinking feeling started low in my belly. "I, well, there was an incident. When I was young, but we were able to clean it up."

"Oh?" The king leaned in. "What exactly happened?"

Now they were all staring at me. The boys curiously, the tutor with sharp interest, even Vray and Norfeld were watching my reaction. A picnic in pastels, surrounded by flowers, foods prepared in bite-sized portions with great effort, and luxury I could never have imagined, and the most interesting thing about the whole situation simply had to be *me.*

I was trapped, I realized. Not in a cage or locked in a room, but I was trapped on this open hill, in a beautiful garden glen, by the high society of the fae. The burning in my back increased, and something pressed in on me, screaming at me to keep it a secret. My palms were so hot, I rubbed them absently on the grass.

"I—"

CAW!

Startling backward and nearly falling, I was saved by a fat shadow of feathers plummeting into my lap.

"Guards!" Lord Norfeld called. The princes squealed in delight as Princess Vray and Master Draedon scooped them up in alarm.

"Puko!" I gasped as he righted himself on my lap. "Your Majesty, I am so sorry."

"You know this bird?" Diamid asked in surprise.

"Yes, he traveled with me from the mountains." I got a firm grasp on his feet, sealing him to my knee. "I am so sorry. He's probably just frustrated he couldn't find me inside the palace. I usually sleep with a window open for him."

"What an odd bird. What did you say his name was?" The king's gaze was now narrowed on Puko's clouded eye. A pang shot through my back, so raw and hot and painful that I let out a small cry.

"*Ah*! Ah, that. He's been called a lot of things since he found me on my journey." I searched for the names the others called him, particularly Eberon. "Troublemaker, Featherbrain, Menace."

"Menace!" the twins squealed. "Can I pet him?"

Melting with relief, I was glad to have a reason to avoid the king's stare. "If he'll let you, I don't mind." The princes scurried from the grasp of their caretakers and rushed to Puko. I thanked him silently for his cooperation in the distraction and vowed to give him a big bowl of cherries as soon as possible.

"Sire?" A guard approached.

The king waved a hand, and the guard retreated.

"You said this creature *follows* you?" Lord Norfeld asked.

"Sometimes. Mostly, he just bothers me for food in the mornings." I shrugged, keeping my tone casual. "It's true what they say, if you feed an animal, it will follow you forever."

"I want to feed a wolf!" Arran yelled.

"I want to feed a *bear*." Alban growled. "My bear can eat your wolf!"

"Ahem." The princess gave the twins a sharp look, and they settled down.

"I'm sorry, I didn't know he was around. I can try to send him away," I offered.

"No, it's fine." Vray sighed. "They need to learn *control*."

"Sorry, Mother."

"Sorry."

"Your Majesty?" A train of servants approached with what must be lunch.

Lunch? There were already plates all around us, barely touched except for Diamid's bowl of grapes and an assortment of sweets the boys had gobbled up. As far as I was aware, lunch had already been served.

"Yes, yes, set it up." He was still staring at Puko but waved the servants forward. With the moment broken, I felt I could breathe again. The rest of the lunch was a painful string of trying to eat between deeply personal questions and figuring out how to phrase things delicately enough for a king. Finally, I was allowed to leave when it became clear the twins needed a nap.

The king still watched Puko.

My seal still burned.

TWENTY-FOUR

INTERESTING

I walked absently to the entryway, still feeling the king's eyes on my back. I had Puko clamped in my arms, willing him to be quiet for once in his life until we were away from the picnic and around the corner.

"Shh," I whispered to Puko absently, shifting my eyes back and forth, watching for Diamid to pop out and grab me. But he never did.

In my distress at getting away from the prying eyes of the hilltop, I must have turned a wrong corner, because suddenly nothing looked familiar.

I took a calming breath and turned back the way I'd come. Surely, I would be able to see the fountain soon; I hadn't passed it but a moment ago.

But I never found the fountain. I walked in circles, panic growing as the hallways around me seemed to move and change, despite not walking very far at all. The ivy-covered walls were alive and rustling with a breeze that came from everywhere and nowhere all at once.

I decided to pick a hallway and stick with it, for better or worse, until I found someone who might be able to help me. I took the brightest, widest one in hopes that I would find a Spring fae. The hallway wound and curved but remained bright. I was hopeful as more sun began to peek through the greenery overhead, widening into a possibly more frequently traveled area.

Instead, I rounded a corner and almost bumped into a familiar face. One that I was in no condition to handle at that moment.

I snapped my attention onto a set of milky white eyes. Her skin was a pleasant pink, her short black hair was still cropped close to her head, and now that I saw her up close, I could see small horns protruding from her temples.

Lady Krissaph inhaled deeply through her nose and smiled. She ran her tongue over her sharp fangs and grinned. She wore a thin gold dress with a neckline that dropped to her navel and a slit on the side of each leg that rose above her hips. All in all, I could see nearly as much now as I could when I'd met her in the bath at the Autumn Palace.

"Well, well, well. Imagine bumping into the famous lost faeling here," she purred.

"Lady Krissaph," I said. I bowed my head like I had seen so many others do as a sign of respect.

"I see you've been in Diamid's esteemed presence. Been probing for information, has he?" She offered me her arm. "Come."

Puko's feathers bristled; he was puffed up like a black cloud in my arms. I didn't know what to do. I was frozen in place, not wanting to go with her, but I was already lost as it was.

"Oh, come on now, I don't bite." She continued to hold out her arm patiently. "Well, I don't bite females. Often."

I took a deep breath and shifted Puko to one arm, taking Krissaph's arm with my other hand.

"Good girl, wise decision." She immediately began walking further down the hallway, and I had little choice but to follow.

"So, young one. You have many mysteries surrounding you, yes?" she asked.

"I'm not the only one," I muttered. Puko cawed his agreement.

"Interesting company you keep, Wren." To my dismay we turned a corner and split away from our original corridor. "This one seems to be full of secrets too."

I glanced down at Puko's white eye. He seemed to be watching Krissaph with it, and it sent a chill through me. I hadn't ever given it much thought, but he had sat faithfully on Mila's shoulder since I could remember. He was certainly no ordinary bird, and I could only imagine what he'd seen in his time.

"Where is it we are going, Lady Krissaph?" I asked.

"A small detour through the lovely palace, then I will safely deposit you at your door. Don't worry, despite what that frigid bitch may have said about me, I won't hurt you." Puko ruffled his feathers and let out a low, gurgling croak that I had never heard before.

"Oh, hush, you," Krissaph hissed at Puko, which shut him up. "Now, I just want a pleasant chat. Is that so much to ask?"

"I don't know what you want to talk about, but if you can get me back to my room, I'll talk with you," I offered.

"Wonderful." She grinned, leading us down a new path. "Now, can you tell me what exactly you keep on your back that smells so sour?"

My spine shot straight, panic running through me, trailed by nausea. "You smell something?"

"Yes, *I* can smell something, though I doubt many others could do the same." She tilted her head to the side. "Does that distress you?"

"Yes," I answered truthfully. "And I'd rather not talk about it."

"I see," she said with a pout. "I suppose it can't be helped then. In that case, would you like to talk to me about your parentage?"

I blinked. That had come out of nowhere.

"Oh, don't be so surprised. Of course who your sire is would be the talk of the Wyldes."

"I don't know anything about my parents," I said truthfully. "And I don't know how I would find out. For all I know, they're dead."

"Hmm, an interesting problem to have." Her lips, painted plum, spread into a slow grin. "But if I have tasted your sire before, I could taste him on you now. Would you care for a tryst in a dark corridor? I know a lovely spot with candles and the most comfortable cushions. If you lay on the red one and throw a leg across the round one, I can reach your—"

"No! *No*, thank you, Lady Krissaph." If any more blood rushed to my face, I would faint. I could barely wrap my head around an outing with Caldon; I certainly couldn't handle whatever Lady Krissaph would try to do to me.

"You're sure?" She frowned. "What a shame. I do wonder what you taste like under all that smoke and despair."

I didn't want to know. Not even a little bit. Well, maybe a tiny little bit.

"So to, um, taste me. You can't just, I don't know, lick my hand or something?"

Krissaph tilted her head back and laughed. She had to hold her stomach she was laughing so hard. I held on tighter to Puko, who let out another gurgling croak.

"Oh dear, how charming. You really did grow up outside the Wyldes." She wiped a tear off her cheek with her free hand and steered us down a new hallway. "I need to taste you on a more personal level than that, Wren. I need you at a heightened state of emotion to do that."

"I'm pretty frustrated and upset right now, won't that work?" I sighed.

A smirk tugged at her mouth. "No, I need to feed from a fairly specific emotion, and it's not frustration. Well, it's not that kind of frustration, anyway."

"I see." I didn't see. I didn't really want to, either.

"Ah, Wren. We're nearly at our destination, and you seem to be leaving me with more questions than answers." She sighed and turned down another hallway. "Here we are, stop one."

She stepped into bright sunlight as the new hallway opened into a stone courtyard with a bubbling fountain and lines of clothes out to dry. Several fae of different sorts who looked to be in service at the palace were happily at work and chatting away the afternoon. They didn't seem to mind our intrusion.

I looked around, unsure of what I was supposed to be doing. "Um, this isn't my room."

"Look up," she said.

I did. There were a few clouds, and the sun was high in the sky. "What am I seeing?"

Krissaph gestured to the mass of black feathers in my arms. "If you don't want Diamid to investigate him further, send him outside until your time in the Spring Palace is done."

I looked down at Puko, who seemed to be nodding in agreement.

I lifted my arms and let him shake out his feathers, then he spread his wings wide.

"Oh, one moment." Krissaph reached over and plucked a stray feather from Puko's tail. "A souvenir."

He turned around to snap at her, a big ball of indignation. But Krissaph was too fast and had already moved out of range. She tucked the feather behind her ear and backed up, letting the raven take off. He soared away and quickly dipped out of sight.

"Now, do you still want to go back to your room? Or would you like to see mine?" She smiled, and a few heads turned our way. These attendants probably thought I was having a rendezvous with Krissaph, and she'd probably done that on purpose.

"Mine, please," I said a little louder than I needed to. "I need to get back to Eberon and Schula."

"Very well." She offered her arm again, and I took it, walking with her through a new corridor.

She seemed content to lead me around in silence for a few minutes, until I spotted a familiar statue in an alcove I knew to be by the baths.

"Ah, I believe this is where we part ways." Krissaph paused to tilt her head upward. "I may be of the Spring Court, but I associate with whom I want. You interest me, Wren. I think you're going to shake a few things up in the Wyldes, and I for one am looking forward to it."

Footsteps passed nearby, and Krissaph backed me into an alcove. She pressed our bodies together in what must have looked to the outside world like a lovers' embrace. I heard a giggle accompany the footsteps as they faded away.

"If you are ever doing something and you need to cover your tracks, you are welcome to claim an evening with me. No one would question it, and I will tell them you were with me all night. That is a promise," she whispered in my ear, raising goose bumps on my skin with her warm breath.

"What would I be doing in secret?" I murmured.

"Anything you want, young one." She backed away, licking her lips. "I encourage your mischief. There are a few important fae in this part of the world who could stand to be knocked off their feet, and I look forward to seeing it happen. I think you can be the one to make it happen."

I stepped away from her and toward the hallway that would lead me back to our rooms. "But I don't want to shake anyone up."

"I don't think you have a choice. You taste of change, whether you like it or not. And, of course, my offer still stands for a midnight tryst." She winked seductively at me, and I took another step away. "The thing about odd birds like yours, they can find their feathers again if you have need of me."

"Thank you, I think." There was no one else in the hallway at the moment, and I wasn't sure whether that was a blessing or a disappointment.

She inhaled deeply and smirked.

"I look forward to whatever trouble you get yourself into. And let me know when that sour thing comes off your back, would you? I'm deeply interested in what smells so curious about you."

She dipped her head and turned away, swinging her hips in a suggestive promise as she wandered down the way we had come.

I took a few deep breaths and straightened my dress. I clutched the quartz at my neck and sighed as I began my walk to the rooms.

Now in a familiar and populated part of the palace, I felt the presence of fae all around me. I felt their eyes on me, and I tried to shake it off as paranoia on my part. I just hoped no one had heard Krissaph's words to me.

My imagination ran wild with the suggestion that I was going to bring change to the Wyldes. I didn't want change; I craved stability. I wanted to settle down and build a nice cabin and find a familiar life with predictable patterns. But in the moment, that felt as unattainable as the stars themselves.

I stopped, blinking the threatening tears from my eyes and standing squarely in front of the door to our rooms.

Between Diamid and Krissaph, I was exhausted, and I desperately needed the help of my friends.

TWENTY-FIVE
FRACTURED DECISIONS

"We need to leave." Eberon paced the common space of our quarters, which really didn't have enough room to be pacing in. Schula had to lift her feet each time he made a pass near the cushion where she was sitting with her feet tucked to one side.

"You need to calm down," Schula soothed. "Panic will do no good now; what we need is your clear head."

"A clear head?" Eberon sputtered. "A *clear head?* This is one hell of a thing to reveal to me now! You knew the whole time. I'm just coming to terms with it. And even Thain found out before we left for Spring! Thain knew, and he didn't—"

"Thain found out under difficult circumstances," Schula said. "He's probably still figuring out his own feelings about it. He learned less than a day before he was sent away on Baeleon's task, remember?"

"Still," Eberon murmured. "He could have said something to me."

Schula sighed. "I know Thain isn't here, but we can handle this. You're supposed to be our compass, I know you can find the right move."

Eberon paused, blinking at the empty space before him. "Right, you're right."

Schula sighed again, turning to my corner of the room. "Wren, you're sure he knew Puko from somewhere?"

"Yes, or he was suspicious of him. He asked me questions about my magic, then Puko came down and interrupted everything. Which may have made things worse, I don't know."

"You see? We need to get Wren out of here before there's an incident. Baeleon will filet us alive if he finds out we were harboring witch magic! Our business in Dwellonmar is done anyway." Eberon resumed pacing.

"Are we allowed to just leave?" I asked.

"We aren't prisoners," Eberon scoffed. "Though, we might be. You know, if they find *witchcraft* carved into the flesh of the youngling!"

"It's not." Schula pinched the bridge of her nose. "Nothing is carved into anyone's flesh, Eberon. The markings are sealing her magic; it was probably done to keep her safe."

"Oh, well, that's fine then!" Eberon threw his hands up. The golden fae looked like he was on the verge of a panic attack. "And you'd know because you knew about this the whole time and didn't find it important enough to, I don't know, tell your triquetram?"

"We don't even know if anyone would care!" Schula countered. "As long as it's removed and any magic in her is settled, nothing will have changed. Wren will still be part of the Wyldes, and the courts can fight for her favor all the same."

"We don't know if anyone would . . ." Eberon sputtered. "Baeleon himself was in the last battle before the witches were cast out! DuVarick was there! The Spring Court king of the time *died* in that battle. Why would they not care?"

"Because Wren wasn't there!" Schula said, getting heated. "That's the entire point, the marks on her back don't define her. She didn't create them, she didn't ask for them, and she wasn't even born when the witches were cast out!"

"This isn't Schula's fault." The pair of them stopped to look my way. My heart was racing, the argument building too high, too fast, and threatening to spiral out of control. "I begged her not to tell anyone. I thought I could handle it on my own. If anyone is going to be in trouble for the marks on *my* back, it should be me."

Schula's shoulders sank, the tension leaving. Eberon's mouth was a grim line, a muscle in his jaw jumping as he clenched his teeth.

"It's not as though she's bringing witches into the Wyldes or performing their magic," Schula said. "Wren is expected to spend time at all the courts and make an important decision. She has a year to do it. We can't just have a two-day visit and call it done. Yes, this has been kept secret. Yes, I should have told you at some point. But we're here now, and our current problem is Diamid, not one another."

Eberon faced Schula. "If Diamid is feeling out any powers she may have, he likely suspects those same powers to be the reason she survived the plague. For all we know, he's right. That kind of power in your court is too tempting, and everyone is going to be after her if they suspect the same."

Numbness fell over me. "I'm not powerful, I'm an accident waiting to happen. There was a fire last time, Eberon. It was out of control."

Eberon slumped down onto the nearest cushion. "Fire I can deal with." He lifted a hand, flicking his fingers upward in a casual display ending in a brief flame that was extinguished a heartbeat after it was called. "My king gutting me because our triquetram hid something like this from him, I cannot."

Schula pursed her lips.

"It wasn't you, though, it was me," I protested.

Eberon huffed out a laugh. "But it wasn't just you, little bird. Schula knew, and that means all of us should have known. Baeleon will not care. A triquetram is an inseparable unit where the actions of one affect all."

Eberon sighed after he said it, then with the smallest jerk of his head, he moved his attention to Schula as if he'd just realized something about what he'd said.

"But I'm not one of you, am I?" Schula stood.

"Schula—" Eberon started.

"No, not this time, Eb." She made for the front door, pausing to turn around long enough to look at him. "I can't replace her. I never wanted to. But this, what Wren went through and what she's hidden, neither you nor Thain are going to understand it the way I do."

The door closed behind her with a solid thud, and Eberon closed his eyes. Quiet engulfed the room, not a sound between us as footsteps faded away into the palace.

"I know I messed up. I should have gotten these marks off me sooner," I said. Realization sank into me like the chill of winter into my bones.

Avoiding the problem was no longer an option, because the consequences were no longer my own. "If I removed them now somehow, would that help?"

"No," Eberon said, so softly I nearly didn't hear him. "In this moment, the fault was mine." He sighed, running a hand down his face.

From my corner seat, I leaned back and rested my head against the wall. The secret had felt so small before. Such a little thing, and I had planned to deal with it soon anyway. Hadn't I?

Had I?

Nightmares about that day when I was ten had chased me for years. The sensation of everything around me burning was so rooted into my memories I could still smell the burning herbs that had been drying over Mila's window. The pops and crackles of damp wood, because it had just rained that morning. The look on Mila's face . . . I had never in my life seen her caught by surprise before. The terror of the moment had kept the markings on my back for so many years since, because I never wanted to deal with what could be let out again.

Shifting from the other side of the room, Eberon stood. "I need to go find her."

"What can I do to help?" I asked, scrambling to my feet.

Eberon shook his head, not looking at me as he opened the door. "This is for me to handle. Wait here. It will be okay."

I wished he'd sounded more sure of himself as the door closed behind him.

There was nothing else to do but hope he was right.

Neither of them came back before a pair of attendants arrived to lay out food on our shared table. I wanted to wait for them, but leaving the room and searching the palace blindly seemed like a bad idea considering this place was designed to confuse and disorient. Picking at a few items, I finally gave up and ate a roll stuffed with cabbage and other vegetables I didn't recognize. When the rest of the food grew cold, I could no longer sit idle and waiting.

Slipping out of our quarters, I made my way down to the lion fountain. The baths were one way, the main hall the other. There were a few people walking in any given direction, but none that gave me an idea of where Schula or Eberon might have gone. With no other ideas, I walked in the direction of the baths and skipped the turn I should have taken to get to them.

I moved to each intersecting corridor, pausing only long enough to decide if I wanted to explore them or not. Deeper and deeper into the palace I went, and no one looked my way, seemingly absorbed in their own business, which was fine by me. It wasn't until I finally crossed paths with a dryad smelling of sweat that I had the thought that Schula might have chosen to run through her training routine to expel some of her distress.

The dryad had come from a long hall with many doors. I looked for any significant markings in this crossing, landing on a peculiar red flower in a vase to become my marker for finding my way back, then made my way down the hall.

Most doors were closed, but through the few left open, I saw more scholarly pursuits than physical. A room of books, a room of fae scrawling notes at desks, a room of maps. Occasionally, my curiosity would be rewarded with someone lifting their head from their work, but no one spoke to me, they simply turned back to their tasks.

The corridor intersected many more times before I found a turn that ended in a single doorway. This one gave me pause. The wooden doors, painted blue and carved with decorations, were as large as the ones in the main hall where all the festivities had been held so far. One lone fae wandered out of the room, passing me with no more than a nod, a stack of books in her arms. Turning in to the short hall, I pushed open the doors and went inside.

A library. I should have guessed from the rest of the rooms in this part of the palace. The walls were lined with books, tables scattered in the middle space offered work surfaces, and a young boy was moving from lantern to lantern refilling the oil.

"Miss Wren, what a pleasant surprise," Master Draedon said, coming up to me with a book tucked under one arm. "Are you perhaps in search of something?"

His clothes were a muted blue today, his beard nearly blending into them. His bright yellow eyes, however, were clear and sharp as they inspected me.

"Good evening, Master Draedon." I bowed my head to the royal tutor, a motion I'd become all too familiar with. "No, I'm afraid I may have gotten myself lost. I was looking for someone, but I'm not entirely sure where they may have gone."

"I see," he nodded, a hint of knowing in his rounded cheeks as he smiled. "I believe I can help you find your way. Somewhere more likely to find your company, that is."

"I don't mean to take up your time," I said, already taking a step back toward the door. "I can retrace my steps."

Master Draedon chuckled, walking with me as I found myself going through the library doors at his side. "I assure you, it is no bother. I was only seeking a book for tomorrow's lessons with my students."

"In that case, thank you," I said, with no choice but to follow along. He took us back through the hall of books and desks, then we arrived at the crossing with the red flower I'd made note of and passed it completely. My head turned, watching the vase as we left it behind.

"Where is it we're going, Master Draedon?" I asked.

"Not far. You'll find your company up ahead," he answered.

How he knew was beyond my imagination, but I kept my curious tongue still until we arrived. Master Draedon stopped at an open, arched entry and turned.

"I will leave you to it then," he said, and we both bowed our heads as he left me.

Sighing, I peered into the room before me. There was no sign of Schula or Eberon, but what I did find was a place meant for leisure. The walls, painted pale pink, allowed vines from the ceiling to crawl toward the floor on round pillars. Some kind of game with painted stones was laid out on a low table, cushions surrounding it, three people playing and chatting. One wall was consumed by paintings, and six more people were lounging beneath them while a dryad played a stringed instrument on his lap. A few more were on the other side of the room, one of them reading something aloud to the others. We didn't have anything like this at Silver Lake. If someone wanted to play a game, you would clear your table and play there. If someone wanted to play music, they played outside while taking a break from work. Even the tavern was a place for food and drink. This room with no other purpose was strange.

"Maybe I can find my way back to that red flower," I murmured, stepping back from the room. A head of long pink hair moved, standing up from next to the wall of paintings, and I realized why Master Draedon had thought I would find who I was looking for in this room.

"Caldon," I said as he padded across the room with a smile, joining me outside the arched doorway.

"What brings you to this part of the palace?" He beamed, eyes dipping to my neck and back. "Did someone escort you?"

In my head, I wanted to scream. The quartz still hung around my neck; I hadn't removed it since the picnic, and I hadn't gotten to clear things up with Caldon yet. Schula, Eberon, and the marks on my back were at the top of my mind, and in a surge of annoyance, this felt like an obstacle.

"Master Draedon seemed to misunderstand who it is I'm looking for," I said as he offered his arm, and I took it while eyeing his profile.

Caldon really was beautiful, and he carried himself with an ease that affected the people around him. The top half of his hair was pulled back from his face, tied into a braid as the rest of it fell down his back. He had foregone the waistcoat I'd seen him in for every other occasion, now wearing something easier, looser, in a faded red that complemented the tones of his skin.

"And how lucky I would have been if he were right that I was the one you sought out," Caldon mused. "Alas, I will lick my wounds later. For the moment, where can I lead you this evening?"

Hells. I couldn't tell him about the fight earlier. I couldn't tell him Schula had run off, or that Eberon had chased after her and left me alone for hours. And I certainly couldn't tell him this all had to do with the witch markings I carried on my back.

Caldon paused us in the hallway. "Something is troubling you."

Well, there is one problem I can take care of right now, even if it is uncomfortable.

"I wanted to ask: Was there another meaning attached to this necklace you gave me?"

Caldon's brows shot up, then his eyes moved to the hallway around us. "Let's find somewhere more private for this conversation. I can see I will need to give you my full attention."

"Thank you." He led us in the general direction of the lion fountain, as far as I could tell. A few turns later, we came to an alcove that held nothing more than a bench and a vase of roses. He helped me to sit first before joining me on the cushioned seat.

"It seems I've realized far too late that you may not know all the customs of the Wyldes yet. For that, I apologize." Caldon bowed his head, bringing it up again with a smile. "There will be many gifts you may receive, but a gift of stone will always mean something. In this case, my admiration of your spirit and the beauty of your eyes. If you would like it, I would spend more time with you than my job as your guide to Dwellonmar would require."

Caldon lifted one of my hands, his lips brushing my knuckles in the whisper of a kiss before letting my fingers fall back to my lap. Thankful for the cage of my ribs to keep my heart in its place, I pulled my bottom lip between my teeth.

So, it was to do with courtship after all. I'd seen it plenty of times. The way the young couples would dance during festivals, the women making trinkets for their lovers, the men performing deeds they thought would sway the object of their affection's heart. There had been a time I'd wanted it too. Wanted it so badly I could have convinced myself that the right human would come along and look past my flaws and still choose me. But that hope had been dashed many years ago, gone by the wayside once my hormone-addled brain left my youth behind and I settled into the peaceful adulthood I had enjoyed until the raid.

And now that it was suddenly an option, I didn't want it. Or perhaps I simply didn't want it with him. Caldon, or maybe Dwellonmar itself, had lifted my head high into the clouds while we'd explored the Spring Lands in that carefree manner of his, but I was always meant to be firmly on my feet.

Slipping the necklace from my head, I held it out for Caldon to take. "I'm sorry, I don't think I'm prepared for something like that. I'm too new to all this, and I have to travel the Wyldes for the next year."

Caldon closed his eyes with a smile, nodding. He curled my fingers back around the stone, pushing my hand back toward my chest.

"There is no call for sorrow, lovely Wren. My feelings are free and easy. I don't want them to be the stone that sinks anyone's heart downward." He stood, offering me his arm again. "Do not worry for my heart; in this city of flowers it will be easily mended."

Taking his arm, I nearly failed to hold back my laughter. Schula had been right; he moved through lovers easily, it would seem.

"You're a flatterer, aren't you?" I teased, and his amusement bubbled into laughter as we began walking down the hall.

"Where shall I take you?" he asked.

I felt lighter with this problem solved. The stone in the pit of my stomach was still there, a boiling reminder that my secrets were cracking the beautiful façade of my new life and I had to fix things before they got even more out of hand. Bryn would have scolded me by now; I could almost hear him trying to liken my situation to some tale or other he'd gathered from travelers or passing drunks. But there wasn't anyone else in a situation like this; there might never have been before or ever would be again. At least this matter with Caldon was settled, however, so I gave my Spring Court guide the only answer I could in the moment. "I think I would like to find my bed."

TWENTY-SIX

FAREWELL TO SPRING

The door closing in the main room startled me awake. The texture of the woven blankets I'd fallen asleep on had pressed their pattern into my cheek as I wiped the side of my face with my hand and opened my bedroom door. Schula met me with a tired smile.

"Are you all right?" I asked, my tone careful.

"Sorry for earlier," she said. "I'll be fine."

Stepping from my room, I noticed in the low light of the last lantern that her hair was damp. The table had been cleaned up when I'd returned from my futile outing to find them earlier, but there was still a bowl of fruit I had snuck into my room. "Are you hungry? I have some pears."

Schula hesitated, her eyes ringed dark and pink.

"You're tired. I can let you go to bed," I said.

"No," she started. "Well, yes, I am. But that doesn't mean I don't want to talk to you. I should explain."

What would Mila do? Or Bryn? Neither of them would have had the reaction I thought I wanted in the moment. My hand reached out, taking hers in mine. "Come here."

Schula let me bring her into my room, closing the door behind her. Sitting her on the bed, since there was little other furniture to choose from, I pulled the bowl off the small table that held my washbasin and plopped one of the green fruits into her palm.

"You look like you need to eat something," I said, and she burst into a laugh.

"I feel like I've said that same thing to you a dozen times in the last few weeks."

"Fair enough." I shrugged. "I feel like I've heard it at least a dozen times."

She smiled, biting into the crisp pear and savoring the juices with a moan. "There are a lot of memories in this place for me. They may just be getting under my skin."

It felt good to sit down next to her, and Schula leaned over to rest her head on my shoulder as she picked at the fruit. The urge to pry into her thoughts was hard to resist, but thankfully she didn't keep me in suspense for long. When she was done with the pear, she set the remnants in another bowl where I had put my own leftovers earlier in the evening.

"I left my home a long time ago, but the first place I ended up at for very long was Dwellonmar," Schula said, lying back on the bed with a sigh. "King Diamid doesn't seem to remember me, or maybe he doesn't want to address it. But he let me stay, a citizen of no court, until I got my feet under me again. Caldon was a big part of it, but so was this city. I think being here reminds me of how much I am not the person Eberon and Thain need the most."

Lying back next to her, I kept my head turned her way. "What was their missing person like?" It had felt so taboo to speak of them before now, the person who'd left a hole in the hearts of my new friends and a cold black band on their thumbs.

Schula closed her eyes, smiling. "A big ball of energy. Someone who charged forward to reach out a helping hand, even before you knew you needed it. I'm certainly no replacement for that."

"That's not true!" I nearly sat up; I couldn't believe what I was hearing. "You more than anyone else have been the hand to reach out for me. All of you, yes, but Thain and Eberon have their own way of helping me. I'm sorry if I haven't said it before now, but you're the one who has settled me in the most. I will be forever grateful for you, Schula."

Her eyes peeled open, her lips pressed thin. "Then I've done that much right, at least. I'm glad Thain found you."

The moment was so charged with emotion that I had to change

the subject. Neither of us seemed to know what to say or how to move ourselves. With a deep breath, I broke the tension with a question. "Did Eberon find you?"

Her brows shot up. "No, he came after me?"

"Of course he did," I said. "He felt awful about it. I know I don't have all the details, but it seemed like he didn't mean to phrase himself that way."

Schula stared up at the ceiling. "I know, I'm to blame too. I shouldn't have left like that when we still have to figure out our next steps about your magic."

The silence settled, neither of us having the right answers. In the low light of the night, and with no more conversation, we had both started to doze off when the front door opened again.

Schula scrambled off the bed, pulling my bedroom door open before I even got to my feet. By the time I made it to the doorway, I found Schula wrapping her arms around Eberon.

"No, I'm sorry," Eberon murmured, his arms around her back. "That was callous of me."

They separated, both looking to me as I entered the room. Eberon was still wearing the same Spring Court fashion he had been in earlier, though more wrinkled and worn than they had been hours ago.

Eberon offered a tight smile. "We leave tomorrow. I've been arranging provisions for travel. It should all be ready after breakfast."

"What did you tell King Diamid?" Schula asked.

The golden fae shrugged, brushing strands of fiery hair from his face. "A story about how pained I was to be away from Thain, that we had business to take care of with a mission he was on."

"Is that okay?" I asked.

"It's the truth, regardless." Eberon gave an empty laugh. "I don't think I can handle this alone. I need him."

Schula nodded, putting a hand on his shoulder. I still didn't entirely understand the bond, but I did respect that they were rarely this separated. I imagined it to be like being apart from Bryn, and the pain of his absence still kept me up at night.

"Any excuses for Wren?" Schula asked, looking to me. "She's supposed to be traveling the Wyldes."

"I fed him something about the season and making longer plans to stay for the spring equinox," Eberon said. "What was it I told them . . . Right. We left in a hurry, and all your things were still in Thanantholl."

"So, tomorrow?" Schula hummed. "Yes, that will be good. We go home and make amends with Thain. Together, we can figure this out."

"Let's get some sleep." Eberon yawned and made for his doorway. "We can say any lingering farewells after breakfast."

A light rain chased us out of the Spring Lands. I was quiet for most of the ride back, and I thought Schula and Eberon knew that was what I needed.

Puko sat on the windowsill next to me the whole way. He didn't leave my side except to eat, and even for that I didn't think he gave himself enough time to find much. He had found me immediately upon leaving the palace, and I was comforted by his presence.

My sleep was restless, and my thoughts wandered. I hadn't gotten to say goodbye to Caldon. Hells, I didn't even know how I really felt about him yet, but I regretted the missed opportunity to be with him. I would be back in the spring, but that still seemed so far away. Did he care? What were a few months to anyone with such a lifespan, after all?

And Krissaph. Whatever games she was playing seemed harmless enough. But I really wanted to know what had happened between her and Schula. Puko didn't seem to like her either. I questioned any decision that involved trusting an unseelie fae. But at this point, with Bryn gone and Mila off who knew where with her coven, my handful of trustworthy friends was dwindling. Maybe Krissaph could help me at some point after all.

Rain drizzled, muddying the road ahead and adding a dreary image to go with my heavy mood. I flexed my shoulder blades and tried to subtly scratch my seal. It hadn't calmed down since we'd left Dwellonmar. I had really hoped that it would.

Schula was right about my seal. The fae courts would find out what secrets I was keeping. I had to decide what to do. Whether I wanted it or not, my magic was straining harder to break free every day. Any more prodding and I would burst at the seams. If the four crowns were going to find out what I could do one way or another, I might as well be prepared to use it.

And Thain. We would be back in Thanantholl before him; the border was much further away than Dwellonmar, and we hadn't stayed long. I didn't know what to say to him, or even if I should forgive him yet.

Too many thoughts haunted me. I wanted nothing more than to curl up on a small bed in a log cabin in the mountains, a bearded giant humming as he whittled away on a piece of wood. It hurt that I could never have that again, and now my life was so much more complicated.

I exhaled sharply and slumped my head against the carriage.

"That was a heavy sigh," Schula said, moving her book to her lap.

Schula was on the opposite end of the same bench I was on. Puko was preening his feathers, scattering little rain droplets on my arm. Eberon was driving the carriage, only stopping us if the rain was more than he wanted for the horse. And I was in the same seat I had been in for days, under a blanket and feeling sorry for myself.

"Did I sigh? Sorry."

"I know what you need." Schula tucked a bit of ribbon in her book and set it aside. "You need a hot bath when we get back. And then you need a good workout. Move your body."

"Maybe." I wondered if all these thoughts could be blocked out by throwing myself at my training. "Schula, will you teach me magic? I still want to learn self-defense from you, but I need to learn control over my magic so I can lift the seal soon and be ready for it. I just want to know what to expect."

She studied me for a moment, long enough that I wasn't sure she'd remember to answer me out loud. "All right. When we're finally off the road, I'm moving you past limbering your body. Combat training and magic control. I'm not going to make it easy."

"Good," I said. "I don't want it to be easy. I want it to be effective."

"You asked for it; don't break on me."

That earned her a sharp look, but I didn't say anything.

"Almost to the gates," Eberon called from the driver's bench. I looked out the window, startling Puko into flight. Light rain still pattered over the Wyldes, but instead of rolling green hills, we were in the endless sunset forests of the Autumn Lands. The smell of wet leaves raked through the air, and I could see tendrils of smoke ahead of us where Thanantholl hid in the valley.

"I hope you're ready for the city. It isn't going to be the same as it was before," Schula said.

"Did something change?" I asked, pulling my head back inside.

"You were a curiosity before, an unknown thing." The white fae stretched in her seat. "Now, the truth has come out to the court, and the gossip has had time to fester. I'm sure you're the talk of the town by now."

"Wonderful." I grimaced, then my mind moved to something else that had had time to fester. "Can I stay with you for a little while longer?"

"Of course." She looked sideways at me. "I hope I haven't done anything to make you think otherwise. It's not Mama Flori, is it? I know she can be a bit overbearing, but she does care."

"No, no, it's not that," I said. "You've been great, and Mama Flori is so nice. I just don't want to overstay my welcome. I still want to find a place of my own at some point. The city is too loud, too many people. It's not what I'm used to at all."

"Ah, well, I knew that was coming. I don't think you should be in such a hurry; you don't even know which court you'll settle into. Stop thinking in human years. You're half fae, and chances are you're going to be around a lot longer than you first thought. Give yourself the year the four crowns agreed to and see where you want to settle first."

"I guess." I shifted in my seat. "I'm just anxious about it all. The new courts, the new fae, the new cities. I just want a quiet little spot in the woods."

"Sorry to frustrate you, but it would be a lot easier for me to help you with that if we knew what court you aligned with," she said. "Try to have a little patience."

A bump in the road shook us both, and the carriage slowed down.

"Right, one thing at a time." I sighed. Puko cawed. The carriage bumped.

My seal itched.

TWENTY-SEVEN
PRACTICE

Fresh air blew through the carriage as we opened the windows wide. The rain had finally sputtered out, and I stuck my head out to breathe in the wet leaves and gentle scent of rain-soaked earth.

"We'll be through the gates soon. They'll want to stop and check us since we have a carriage, but it shouldn't take long," Schula said.

"You two all right in there?" Eberon asked as we slowed to a stop.

"We'll be fine," Schula answered. She stood and pulled our windows closed, shooing Puko out. He knew his way home by now, or he could ride on top until we got there.

"I'll be ready." I sat, anxious to get moving. I fidgeted, done with being stuck in the little carriage.

The guards at the gate peeked into the carriage and then waved us through. Eberon steered Boxfield through the streets, and I could tell from his constant grumbling that we were garnering a lot of attention. I was glad to be inside with the curtains drawn.

We rode to Schula's apartment in silence, ignoring the feeling of fae outside watching us. When the carriage pulled to a stop, I barely had the door opened when it was pulled out of my hands and thrown wide.

"Wren, did you get thinner? Come, Mama Flori has lunch upstairs. You will come eat now." The wrinkled gray face of Mama Flori beamed up at me as I was half dragged out of the carriage toward the stairs that led to the apartment.

"Mama Flori," I protested, "I can walk on my own."

But she didn't really listen. She just turned to Schula and Eberon, who were both trying to contain smiles, and wagged a scolding finger at them. "You didn't feed her on your trip, did you? Boys! Boys, come get their things and bring them up now."

Her two sons, also wrinkled gray mole-like fae, emerged from the shop covered in flour. "Yes, Mama."

"Mama Flori, we did feed her. It's only been a couple weeks, and I promise the Spring Court did not starve us." Schula was nearly in tears laughing as I was dragged up the stairs.

"You don't try hard enough," she insisted. "Wren, come."

Through the door, I smelled her baking. Schula's table was piled high with breads, pies, tarts, and other dishes that were still covered so I couldn't see what they were yet.

"You eat, go ahead." Mama Flori sat me in a chair and began unwrapping food and placing it in front of me.

"How did you know we were here?" Schula asked, coming in after us.

"The bird came, and I knew. Come and sit down, Schula. You need to eat too," Mama Flori said.

Schula and I endured Mama Flori's scrutiny, and all I could think was how good it was to be back in Thanantholl. I glanced out the window at a smug-looking Puko, who had somehow gotten a bowl of breadcrumbs and was gorging himself.

After her sons carried up our luggage, they helped calm their mother down enough that we could convince her to wrap up the rest of the food for later.

Eberon barely took one step through the door with our last bag when Mama Flori shoved two pies neatly tied up in a parcel into his arms. The boys finally dragged Mama Flori back down to the bakery, and we were left in peace.

Eberon set the pies on the table, folding his arms and looking out the window. "Well, we're back. Now we need to deal with . . ." His words trailed off, but after a moment both Schula and Eberon were looking my way. My eyes dipped down to the table, tracing the lines of the wood with my gaze instead of looking at them.

"I know," I said quietly. "There's no going back now. I have to face these marks so I can move forward."

"So we can all move forward with our heads intact," Eberon said, then he smiled. "I'll go see what I can learn of Thain. He needs a good earful for not telling me about all this, anyway."

Something in me numbed. Dwellonmar had made all the problems of Thanantholl feel so far away, but now that we were back, everything felt fresh again. Thain and I arguing, my cowardice in hiding the markings from the others. From him. I couldn't blame myself for being afraid at first, but standing in those woods when I'd talked to Thain about the witches for the first time, I'd known this would be significant somehow. I just hadn't wanted to face it, and it had been foolish of me to think I could take care of it all by myself before anyone found out. I'd lasted, what, two days? And then I'd dragged Schula into it.

"We can dwell on what's done, or we can move forward." Schula interrupted my spiraling thoughts. "Bath, stretch, take a look at that seal, hmm?"

"Well said," Eberon mused, then he heaved out a breath and stretched out his shoulders. "I'm going to see what I can learn for now. I'll send word as soon as I know where Thain is."

"Thanks, Eb," Schula said, and she walked him to the front door and locked it behind him. Turning so her back was against the door, she let a slow smile spread across her lips.

"What?" I asked.

"I'm going to do so many things to your body you'll think you sprouted new muscles to ache," she teased.

"Why are you so cruel?" I whined, but she was already pulling me up off the chair. I groaned but let her push me toward the bathroom. She started the water running and popped out of the room. "You get in first, I'll be right back."

I didn't wait for the water to finish filling the tub before I dropped my clothes to the floor and started cleaning myself. I was almost done when Schula came back in with fresh towels, setting them on the shelf before stripping off her own travel things.

"I put a couple of logs in the fire," Schula said, tossing off her own clothes while I finished rinsing my hair and got into the steaming water. Soon after, she sank into the water with a sigh, quietly sloshing the sides of the tub as she sat. My eyes trailed down the scars on her back for a moment before I turned my attention away. Someday I would be brave enough to ask what had happened. Someday.

She stretched her arms out in front of her. "So, you think you're ready to release that seal?"

"I'll have to be, won't I? I just want a little training so I don't, you know, catch on fire again."

Schula snorted. "If you do, I'll put you out."

I huffed a laugh. "I'm glad you'll be there."

"Me too." She yawned. "Everything has been brighter since I met you, so we can't have you go burning yourself alive now."

Clean and rested, we wrapped ourselves in towels, and I put a pot of tea on the fire. Once my hair was free of tangles, I braided it out of my way, and we drained our mugs.

"Here." Schula handed me a cloak. "Pull it over your face a little. I hung it over the stove, so it should smell more like smoke than like you. It might help stop prying eyes until we get out of the city."

"We're leaving Thanantholl? We just got here." I frowned, pulling the cloak around my shoulders.

"We're going to run some of the dirt paths outside the gates," she said. "No one is going to bother us there, and if you have any mishaps with your fire, you'll be less likely to hurt anyone."

"Oh." I pulled the hood up and took off my smoky quartz. It was probably safer here, and I'd hate to lose it in the woods.

After that, Schula dragged me outside. A light breeze rustled the trees overhead, shaking fat leaves over us. She'd been right about the cloak, it helped, and we were able to avoid attention as we slipped through back paths and lesser used roads until we reached the front gates. The guards nodded us out, and Schula started us down a faint dirt path through the trees.

Admittedly, I was nervous to do anything with my magic, but I was frustrated and ready to do *something* about it. Part of that must have shown on my face, because Schula was relentless in our workout. She had me run with her along narrow paths, barely bigger than game trails. But they did the job, and soon enough I was sweating despite the autumn chill. Unfortunately, if you weren't paying close attention, you'd get stuck by the thorns that covered the ground, requiring you to lift your feet higher and choose your steps wisely.

By the time we stopped, my lungs ached for air. Schula handed me water, and we started stretches in a clearing outside of Thanantholl, not too far off the road. At least the walk back wouldn't be as long. She then proceeded to contort my body and hers into some impressive shapes while describing how to control my magic. My body was every bit as sore as the first day she'd had me stretch, and muscles I didn't know I had screamed at me to stop, but Schula didn't let me.

"I can't stay standing like this much longer." I was trying very hard not to whine, but I didn't think it was working.

"Hold it for just a little more," she said, pressing her knee into my back. "You're going to know this stance in your sleep or die trying."

"Great," I grunted. Puko sat overhead watching us with casual raven amusement.

"All right, relax." No sooner had the words left her lips than I fell to the ground. "You wanted this."

"I know," I said. "I'm ready, just tell me what's next."

"Well, I don't know much about human bodies," Schula admitted. "Maybe you do need a break. Next, we can meditate."

"We can what?" I didn't bother moving.

"We're going to work on your calm and concentration. If you don't have control of your mind, you won't have control of your magic."

"That makes sense. Magic is tied to strong emotion, right?" I asked.

"Yes, it is." Schula pulled me into a sitting position and sat down beside me. "If you can keep calm, you can control magical outbursts. We start with this, and then when you're ready, you can handle whatever releases with your seal."

"Hopefully," I mumbled.

"You *can,*" she insisted. "And you will. Now, close your eyes and get comfortable. Clear your mind. I want you to picture your inner sanctum. This is where you need your mind to rest, the center of it all, the house for your magic. Make a calm place with no noise. Be at peace, we're going to breathe."

And breathe we did. She counted to three slowly, and we inhaled. Three again as we held our breath. Three one more time, and we released the air. Then we repeated the process again, and again, and again.

I tried to picture my serene place. At first, I thought it would be a forest, but a forest is anything but quiet. You can't walk without breaking sticks, there are birds and squirrels and wind and leaves. I let the forest go and moved on to something else.

"You're doing well, keep making that place in your mind," Schula said softly.

The quietest place I'd ever been. I nearly shouted when my mind fell into a frozen lake. The lake Thain had pulled me from. I winced but kept my eyes shut. Quiet, but not peaceful. I moved on again.

"Keep trying," Schula said.

Now I made the place *I* wanted. A little log cabin in an open field. Just big enough for me. I built it like Bryn would have. I pictured every cut log, every stone in the floor. I gave it a hearth, and I kept building. A loft, just a little one, with a warm bed near the chimney for heat. Below, I had only the bare minimum of possessions. A wooden table, a chair, a shelf, and a cooking pot. An axe sat by the door, and a cloak hung above it. There, my little cabin. My home, my serenity.

"There, right there," Schula said, pleased. "Whatever you've found, hold on to it. That is your magic's home. You are making it a place to live, a place for you to be with it."

I sat in my cabin just as I sat in the forest outside Thanantholl. On the floor, legs crossed, eyes closed, breathing. My leg cramped, and I went to move, but Schula smacked me without dropping the count. If I opened my eyes, I'd get smacked again. My back strained, and I was ready to scream, but I sat there breathing like she told me to.

"All right, that's enough for today." Schula stopped us, and I fell onto my back. It had felt like days that we had sat there, sitting in our quiet places and breathing. When I opened my eyes, the sun had hardly moved.

"You did well. I can tell you made a good place to keep your mind." Schula stretched. "Hold on to it, because you're going to do this again before bed. And in the morning. And after lunch."

"That often?" I rolled onto my stomach, laying my face in the cool grass.

"Yes, that often," she said. "As often as you can. Do it in the bath, before sleep, when you wake up. Do it whenever you have a spare moment."

"You told me to practice my combat poses whenever I had a spare moment," I said.

"Do both. I do. The more you do it, the better you'll be." She stood. "Now, get up. You've had a rest, let me show you how to hold your hands for an impact."

"Great," I moaned.

Caw.

And we did the entire thing again.

Placing my hand on the metal railing outside Schula's apartment first thing in the morning was a mistake, I realized as I pulled my wet palm away from the dripping wet metal.

"Ugh, it rained." Wiping my hand on my pants, I made it to the bottom of the steps without the use of the railing. Puko landed on my shoulder, and I nearly fell sideways.

"A good many things are wet this morning!" Mama Flori called from the corner of her shop. She was shaking out an empty flour sack before adding it to a folded pile next to her. "It tends to rain a lot around here."

"I've noticed." I moved to stand next to her, picking up a new sack from a crumpled pile and shaking the loose bits of flour out of it. Puko ruffled his feathers indignantly and took off for the railing in front of the apartment upstairs. "You didn't need a free ride anyway, you silly thing," I called up to him. "You're the one with wings!"

Mama Flori chuckled, picking up the next sack.

"Thank you, lovely. I'm sending these back to the mill today, and I try to get the old bits out as much as I can first." She scrunched up her little mole nose, holding back a sneeze. "Whew! And what are you up to this morning?"

"Schula went to Pearl Street for a few things, so I'm heading out to find some firewood."

"Wet as it is?" Mama Flori asked, folding up her current sack and grabbing another.

"Like you said, it rains a lot around here," I mused. "It will dry. Mostly, I think I want to get some fresh air, do something with my hands. I'm used to a lot more time to myself than I've gotten since coming here."

"Well, don't let me keep you, I can handle a few sacks. Go! Enjoy the day." Mama Flori chased me off with a smile, flapping an empty sack at me as I pulled Bryn's coat tight. I walked the path out of Thanantholl, axe on my hip and a basket in hand in case I found anything I wanted to bring back with me.

Puko made his way overhead, staying just in sight so I knew he was coming with me. I'd become familiar with the route out of the valley over the past few days; it would just take some time to walk it. When I went out with Schula, I'd been using the cloak to hide myself from unwanted attention, but today was about me, and I wanted Bryn's coat and the feel of the axe in my hands.

I'd gone over the rules of taking things from the forests of the Autumn Lands with one of Mama Flori's boys who liked to come out here often. The same foraging courtesies I was used to in the mountains applied, so that wasn't hard to remember, but the trees were another matter. He described the trees as "part of the land," whatever that meant. I would have to limit myself to what had already fallen, but that was enough on its own. Today was less about the wood gathering and more about my thoughts.

Out of the city proper and into the trees, I was pleased to leave the gates and staring guards behind. Puko landed on my shoulder once we were away from Thanantholl, and my boots crunching the leaves underfoot with the earthy smell after the rain was everything I needed. I carried these sounds, these smells, in my soul with me. This was what I craved, the Mother's living world around me and my own two hands to work with.

We enjoyed the walk for a while until I came across a fallen branch large enough to do something with. I made quick work of it, the motions that were so familiar to me coming to my arms like an old friend. I came out of it with five good-sized pieces, bundled them with some rope I'd brought, and settled them on my back.

"What do you think, Puko? Does it remind you of home?" I asked.

Caw.

My boots crunched through the leaves as we kept going. Since our return from the Spring Lands, I had thrown myself into working on control. Eberon hadn't found Thain yet, and after finally getting the opportunity to ask Baeleon directly, he still had no answers. Thain would return when he returned. A frustrating response that had only turned Eberon into more of an anxious mess. My stomach had twisted at the news, and I craved the chance to just talk to him.

Coming back to Thanantholl had made me realize just how comfortable Thain and I had been. Even crossing the mountains and camping together had been comfortable. The way he moved, the way he spoke, even the way he smelled was now familiar to me. The fight we'd had was eating me up inside. How did Thain feel about it? Would he come back from his task with a clear head, or would this be the moment he revealed me to the Autumn Court?

Puko circled overhead, having come and gone from my shoulder at whim. This time he shifted to the south, and I changed direction to walk underneath his path.

The trees thinned here and there, but the blue vines that traced the edges of every corner of the Wyldes never relented. Once I climbed over a terrible patch of them, I was welcomed by the sight of leaves I'd seen before.

"Sweet potatoes," I exclaimed, kneeling before the patch of greenery. Once Eberon found them on our way to Thanantholl that first time, I couldn't get the taste out of my head. But I wasn't entirely sure I'd identified the right leaves, and I had to carefully pry one out with my axe to confirm. With great joy, I pulled out a long red tuber, revealing several more behind it.

"Did you spot these from all the way up there?" I asked, tilting my head to the sky.

Puko didn't answer, but I did make a mental note to give him some later. With my basket now full of sweet potatoes and still more than I could carry left for others to find, I gave up on searching for more fallen branches and made my way back to the gates of Thanantholl.

Finding my way back wasn't hard; I'd been keeping track of my steps and stacking stones for markers. But it was still a relief to see the familiar slope, the beginnings of the cobbled roads, and the two guards posted on either side of the entryway.

Puko flew high, making his way back without me.

"My company is only good while I'm useful finding you food, is that it?" I asked, watching him fly off.

At the gate, the guard didn't do much to stop me once he had a look at my face. Keeping my expression even, I let them make their comments about me and moved on. It was getting old, hearing again and again how I'd been found with the humans.

I didn't feel particularly lost; I was living there. But Schula had warned me that the most favored hobby in Thanantholl was gossiping. So I let it go as I began to walk away, heading back to Schula's apartment with my findings.

"Didn't the Ravager find her?" one said, still talking about me as I passed. "He just missed seeing her too."

The Ravager. Thain had such a title, didn't he? I'd heard it in the Autumn Palace. My head whipped around, staring at the guards, who looked in my direction. "He was here?"

They looked at each other, then the taller one shrugged. "Might have been an hour ago."

I took off running. As fast as I could manage with a basket on one arm and an armful of split wood tied to my back. Passing bridges, people, shops, and many houses, my feet raced faster than my mind. Before I knew it, I had veered completely off the path to Schula's apartment and I stood before a gate leading to a small blue-fenced yard, in front of a house with a blue door.

Thain's house.

My chest was still heaving, pulling in all the air I could from my dash across Thanantholl, as I pushed through the gate, hand stopping as I reached for the handle of the front door.

What was I doing? I was hardly the first person he would want to see. Before I could question my motivations, the door swung inward.

"Miss Wren," Wairen said. "It is good to see you."

"It's good to see you too," I echoed, but my eyes were darting around Wairen for any sign of life inside the house.

Wairen took notice, stepping aside and looking over their shoulder. "What are you looking for?"

All the breath emptied out of me, and I took a step back, composing myself. "Thain. I heard he has returned."

Wairen nodded. "Eberon said the same thing when he ran off."

"Eberon was here?" I asked, then I noticed the pile of blankets and pillows taking up the armchair by the hearth that Thain favored.

"He has been here each night," Wairen answered. "Until a little while ago. Eberon can feel it when Master Thain isn't too far away."

"He can *feel* it? No, I mean thank you, Wairen. Do you know where Eberon went?" I asked.

Wairen thought for a moment, looking out the door behind me. "The king. Yes, that was the right direction. Master Thain goes to the palace when he returns from duties, he does not always return home first. I believe they are both at the palace."

"Oh." The energy that had spurred me through the valley had now completely left me. Of course he was with King Baeleon. The task that had sent him away for weeks had been from his king, of course he would have to see his king upon his return.

"Thank you, Wairen. I'll go let Schula know," I said.

Wairen tilted their head to the side. "Will you be returning to your room? Master Thain has told me to make sure everything is ready for you."

What did that mean? *What does that mean, Thain?*

"He . . . what?" I managed. I didn't know what to do with my hands, my feet. I fidgeted with the basket on my arm, the rope digging into my shoulders where I'd secured the wood.

"Master Thain told me to make sure everything is ready for you," Wairen repeated.

"No, I heard. I mean . . . thank you. I should go," I said, and Wairen waved me off as I retreated through the garden and out the gate.

Schula. I should tell Schula what had happened. And I should do something with this wood, and the sweet potatoes, and . . .

And myself. I needed to find something to do with myself, because my insides felt turned wrong-side-out and nauseated and numb all at the same time.

TWENTY-EIGHT
THE UPPER HAND

A key in the door jolted me awake. Schula's bed was warm, and rain pattered outside the window in soothing drops. Puko had been allowed inside for the night, and his only reaction to the key at the door was to conjure up an annoyed croak and burrow deeper into his own feathers.

The door opened, and I was already one foot out of the bedding. "Is he all right?"

Schula closed the door behind her with a yawn. "That took so long! Yes, he's fine. Go back to bed, I'll tell you everything."

By the time I'd reached the apartment after hearing the news of Thain's return, Schula was already there with the box of tea leaves she had gone to Pearl Street to buy, a steaming hot cup in hand as she sat in the open window watching the leaves fall. She'd nearly dropped her cup when I'd shouted the news from the bottom of the stairs.

She'd gone to the palace to learn more, and I'd stayed in the apartment until they were done. Because they were the triquetram, and I wasn't. And it was torture. I had eventually given in and gone to sleep.

I sat back down on the bed, and Schula fell into it with a moan.

"Beds are so good. Beds are a blessing from the Stars," she mumbled into the covers.

"What happened at the palace that took until the middle of the night?" I asked.

Schula rolled over. "Not a task we have leave to speak about to anyone else, you understand?"

"Yes."

"Good. I won't go into too many details, but there is something happening at the borders to the Wyldes. We aren't sure why, but it has to do with things coming in and out of the wards."

The wards the witches made. My heart sank; my face fell.

"This doesn't mean it has anything to do with you." Schula slipped under the covers. "It's been happening slowly for the last few years, well before you crossed over. It's just that now it's getting worse."

"When can I see Thain?" I asked.

"Tomorrow. Or is it today? In a few hours," she settled on. "We're all exhausted after a long night of discussions. Just let me sleep this off and we'll get ready to meet at Eb's place for a late breakfast and some catching up."

It wasn't the end of my anguish, but it was an answer I could respect. "Right, everyone should get some sleep first." I just didn't know if I would be able to join them, now that I was all riled up.

"Oh, and Baeleon has a message for you," Schula said, snuggling into the pillows.

"Is it Dwellonmar? Have I caused trouble by leaving so soon?"

"Nothing is wrong." She yawned. "Baeleon received word from the Winter Court. You are cordially invited to the winter solstice festivities in a few weeks. It makes sense; they probably heard about your invitation to the spring equinox."

"Oh." My shoulders relaxed. "Right, we were expecting that. Are you and Eberon coming too?"

"Eberon and Thain will go. We'll accompany you through all the Wyldes for the next year, but there are places I will not go."

Lying down on the bed next to her, I nodded. Schula might not have shared the details yet, but I had already guessed as much.

"Is there anything I need to pack for the Winter Lands?" I asked, but I was met with silence. "Schula?"

The snow-white fae had already fallen asleep, her even breaths warming the pillow pressed into her cheek.

"Good night, Schula." Resolving myself to several hours of quiet and racing thoughts, I folded my hands over my stomach and stared up at the ceiling.

Thain was back, and I could finally resolve things with him. I just wasn't sure if that meant a pit in my stomach or a lightening of my heart, or both.

The squeak of the wardrobe door roused me. Sun fell across the floor in bright dashed lines where it poured in between the curtains.

"I didn't mean to wake you," Schula said, pulling the sleeve of something from the wardrobe and then dropping it again.

"No, I'm ready. Is it time to go?" Puko was gone, probably already let out for the morning. Schula's hair was damp, meaning I'd managed to sleep through the sounds of the bath as well.

"Soon enough. I was just looking for something to wear." Schula's mild interest in the fabrics before her turned sharp as her eyes darted to the bed. "Actually, if you're that ready to face Thain . . ."

A wicked grin crossed her lips, her fangs taking on a sharp gleam.

"What are you plotting?" I threw a pillow at her, and she caught it easily, laughing.

"You could strike first. He won't be ready yet."

"Strike first? I wouldn't survive a fight with Thain," I protested.

"No, no, I mean to catch him by surprise." She smiled. "Come on, what do you say?"

"Okay, but I want to know what you're plotting," I said.

"Excellent." She clapped her hands together. "Let's play a little game of deadly dress-up, shall we?" She turned to her stash of clothing, throwing the other wardrobe doors open and basking in the fabrics. Schula's wardrobe had two sides to it. The front held her everyday clothing. Her preference for leggings and tunics made for comfort and function. In the back, however, I saw the eccentric side of her.

"What precisely do you mean by deadly dress-up?" I asked.

The first thing she pulled out was a corset and skirt, not unlike what she'd worn to the River's Edge. There was no way I could fill out the cups, so I shook my head. Schula just shrugged and dove further in with determination.

"Deadly dress-up is when, if looks could kill, you have the right look for the job." She shook her hips excitedly as she sorted her clothes. "Take off that tunic and get over here."

It wasn't long before she had me stripped down to my underthings and standing in front of her.

She put me in lace, in leather, in things that were mostly straps. Scandalous things that would have had me stoned by the humans, even in Sulls. But I found a small thrill in wearing them all. They made me feel strong. They made me feel like a creature of the Wyldes.

Of course, me being willing to leave the apartment in such an ensemble was another matter. What Schula finally settled on was the closest thing to my comfort zone that she had in the back of the wardrobe.

My leggings were a second skin. Black leather, they laced from my boots to the waistband, exposing a sliver of skin under the black cord all the way up. The top was little better. It was bloodred and woven from silk that clung to everything. The neck laced closed, but it stopped low over my breasts, exposing the bit of cleavage I had managed to put on my bones over the past weeks.

"I've never seen anything like this before." I turned, looking at my reflection from another angle. "Where could this possibly be in fashion?"

"The Summer Court. Here, turn." Schula plucked the ties that kept my hair in place and began to unravel one of my braids.

"What are you—Schula! What are you doing?" I scrambled to cover the other side of my head before she got to that as well.

"Letting your hair down," she answered, then she paused. "Actually, this is up to you. I'm sorry, Wren, I got too excited dressing you up. I know this is a tender thing for you, and the decision is yours to make."

Half of my hair was nearly undone anyway. My fingers pulled the braid apart, making practiced work out of the curls. The deep brown strands still smelled lightly of soap. With one side of my reflection still adorned by the braid I used to shield my ears and the other side loose around my shoulders, I stared for a long breath.

"I can put it back," Schula started.

"Leave it." Pulling the other tie loose, I set it on a nearby table. "Leave it down; my ears don't show unless I move it a lot anyway."

Even through the mirror, Schula's smile dazzled. "Understood."

My hair was left loose, still covering my ears but wild and free and foreign to me in the mirror. I never left my hair unbraided. It was a shield between my secrets and the rest of the world. But no one here needed shielding from who I was and what had happened to me, least of all Thain with his own scars and his eyes that saw through me anyway.

Schula painted my lips black and put a line of kohl against my eyelids.

"Why am I dressing like this?" I asked. "For a simple breakfast."

"To throw him off. I've been with Thain and Eberon for fifty years, and I know their tastes well." Schula had decided today was a day for the back of the wardrobe, and she'd dressed up too. Tight red leggings with golden buttons and a loose golden tunic that tied at the sides. Much like the usual Thanantholl style, but there was something sultry about the way she wore it.

"And I'm appealing to his tastes why?" I inspected my neckline in the mirror to see just how much skin was exposed from every angle. A light blush graced my face under my freckles, but I felt very daring all the same.

"Because he deserves a little torment for losing his composure," Schula answered, eyes crinkling with merriment. "And because I want to see him squirm."

That I could affect anyone simply with the manner of my dress seemed ridiculous. But maybe it would be another new experience after so very many realizations since coming to this place. Wanting things was a dangerous game, promising nothing but disappointment. That was how I'd viewed the world. What was easily grasped, already at the fingertips of others, would be an impossible stretch for me. But that was Silver Lake, and this was the Wyldes. And if I was to be a part of the Wyldes, then whatever was within reach of others was also within reach for me.

"Are we ready then?" I asked.

"Wait." She ran to the table on my side of the bed. "Wear this."

The gray stone glinted with polish and care. But it also carried meaning.

"The necklace from Caldon?" I asked.

"Yes, it matches the outfit." Her too-innocent tone indicated additional motives, but I let it go.

"All right, it's on. Ready now?" I asked.

"Yes." She ran a tongue over her fangs and sauntered to the door, opening it for me. "This is going to be *splendid*."

"Here we are. Shoulders straight, chin up," Schula ordered, and I obeyed. I didn't know what to do with my hands, so as she knocked I clasped them behind my back. A moment later, Eberon was at the door.

"Schula." He blinked, then spotted me and began sputtering. "What—*Wren*?"

"Are you going to let us in?" Schula asked.

Eberon narrowed his eyes at her. "Of course, you unseelie vixen."

Schula scoffed. "You know I'm not."

He stepped back, letting us inside even as he shook his head. "I see you got into Schula's wardrobe, little bird."

"Where are we headed? The study?" Schula purred, thoroughly enjoying herself.

"Er, yes. By all means, follow me." He closed the door behind us and let Schula and I lead the way. "He's going to know this was your doing, Schula."

"I don't care," she sang.

The study was just as we had left it, save for a platter of fig pastries laid out on Eberon's desk already missing one or two morsels. The bookshelves behind the desk looked more disordered today, as though someone had been rifling through the tomes for something specific, and the armchairs around the room had been pulled up for all to be able to sit.

And there, at the far edge of the desk, was a giant midnight fae in an armchair. The sight of him slammed into me, and the ache of our argument suddenly paled in comparison to the ache left by missing him. He was *here*. Right here, and I could reach out and touch him if I wasn't such a coward.

Even the scent of him was familiar, that of someone who spent much of his time around campfires and in the trees. His shirt was open in the front, and he'd laid his head back with his eyes closed. He looked worse for his time on the border, exhausted.

"Took you long enough, Schula," he grunted, but when he opened his eyes and lifted his head he stilled, eyes on me.

Schula cleared her throat loudly. "She's here for a serious discussion of the border affairs, and whatever business you two still have can be handled afterward like adults."

My mouth went dry, and I put my hands behind my back again because I didn't know what else to do with them, but I held my ground and stood just as Schula had told me to. Chin up, back straight, my face a mask of indifference. Thain stared at me for a long time, and I nodded in agreement with Schula. His eyes drifted from my painted lips, down the line of curls that rested over one shoulder, to the stretch of skin down the sides of my legs. In the end, his silver eyes settled on the smoky quartz at the column of my neck and stayed there.

"Right, let's compare notes then." Eberon took his seat behind the desk and rubbed his temples, strands of scarlet hair falling in his face. "We didn't get to cover this in Baeleon's meeting, Thain, but while you were gone the three of us went to Dwellonmar for Galavan's funeral service. Schula and I poked around for anything about the wards we could find. As far as we can tell, Diamid wasn't hiding anything from the other courts about the circumstances they found the body in. None of his advisers seem to know anything about the problem with the wards either. Out of the three of us, the only one to discover any suspicious behavior was Wren."

Thain raised an eyebrow and glanced up from my necklace to my eyes as Eberon continued.

"It would seem the fair king of the Spring Court has a deep interest in the 'found youth,' as they call her. His people entertained her, took her around the city, and of course were as appealing as possible. The one to raise our suspicions was Diamid himself. He invited Wren to a private meal and was quite forward with questions regarding her magic. It was Puko who disrupted them."

"Of course he's interested in what powers she has, all the crowns will be," Thain murmured. I didn't miss that his claws had extended slightly and were peeling tiny ribbons of varnish off the arm of his chair.

"No, it wasn't quite right," Schula added. "It seemed like he had more at stake than a new fae and what he had to gain from her choosing the Spring Court."

"Then suspicion of tampering with the wards is off him, or his court at least, but now we have a problem with Wren?" Thain asked.

"It's not enough to go off for now, but I'll be very curious to see how the other courts react to her." Eberon leaned back in his chair. "And with this business at the borders, everyone is going to be on high alert for anything out of the ordinary once word spreads of the wards."

Quiet contemplation overtook us. Schula picked at a pastry, putting one small flake at a time on her tongue as she thought. Thain stared into the space before him, swirling something in his cup. Eberon had one arm resting on the desk, tapping a finger absently. It was me. I was the thing that was out of the ordinary now, and it was time to deal with that.

"I need to break this seal," I said. It felt as though the silence of the room had shattered. The fear I'd built like a wall around the markings down my spine was nothing compared to the fear of what their presence might cause to happen. To me, to these people who had taken me in with kindness. It was time.

"You're sure?" Schula asked.

No. "I think so."

Thain hadn't taken his eyes off me since I'd sat down. I didn't think I'd looked away from him either. When he spoke, his low timbre directed at me for the first time since he'd left for the borders, it was with a softness I hadn't expected. "Then we will figure out how to remove it."

It felt like a peace offering, and I was ready to reach out and take it. "I should have brought it up before, and I'm more sorry than you know that I didn't. I was scared."

"You had every right to be," Schula said.

"That can be our next move," Eberon said. "If it's all right, though, I want to get back to the wards."

Thain nodded, his eyes still on mine. "We can finish this later."

Good. It felt so good to think there was hope at the end of this for me and Thain to reconcile. My shoulders relaxed, and I was able to smile as I reached for a fig pastry from the tray. "Agreed."

"You described the investigation in detail at Baeleon's meeting," Schula said, moving us forward. "But not what you think caused the problem in the first place. Any ideas?"

Thain tilted his head, eyes drifting to a paper under the corner of the tray of food. He pulled out a map, tapping once on a spot at the borders. "A Winter patrol took up the watch for now. More things are slipping through, like whatever it is we were trying to hunt down after Galavan."

"That's most of the meetings from last night," Schula leaned over to murmur in my direction. "You didn't miss much. For as long as it went, it was a lot of arguing about stomach wounds and things that could make them."

Thain continued. "It seems everyone in the Wyldes sent people to investigate not only the death but the situation of the magic."

"Who?" Eberon asked.

"Aithne, Asher, and Reghan. Took us a day to work together in the first place, then another to get on the right trail." Thain sighed. "I would have gotten more done alone."

"Asher," Schula hissed. "I hope you used him as bait for whatever killed Galavan."

"The opportunity didn't come up." Thain let the smallest of grins turn the corner of his mouth upward. "Believe me, I was looking for an opening. The only trail we had to follow was scent. No footprints, no hint of anything else. At one point, we thought we found a piece of ripped flesh in the bushes, maybe something useful, but it was too old. Galavan died in a crater of blood, and not a damned thing could be traced going in or out of it except Galavan."

"It's not like Galavan to put up no fight." Eberon was twisting the black band on his thumb absently. "Or anyone watching the borders."

"Unless it was something without a corporeal form," Schula added.

"That's what Aithne figured out first, not that it took long once we all saw the site. We covered that before you arrived yesterday," Thain said. "In the end, we had to give up the hunt after a couple days of sleeting rain. Everything was gone. At least we could survey the extent of the damage to the wards after that."

"And what is the extent of the damage?" Eberon asked.

"All of the Summer Lands' southern border is exposed. The Spring Lands to the east are half intact still, same for the Winter Lands to the west," Thain answered.

"What of the Autumn Lands?" I asked.

"The Autumn Lands touch only the open ocean and the rest of the Wyldes. The wards don't exist up here," Schula said. "Not that much would be able to cross moving water like that anyway."

"As expected, this is going to require more manual guarding while the damage is investigated and repaired," Thain added. "Every soldier and scholar can expect a summons from the crowns any time now, particularly full triquetrams."

"And us?" Schula asked.

"Guard duty of a different sort." Thain jerked his head toward me.

"I knew we kept you around for something," Schula teased, patting my back.

"So, we're to continue touring the Wyldes with Wren?" Eberon asked. "I highly doubt that to be His Majesty's only order."

Thain drained his glass and set it on the desk. "This was done by someone with knowledge of the wards. Most likely a group, considering the effort it took to construct them in the first place. We continue the rounds and rule out the obvious fae powers first. If we can't find our enemy in the Wyldes, we find them in the outer lands. But our first task is to feel out the other courts under the guise of escorting Wren."

All eyes turned to me.

"Will that seem a little suspicious?" I asked. "If you're someone the king would normally send to investigate, won't it be odd if you aren't at the border?"

"The other crowns and who knows who else will be poking around for the same thing we are. They'd be stupid not to." Eberon rubbed his temples.

"Everyone will know what we're up to, but they'll let us do it anyway."

"So, are we to head out again?" Schula sighed. "So soon after arriving home?"

"As soon as we can," Thain said.

"This is a more extensive trip; give me two days," Eberon said. "Pack for every occasion. Wren, you'll need a wider selection of clothing. We can start with Winter since you've received an invitation to their solstice."

"I'll take those two days to try and deal with—that is, to bring out my magic," I finished awkwardly.

Schula's expression of sympathy only made me feel worse. I should have done this weeks ago.

"Tomorrow," Thain said. "There were a few books in the library when I was looking for witching marks. Some of them might be useful for removing the seal."

"Good call," Eberon murmured. "Right, I'll begin preparations if you three can handle the rest."

"Well, that's settled," Schula said, standing up. "Thain, take Wren to Maple Way and talk it out."

"Maple Way?" Thain asked, something odd in his expression. He darted his eyes to me. I sat a little straighter and lifted my chin.

"I will not repeat myself." Schula glared at him, a blizzard in her voice. Eberon was suddenly very busy cleaning the breakfast tray from his desk.

Thain looked me in the eye, gaze darting briefly to my necklace and back. "She's right. I believe we are due an exchanging of words."

I nodded, swallowing the lump in my throat. Schula gave me an encouraging look and waved us off. "Go on, Eb and I have preparations to make. Be ready for one last trip to the River's Edge before our travels! I demand *dancing*." Schula twirled as if to demonstrate her need of it.

And with that, we dispersed. Eberon and Schula went in one direction, and Thain and I another.

TWENTY-NINE

TEA

Walking beside Thain, cloak drawn around my shoulders against the dripping sky that had begun while we were in Eberon's study, was easy. Familiar. Tinged with the strain of the fight, to be certain, but healing from seeing him again and the calm between us at breakfast. This was it, this was my chance to tell him that I'd missed him, and that I was sorry.

Chest drumming steadily, I closed my eyes and drank in the scent of him. The smoky edges that the rainfall couldn't quite erase, the way he wore the simplest things and used just enough words. My fingers drifted to the quartz around my neck. Caldon spoke with a flourish, and he was dazzling and social. All the things that would have the young ladies of Silver Lake tripping over themselves. Thain was none of those things, and yet I found myself wishing he was the one who had shown interest.

My pace stumbled. *Do I feel that way about Thain?*

He was comfortable to be around, to be sure. With that thought in mind, so was Eberon. So was Schula. Even Mama Flori now counted as one of those comfortable people. My circle of people had grown significantly, but not all of them made me feel the same way. Some of them made me feel as though I was reaching for something new, something I couldn't have before. It was thrilling. It was terrifying.

Thain seemed lost in his own thoughts as we walked through Thanantholl's winding streets. Though neither of us spoke, his subtle directional changes were enough for me to follow his lead to this shop Schula had insisted we visit.

Maple Way, a tea shop, was in a calm corner of the city, surrounded mostly by residential streets and a few public gardens. It stood apart from the surrounding homes with its cheerful yellow walls and beautiful carved chairs on the front patio. Inside, screens and potted plants divided the tables from one another, giving us the privacy that this conversation needed.

We were seated quickly in the darkest corner, which was still brighter than the inside of most buildings I'd been in. To my left was the shop, where a nymph brought trays to the guests. To my right was a large window with a view of the water behind the building.

Thain, for his part, looked utterly unsettled. I supposed Schula had accomplished that much when she'd dressed me today, and I had to admit that I rather liked it. Unfortunately, I was unsettled too and couldn't enjoy the feeling as much as I would have liked to.

I'd taken so long looking through the list of teas that Thain had the server bring us her recommendations. Now the menus were gone and there was nothing between us save for our impending awkward conversation.

"Welcome back. It occurred to me I hadn't gotten to say it yet." I let my fingers trace the design painted on the table so neither of us could see that my fingers were shaking. I was both eager to settle things between us and dreading the encounter altogether.

"I wanted to apologize for my behavior." He shifted in his seat. "You don't owe me anything, not even answers. I shouldn't have thought of them as mine for the taking."

"And I shouldn't have hidden something like that to begin with," I said. "You told me you were on bad terms with the witches from the beginning, and I still hid this part of me. I was scared. I'm still scared, if I'm being honest."

"Not of me, I hope." His words were layered with something else. Almost defensive but not entirely directed at me.

Scared of Thain? No, I wasn't. But I realized in that moment how many people probably were. He was capable of physical feats I could barely imagine, and his king seemed to use him to flaunt his power and handle the worst of tasks. What must the rest of the Autunm Court think of him? They'd named him Ravager. Apart from Eberon, Schula, and Wairen, I didn't think I'd seen anyone interact with Thain at all.

"No, not of you," I answered with a softness that surprised me. "Of me."

His jaw tightened for a moment while he rolled my answer through his thoughts. "What happened before—the fire you mentioned—it won't be like that again."

"We don't know that for sure," I answered. "Schula has been working with me. I've made this space in my mind as she told me, and I've been practicing. But it still scares me. Last time was so terrible."

"This time you will have me," he replied, "and there is nothing that you could lose control of that I wouldn't be able to handle. If you fall, I will catch you."

And as simply as that, a mountain lifted off my shoulders. My breath caught in my throat, and a sudden tear rushed out of me. Wiping it away with the heel of my hand, I kept my other fist clenched in my lap. He was right. *He was right.* These people, this place, were nothing like Mila's cabin. Whatever had erupted from me before was not of the mountains, it was of the Wyldes. This was where it all began, and this was where it would have to end.

"Thank you," I whispered.

He fidgeted a little as he glanced around the shop. He looked too big to be sitting in the delicate chair across from me.

"Was there something wrong with coming to this shop?" I asked. His reaction to it in Eberon's study was one thing, but he'd definitely grown warier of it as it had come into view.

"I have certain memories of this place. This is where Schula made me apologize to her when we first met," he said. "I may have overreacted to her upbringing when I found out about it."

"Oh." The corners of my mouth turned upward. "That does sound like her."

"You learn quickly." His mouth slanted in a grim line. "But I'm glad you came. I wasn't myself that day; I didn't want you to see that from me."

"I don't want to push you away, any of you. Schula tells me it would have torn you up inside if we didn't reconcile. I wouldn't like it either; you three mean so much to me." I looked out the window instead of at him, waiting for an answer but not sure what I wanted to hear.

"Schula thinks she knows a lot more than she does," he grumbled.

I looked at him, surprised. I opened my mouth to say something, but the server had arrived with our tea. She set a cup down in front of each of us with a soft smile and left quickly, as if she could sense the strained aura around us. I gave her a small smile as she disappeared behind a dividing screen.

Thain sighed when she left. "I didn't mean that. Of course I want to reconcile. Schula is just a busybody. Let's move on before I make more of a mess of things. Why don't you tell me about your time in Dwellonmar?"

I took a sip of my tea and kept the warm cup in my hands. It was a gentle flavor: jasmine sweetened with honey. I watched the dregs float in the bottom of my cup while I thought about an answer.

"Dwellonmar is lovely, an everlasting spring." I played with the rim of my teacup with a thumb. "Beautiful, of course, but it wasn't Thanantholl. The Spring fae, I think they do everything at their pace. It's like they're all waking up from a long sleep, which I suppose is the very nature of spring itself, but how do they get anything done? I mean, here it's rushing around, it's full of life, it's that last burst of energy before winter sets in, only it isn't *going* to set in. It's fires and food and leaves in the wind and rainy afternoons under a blanket with a book. Nothing here ever really sleeps, someone is always doing something. And I think I would miss that."

Thain blinked, his face unreadable as he stared at me. I fidgeted in my seat under his gaze and took a long sip of tea.

"That was perhaps the most words I've heard you say all at once since we met." Thain's face cracked into a wide, genuine smile that lit up his face for an instant before it flickered out again as quickly as it had come. "I don't know that I've ever gotten an outside perspective of Thanantholl before. So does that mean you didn't like the Spring Lands?"

I swallowed my tea and the lump in my throat and thought about my answer.

"No, they were wonderful, but I don't think I've seen enough of them to really know what it's like. Everyone seemed to be putting on a show for the 'found youth' and not letting me explore it little by little. At least here in Thanantholl I got a good, slow look at it all before the news of me got out."

He nodded slowly, taking my words in one by one and thinking them over. "I don't think you can expect to escape the interest of the people wherever you go; it would be better to present yourself for them to see easily, and eventually the novelty will wear off. But you'd be wise to take their affections with caution, as it's in the interest of each court to gain your allegiance. Have patience. It will calm down in time."

"I hope so." I sighed.

Thain slowly stirred his tea, watching my neck. My throat bobbed as I swallowed; he was making me nervous for some reason.

"Is something wrong?" I asked.

"I was just looking at that stone." His nostrils flared slightly. "Where did it come from?"

My fingers brushed the cool stone absently as I realized he was talking about my necklace. Warmth rose to my cheeks, remembering what sort of things a stone like this might imply.

"Caldon, the king's representative in Dwellonmar who took me around the city. It was a present." I played with the chain it hung on and watched Thain.

He shifted in his seat. "Did Caldon tell you what it means?"

My throat bobbed again, and my heart raced. I did *not* want to be discussing Caldon with Thain, but here we were. "I addressed it with him before we left," I answered.

"What did you tell him?" Thain asked. He still hadn't touched his tea.

It was all I could do not to stare at him. Pulling my cup to my lips, I took a long drink. Why was Thain bothered by this? Could he be jealous? Surely not. But was he?

"Does it matter to you what I told him?" I asked.

His brows lowered. "And if it does?"

I licked my lower lip of the last drops of my drink, Thain's eyes tracking the movement. I set my cup down on the saucer, the gentle clink the only sound between us.

"I did not share his sentiment," I finally answered. "My preference will always be for someone who can find enjoyment in quieter places."

Thain had no answer to that, and I had no more to say. With my cup empty and his yet untouched, the arrival of the server to clean up my things startled me. The nymph offered a pleasant smile before asking if I'd like anything else and whisking away my empty cup when I declined.

"I should take you back to Schula's," Thain said, his eyes moving to the window. "The rain has already let up, and I want to go find those books at the library."

"Right." I stood. "Thank you for the tea. And for helping me with . . ." I didn't want to mention the marks any more than necessary. Considering the incredible hearing of most of the people in Thanantholl, it would be foolish to think we could never be overheard.

"Of course," he added, and we made our way to the front of the tea shop. "I suppose we'll see each other tonight at the River's Edge."

"I hope Schula goes easy on me this time," I mused. "I'll be useless for stretches in the morning."

"I hope you're ready for tomorrow." Thain chuckled. "It won't be so easy as a night of dancing with Schula."

"And I hope you're ready for tomorrow. The last time I did anything with my magic I almost burned down a house." I eyed him sheepishly.

"I once cracked the top of a mountain with my triquetram when it was whole." He grinned, a dangerous glint in his eyes. "I think I can handle a burning house."

THIRTY
A DANCE OF TWO HEARTS

Thain walked with me until we reached the street that would lead me to Schula's apartment. I felt light, like a weight had lifted off my shoulders. There was already pressure from the courts to be swayed to their side, and pressure from Baeleon to learn magic. There was even the very real pressure of my seal that burned my back and begged to be released. But now at least there was no pressure from the strain between me and Thain, and the fluttering warmth of hope was enough to let some of the other pressures fly away from my mind.

We said our goodbyes, and I walked the short few blocks back to Schula's apartment by myself. Some stared, but I ignored them as I hurried back. I climbed the stairs quickly, until a weight dropped onto my shoulder and nearly knocked me over the railing.

"Puko!" I hissed at the fat black bird that had landed on my shoulder. "I know Mama Flori gave you bread this morning. You'd better not be begging for food."

Caw!

I rolled my eyes and continued up the steps with the raven on my shoulder. The noise was sufficient to announce my return, because Schula was swinging the door open as I reached the top.

"Well? What happened?" She didn't wait for an answer before pulling me inside. She waved Puko off to his usual windowsill and sat me down at the table.

"It's okay now, we're fine. We both apologized, and he said he was sorry

I saw that side of him." I beamed at her. "Tomorrow, he said he would help me with the seal."

"His beastly side?" Schula murmured. "He can be wild when he's riled up. When he pulls that out, it's hard for him to put it away. I suppose the Stars made him a little more beast than the rest of us."

"What does that mean?" I asked. "I've had so many questions about that since I first saw Thain. Back in the mountains, I couldn't read him at all. Sometimes I still can't."

"When you first met Thain, he had just slain a band of raiders, right?" Schula asked.

"He killed them all in only a few minutes. It was probably quite a sight to see."

"Right," she said. "And do you remember how he acted after? Did the Thain you met then seem to be the same as the Thain you know now?"

"No," I said. "He was really unsettling, actually. He was quiet, not that that's new for Thain, but he was too quiet. And his movements were so . . . precise, maybe? Deliberate? Looking back, he really wasn't the Thain I've come to know."

"He was pulling himself back from the thrall of battle." Schula nodded, running a tongue over her teeth. "The more he fights, the more riled up that side of him gets and the harder it is to pull back."

"I didn't know," I said quietly. "Is it hard on him?"

"That's hard to say," she said. "On the one hand, it's a part of him. I wouldn't want him to go around hating part of what he is. On the other hand, I've seen his struggles to contain it on the battlefield. You'd have to ask Thain if it's hard on him, I'm not sure."

"You've seen him on a battlefield?" I gasped. "I mean, I guess I knew that. Old as he is and as much of a history of war as the Wyldes have, of course he's been in battle."

"Oh, he's been in battle. He's terrifying too. One of the best soldiers in the Autumn Court. The problem is, you can't control him once he really lets go, you just unleash him in the right direction and let him do his worst."

Something about that sentiment seemed sad. Sad that anyone was simply a tool to be unleashed. I might not know what it was like to be that useful to my people, but I knew what it was like to be thought of as less of a person and more of a thing to be dealt with. "I'd hate to see that," I murmured.

"No sane person *wants* to see war," Schula said. "But if it comes to it, be glad Thain is on our side."

She hummed, eyeing her open wardrobe doors as a grin spread across her lips. "I'm glad you two made up. This calls for a celebration before tonight."

"Schula." I could already see where this was going.

"Let's go look for some new clothes!"

Dressed in dusty rose with silver slippers and borrowed silver bangles, I was giddy as we walked to the River's Edge. Schula walked beside me draped in a dramatic red gown, practically dancing us there. Not even the murmurs that trailed after me could bother me tonight.

When we rounded the last corner, the River's Edge came into view. The tables dripped with candles and fresh white flowers, just as they had the night I'd arrived in Thanantholl. A few diners danced to a light, fast violin tune, their beautiful gowns and coattails swirling around them as they moved. Everything shimmered in the fading light. When we were close enough to hear the music, Schula took my hand and placed a palm on my back before dipping me to the music as the dancers did the same.

"I love this song," she purred. "It's been so long since I've been dancing. We should go one night, you and me. Leave the other two behind."

She danced us to the front gate, where the closest diners watched us as she spun me around.

"Should we dance instead of dine tonight?" I teased.

"Another time," she said. "I want food slightly more than I want to dance just yet, and we need to get a table. It looks like Eb and Thain aren't here yet."

A server appeared with a smile.

"Welcome back, Lady Schula and Miss Wren." Marila, the watery fae from last time, greeted us with a bottle of wine. "Lord Eberon has already contacted us. We were informed to greet you with wine and the first course if you'd like it, as he and Lord Thain are running late."

"Oh, are they?" Schula raised her eyebrow and inspected the label on the wine bottle in Marila's hands. "I suppose I can forgive them, as long as they don't dally too much longer."

Marila snorted. "I'd hope so, this is our last bottle of this vintage, and it's very expensive."

"Cheeky tart." Schula laughed. "Lead me to a chair, because I am in great need of that wine!"

"As you will it, Lady." Marila grinned, and with a chuckle she took us to a nice table for four at the edge of the water. I sighed as I sank into the plush cushion, watching the rising moon reflect in the rippling river.

"Ahh, that's what I needed after a long week." Schula barely let Marila finish pouring her glass before it hit her lips.

"I'll send for a treat while you wait on the others. You just sit tight and enjoy yourselves." Marila smiled and glided away.

"This place never gets old," Schula said and glanced over the water that gently carried away fallen maple leaves. "Eb and Thain had better get here soon, or I'll start without them."

"I wonder what would keep them," I murmured.

"Court details, most likely." Schula shrugged. "They'll be here soon. Eb always arranges for me to have wine when he's going to be late."

My heart caught as I heard a new tune start up. The violinist was wonderful, and I was filled with a rush of movement as the notes peaked and dipped in a jolly tune.

"Ooh, I like this song too." Schula knocked the rest of her wine back and set the glass down. "Come on!"

It felt as though my feet barely touched the ground as we raced into the open courtyard, and Schula didn't take no for an answer as we twirled over the stone floor. Every so often, a particular arch of notes seemed to signal to all the dancers to stop and twirl in place, then she would dip me, and the dancing would start all over again.

I was breathless when the song was done, but soon another started, and Schula continued to dance with me. I was glad for the soft new slippers I had bought, because my feet were going to be sore when I was done. Not that I cared—for once we were both enjoying ourselves without worrying.

We paused between songs as Marila brought Schula over a fresh glass of wine. Schula laughed and took a slow drink, closing her eyes and inhaling. She licked her lips and smiled when she was done.

A new tune was starting, and she winked at me. "I think I'll sit this one out."

"Okay," I said, about to follow her back to my chair when a warm hand rested on my shoulder. I spun, my heart still beating from the fast-paced dance we'd just finished, and looked into a pair of molten silver eyes.

"Thain," I whispered.

"I'm sorry we came late."

I glanced at Schula, who was retreating to our table, wine in hand. Eberon was already there, pouring himself a drink as well.

"I think we're in the way," Thain said.

I looked around us, seeing how every other pair had started dancing again and we stood still in the middle of it.

"May I have this dance?" Thain gave me a ghost of a smile.

I grinned and took his hand.

Dancing with Thain was completely different from dancing with Schula. Schula was energetic and firm in her movements, but Thain was as I had always seen him in the Wyldes, fluid and precise. He moved like a big cat, graceful while the violin sang us a song of wind and rain and leaves.

The glow of soft lights and the faint hint of stars overhead added a thrilling veil to the courtyard of swirling silks and fallen leaves. Thain's hand was warm on my back, his chest solid under my palm, our other hands entwined as if they were made to fit together. Warmth swirled between us, enveloped by the chill of the evening outside of the bubble we were in. His expression soft, my chest pounding, our bodies moved together to the sweet cry of the violin.

The usual ferocity he carried at the edges of his features was gone tonight. His breath fanned my neck as he leaned down to murmur near my ear, "You look happy tonight. It suits you."

"This place suits me." *You suit me.*

I bit my lip, resisting the urge to pull his hair loose from its ponytail. He rarely wore it tied back outside the city, but since we'd arrived in Thanantholl I hardly saw it down anymore.

He leaned closer still and whispered, "I see you left that quartz at home. I will have to find you something more suitable to replace it."

Our faces were so close now, I didn't know where to look. From his eyes, burning with something I couldn't place, to his mouth as his lips moved with his words.

The music stopped, and we pulled away.

"Would you like to sit down?" Thain asked.

"Yes, please," I answered, tired from Schula and breathless from Thain.

Thain offered me a hand, and I took it. He was warm, and his palm had a rough edge to it. I sank gratefully into my chair and drank whatever red substance Schula handed me with relief.

"Wren, Schula, you two look splendid tonight," Eberon said, raising his glass. "I'm so glad to be all back together again."

"Me too." Schula feigned a swoon before turning to Thain. "You wouldn't believe what a boor Eb is when you're gone."

I busied myself with my wine, trying to hide my smile as Eberon made several indignant noises.

"It's all right, Eberon. I missed you too," Thain said. "You three are much improved company to Aithne, Asher, and Reghan."

"I'm sure we are," Eberon drawled. "But rather than dwell on them, why don't we speak of something lighter?"

"Good evening." Marila approached with a basket of fritters and a fresh pitcher of cider. "Let me tell you about what our chef has prepared tonight."

Dinner was a whirlwind of conversation, dancing, food, and drink. Lots and lots of drink. I was more careful this time to not let it go to my head, and I had plenty of water between glasses of wine.

We didn't talk about the Spring Court, or what had happened on the border, or even the impending trip to the Winter Lands. Instead, Eberon dominated the conversation with cheap court gossip. It was blissfully easy to enjoy the sound of his voice while Schula chimed in with all the right reactions to spur him on. The cider was tart and cool and made my head feel underwater after a while. Thain looked content to just listen to the others. I supposed I did too. This was exactly what I had been craving for more than two decades, and I didn't even have the words to sum it up. This was perfect.

The evening grew into night, and even though I was exhausted, I was reluctant to leave. Schula finally announced that she was going to fall asleep at the table if we didn't go home, so that was what we did. Thain stood when we left. He seemed to have something to say, but Eberon put a hand firmly on his shoulder, and Thain stayed silent. Schula and I waved our farewell and left through the front gate with a smile from Marila. Our pace was easy and blissfully alone as we made our way from the River's Edge.

The walk was hard on my feet, but I was still riding a high of emotions from the night, and they didn't bother me too much. I grinned like a loon as I helped Schula drag herself up the stairs to the apartment. We were welcomed home by a huge raven on the stair rail, feathers puffed up, disgruntled to have been woken by half-drunk fae coming home.

"What're you lookin' at, bird?" Schula asked. Puko ruffled his feathers and turned the other way.

"Come on, Schula, I think you need to wash your face and go to sleep." I held in the amusement as much as I could.

"Mmm," she groaned and pushed open the door.

Inside, I managed to get Schula to wash her face while I struggled to unlace us both from our elaborate gowns. Once they were off, I draped them over the kitchen chairs and got Schula into the bed. I threw fresh logs in the woodstove and crawled under the covers myself.

"Wren," Schula mumbled, already half asleep.

"Yes?" I yawned.

"It won't hurt my feelings if you move back in with Thain," she said.

I wasn't sure what to say to that, so I said nothing.

"I'm an adult, I can take it." She yawned. "I know how he feels."

"You're drunk, Schula," I said.

"Half drunk," she corrected. "And I know what I'm talking about. It won't hurt my feelings. Not if that's what you really want. I want you to be happy."

"You make me happy," I said. "All of you do."

"But not like Thain." She closed her eyes. "I shouldn't have pushed Caldon on you. I was wrong, you never needed him, you had *him*. But maybe he did. He needed that push."

"You're talking about too many hes," I said. "I don't know what you're saying."

"Oh, s'okay. You don't have to know, he does." She rolled over and snuggled deeper in the blankets. "It's okay to want things, Wren."

To want things. To want . . .

"G'night, Wren." Schula's words were muffled by the pillows.

"Schula?" I nudged her lightly, but her breathing had already evened out, and her mouth was slightly open.

I sighed and scooted down in the warm blankets too. "Good night, Schula."

It took me a while after that, but I finally fell asleep.

THIRTY-ONE
BURNING

I decided I very much liked dressing how *I* wanted. Since coming to the Wyldes, I had been put into the proper outfit for every occasion. Before that, I'd worn what everyone in the mountains expected me to wear. After yesterday, I'd decided that clothes had a certain power, and I wanted to dress for myself. I was still finding out exactly who Wren was.

Schula happily opened her wardrobe to me. I liked the function of the tight leggings of the Autumn Lands, so I borrowed a pair in brown suede. These decidedly did *not* have a line of exposed skin from hip to ankle like last time, though. Not that it wasn't an option in the back of her closet. I also chose a baggy white tunic that laced around my middle a few times to draw it in. It fell almost to my knees, but it flowed around me and was quite comfortable. The only things I couldn't get used to were the boots that didn't protect my legs, so I pulled my old worn boots up to my knees and left with Puko perched on my shoulder.

"Are you sure you don't want me to come with you?" Schula asked, sitting at the table with a steaming cup.

"The wine is still pounding your head," I reminded her in low tones. "I've taken on plenty of the chores while Bryn drank himself sick after a festival. I'll be just fine."

Schula started nodding, then nodded much slower with a groan. I left the apartment with a smile.

It was cool enough that a light cloak kept me warm and helped me cover my face, and I was hardly stopped on my way.

Navigating Thanantholl was becoming easier, or at least I could get to a few key places. Schula's apartment wasn't far from a main road, and I took it to the front gates. Like Schula, Thain didn't want to risk a magical accident in the city.

I spotted him before he saw me. I thought. He always seemed to be enviably aware of his surroundings.

He was dressed in black, of course, and he leaned against a tree near the entrance waiting for me. The guards at the gate were clearly in awe of him as they spoke to him, taking turns keeping a set of eyes on the road. Thain obliged them with what sounded like tales from past battles, but when he spotted me coming up the road, he stopped. The guards straightened at their stations, now paying more attention to their job. I could tell they were still listening intently, though.

"Were you waiting long?" I asked as he stepped forward.

"Not at all. Let's go." We walked out of earshot of the entrance.

Earshot for fae was a pretty good distance, so we walked several minutes before we broke the silence. I was too nervous about my magic to say anything. Thain was going to have to do the talking, which could have been a problem because he hadn't done all that much talking since we'd reached the city. Thankfully, he was ready to teach.

Thain pushed forward through the trees like he had a precise destination in mind, the dusty blue vines that covered the wild places doing their best to trip me as we moved through them. He walked us a good distance out of the valley and well away from any roads until we pushed into a clearing. I nearly stumbled into him, but Thain had already turned to steady me with one hand as we stepped free of the vines.

"This place is empty," I observed.

"I spent time opening it up," Thain explained, and I watched him cross to the other side, where he bent over to pull a vine loose from the rich dirt, tossing it to the edges where the trees were. Thain righted himself and turned around. His hair was loose around his shoulders today, his features softened from the tension of the city, the top of his black shirt left untied, offering a glimpse of his broad chest. "I told you before," he soothed, "I won't let it get out of hand. You're safe with me."

Of course I was, and I could have melted at that.

It's okay to want things, Wren.

"About last night," I began, but he had already stepped in front of me, pausing me with a shake of his head.

Thain lifted one hand, brushing my cheek with his thumb, his other fingers barely touching one of my braids. My hand reached up to cover his, pressing my cheek into his touch with all the ache and wanting that had been building up between us.

"Last night was more of a treasure to me than you know," he said. "You frighten me."

My lower lip dropped open, but no thoughts formed enough to spill out. Thain? Afraid of me?

"You are a breath of life." Thain's tone pulled out something soft in him, something raw that I'd never heard before. "The light of a new dawn, and the blooming of new things in a sea of days that do not change for me. You fit like a piece of my world. As Eberon fits, as Schula fits."

"Yes," I hurried to answer. "I know exactly what you mean."

Thain's hand dropped from my face, slipping from my fingers as our hands fell to our sides.

"To pursue this thing between us, there will be no going back," Thain said. "You have all of the Wyldes at your fingertips, and once the markings on your back are no longer stopping you from fully experiencing yourself, you will find your happiness. That happiness might be in a place where I am not, and I will not keep you from it."

He might as well have taken my axe and carved it through my rib cage. "We don't know that I'm not meant for Autumn."

"And we don't know that you are." Thain let a breath hiss out of him slowly, closing his eyes. "What I want to say is that there must be an order to this. First, we take care of the seal. Then, you find your footing with your magic and with the lands of the Wyldes that call to you. Then, we address this."

He was right. Mother, I wished he wasn't, but he was right. "Okay," I managed.

"That being said," he continued, "I know we will have this connection."

"How?" I asked. "You said yourself that—"

"I said the logical thing to say," Thain said. "And now I say what I know in my heart to be true. Because the alternative would be something that would break me to bear."

The small space between us was filled with so much. Short breaths, beating hearts, and the looming uncertainty ahead.

Circling overhead, a black shadow found the clearing.

"Are you here to watch?" Thain looked up at Puko, who flapped his way down to a branch at the edge of the trees. We each took steps back, gaining some much-needed air from the tension we had just created.

"No distractions," I told the bird, who ignored me to pluck at something on his tail feathers.

My fingers shook. I turned to Thain and clasped my hands behind my back.

"I found enough in the scrolls at the library to help with the markings, so this should be straightforward," Thain said.

"Good. I don't think I could handle complicated right now," I said.

"All right, then show me your meditation. I need to watch how your magic settles into it. We can save removing the seal for after I know you have a good handle on things." He leaned against the tree again.

"You can see that?" I asked.

"I can. Now: sit, breathe."

I rolled my eyes and sat on the ground, moving sticks and rocks out from under me. I breathed, just like I had that morning, and the evening before, and every time Schula caught me with nothing to do. I sat and found that place, my little cabin in an open, grassy field. My warm fire and my cozy loft.

"Good, keep going. Focus everything inward, you're a tangled mess." He kept his voice low and soothing.

I had no idea what he was asking, but I tried anyway. I sat on the floor of my cabin just as I sat in the woods.

Inward.

Inward.

Inward.

"There, right there. Stay there, I'm going to try something and see if you notice. Keep your eyes closed." I could hear Thain shift from the tree to closer by my side.

I kept my focus. I stayed in my cabin.

Next to me, the fire flared, and I nearly jumped out of my skin. A huge burst of heat rushed into me, and my whole body jerked. I lost all concentration then and opened my eyes as I fell over into Thain's lap.

"What was that?" I panted, pulling myself upright.

"Are you all right?" He helped me sit upright. "Sorry."

"What happened?" I asked, now rubbing my arms ferociously.

"I reached out my magic to yours. To . . ." He drew his brows together. "Feel it out? Your fire is strong, but it tastes different than Eberon's."

"How can you feel or taste my—" Gasping for breath, I was suddenly freezing. Pain, pain and cold rolled down my limbs, across my skin. Everywhere except my spine, which burned.

"You're sweating." Thain put a hand on my forehead, and it might as well have been a hot iron. I sank into it, sighing with relief from the warmth, and his expression sharpened. "Are you cold?"

"It hurts. The magic." I gritted my teeth as another wave of icy pain rolled over me. "It's cold, and it wants out."

This was just like before. Mila had prodded the seal somehow, like poking a hole in your waterskin, and the pressure had forced out what it could as hard as it could. Except everything about this was worse. The Wyldes were already messing with the markings and had been since I'd stepped foot within its borders. Now, that intensity was translating into pain.

"Try to center yourself again," Thain said. "Breathe."

I closed my eyes, willing the pain away, and tried to think of my little cabin. My stomach was twisting in my knots. I lurched forward and spilled my breakfast onto the forest floor. Thankfully, Thain pulled me backward a bit to avoid the mess.

I gasped in a huge breath.

The pressure filled me up. My skin was ready to rip open. split at the seams. A hand shot up the back of my tunic, and he hissed.

A growl erupted out of him, and Puko was making his alarmed croaking sounds. Thain lifted me and covered me with my cloak, hiding my face. Then he ran. His arms were bigger than my legs, and he easily swept us through Thanantholl. I was rolled into his chest and couldn't see the guards at the gate, but they didn't speak a word as Thain ran past.

I'd had no idea the fae could run like this, or maybe it was his own wind that carried us through the streets. I heard a few shouts of surprise, but no protests. The shivering increased as I continued my own battle with the magic that was about to explode around me. I sobbed, and he gripped me tighter.

"Hold on." His chest rumbled with the words. "Keep doing your breathing, focus on that."

I swallowed and nodded into him. I brought up Schula's voice in my head counting *one . . . two . . . three . . . one . . . two . . . three . . .*

"Good, Wren. You're doing good. Keep breathing, keep it in," he rumbled.

The sounds of the city flowed by me, but I barely registered them. I knew we traveled over bridges and around corners, but where we were I had no idea. It felt like hours as Thain ran with me in his arms, but I knew the pain was skewing my perception of time. All I could do was count. *One . . . two . . . three . . .*

His body slowed down as he stopped somewhere. There were mumbling voices and a panicked knocking of wood, and soon after that I felt more hands on me.

"What in the hells?" It was Eberon. "Inside, by the fire."

"Wren?" Schula's voice was panicked.

"Schula, cool her back. Eberon, her body is freezing," Thain ordered.

I was set on a cushion by the fire in Eberon's house. A gaggle of other fae from the house were staring from every doorway.

"*Out*," Thain snapped, and they scattered.

"What happened to her?" Schula's cool hands ran up my shirt and over my seal and sucked in a breath. "She's scalding!"

"I reached out my magic to hers," Thain answered.

Eberon held my hands and forehead with his blissful heat. "Are you sure that's all you did?"

They were in danger, and all I was managing to do was shiver uncontrollably while trying to contain my burning power and not throw up again.

"Help me close it," Thain pleaded. "This is so much larger than expected. She's not ready, and we have to get her somewhere safe to open it."

The strain in his voice hurt to hear. I had thought the pain could get no worse until that moment when my heart tore open and bled for my stupid secrets.

"Are you insane?" Schula hissed. "The pressure is killing her!"

"She's here because of me!" Thain's tone sharpened. "I brought her here. I convinced her to come to Thanantholl. She's only being dragged around the whole of the Wyldes because I found a lost fae and took her to my king. Now all the courts have eyes on her, and she's burning herself up to remove these wretched markings because of *me*."

"Do it," Eberon said, straining to warm my face. "She's not ready. Thanantholl isn't ready. What do we need to do?"

"It's a simple in-and-out of power. Her magic is trying to come out; we push it back in and add strength to the markings." Schula moved to cover more of my markings with blissful ice.

"That won't affect how the seal works?" Eberon asked.

"I put a little power into it when she first crossed into the Summer Lands," Schula said. "It worked then."

The next sensation I had was like being put in a bubble. I screamed, but my voice didn't come out, or I couldn't hear it over the rushing in my ears. The magic was being pushed back into me, and it was like daggers of ice against a flood of fire that wanted out so badly it would rip me in two to escape. The seal was being repaired, or reinforced, or whatever needed to be done, and at last the pressure was easing. Eberon's heat was finally seeping into the skin on my forearms where he held on, and Schula's cool fingers relieved my back.

Everything throbbed with magic. It clawed at the edges of the seal, trying to get out again. Thankfully, the pressure was muffled under whatever they did, because I finally felt I could breathe.

"It's a patch job, but it will hold for a while," Schula said.

"She has to let this out somewhere." Eberon ran his hands along my arms as he spoke softly, a furnace warming my frozen skin.

"The Sangolins," Thain said.

Eberon scoffed. "DuVarick isn't going to just—"

"He isn't going to know." Schula cut him off.

"Schula, you don't have to come," Thain said.

"I'm coming no matter where it is," she insisted.

"Then pick somewhere else!" Eberon snapped.

"Where else can she let out this much fire and not set the Wyldes aflame?" Thain asked.

Eberon pressed his jaw shut, frowning at the others. I wiped the sweat off my brow, still breathing slowly as though I were meditating. *One . . . two . . . three . . .*

"The Sangolins are a wasteland of rock and snow." Schula placed a cool hand on my forehead. "You can burn it all off and no one will be hurt, do you understand, Wren?"

I nodded weakly.

"It's perfect." Thain gave Eberon a look.

"DuVarick isn't going to like this," Eberon grumbled.

"I can handle DuVarick," Thain said, low and dangerous. "She's invited to the Winter Lands at any rate."

"Not for this!" Eberon said, exasperation seeping from every word.

"What will he care? We were on our way to him anyway." Schula continued to rub soothing cool circles on my skin with her fingers.

"A show of power like that? He's going to want . . ." Eberon looked at me. Then Thain. Schula avoided eye contact.

"Even he has rules to follow," Thain insisted.

"Who?" I blinked. I was going to ask more, but my head was swimming. Schula's concerned face swirled in my vision, and then everything went black.

THIRTY-TWO
PAIN

The trotting of a horse is a distinct sensation. It bounced me in rhythm to the hoofbeats, and I was vaguely aware that I must be tied to the saddle. I certainly would have fallen off by now otherwise. Odd that I would be tied to a horse when my last memory was blacking out in Eberon's home.

The sun against my eyelids was bright, and I didn't think I'd enjoy the light just yet. Instead of looking around, I used my other senses. Wherever I was, it was cool. Even Thanantholl with its perpetual crisp air was warmer than this. My tongue was dry as a bone, and stiff. I hadn't had anything to drink in some time, I was sure of it. I fluttered my eyes open, and I saw midnight.

"Thain," I murmured.

"You're awake," Thain said softly, then he raised his voice and looked to the side. "We're stopping."

I glanced around, blinking in the bright light. I was riding Boxfield. He slowed his trot to a stop in a rocky field with snow dusting the ground. I could see sharp mountains in the distance, nothing like the mountains I'd grown up in. These were jagged and cold.

Thain undid the straps holding me to the horse and picked me up gently. I winced; my back still burned.

"How are you feeling, little bird?" Eberon asked.

"Sore," I murmured. "I feel like my back is melting off of me."

"You've been in and out of it with delirium," Thain noted.

"She seems better today, thank the Stars," Eberon added.

"I bet you're thirsty." Schula brought a waterskin to my lips, and I drained it while she rubbed her cool hands to my seal.

"Thank you," I croaked.

"We need to keep moving," Thain said, his voice low as he started walking away.

"Surely you aren't going to walk her to the Sangolins," Eberon said. I tilted my head to see the fiery golden fae. His clothes were wrinkled, his eyes ringed with exhaustion.

"We can't keep riding Boxfield this hard, and we're getting close to the trees," Thain said, still striding in the direction of the mountains. "Send him home. I'll take it from here if she can hold on."

Eberon adjusted me onto Thain's back, where he could carry me more easily.

"Go on home, boy." Eberon took a pack off Boxfield and slapped his haunches, sending him into a gallop the direction we had come from.

"Puko?" I asked.

"Mama Flori will leave out food for him," Schula said. "I told her before we left."

"Okay," I said. I hoped he stayed, for his safety, but knowing him he probably wouldn't.

"Hold on tight," Thain said.

Wrapping my arms around his neck without choking him, I concentrated on not feeling more nauseous than I already was.

Thain ran. He ran *fast.*

There had to be a better way to describe his graceful gait through the countryside, but I was at a loss for words. When I dared open my eyes, I got glimpses of the rocky ground rushing by, which did nothing for my spinning head. I preferred staying in the dark.

We went fast where there was room to run and slower where too many rocks and plants were a hazard. I concentrated on keeping my seal intact, pushing back at the power trying to claw out of the magic bubble they'd put it in. I knew I felt hot, and I could tell that I was affecting the others too. I caught glimpses of sweat on each of them, and while I couldn't tell on Thain's dark skin, I could see that Eberon and Schula were flushed.

"It's getting dark," Schula said. "We need to get inside."

"Do you have somewhere?" Thain asked.

"Yes, this way."

I felt us veer to the right, running dangerously close to a tree line that had finally appeared as we drew closer to the mountains. Schula led us to a rocky outcropping that had a solid wooden door built into it.

"It's no palace, but climb on in." Schula held the door open, and Thain carried me through the door first. I let my eyes adjust, but once the door closed and we were in pitch darkness, I wouldn't be able to see at all.

The walls were limestone; we were in a cave. There was enough room for all four of us to lie down on the ground for the night, but that was about it. I nearly missed the two small vent holes near the top of the wall that allowed fresh air in.

"All in?" Schula asked as she tugged the door closed behind her without waiting for an answer. My heart jumped in the darkness until a tiny flicker provided enough light for my eyes to see by.

Eberon held a tiny flame, barely the flicker of a candle in his palm.

"Normally, we wouldn't have a light for fear of the flesh hounds," he explained. "But this won't add any more heat than we already have, so it should be fine."

I shuddered. "Why are they called flesh hounds?" I asked.

Schula looked between Thain and Eberon. Finally, Eberon cleared his throat.

"They hunt the flesh of warm things to adorn their own frozen bodies. I think we can leave it at that," he said.

"Are we in the Unclaimed Wyldes?" I asked. Surely something like that would only be in the dark, frightening places no one laid claim to.

"We're on the edge of the Winter Lands," Schula told me. "It's large and spread out, this place. Most people here live in the Winter's Teeth, the mountain range to the west. The things that live down here by the plains mostly go unchecked. We should reach the Sangolins tomorrow."

Listening for any sounds outside, I felt a little better when nothing unusual came up. "So, we're in this cave because of the dangerous things that live here?"

"The rules here are pretty similar to traveling in the Unclaimed Wyldes," Eberon explained. "When we're in the Winter Lands, don't travel at night, don't light fires, don't go deep into the tree line, and when you're between safe places, don't stop moving for long."

The horrors of the Unclaimed Wyldes had been bad enough, but the Winter Lands didn't sound any better. In fact, they were almost worse.

Eberon pulled food out of the pack and passed it around. We ate in near silence, not speaking much and certainly not about our current predicament.

When we finished eating, we sat in more silence. All I had to focus on was my own horrid imagination of all the things that could be lurking just outside the door, ready to tear me into pieces.

"I'll take first watch," Thain said, breaking up the quiet. "You three get some sleep."

He sat right next to the door, his ears trained on the outside world.

Eberon handed out blankets, making the ground more bearable to lie on, then he extinguished his little light.

I lay down, trying to get comfortable. Despite the snow outside and the cool walls of our safe spot, I was still hot. I tried to bring myself to sleep. My body and mind were exhausted from fighting my own magic, and I was ready for the darkness to relieve my fight, but I couldn't quite reach that point.

I tossed and turned, rolling several times on my blanket. At one point, I took off my boots and scooted my blanket away, trying to embrace the cool ground beneath me. I sighed, trying to lie still enough to simply drift off.

I shivered as something slipped up the back of my shirt. Icy fingers pushed the material out of the way, and a cold body pressed against my back. Schula wrapped her arms around my middle and settled in.

I shuddered with relief. When I closed my eyes again, I was finally able to drift off.

THIRTY-THREE
RELIEF

When I woke up, I was nearly wriggled out of my clothes. My leggings were pushed off my hips, only barely hiding all the parts your pants are meant to keep hidden. My shirt was bunched up to my armpits, one breast hanging out of my breast band.

My eyes snapped wide, and I yanked down my shirt, reaching inside to adjust the breast band again. I was beyond thankful for the darkness that blanketed us. I gently removed the cool arm that was still draped across my stomach, likely the reason I'd wrestled out of my clothes to get to the relief of her touch in my sleep, then I yanked my leggings up where they belonged.

Schula groaned, rolling over and rubbing the sleep from her eyes. "Is it morning?"

"Shh." Eberon lit his palm, flickering light through the room. He motioned to the door, and that was when we all heard the shuffling on the other side of it.

Thain was on his feet in an instant, and Schula and I scrambled to follow suit. Schula mouthed in the dim light, *Flesh hounds?* and looked to Eberon for an answer. He nodded.

Thain seemed to grow, his fingers sharpening into claws, his fangs growing larger, and his eyes almost glowed. His glamour was starting to fade.

"Eb, open the door," he commanded.

Eberon let his fire go out and pushed the door open. In a blur of midnight fury, Thain was outside and tearing into something. I saw blood splatter right before Schula covered my eyes.

"Come on, Wren." She grabbed my arm and led me out. "We're running on ahead."

"I'm staying with Thain in case he has trouble coming back to us," Eberon said. "Go on, we'll catch up."

Schula practically dragged me through the door. Thain had pushed the fight into the trees, the one place they'd told me not to go in the Winter Lands. The thing he was fighting was huge.

Through the jagged branches and thick trunks, I caught glimpses of a horrid creature. The stench of it stung my nose with rot and decay. It was shaped like an enormous wolf without fur; its gray skin sagged, but underneath the skin, ropes of muscle gave the creature bulk. It was a surreal combination of decrepit and ferocious. Its eyes were small and dull; it must have relied on its other senses to hunt. On its back hung strips of bloody skin, laid across its spine like grotesque adornments.

I swallowed a scream, and Schula lifted me off my feet, pulling me onto her back and running in the opposite direction.

"Was that one of the flesh hounds?"

"Shh, it's okay." She held me tight as she ran. "They aren't usually that big, but Thain can take care of it."

The sounds of ripping and tearing and snarling finally faded behind us. Tears stung my eyes, and as much as I would have liked to say it was the cold wind in my face, it was partially because I was so upset with myself.

I was the reason everyone was here. I was the reason the flesh hounds had chased us. I was the reason they were so worried. I couldn't even keep up with them on foot, and Thain or Schula had to carry me.

I decided in that moment to never be weak again. I vowed to myself to master my magic. I would conquer this thing eating at me inside, and I would tame it. I didn't care that I was half this or half that; I had enough of the Wyldes in me that I could run as fast as the rest of the fae, be as strong as them, be as smart as them. I would learn it all, if I could just make it through this one obstacle.

I looked up at Schula through my wild hair. I could feel her heart pounding against her rib cage. Probably the strain of dealing with me and the knowledge of the creature we'd left behind us.

"Are there any of those flesh hounds around us now?" I asked.

She tilted her head a bit, listening. "No, none."

"I know I'll slow us down, but do you think I could run?" I looked ahead to the cold gray mountains that had drawn steadily closer since yesterday.

"Are you sure you want to? I'm fine carrying you," she insisted.

"I'm sure." She set me on my feet, and I began running beside her instead. We had to go slower than before, but I was much happier using my own feet, as long as I wasn't putting us in danger. The terrain wasn't too bad, mostly flat, you just had to watch out for the rocks. My back still burned, but the cold air was helping immensely, and running distracted me from the discomfort.

I started to tire, but I kept pushing forward. Sweat beaded my forehead, and my legs ached, but we kept going. We ran for probably an hour before I just couldn't go on any longer. I was exhausted, and no amount of fear was going to keep me running anymore. It was too hard to fight my seal and spend so much energy running at the same time.

Schula scooped me up and kept going, speeding up. "We're very close, just hold on."

The fight to keep myself contained was growing more difficult. Whatever magical patch job they had done on me back at Eberon's house wasn't going to last much longer.

The sun was finally high enough for us to feel some warmth as Schula carried me up a gentle slope. The mountains had crept up on us, and from the look of them our gentle slope wouldn't be so gentle soon. Luckily, we turned north. It looked like Schula meant to skim the edge of the dark range. Their jagged edges and towering peaks reminded me of teeth biting though the world. I remembered something Prince Alban had said at the Spring Court: the Winter's Teeth. I shivered; this must be them.

"Wren, we're not alone," Schula murmured in my ear. "Don't be alarmed, but I don't think it's Eb or Thain."

I stiffened in her arms. "What do we do?"

"We keep going," she insisted. "We just go through a small patch of trees and we're almost there."

"Why is this place so special?" I asked, straining to hear the other presences that Schula had noticed.

"In the past, many powerful fire fae have come here to burn themselves out, so to speak." She broke through a line of trees and dodged a fallen trunk. "There is a place here for you to burn safely. There is absolutely nothing there to burn. Not one blade of grass. Thanks to that, none of the animals bother with it either. You are safe to cause as much of an explosion as you'd like. I'm also told the deep snow is refreshing, but I wouldn't know."

"I see," I breathed. We pushed out of the trees to the edge of what looked like a giant crater. It was probably half a mile wide, and the edges were steep. Schula didn't hesitate to jump off the flat edge and slide down toward the middle.

It was deep, and near the bottom it was filled with snow, an unbroken surface of flat white flakes that we tore through.

"I thought the Sangolins were plains?" I asked.

"They are, this is just a crater at the edge of them. There isn't really anything of note in the plains except this crater, so any time someone mentions the Sangolins, they're probably talking about this place."

We neared the middle of the crater, and Schula slowed.

"I'm leaving you here. Let it out, and I'll be right back." Schula smiled and stroked my hair. "You'll be so much better, just let it out. I'm going to undo the seal now, then all you have to do is let go, okay?"

"Okay," I breathed.

She ran her hands up my back, tracing it with her icy fingers and muttering a long string of words under her breath. I could feel it, like a thread unraveling. The seal that had always been there was falling away, and it was disorienting. Suddenly, I felt so much less stable than I had before, and that was saying something.

The burden of holding everything in was now squarely on my shoulders.

Schula's eyes popped wide open as she looked at me as if for the first time. "Wren."

She placed her hands on either side of my face and pressed a gentle kiss to my forehead. I could feel her. Finally, really feel her presence as a fae.

"I'll be right back," she breathed. "I just need to take care of whoever is behind us, and I'll be back the second you're done."

Schula squeezed my arm and ran. She left me in snow up to my knees. She ran back through the tracks we had made, back up to the edge of the crater and out of sight.

But all I could feel at that moment was power.

My back burned where the seal had been, but it felt so good to be rid of it. I stripped off my top, not giving a damn about where I was, and I laid my marked skin directly on the snow. Snow melted all around me, soaking through my remaining clothes and soothing the burn that hadn't really stopped since I'd taken my first step into the Wyldes.

Tears streaked down my face at the relief, and I let go.

Fire. Burning flames engulfed me but didn't burn me. The bright red flames licked my body and decimated the snowy landscape around me. I was quickly turning the crater into a small, shallow lake.

The feeling of release was euphoric. It flowed through me, the power to burn. The well of it was almost endless; I felt like I could burn forever. I burned harder, trying to reach it. Flames were licking up the entire crater, eating up the snow and quickly turning it to water. I took a deep breath. Finally, finally everything was clearer. The veil was lifted, and I was breathing for the first time.

Rolling over, I sat up. My boots, my leggings, and my breast band had not burned off. I had thought they would. I had no idea where my tunic was, though.

I pushed the power out a little harder, engulfing more of the crater. It felt *so good* to let it out. I smiled as I sank deeper and deeper into the bottom of the crater as it filled up with water, and I lay back in it.

I closed my eyes and focused on burning it all out of my system. I would recover it over time and work with it in smaller amounts, Eberon had told me.

My butt hit the bottom. Something solid, not snow. I got onto my knees and inspected it. I ran my fingers along it, feeling the rough, cold surface. Ice, it was ice.

I pushed slush and debris away from my hands, opening a window into the ice below me. It looked like the ice over Silver Lake in winter, dark and still under the surface. Undisturbed for who knew how long. My fire was quickly melting it, though, and I took several steps back. I didn't know how thick the layer of ice was, but I didn't want to find out. A bath was one thing, but to be suspended in a large body of water again only terrorized me with memories of almost drowning.

I tried to rein it in, slow down the burn, but I couldn't. I started to panic as I couldn't stop the fire. I felt like a little girl again, standing in Mila's yard and burning everything around me. My panic rose higher as I realized more heat was pouring out of me, melting the ice underfoot.

I ran through the water as well as I could. I ran in the opposite direction of Schula, not wanting to hurt her. I left a trail of melting ice in my wake.

A rumble rippled through the ground. I felt a horrid presence under my feet and ran faster. Somewhere behind me, Schula screamed. I wanted to go to her, but I was afraid.

Burning harder and running faster, I raced for the far edge of the crater. My heart skipped a beat as I felt the bottom of my well of fire. I wasn't close to it, but I could feel where it was now.

I reached the far slope of the crater and began to climb. A rumble of annoyance under the ice terrified me, but I climbed up and out of the crater, gaining distance from the thing below the ice.

I sank to my knees once I was on the ground again. My heart banged in my chest as I struggled to control the fire. My breathing grew labored, and my muscles strained.

It was the worst fight of my life, the fight to gain control of the fire. I was scared and alone and burning. Everything was burning.

Time passed, and my fire had finally slowed down. It was still out of my control, but it had slowed enough for my magic to reach other places. Searing pain hit my ears at the same time, and I screamed.

I reached up to clamp my hands over them to counter the pressure, but I was horrified to pull my hands back and see blood. I reached up again to stop it, but that was when I felt the tips. Long, pointy tips were rapidly sprouting where they would have been had they not been cut off when I was a baby. They felt foreign, bizarre.

Next, my very bones threatened to crack with the strain my magic was putting on them. And my eyes, I could see everything. Not that I couldn't see well before, but now I saw *everything.* Every speck of sand on the ground, every tiny piece of ash that I was burning from the plains around me in the air.

I didn't know how long I lay there screaming in pain and burning up, but I did feel it when I finally stopped.

It wasn't gradual, either. It was sudden, like running into a wall.

I choked out a gasp, tears staining my ashy cheeks as I looked around. In the distance, I saw several forms. More than my three fae friends, but close to the same size and shape.

Then the howls started. Nasty, growling howls. Hundreds of them. My heart sputtered as I realized I had probably drawn every flesh hound for miles to us.

The ground shook, a tremor from below. The thing under the ice was angry, I could feel it. It rammed its body into the ice above it. It terrified me, and I just wanted to find my friends and get away.

I tried to sit up, to pull myself toward where Schula was, but it was useless. I had spent more than just my magic, and I was barely hanging on to my consciousness.

Footsteps from behind me caused me to push myself to roll over. My eyes met a huge fae with an unsettling grin on his face.

Three more were behind him, and beyond the crater were yet more.

"That was quite the show," he snarled. "I think my king will want to see this for himself."

"Wait," I choked.

"Wren!" I could hear Schula's screams across the crater. My ears twitched painfully, and I could hear sounds like fighting.

"Schula," I breathed.

"Oh?" The fae in front of me leaned down, his face twisted into a dark smile. "Did you just say Schula is on our lands?"

I swallowed, squeezing my eyes shut as a tear escaped.

"How interesting." He stood straight and turned slightly toward the fae behind him. "Bring her too. Follow behind at a distance, keep her away from this one."

"Yes, Asher." They saluted and ran, skirting the edge of the crater and sprinting toward Schula.

"Now, you're coming with me, little one." He leaned down until I could see the cruel glint in his black eyes. "DuVarick will want to see you for himself."

THIRTY-FOUR
THE WINTER LANDS

Asher was huge. Maybe even taller than Thain. His black hair was cropped close to his head, and his pale gray complexion looked haunting with his black eyes. And he was *fast*. He sprang into action almost immediately after telling me I was coming with him. Three flesh hounds had crept near, snarling and ready to attack.

But the fae that Asher commanded were ready. They sprouted fang and blade and claw, ready to pounce if any of the creatures got too close.

I was terrified. The hounds were huge, and I got a gruesome picture up close that I hadn't gotten when we'd left Thain fighting one in the trees.

Here in the open I could discern exactly what pieces of torn flesh the hounds had adorned themselves with. One had a strip of neck and ear over its back along with what must have been a length of scalp. I distinctly saw fingers on another. Old, dried blood striped their grotesque hides. It stung to look at them. To smell them was worse.

Instead of healing over, damaged skin seemed to remain open. It festered, dripping pus and infection. The scars I could see told me the wounds would heal eventually, but the marred and open flesh told me it wasn't a quick or pleasant experience.

One of the hounds closest to me had a mangled jaw with maggots crawling on it. It did nothing to ease my nausea.

It was awful. The smells, the sounds. My newly heightened senses were making me sick, and I kept my eyes shut tightly. Asher assigned one of the fighters to bind my hands and hold me in place while they fought the hounds. He did so, none too gently. I couldn't have run if I'd wanted to, though. I was absolutely drained of energy. I couldn't even light a candle right now with my powers.

I strained, trying to hear or see what might have happened to Schula, but I couldn't tell where she was or if she was even alive. She had to be alive, right? Asher had ordered his soldiers to bring her with us.

I screamed once, when a flesh hound broke the line of defense and came bounding toward me. Asher himself caught the thing, ripping its throat out with his claws. Its blood dripped down his arm, and he looked me straight in the eye as he smiled and licked some of it off his bicep, still holding bits of its flesh in his hand as the body twitched on the ground at his feet. He chuckled at my reaction.

I clamped my eyes shut for the remainder of the fight. Even though I could feel warm blood splatter my face. Even though I could smell the pungent scent of punctured intestines, signaling a gruesome death nearby.

It felt like ages before it all died down. I finally pried my eyelids open when I was hauled to my feet. Bodies littered the ground around us. There were probably a hundred dead flesh hounds lying between two dozen fae all answering to Asher. Three of his fae had fallen and were being carried off.

"Come on, you." Calloused hands yanked me forward, and my feet left the ground as my assigned guard grabbed me.

I was lifted and thrown over his shoulder, now fully realizing I was wearing only my breast band and pants. Filth from his skin and blood splatter from the fighting coated my exposed stomach.

My view was of the ground behind the brute carrying me and little else. I twisted my head and could see the boots and legs of other fae, and we were moving.

"Put me down!" I kicked my legs and did everything in my power to disrupt my captor while my hands were still bound.

"Shut up and stay still," he grunted.

"Put! Me! Down!" I screamed, willing my flames to come to life around me, but I was still empty.

"*Silence.*" Asher's cold voice rang through the field, and I stiffened. In a flash, his powerful hand was gripping my face, his palm over my mouth and his claws digging painfully into my cheeks. His eyes came into view as he lifted me by the jaw to meet his eyes, my lower half still over the shoulder of his soldier.

"You listen to me, youngling. I will tolerate nothing but obedience from your *disgusting* kind. You will remain silent for the trip to the palace, and you will hold your tongue in front of His Majesty, or your friend will be the one to pay the price."

He jerked my face roughly to the side. Over his shoulder, I could see in the distance where two of his fae were carrying a limp Schula in their arms. I gasped as I saw the trickle of blood flowing steadily from her temple.

"Do you understand, half breed?" He jerked my gaze back to his cold eyes.

Glaring at him, I refused to give him an answer.

He grunted and dropped me, walking back to the front of the group. My body smacked against hard shoulder blades as I fell fully over my guard's shoulder again.

My heart pounded. What was I supposed to do now? I was going to see Asher's king. That must be the Winter King, right? And I was expected; Asher just didn't know who I was. Right?

But where were Thain and Eberon?

And was Schula all right?

I let myself fall limply against the Winter brute's shoulder as the fae under Asher marched. We made our leisurely way to the looming Winter's Teeth.

I wasn't sure if they were hesitant to face what was ahead of us, which didn't seem like Asher, or if they were letting someone, or something, catch up to us, which I didn't want to think about either.

Light snow that had crunched underfoot was quickly turning to packed ice as we neared the mountains. The fae didn't talk, they didn't march out of line, and they all deferred unquestioningly to Asher.

I would be completely bored if I wasn't scared out of my mind.

The sun, which had been high overhead, was starting to dip into the afternoon. Enough that I could tell we were heading further west. I squirmed on my guard's shoulder, trying to see Schula from where I hung upside down. He took one giant hand and smacked my backside, and I yelped from the force of it.

"Stop moving," he growled.

Maybe it was all a big misunderstanding. Maybe the king would recognize me and let us go. Maybe.

Asher had called me a half breed. Maybe I'd never really escaped that after all.

A cold tear streaked from my eye to my temple and dropped to the ground. I furiously tried to wipe at my face with my bound hands.

It was different now. Even if I was going into danger because of what I was, I wasn't the same lost girl I used to be. Now I had fire. Now I had friends. And I was ready to fight. I was ready to take control of myself.

My newly healed ears twitched as a whisper reached them. Far in the distance, very softly, I heard a familiar caw. My throat tightened as I nearly cried out for Puko. I swallowed and choked out a laugh. A quiet and strained sound.

"What is so funny?" the brute growled under me.

"Nothing." I grinned watching a tiny black speck in the distant sky.

My heart soared to him as Puko followed safely behind us. If a half-blind bird could track me down across the Wyldes, then I could get us out of this.

I wasn't alone, and this time I was going to bow to no one.

THIRTY-FIVE

ICEHOLD

There was nothing but time available to me, and it needed to be used wisely. I let the full weight of my body sink onto the fae carrying me, and I meditated. Under the circumstances, I thought my focus was pretty good, but with every step I had to fight for control.

In the little cabin in my mind, I had some cleaning up to do. Whatever I'd done when it had all spilled out of me had had disastrous effects in my head. The cabin was distorted, and I couldn't focus on any one part of it at first. I began the task of reconstructing it until finally I could settle myself back inside.

But everything was different.

Just like my physical body, my magical body was more sensitive. Sounds, feelings, everything was amplified. Schula had once told me that magic could reach for other magic in this place, so I sat down in the middle of the cabin and meditated.

One . . . two . . . three . . .

I could nearly hear Schula in my head, sitting outside Thanantholl and instructing me.

One . . . two . . . three . . .

On the edge of my hearing was fluttering. The sound of a preening bird.

Still counting and doing my breathing, I carefully stood and walked to the window. I hadn't constructed anything around my little cabin but an empty field, so with nowhere else to land, Puko sat on the ground, staring at me with his milky blind eye.

Of all the things I'd thought I could reach out to from here, this bird was not one of them. I opened my mouth to call out to him, but nothing came out. It dawned on me that I couldn't speak in here, so I went to the door instead and reached out for him.

He opened his beak in an empty caw and hopped a few steps toward me, but he kept his milky eye trained on me, unblinking.

I reached out my hands to pick him up, but he pecked my wrist and backed away with another silent caw.

I don't know what you want. I shook my head at him.

He shook his head back at me and took off. I watched him go until he was a speck in the sky.

Puko was no ordinary raven, that much I had always known. But what he was doing here—whether it was him or a figment of my mind—would remain a mystery for now. I retreated back into the cabin but left the door open in case he returned.

Then I sat on the floor once again and focused.

One . . . two . . . three . . .

Then I felt the subtle warmth. Floating just above my shoulder was a tiny thread of fire. I almost didn't notice it, but as soon as I reached out to touch it, I felt it sink into me.

My heart skipped a beat. It was *my* fire. It was a part of me. It was coming back.

I was jolted by a large bump in the road. My eyes, my real eyes, flew open. I blinked, looking around. We had begun to climb the foot of a mountainside at some point, and we were traveling uphill. I craned my neck, trying to see Puko or where the brutes carrying Schula were, but they were nowhere to be found. Trees and boulders blocked my view, and a cold wind whipped my braids around me.

Closing my eyes again, I focused on sitting and counting, reaching around me for more tiny threads.

I slowly pulled little wisps of fire to me. Tiny bits of myself that were sinking back into where they'd come from.

When I couldn't find any more around me, I took inventory of what I had been able to get back.

It was tiny. A small ball of heat inside me that could cook a meal or maybe light a fireplace. I settled the little ball of fire deep within myself and opened my eyes again. I didn't know how much time had passed, but it was getting dark. The mountain peaks were tall around us, looming with a threatening height and sharp evergreens growing tall toward the sky. Our pace had picked up. I heard Asher mumble something in the front of the group, and we began a gentle descent.

I was afraid to know exactly how high we had climbed to already be heading downward again, but hopefully we were heading somewhere safe for the night. I thought about the flesh hounds and shivered.

"Getting cold, warmblood?" My guard (who still didn't have a name, so I'd started calling him Brute) chuckled at me.

"Where are we going?" I asked softly, not wanting to get in trouble for talking now that we were closer to Asher. The last thing I needed was his attention.

Brute shrugged. "Icehold."

Which was no answer, since I had no idea what or who Icehold was.

The slope continued for a while, and I watched the sun dip dangerously close to the mountainside. It was getting too dark and too cold for my comfort, and I held my breath with every moment that passed, hoping we were almost to shelter.

Finally, the movement at the front of the group behind me changed. Asher called out something about formation, and Brute moved us to the back of the line.

I craned my neck to see where we were, and finally a structure of sorts came into view. Carved stone sprouting right from the mountain itself opened into a gaping maw that descended into the rock. Countless stairs went down, down, down into a dark cavern. Instead of cave walls, though, everything was carved. Inlays of gold, silver, and jade depicted fae, monsters, the mountains, and animals I had never seen before.

My jaw dropped, forgetting for a moment that I was being taken against my will into the depths of the Winter's Teeth. My eyes covered every inch of wall, of ceiling, of pillar that they could reach. Soft curves, intricate details, smooth edges. They put Bryn's little wood carvings to shame. A lump caught in my throat as I inspected the tiny gold inlay depicting the embroidery of a young girl's elaborate gown.

It went on like that for as far as I could see in the fading light. We walked for a long time down those stairs, and I wondered how any of them could bring themselves to step on such glorious decoration as though it were an old, worn rug. I wondered what kind of people could have carved all of this.

The descent finally ended with a torchlit gate. Two guards dressed in black leather opened the metal bars as Asher approached.

A scent hit my nose, and I winced as I realized they were burning their hands. The gate was solid iron. Would that burn me now too? What would affect me differently, now that I had come into my skin?

The guards didn't flinch; they just stared stone-faced ahead and didn't so much as glance at the half breed being hauled past them.

We kept marching through the gates and into what could only be a city, but there were no separate buildings.

Icehold.

Everything, like the grand staircase behind us, was carved from the mountain. There was little made of wood, and there were candles and oil lamps *everywhere*. In lanterns, in windows, on shelves carved outside of doorways seemingly for the express purpose of holding light.

Eyes peered at me from around corners and through windowpanes. The Winter Court for sure. The thing that struck me as odd was their clothing. It all looked so shabby. Hand-me-downs of hand-me-downs, garments I was more than familiar with. It made me realize I hadn't seen one item of patched clothing since entering the Wyldes until now. If this was their common citizen, the Winter Court was far poorer than either Autumn or Spring.

We continued through the streets, pushing fae who were brave enough to be there out of the way and heading toward something I couldn't see around Brute's shoulders.

Then I started seeing silk.

And gold, and veils, and flowers. Money. It was as though we'd stepped through a curtain and found the upper class. The difference between what

I had been seeing and what I saw now was staggering. And the clothes . . . I remembered Eberon saying that the clothing style here would be eccentric, but I hadn't been prepared for this.

The females in this area wore fine lace or thin silk veils that covered their whole bodies to the floor and were held in place by ornate circlets on their heads. Beneath the see-through layer, they seemed to be in competition with one another as to who could wear the smallest amount of clothing despite the freezing temperatures. Every bit of fabric was covered with beadwork or embroidery. *At least I won't be too out of place with my missing tunic.*

The males were little better. Other than the leather-clad warriors, the fae in this aristocratic district walked around with no shirts and a finer version of the kilted wraps that the human plainsmen favored in battle.

What they lacked in cloth on their bodies they made up for in jewelry. Rings, ear cuffs, bracelets, necklaces, and items I couldn't even identify adorned them like jewel boxes. Even King Baeleon's court wasn't this extravagant.

The deeper into the richest part of the city we went, the more activity happened around us. Lanterns were being installed, decorations strung on thin ropes to be hung above us, crossing back and forth overhead.

"What is happening?" I said more to myself than anyone else, but Brute graced me with an answer anyway.

"Solstice preparations," he grunted.

I stared, bewildered, as we marched on. The ever-changing but ever-the-same carved walls still held my fascination over everything else. When I was thoroughly lost from the twists and turns of the carved city, we halted in front of another grand gate made of iron.

This one took four guards to open, and again I could smell the damage to their bare hands as we passed. The gate took us to an open doorway, which took us through a grand carpeted entrance, which took us through a series of lavish halls.

I was lifted and set on my feet in one swift motion, showing me the gilded door we had just passed through and an opulent room. I hadn't realized how much blood must have been flowing to my head, because as it rushed to the rest of my now upright body, I nearly fainted. I was still seeing spots when a gnarled voice spoke.

"Asher," it drawled. "What have you brought before us?"

The big gray male kneeled before a dais, on which was a grand throne of marble. A smaller, only slightly less elaborate throne sat empty next to the first. The fae who could only be the Winter King sat with disgust and disinterest as he looked down his nose at his servant.

His skin was the palest blue, almost white, and his eyes were piercing. His hair was a smoky gray, and it fell around his shoulders with a few small braids adorning it. Unlike his court, he wore little jewelry, a single pendant and three rings. Behind him stood two thin wisps, almost shadows with white eyes. It was difficult to make out their shape in the low light of the room. When I tried to focus on them, I got a sharp pain behind my eyes, and they seemed to be ever-whispering though I couldn't understand a word of what they said.

"My king, I bring you something we haven't seen in these lands in an age."

Mumbles pricked my ears and told me the room held more than just the captivating figure in front of us. I glanced around, quickly taking in the forms of more Winter nobility before focusing again on the fae on the throne.

A hand grabbed my bound wrists and yanked me into the light, leaving me to stumble on the white carpet at the King's feet.

"We found this half breed in the Sangolins without your permission." Asher bowed his head. "She was burning off a considerable amount of fire in the crater."

The king tapped a finger on the arm of his throne for a moment before he leaned forward and his nose twitched. The wisps behind him thrashed and hissed, whispering even more fiercely in his ears.

"*You*," the king rumbled and stood suddenly, bringing his court to their knees around him. "How did you come to exist?"

I had no clue how I was supposed to answer that. None at all, so I tried to say something that might lessen his wrath at me.

"I don't know my parents, Your Majesty. I was raised by humans.

Please, I am here with your permission. I was traveling with an envoy from the Autumn Lands, I'm—"

Smack.

Asher stood over me in a flash, backhanding me. I spun and fell to the ground, landing on my shoulder hard as I cried out from the impact. I gasped at the sharp pain, the eye on the right side of my face watering in protest.

"That is not the answer King DuVarick asked for!" Asher roared.

"She was traveling with others?" the king asked, still not taking his piercing eyes off me.

"Yes." Asher bowed his head and took a knee once again. "Sire, it was Schula."

The roar that echoed in the room could have shattered bone if we weren't all fae as the Winter King leaned forward, baring his fangs and howling out in fury. My stomach lurched watching the wisps writhe and dance at the display.

"Throw this one to the below. We will deal with her later. We will have Schula in front of us *now*."

So the king ordered, and so I was taken away.

The room still spun as I was carried out by Brute, and I cried out for Schula. Her still-limp body was carried by me as I screamed. She didn't wake up; she didn't even twitch.

Still, I screamed for her as I was carried down a narrow hall until she was out of sight.

Until I was out of sight.

Until I noticed I was being taken somewhere even the torchlight wouldn't touch.

As the last flicker of distant fire left us, so did my raw voice.

Brute threw me onto what must have been a straw-covered floor, and then it was just me.

Me, and the below.

THIRTY-SIX

THE BELOW

My skin was cool, but I didn't feel cold.

My stomach was empty, but I couldn't be moved to look for food.

My heart hurt, but there was nothing to ease the pain.

I had spent a very long time hitting and screaming and clawing at the door, and now I had nothing left to offer the darkness but a hopeless shell. I couldn't help Schula, I couldn't find Thain or Eberon or Puko. I couldn't even help myself.

I didn't know how long I sat on the cold ground staring at where the door to my prison must be. Not that I could see it. Not that I could see anything at all. All there was, all I could sense, was me, the hard floor beneath me, and darkness.

I would sometimes hear a soft clicking noise, but with the echo I had no way to know where it came from. Though it was quiet, it was a grating sound against the silence that blanketed me. I shivered when I heard it and was left with a sense of unease when it stopped.

My stomach made a noise that sounded like a roll of thunder in the empty space. With my new ears, I could hear a slight echo of every movement I made. That must be because I was in a large space, right? Perhaps more cave or another carved portion of the mountain.

I traced the lines of goose bumps on my arms as I continued to stare into the blank space that was the door.

What was happening to Schula right now? The Winter Court didn't seem to like her for some reason.

And where was Thain? And Eberon? They should have caught up by now. Maybe they had, maybe the Winter King had sent them away.

I would even cry out in joy for Puko at this point. His soft feathers were a familiar comfort. They reminded me of home and of Mila.

My stomach growled again. I sighed and sank until I lay on the floor, curled into a tight shape for warmth.

And I slept.

I woke up with the sensation of gravel pressed into my cheek. Sitting up, I gently picked the pieces off my skin, trying to orient myself to the door. Then I heard the clicking again.

I stopped to listen. It went on for only a few heartbeats before it stopped once more.

I let my muscles relax. I hadn't even noticed when I'd tensed them.

Then I continued to stare, rubbing my fingers over my hands. The small cuts I had given myself when I'd tried to claw my way out of the darkness were already gone. I was sure there were flecks of blood still on my fingers. But now I just sat and waited for a sign of life to come my way.

Maybe they would bring food. Maybe DuVarick would send for me.

Maybe they would toss someone else in here so I wouldn't be alone.

There wasn't much for me to do, so there I sat.

And waited.

In the darkness.

This was stupid. I couldn't claw my way out. I couldn't see. I was back to being the same stupid, helpless girl I'd been in the mountains.

Furious, I smacked my fist on the door in front of me, and a spark spit out of my hand and landed on the ground, extinguishing itself instantly.

I gasped.

Fire. Had I imagined it? But how had I made it happen? Eberon had intended to teach me about fire magic, but we'd never gotten the chance. I had thought I didn't have a way to make it happen, but maybe I could try some things. It wasn't like I had anything else to do.

I stared at my hand. Or where my hand probably was since I couldn't say for sure. I tried to imagine another spark coming to life in my palm. Nothing. I tried making a fist again. I tried hitting the door again. I tried moving my hands like I had seen Eberon do. Nothing.

I stood, getting angry now. Just when I thought I could do something about my situation, it was yanked out from under me again. I flexed my hands, I hit the wall, and I yelled.

"Why won't it work!"

My voice echoed through the cavern, as did the sob that followed. I felt the tear streak down my cheek, and I even heard the soft splat as it hit the floor.

I sank onto the cold ground. Yelling and cutting open my hand wasn't going to get me anywhere, but neither was sitting here. If only I had something that would help me find my way back to the door if I went exploring, I would feel better about moving from this spot.

Then the clicking was back. My back stiffened until it passed. I sighed, quietly scolding myself for making so much noise. Or maybe it was in my head.

I was frustrated. I was tired. I decide to try and get some sleep. I usually handled problems better in the morning. Whenever that was.

I lay down again and thought about fire until I fell asleep.

When I heard the footsteps, I thought I was imagining things. I scrambled to wake up and be on my feet, ready for whatever was coming through the door. Another prisoner? Brute? The king?

I slid my feet into the position Schula had drilled into me and waited. I did my breathing in the back of my mind. *One . . . two . . . three . . .*

The door swung open, and I was nearly blinded. I remembered that when I'd been thrown in here, the light was so dim outside the door that I could barely see my fingers in front of my nose, and now it was bright enough to stun me.

I was yanked by the arm until I fell forward. A huge pair of biceps was the first thing to come into focus, and I recognized with more than a small amount of fear that they belonged to Asher.

My throat tightened, and I allowed myself to be carried away. My eyes focused painfully as I tried to peer through my eyelashes to let in the smallest amount of light I could. I couldn't tell where we were going, though, and all the hallways looked the same as we passed by.

It wasn't long before I was thrown onto a carpeted floor. Ignoring the pain of my eyes in the light, I looked wildly around me. I was in some kind of private office chamber. Asher stood guard by the door. In front of me was a large desk, and behind that was DuVarick. Those wisps, shadows, or whatever they were lined the wall behind him, and this time there were more of them. Angry and dancing and whispering just beyond understanding.

I sucked in a breath and watched the king. He stared back at me unblinkingly until finally he waved his hand and about half the candles around the room extinguished themselves, the wisps dancing in delight.

"How did an abomination like you come to exist?" DuVarick asked slowly.

I swallowed and answered exactly as he wanted me to this time. At least until I had a better grasp of what was going on.

"I don't know my parents, Your Majesty. I was abandoned as a baby."

He grunted and folded his hands on the desk in front of him, leaning forward. "You look just like *her*."

From the corner of my eye, I saw Asher move his head to look over his shoulder. I would remember that to think about later. More importantly, the only *her* I might look like should be—

"My mother?" I breathed. I clamped my lips shut, hoping the outburst wouldn't earn me another slap from Asher. Who could I look like, if not someone of my blood?

The king glowered at me.

"Do you even know what you are?" DuVarick sneered.

"The foundling?" I whispered. "A half fae?"

He snorted and stood from his desk. "Leave us."

Asher bowed and left, closing the door behind him.

My heart was thundering in my chest. I didn't want to be alone with the frightening Winter King, but he knew my mother. He had the answers I had been looking for all my life, and I wanted them badly.

DuVarick paced behind his desk a moment, then came around to where I was still on my knees on the carpet.

"Stand," he ordered. And I did, slowly.

DuVarick stood tall, with broad shoulders but a lean build. Looking at him closely, I noticed a surprising lack of scars for a fae so old. His clothes were of a very fine material but in a simple design. Like many of the other males in his court, he had no shirt but wore a kilted garment around his waist and short boots somewhat like the Autumn Court's.

He approached as I stood and raised a hand. I flinched, thinking I was going to be struck, but he did something much more surprising. He stroked my hair, from my temple to the braid over my shoulder. Even though I must have been a filthy mess with strands of hair pulling loose, he stared at it with fascination. I was suddenly very aware of the breast band and torn leggings I wore in his presence. My dirty skin and scratched-up hands needed a bath.

"You have her hair," he said softly. "And her nose."

His eyes trailed all over my face. It was awkward to say the least, but I had to know more. I had to take a risk, and maybe he would give me what I'd been looking for.

"What was her name?" I asked, pleading.

The king's soft face turned hard and dark as he snatched his hand back. He frowned as he walked around me while I stood perfectly still.

"You shouldn't exist." His boots made soft sounds on the carpet as he circled me slowly, leaving goose bumps crawling up my back. The corners of the room whispered harder, mocking me with their non-words as the wisps' disorienting lines blurred with the dim room.

I jumped as a finger traced the place on my back where my seal had been. He took his time, running over every line that had been there. "So, that's how she fooled them."

I didn't know what the seal had done to fool anybody, but I knew better than to say it.

DuVarick continued circling me, inspecting me for who knew what. He stopped to my left and leaned in, raising my heartbeat to a painful level as I felt his presence right by my face. I felt his fingers brush my hair again, but I didn't move.

He lifted a braid, pulling it away from my newly formed ear, and let out a low growl.

"We knew what you were the moment we smelled you, but we had to see it for ourselves," he said.

I was afraid to ask what he saw, so I remained still and silent.

He dropped my hair and walked slowly back to his desk. I let out a slow breath as he sat back down.

"What to do with the abomination of a betrayer. Shall we skin you?" He tilted his head as he watched the blood drain from my face in horror. "No, the other courts will complain. Pestering, pathetic, spineless. Perhaps we should keep you as a sort of pet? I'm sure you'd be obedient enough after a few more days in the below. They always are."

I swallowed hard and couldn't keep my composure any longer. I wasn't going to stand around obediently for him, and I would start proving that to myself right now.

"You can't keep me here, I haven't met the Summer Court yet," I insisted. "And I'm due back in Spring for the equinox."

My words were met only with a cackling mockery. "Fools," he said, leering. "They don't know what you really are. With your tricks gone, you have nothing to hide the sin that you are. You're lucky we have a personal stake in your existence or you would have been slain the moment you stepped on our lands. Don't think that fool Baeleon would have done any better. When word reaches him that you tricked him, he will want you and those that found you on the end of his sword."

Thain. My heart thudded.

"What is wrong with being half fae?" I asked, my voice rising. "Let me face Baeleon and I'll find out for myself!"

"Half fae?" he laughed darkly. "Not a damn thing. *Asher*!"

The door opened almost instantly, and Asher appeared in the room, ready for orders.

"Take her back and give her something to eat until we decide what to do with her."

"No!" I screamed, but Asher had no difficulty grabbing my arms and twisting them painfully behind my back.

"Yes, my king." Asher bowed.

"Wait! Where is Schula? Who was my mother?"

DuVarick had given me a tiny taste of who I was, and I needed more.

But my answers wouldn't come, because Asher dragged my flailing body back to the below.

And once again I was alone.

THIRTY-SEVEN
COMPANY

I was thrown into the below with a stale roll of bread. It took me a long time to find where it had landed in the dark, and I devoured almost all of it. With more than a little willpower, I was able to set aside some for later, since I didn't know when I'd be fed again.

My mother. DuVarick knew her. Was she from the Winter Lands? Or was it something else? Why did he have such a problem with my existence? And what about me was a trick that would make King Baeleon want to kill me?

And where were my friends?

I sighed, the thoughts chasing each other around my head and making it ache. I leaned against the door and closed my eyes, rubbing my palms over my sore temples.

I let out a slow breath, the same one I let out when meditating. Back in my cabin I went. At least in my mind I could see where I was, unlike the darkness that surrounded my physical body. I tilted my head back and breathed.

Things were still different. Ever since my seal had been lifted and my magic flowed everywhere, things seemed off. Distorted. New. Even in the cabin in my mind, my senses picked up on things I hadn't been able to before. The fire I could feel and touch and move when I was meditating was sharper. Clearer.

Experimentally, I tried to conjure it in my hands. With a little concentration, a light flickered to life in my palm. It didn't burn me, and it didn't feel hot, but it felt heavy as though it had a physical presence I could hold and carry around. I couldn't remember if this was what the fire had felt like when it was burning in the crater, but the sensation was fascinating now that I had time to really pay attention to it.

I played with it in my hands for a while. I was still breathing to keep myself meditating, but it was so second nature by now that I could start to do other things. Maybe if I wanted to learn more about myself and my fire, I was going to have to do it on my own.

I willed the fire brighter, which worked a little. I practiced making the flames rise higher and then burn low. I tried to get it to float above the ground or off my hand like Eberon, but I couldn't manage that trick. This was all in my mind, and I wasn't able to get this far in the real world yet, but maybe the practice would help.

I was trying to get the fire to burn higher but narrower like a pillar in my hand when I heard the clicking. Only here, it was so *loud.* It was alarming to hear when I was safely in my cabin, and I dropped the flame, which sizzled out, nearly jarring me out of the cabin. As I stabilized myself and the clicking finally stopped, I dared to peer outside the cabin door.

I was still surrounded by a grassy field. A light breeze fluttered through the air, and the sun shone brightly overhead. But in the distance, I could feel two specks of something. Light? Magic?

The white one was much closer than the other, but it seemed to be crying out in pain. Not with a sound, but with a feeling somehow. I couldn't quite pinpoint where it was to help it, so I had to turn my attention away.

The other spark was black. It was a smoldering ball of hate and despair, and it was so very far away. But while it should have been a faint feeling from where I stood, I could feel it just as easily as I could the white spark.

The clicking, though, it rang through my clearing so clear and loud. I ducked back into the cabin and looked behind the door where I would keep an axe. There wasn't one, but with a little focus, one appeared, and I took it with me to investigate.

Back out the door and through the grass I headed to where I thought the clicking was coming from. As I grew close, a yellow presence began to form. It was shapeless, and as it seemed to recognize that I was there, the clicking stopped.

If the white spark was pain, and the black spark was hate, then this formless yellow aura was curiosity. It came closer, and I took a step back, drawing my axe up.

"Stay back!" I tried to yell, but no sound came out.

The yellow presence didn't seem to be able to talk. Instead, it sent feelings toward me. First, I felt its amusement. There was no laughter to be heard, but I could feel it in the air. Then it wanted me to wake up.

Wake up? I'm already awake.

There it was again.

Wake up.

I shook my head; I didn't know what it meant. It sighed. And then I was slapped by something. Hard.

My eyes flew open. My real eyes. Darkness surrounded me. I brought a hand up to the cheek that had been slapped, expecting to feel a sting, but it was fine. No sting, no swelling, no sign of being hit at all.

Slowly, I got to my feet. Then I heard it again. The damn clicking. Not as loud as it had been in my head, but it was still there.

Clenching my jaw, I balled my hands into fists and took a step forward. If I went after this stupid clicking, I would probably never find my way back to the door again without Brute or Asher coming for me, but knowing where the door was would do me no good if I went insane first.

Walking slowly in the dark, I discovered the ground was relatively flat. I did have to avoid slipping on loose sand or gravel, but I was otherwise able to walk on my own. I couldn't pinpoint the sound, but I could follow its general direction.

I kept my steps slow and quiet as I continued toward the noise. Sometimes it would stop, but it would always resume eventually. I would wait a few minutes for it to start, as it normally did, but if it looked like it would be a longer wait, I would sit down.

I sat with my knees tucked under my chin, rubbing my palms on my upper arms for warmth. And then it started again. I rose, walking once more toward the clicking. My heart pounded the closer I got, and my stomach rumbled. I wished I had brought the rest of the bread. I'd probably never find it again, but it was too late to turn back now, and I had little choice but to press on.

It went on like that for hours. It frightened me to think what else might be in such a cavern, but finding out now was better than finding out while I was asleep and defenseless.

My foot hit a pebble. A small act, but in the silent cavern its noise would alert whatever was ahead of me to my presence. My stomach dropped as the clicking stuttered, interrupted by the clearing of a throat.

Someone was here.

"You can speak up now," a raspy voice called out. "I think you've tracked me long enough for the both of us."

The voice was male, and it sounded like it didn't get much use these days. It sounded like Bryn when he would go out drinking and singing the night away and could hardly talk the next day.

When my heart calmed down, I cleared my throat in turn. "Who are you?"

"Hmm, telling you wouldn't do much good. Nobody would remember my name anymore. Who are you?"

"That's not very fair. You want to know who I am, but you won't tell me who you are first?"

After a pause, the voice answered again. "All right. I go by Nassir. Now, who are you?"

"I'm Wren. What is this place?" I asked.

"You haven't figured it out by now? The below is a pit for lost things. If you are in here, then DuVarick doesn't want anyone to remember you."

Well, that seemed about right.

"Is it you making that clicking sound?"

"Yes, it's how I get around without my sight," he said. "I make a noise, like the clicking of my tongue, and I listen for the echo off the walls."

I didn't really get it, but it was a better explanation than nothing. "How big is this place?"

"Depends on what you mean by big. It is bigger now than it was when I first got here." Nassir made a shuffling sound, maybe something like sitting down. "What did you do to get on his bad side?"

"I don't actually know." I sighed, sitting as well. "How long have you been here?"

"Who knows? Time passes differently when you live this existence of darkness. I'm sure it has at least been several years. A thousand, maybe?"

He said it with such ease, but my heart dropped at the implication. "A—a thousand years?"

"Perhaps more, perhaps less. I have no way to know."

"What is it you did to be put here?" I asked. "You don't have to tell me if you don't want to."

"Oh, I've committed no crimes. DuVarick is proud of his prison for criminals. You don't get sent to the below for crimes; you get sent to the below to be forgotten."

"Right."

"I will give you one reason I'm here," Nassir offered.

"Is there more than one?" I asked.

"Hush. Do you want my reason or not?" he asked.

"Yes, sorry."

"I'm here because I'm an artist," Nassir answered. "I did some carvings for the city. I don't know if those carvings still stand, but when I was done DuVarick went to great effort to make sure I could do no more such art for another king. He was determined to keep my masterpieces for himself."

"That's awful," I said. "So, he threw you in here?"

"Hmm, among other measures, yes," he said.

"How have you lived this long? Do they feed you? Do you get water?" I asked.

"I find food. There is plenty here if you know where to look. They may think I'm dead, they haven't come for me in so long," Nassir said. "Would you like to know where the water is?"

"Yes!" I said, a little more eagerly than I had intended. "I mean, if you don't mind. Sir."

"Haha, you're a funny one, Wren. Come, I'll show you the water, the food, and the hole. It will be nice to have company for a time."

"The hole?" I asked.

"Well, it might be a hole, or a cave, or a window. Not too sure. More importantly, all this talking has made me thirsty. Follow me."

And so I did.

THIRTY-EIGHT
LIGHT

Nassir was slow to move, but his clicking let me know I was following in the right direction at least.

We went down what might have been a shallow incline, and then we made a wide turn of some sort.

"Hold out your right hand and you can touch the wall there; we'll follow it to the water," Nassir said.

I nodded, realized that he couldn't see me, then answered, "Okay."

The rock wall was rough and bumpy. The texture had a lot of sharp points to it, and I had to be careful to touch it only lightly as we went along for fear of slicing a finger open.

I heard the water before we came to it. A slight trickle, the quietest of brooks bubbling somewhere ahead.

"I hear it!" I said excitedly.

"Do you see any light?" he asked.

I blinked. I did! It was barely a faded gray, hardly distinguishable from the dark around me, but assuming it wasn't my imagination, I could see just a touch of light coming from somewhere.

"I think so, barely," I answered.

"Ah, so I bet it's a window after all," Nassir hummed to himself.

We went further ahead, and I could smell the difference in the air. The gray even turned a shade lighter, and my heart sped up as we got closer and closer.

"I think it's melting snow from the outside. It's quite cold, and it only drips sometimes. I think that is when the sun is out," Nassir explained.

"That makes sense, I don't know where else water might come from and land in a cave like this." I nearly slipped on some loose gravel underfoot, but I caught myself and moved forward more carefully this time. "Nassir, do you have any kind of magic? I mean, earlier when I was meditating, I heard you in my head."

"I'd say you're the one who was in my head. I was minding my own business when you pushed up to me. You are the purple bird, yes?"

"Purple bird? I don't know, maybe? Are you the yellow fog?" I asked back, confused.

"Probably. I haven't meditated in quite some time. I doubt I look like much of anything anymore. We'll take a look at why you're leaking all over me in a minute, first let's get some water and I'll show you how to find lunch."

"Leaking?" I blinked in surprise. "I didn't think I was leaking anything. I hope you mean magic."

"Here we go, lean down here and have a taste." Nassir made a splashing sound, and I followed it eagerly.

Water.

I drank. I scooped it in my hands and couldn't bring it to my mouth fast enough. I drank until my belly hurt and threatened to spill it all back out, and then I drank a little more.

"Slow down, you'll be sick," Nassir said.

"I can't help it." I sighed, leaning back away from the water. "It's been days."

"Hmm, well, how about one of these? I bet you're hungry too."

He put something in my palm. I was afraid of what it might be: it was cool and had a slightly squishy texture with an unappetizingly moist surface.

"Uh, Nassir?"

"It's only a mushroom." He laughed. "Perfectly safe to eat, I assure you."

Relieved, I popped it into my mouth. Now that I knew what it was, the texture wasn't nearly as unappealing. It had a bland taste, but it would fill me up, and I was grateful for it.

"Along with the mushrooms that grow here, I sometimes find cave lichens and the occasional insect. Sometimes a rat is able to make it this far, but that is a rare treat." Nassir splashed a bit, presumably getting some water for himself, and I settled against a part of the wall.

"Thank you for bringing me here. I don't know how long I would have lasted if I kept sitting by the door." I pulled my knees up under my chin and wrapped my arms around my legs. "I don't think my friends can get to me, even if they knew where I was. I'm not sure what to do now."

"Not much *to* do," Nassir said. "Can't get out, can't call for help. Looks like you're stuck here, same as me."

I played with a part of the rough-textured wall as I leaned my head back.

"Until they drag me back out again, anyway." I sighed. "I wish I had my fire."

"Fire?" Nassir perked up. I thought. At least, he sounded more interested than he had since I'd met him.

"Yeah, I have fire magic, but I can't get it to work."

"Fire," he said in wonder. "Wren, go back to the place in your mind where you found me. I'll meet you there as soon as I can. I'm a little rusty, but I'll try my best."

"What? Why?" I asked.

"I can help you. Stars, what I wouldn't do for the feel of true warmth again after all this time. I'll help you, and you can warm us both up. Maybe we can roast a few of these mushrooms. I wonder if they would taste any better that way."

"You think you can help me?" I let myself get a little excited.

"Only if you meet me in your mind. I don't know how much training you've had, so I need in there to assess what we're working with."

"Right, okay." I sat up, taking the familiar position and closing my eyes.

I took in a deep breath and began.

One . . . two . . . three . . .

I pictured the little cabin in my mind.

One . . . two . . . three . . .

I found myself inside it as everything came into view.

It was just as I had left it. I stood in the center of the room, but as soon as I felt my breathing could stay steady and I could move around, I went out the door. Outside was the shapeless yellow mass that I now knew to be Nassir.

"Hello?" I called, and I found I could speak this time. It had come from my real mouth, but I could still stay in here if I concentrated.

"There you are. I see the problem. You need to shut your door. No wonder you're fraying all over," Nassir said.

"My door?" I turned my head to see the cabin still open. "I didn't think it mattered."

"Everything here matters. You can't leave your mind wide open: people you don't want inside can come in, and your essence can leak out."

"Oh," I said, turning back to close the door. "I didn't know."

"So, a cabin, eh?" Nassir's foggy shape floated closer. "Simple. I like it. Some of the young ones have the most eccentric tastes."

"You can see it?" I asked.

"Well, *I* can. But I'm old. I suppose if I'm going to do this again, I should start meditating." The form sighed. "So much for my small attempt at sabotage."

"Sabotage? Who could you sabotage by not meditating?" I asked. "I thought it was dangerous to not meditate."

"Hmm, it's irresponsible, but I'd happily give up whatever magical strength I have left if it meant sabotaging him. Come, sit down, and I'll see what you're doing with that fire," Nassir said.

"But who are you trying to hurt?" I asked again.

"I doubt it would be good if I told you, so I won't. Now, do you want to do this or not?" Nassir was getting impatient.

"Fine, fine, I'm sitting." I sat on the grass and focused on my breathing, and I felt Nassir settle in beside me.

"Good, you've got that down. Now, show me how you pull out your fire."

After a little focus, I felt the gentle weight and warmth of flame form in my hands.

"I got it!" I grinned.

"Ah, what a mess. All right, firstly, you're too calm. I'm surprised you managed to bring up anything at all. Fire is hot. It's passion and anger and rage and excitement. *That's* what you should use to bring it out."

"My *emotions*." I smacked my forehead, extinguishing the little fire. "Of course! Cosimo told me something like that once when Thain took me to the library."

Nassir sucked in a breath. "Thain? He lives?"

"Yes, you know him?" I blinked. I knew Thain was old, but I hadn't considered that another ancient being might know him from hundreds of years ago.

"Sort of. I know *of* him. He was a promising young warrior in the War of the Wyldes. Fierce, to say the least. I paid little attention to the gossip from outside of the Winter Court once things were settled, and never heard what became of him. I suppose it's nice to hear he has survived."

"Oh," was all I could manage to say.

"Ah, but nostalgia aside, try again with the fire. This time, bring it forward with passion. Energy," Nassir said.

Energy. I could do that. I thought. Most of my life had been a calm mask, no wonder my magic wasn't coming easily to me. Now it was time to try something new.

My nose twitched as I focused. My heartbeat quickened and my brows knit together in concentration. Emotions that might evoke the spirit of fire . . . I focused.

The first time I saw the Wyldes.

The exhilaration of felling my first tree.

Chasing rabbits down the hills.

Schula finding me struggling with Puko in the bath, revealing my seal and scaring me half to death.

"Good, much better," Nassir said.

My palm was *hot*, but it didn't burn me, and somehow, I knew it wasn't going to no matter how hot it got. The fire was bright, and tall, and . . . purple.

"Why isn't it red?" I asked.

"That is a good question," Nassir answered.

"You mean you don't know? What's wrong with it?" I asked.

"Presumably nothing. Although I'll admit I haven't seen anything like this before. *Oh*."

"Oh?" I was beginning to panic. "What does that mean?"

"Can I see your ears?" Nassir asked. "Not here, your real ears."

Panic and the bitter hint of sorrow filled my throat. "Okay."

The shapeless yellow fog looked at me curiously and then disappeared. My eyes opened to the dark cavern around us. I blinked several times before fully remembering I couldn't see. Then I looked roughly where it felt like Nassir might be sitting.

"Can I touch your ears?" Nassir asked. "It's the only way I can really see them."

"Yes," I said, pulling my hair out of the way. "Go ahead."

Nassir's fingers were cold, but they were also very gentle as he ran the calloused tips along the shape of my ears. I didn't know why I was so embarrassed by the act, other than the fact I hadn't gotten to see them yet myself since they'd grown, and the sensation of them even being there was truly bizarre.

"Well, this is an interesting surprise," Nassir said. "Wren, I think we need to start from the beginning, because I'm truly not sure how you came to exist. Please, tell me your story, I want to know it all."

"My . . . my whole life until now?" I asked. "There isn't a lot to tell. What's wrong with my ears?"

"I was there when they were exiled . . ." Nassir murmured. "I'll collect us some food. Why don't you start us a fire, now that you have the hang of it, and I'll explain everything after you tell me your tale."

"Okay," I agreed and tried to focus on my hands. Nassir shuffling around nearby was a distraction, and so were my mixed emotions, but I finally focused on the right energy, and a small flame came to life in my palm.

I was elated to see it was red. A normal, flickering, everyday red fire.

"I did it!" I called. Nassir's shape was coming into view. I finally got a look at my only companion in the darkness.

"Ah, I'm done too. Hold on." Nassir came close, and I studied him. His skin was pale but at one time might have been the same color as mine. His hands were scarred and calloused, and full of mushrooms and a greenish plant I didn't know. His hair was long, white, and unkempt down his back, and a beard fell from his chin to his chest in a similar fashion. It was his eyes that made me gasp, though. They were as white and blind as Puko's left eye. I knew DuVarick must have done it. This must be the extra measures he'd taken to ensure Nassir couldn't create more art. My shoulders shook with anger for a moment, but the flames flickered, and I had to concentrate to keep them up.

"Nassir, your eyes."

"Don't worry for me, it happened long ago, and I can get by perfectly fine without them. Being blind has not stopped me."

His words didn't make sense until he leaned down and gestured above us. I looked up and finally realized why the cave walls had such an unusual texture.

Nassir had done a lot more than a few marvelous carvings for the Winter Lands—he had carved the grand staircase, I was sure of it. Every inch of cavern wall around us, as far up as I could touch, was sculpted in beautiful scenery. Fae, creatures of the Wyldes, places I had never been to, plants I had never seen. Not one tiny portion of the wall was left uncarved.

"Nassir, you did it. The stairs." My voice shook as I stood, scattering flame along more and more of the wall. This place was huge, and he had carved all of it. Even now, with light to follow, it would probably take me an hour to walk back to the door, and he had carved it all. Blind, in the dark, forgotten and hungry and cold. Nassir had done it, not knowing if anyone would ever see it.

"Aye, it was me," he said simply.

"Why? Why would DuVarick cast you away? Just for your art? Just to never have you create like that again?" My voice wavered.

"I'll tell you what," Nassir offered, "if you give me your story, I'll give you mine."

"Deal." I nodded slowly, wiping my eyes free of any more tears.

"Good. If you can start from the beginning, I'll try not to stop you with too many questions. When you're done, I might just be able to tell you why DuVarick would put you in here."

"All right," I agreed. "From the beginning."

I took a deep breath and told him.

THIRTY-NINE
A FRIEND

I sat on the rocky ground of the cavern, holding two handfuls of fire and watching the light dance on the carved murals over us. I was sad to look at Nassir, imprisoned for so long. His form was thin, but not enough to frighten me for his safety. No thinner than myself most winters. But more nourishment would clearly do him good. Was this what Mama Flori had seen when she'd looked at me?

Nassir sat quietly while I gathered my thoughts, which I was grateful for.

"I suppose this story starts with me being found in the mountains by a wonderful human named Bryn."

And so I told Nassir about Bryn. Everything from his charms to his vices and how we went about our daily lives.

Then I told him about Mila. I covered my education with the witches. I talked about the villages, and our occasional trips to Sulls. I covered the uncomfortable memory of setting fire to Mila's roof when my seal was first released, and then he stopped me to talk more extensively about my seal.

"Do you still have it?" he asked.

"No, it's gone now. It was removed just before DuVarick's guards took me," I explained.

"Ah, and that clears up more of the puzzle. Do you know when exactly it was put on you?" Nassir asked.

"I had it when I was found," I said. "It was off briefly when I, um, when the fire happened, but it was put back quickly to seal my magic and stop the fire consuming me."

"Mmm. And this time, when it was removed for good, did you feel any different at the end?"

"At the end?" I thought about it. "I felt tired, I guess. Some things changed. I think I became more fae. My ears grew back, at least, and I feel a little disoriented, even now. It feels as though I'm not in my own body, and I'm still getting used to walking properly."

"By the Stars, that's what it was," Nassir mumbled. "Go on, go on. Tell me how you came to be in the Wyldes."

Then I told him about Thain. He snorted at the mention of the raiders that had burned Silver Lake and grumbled when the villagers didn't save me from drowning. He nodded approval for what Thain had done and listened intently when I described the little outpost I'd stayed at where I'd met Schula and Eberon.

I told him about my time in Thanantholl, the visit to Dwellonmar, and finally I told him about the magic training that had led me to the Winter Lands, where I'd been captured the moment my fire burned out.

I leaned over to drink my fill of water after all that talking. Nassir only sat quietly, contemplating my story.

I kept one hand free to hold fire. I could feel my resources depleting slowly, but I wasn't ready to give up my sight again just yet. I pulled some more mushrooms free and began roasting them for later while I waited.

Nassir took a piece of plant from the earlier pile and gnawed on it, not really eating it but moving the stem around in his mouth. A fidget, I guessed.

Finally, I couldn't take it anymore. "Did I say anything that might help you figure out why DuVarick would think I shouldn't exist?"

"Yes." He sighed. "Although I don't want to say until I'm sure of what you are."

"What I am?" I asked. "What am I? Am I not half fae?"

"Hmm." He paused. "Let me try to remember something a little longer. More importantly, little Wren, I don't think you are half of *either* thing you thought you were."

"What do you mean?" I asked, panic rising in my throat. "I'm not half fae? I'm not half *human*?"

"I don't think so, not quite," Nassir said. "But I can't place one of the scents on you. I know I've encountered it on a rare occasion before, but forgive my memory. It has been some time since I've encountered much more than this cavern."

I took a shaky breath. "How would no one have noticed before DuVarick and Asher that I was something other than half fae? How could I have gone until now and not had a clue?"

"The answer lies in your seal. It would seem it suppressed far more than just your magic. You didn't fully grow into your intended body until that seal was broken completely. You were so locked down under its influence that I'm sure freeing your magic was quite painful. I would assume you were so obscured by it that no one was able to detect your true nature. Surprising, really, that Baeleon or Diamid didn't scent it out. A very powerful witch must have sealed you."

The breath vanished from my chest. I stared down through the magical fire dancing in my palm. My hands were now free of a few small scars I had gotten over the years, and it was unnerving to see my skin so empty of them. My fingers even felt a hair longer.

"What else could I possibly be if not human?" I mumbled, then I gasped. "I'm not something horrid like that unseelie wraith creature, am I?"

"I don't think so, although I don't know what creature you speak of. But I'm growing more and more certain, with more and more dread in my belly, that I know one of your parents," Nassir said. "You have told me an important story, Wren. Now I'll tell you an important story, and after both our stories have been told, I think we can give each other some answers."

I didn't know what answers I could give him, but I burned the fire in my hand a little warmer, ready to settle in and hear his tale.

"A long time ago, when I knew the warmth of the sun on my face and the snow under my feet, I was the son of a farmer," Nassir began. "My father was forever butting heads with me over my carving. I would dig designs in our furniture, the windowsill, the doorframes. I would even draw designs in the dirt with rocks or sticks when I was supposed to be watching the goats. He never understood, and I never accepted the life of a farmer."

I gave a small smile. Bryn had done both, and he'd loved his life well. Woodcutting by day and carving by night. I wished Nassir and his father had considered that an option, rather than fighting over it.

"It went on like that for at least a century. I traveled a bit here and there. A few months in the Summer Lands. Too hot for me, but the flowers are beautiful. I spent time in many parts of the Wyldes, but I always came home. Anyway, my days were growing stagnant again, and my father and I'd had just about enough of each other, when I felt an odd sensation. A pull, as it were. Something in my bones ached, like they knew a storm was coming, but I wasn't afraid. If anything, I was excited. So once again, I left. This time, I had a direction and a feeling, and I made my way to Icehold."

Nassir coughed and leaned down to drink. He was probably going to need several water breaks. I doubted he'd spoken out loud to himself in the darkness, and his throat probably wasn't used to so many words at once.

"I arrived in Icehold, and it took no time at all to run into a young male with piercing blue eyes. I have forgotten much of what he looks like over the years, but I will never forget those eyes."

"DuVarick." I shivered. I had seen those eyes too. I wondered if they had always been so heartless.

Nassir gave a sad smile. "His father was already dead, and he was the new chosen ruler of the Winter Lands. The magic of the lands chooses who sits upon the throne, so this place must have seen something great in him at the time. A balancing of his father, perhaps, or none remaining within Icehold worthy enough to take the crown. His mother and uncle acted as regents until he came of suitable age, or so was their excuse. Personally, I can not believe you could be chosen to guide any corner of the Wyldes if not ready, but in grief and upheaval, DuVarick allowed it. You can imagine our surprise when we found ourselves running through the streets, searching for something but not knowing what, and bumping into our triquetram in the middle of Icehold."

I gasped. "You're his triquetram? And he imprisoned you?"

"Slow down now, I'm not to that part yet. We're still at the beginning, when we were young and optimistic, out to make a change in the Wyldes," Nassir said. "Now, before, when I said I doubt anyone knows I'm still alive? I'm not certain of that. I know that *I* can tell DuVarick is alive, but he has not desired to see me in years. I fear by now he is so consumed by his own lust for power that he has all but forgotten that a string of it is attached to me."

I ached for Nassir. Watching Schula and especially Eberon while Thain was off at the borders had been hard; I couldn't imagine being imprisoned by your own triquetram. It must have been heartbreaking.

"Years passed, and DuVarick was properly crowned. It was a ceremony for the show of it, as by that time everyone had fully accepted him as the ruler of these mountains, and they loved his power. His power was their power. Icehold was stronger under him than it had ever been, and it grew. The Winter fae had never accumulated in such mass before. Unlike the other courts, Winter was an isolated land. Pockets of fae would live where they could, but the mountains are harsh, and the unseelie creatures that live here are deadly. Under his aggressive push for advancement, Icehold hungrily carved itself from the mountains around it into a large city. It was a time for inventors and builders of tools to thrive. We used to spend a fortune to buy food from the other lands, but DuVarick demanded we find a way to farm crops and not just livestock. He demanded it, and his people found a way. He demanded strong buildings, innovations to improve daily life, and combat prowess. His army grew strong and went on regular hunts to cut back the unseelie in his lands. Yes, DuVarick was well loved. At least, for a time."

Nassir wheezed and drank deeply from the water again.

"Nassir, if you need to take a break, we can."

"No matter what wrongs he has committed, he is still my triquetram. My responsibility. And I'll have his story told. And mine."

"I understand," I said. "Please, I'm listening."

He nodded and continued. "It seemed only one person had much of a problem with how things were in Icehold under DuVarick, and that was his uncle. Power can be a difficult thing to give up, Wren, and his uncle took it hard. Omber the Wise, he was called. He never liked me.

From the beginning, he discouraged his nephew's association with the son of a farmer, but DuVarick wouldn't hear it. We were triquetram, and his power was stronger with our bond."

"So Omber had gone from regent of all the Winter Lands to, what, DuVarick's adviser?" I asked.

"Yes. DuVarick's mother had died under circumstances that never felt quite right to me. They said she died of an illness, but I never believed it. DuVarick took it hard, and over time his resistance to Omber's influence grew thin. Since DuVarick's rise to power, I had been given the chance to carve out the great entrance to the city. My every ambition was coming true. I was making my art, and my skills grew exponentially. I had a team of artists and builders at my disposal, and our sole job was to make Icehold as great as we could. Build new homes for the fae coming to live here. Display our skill and power with sculptures and murals wherever we could. It was everything I could have asked for." He paused for a moment. "Tell me, does he still surround himself with those shadows?" Nassir asked.

"You could see them?" I asked.

He nodded. "So very many people around him whispered influence into his ear. Evil, desperate, greedy things. The Wyldes are a land of magic, young one. What you whisper hard enough, long enough, can find a footing in our world. Unseelie things, forming from hate or greed. And so they still haunt him, do they?"

Nassir sounded so deeply sad. He sat still a while, letting so much time pass I wondered if he should be left to his private moment of reflection. This story had to be difficult to tell. He finally took a drink, then sighed and ran his fingers through his matted hair. "Omber's influence was strongest of all, and he eventually convinced DuVarick that I was a weakness. I still don't know how he did it. To convince someone that their triquetram would drag them down? Ludicrous. But with the pressures of rulership and the loss of his mother, I suppose DuVarick would grasp at anything to secure his position."

"And he had you thrown in here? Just like that?" I asked sadly.

"No, not right away. I suppose I should have kept a better eye on how he was doing. It's partly my fault that I didn't see it coming. We had both been kept so busy with our work that the time we spent together grew less and less. It began with canceling outings we had planned. Trips to view the far corners of the Winter Lands and secure the boundaries. I would find out later that he'd gone without me, and we would fight about it. Then it grew to state dinners. I was no longer at his side when emissaries from the other courts visited. It was like he was ashamed of me. I heard the whispers in the streets. It was odd that DuVarick would shun his only triquetram. I must have done something wrong. It couldn't have been DuVarick, everyone loved him. It must have been me."

I reached out and squeezed Nassir's hand. He gave me a smile and continued.

"Of course, it led to a fight. He accused me of being weak. He didn't know how such a powerful fae could be paired with someone like me. The Wyldes always put like fae together, not someone like him with someone like me. I couldn't take it. I left. I went back to the farm and spent some time with my father to cool off."

Nassir laughed, and it echoed around us.

"For once, we didn't fight. Father just let me watch the stupid goats and said nothing of my years away in Icehold. Eventually, I cooled off, and I went back to make amends. I just couldn't be apart from him any longer. My triquetram, a piece of my heart that lived and breathed outside of my body."

"And that's when it happened?" I asked.

"He could feel me coming, of course, and he had people waiting at the gate. At first, he would bring me out of here and talk with me on occasion. Let me see what was going on in Icehold without me. Then the visits became less and less frequent. Then there were none."

"That must have been terribly lonely. I'm so sorry, Nassir." I wiped my damp eyes and sniffed. "You think it was Omber?"

"Oh, I know it was Omber," Nassir said. "But DuVarick was too sick and too deep in his poisonous words to notice. I couldn't say anything to him, he wouldn't listen. In the end, he declared I was of better use to him nearby but out of sight. He could still reap the benefits of my powers, and none would be able to use me against him. So here I remained. Usually alone, occasionally with another prisoner, although I never bothered to speak with them since they came and went so quickly. That is, until someone came along that interested me in another way altogether."

"Who was it?" I breathed, leaning forward.

"It was our third. My sweetest Lark. My triquetram."

"Your triquetram is whole?" I asked, then an image of two hands on a marble throne crossed my mind. "The king wears two black rings."

Nassir snorted. "Of course he renounces me. I suppose I'm as good as dead to him anyway. But sadly, the other ring is true. I felt it, the day her light went out. Sweet Lark. A purple star in my endless night. I didn't eat for days after that. DuVarick didn't either, I suspect. He even came down to this doorway himself twice after it happened, but he never did come in."

"I'm sorry," I said. "I can't imagine how that must have been for you."

Nassir sighed and reached out for one of my hands. I held his hand with my empty one. He clutched it tight and brought it to his lips in a kiss that brushed my knuckles.

"I'm sorry too, Wren. Because I think Lark was your mother."

FORTY

LARK

My breath caught in my throat as Nassir said the words. My mother. He knew her.

"I knew it instantly. The first moment she stepped into the city, it was the same tug I'd felt to seek out DuVarick." Nassir leaned back with a smile, reminiscing. "She was full of energy. Stubborn too. Her aura was different, but that was to be expected. After all, she wasn't fae."

My heart thudded. I felt a pang at my mistaken identity for all these years, but if Nassir had the truth, I was going to find out.

"What was she then?" I asked. Patience wasn't one of my virtues.

"I hadn't encountered one of her kind in person, though from time to time they do wander into the Wyldes, seeking to share knowledge and attempting to form a mutual relationship. Not often after the war, of course, but from time to time. But we have a long, uncomfortable history with one another, and soon enough they leave," Nassir said. "Or are slain. One way or another, they do not stay for long."

The idealists. The ones who thought they could mend an old rift and gain knowledge for it.

"Lark was a witch." My voice shook. "But . . ."

Thain would hate me.

Thain would *hate* me. He had a personal history with that war. He had seen witches do awful things to his people.

They would all hate me.

Schula, she'd made a face right before she left me in the crater. I'd thought she was acting strange. She knew. She'd found out when she lifted my seal.

Oh Mother. Oh Stars. Did she hate me too?

"Wren, are you all right?" Nassir asked, reaching out for my hand again. "Stay calm, I will tell you everything. This does not mean you are hated here. Half of you is still of the Wyldes."

"What if this is how I survived the plague?" I whispered. "They'll think it was witchcraft that saved me. What if it was?"

"Wren, calm down," Nassir said firmly. "You can tell me about this plague later, but I assure you that as a baby you had no control over your powers. Lark was a righteous person, and she would not have her own child part of an evil plot. It was not your fault; it was not her fault. Just let me tell you what I know."

I took a breath. Then another. "All right, yes," I said. "Sorry, I'm fine. Go on, I want to know more."

Nassir paused until he was satisfied that I had calmed down, then he leaned back again and sighed. "Lark met DuVarick first, of course. I could feel them together. Thriving, getting more and more powerful."

"How is it that a witch could be triquetram with a fae?" I asked.

"It's uncommon, but it does happen. Your triquetram is almost always your equal in power, but that doesn't mean equal in race or status. It's as the Stars will it to be." Nassir shrugged.

"Okay, so your triquetram was whole, and that made you all stronger. Right?"

Nassir nodded. "I had long ago ceased to meditate. I thought if I was weaker, DuVarick could not benefit from my presence. But even in that low state, I felt the pulse of energy from them flowing into me. I could deny it no longer, I itched to meet her, and evidently the same was true for Lark."

"You met her? In here?" I asked.

"One day, when DuVarick was out on a diplomatic errand, she came down here. It took some time, but with the pull of our powers she eventually found her way to me. I was waiting at the door, and the moment she opened, it she flew into my arms, hugging me." He smiled sadly. "And that was that. As far as she was concerned, we were family. She stole away whenever DuVarick wasn't looking to come see me. She told me about herself, and I told her about me, though I don't like to talk about it; she was very good at prying the stories right out of me. Against my wishes, she begged DuVarick to free me. They argued often about it, but as you can see, DuVarick won in the end."

"That's awful," I said.

Nassir waved away my concerns. "DuVarick's mind is twisted far from what it once was. He has allowed it to become so tainted by his emotions and his uncle that there is no coming back from it. And those shadows do much to keep him out of touch with what he knows to be true."

"Then, what happened to Lark?" I asked.

"She disappeared. One night, she was simply gone. I felt DuVarick's rage. I was saddened, but glad she'd escaped his clutches. No matter how much he might have cared about her as his triquetram, he cared about his power more, and now she was a part of that. He was furious when she left."

"Why did she leave?" I asked.

"I never did find out," Nassir said. "But it was months after her disappearance that I felt her life fade. It nearly stopped my own heart, it was such a painful loss. I suppose I had always harbored hope of seeing her again, once more before her mortal lifespan ended. Even by a witch's standards, she was lost to us far too soon."

I sat quietly, not sure how to absorb it all.

My mother. A witch.

I was part witch.

Right?

"How can you be certain that I'm her daughter?" I asked.

"When you first arrived, I thought my mind was playing tricks on me. I thought you *were* Lark, come back to me after all this time. Your spirit is very similar to hers, your magic feels almost the same," Nassir said. "Perhaps a bit more of the Wyldes in you, but close enough to fool an old fool like me. My first thought was that witches simply had magic that felt that way, but as I observed you from a distance and realized you were not Lark, I could still feel the faint echoes of my triquetram coming from you.

You are also the right age to belong to her, and her death coincides with when you were left in the mountains. I had to piece it all together, but when you came at me in my mind, a purple bird of fire, I realized you had to be connected to my Lark. Your story simply confirmed a few things."

"You're sure?" I asked again.

"I am sure," he said. "And tell me this, Wren, how did DuVarick behave around you? He mentioned you look just like *her*, right?"

"Yes, he did," I answered.

"The only obsession I have felt from him in decades was when he was with Lark. I'm convinced, and I think he is as well. If anyone was going to recognize the offspring of Lark, it would be us."

"But why didn't you come forward when I first arrived?" I asked. "We could have figured all this out before now. I could have warmed us with my fire, and . . . and . . ."

"Ah, for that I am sorry. First I thought you were a trick of my mind, and then I thought you were a trick of DuVarick's to finally tip me into insanity," Nassir admitted.

"Oh." I let the fire fade from my palm with a sigh. It had drained a lot from me, as had Nassir's story. "I don't know what to do now."

"There isn't much to do but wait for DuVarick to come for you again."

"I suppose I should be a little closer to the entrance then."

"We can go that way. I will follow, but I won't get close enough to be seen when one of his men opens the door," Nassir said.

"Good idea." I stood up and brushed dust off my clothing. "With the light, it should only take me an hour to get back there, maybe less."

"Far less, I'm sure," Nassir offered. "I'll gather a few more plants to eat and be there with you after a while."

"Right, I'll go back in case they come for me again."

And think of a way to use this new information to get out of this mess.

The rest of the day, or morning, or whenever it was, went quietly. Nassir and I both had a lot to dwell on. We ate. Nassir appreciated the roasted food as he hadn't had such in a long time. I gave him the last bit of bread I had saved earlier when I didn't know where my next meal would come from. He savored it, and it pained me to think when his next bit of food would come that wasn't mushrooms or insects.

I thought a lot about Lark. About the kind of person Nassir said she was. One of her last desires was to free him. Could I do that? If I could find a way, I wanted to.

After a time, we decided to sleep. I was exhausted emotionally and physically, and I didn't have a problem drifting off on the hard ground.

The cool cavern chilled me as I slept. I didn't know how long I was out, but when a clicking sound disturbed me, I grumbled and rolled over.

"Shh, I'm still sleeping, Nassir."

Tap tap . . . tap tap.

My eyes flew open when I realized it wasn't Nassir's clicking but a new tapping sound that had bothered me.

I sat up in my cabin and instantly realized my body must still be asleep. I was alarmed but kept myself under control as I looked around.

There at the window was the tapping sound. A fat black bird with one milky white eye was trying to get my attention.

"Puko!"

I ran to the window, throwing it open and gathering him inside. "Puko, how are you here? Where are you really?"

He screeched in my ear and flapped clumsily over to a chair, where he perched on the arm closest to the fireplace, preening.

"But how are you here?" I sighed, frustrated.

Caw!

He puffed out his chest and took off, flapping back through the window. He settled just outside again and pecked at the windowsill.

CAW!

"What? I don't understand!" I pleaded.

Then I was snapped awake. Really awake.

A tendril of panic entwined my insides before I realized it was Nassir shaking me in the dark.

"Wren, Wren, are you okay? Was it a nightmare?"

"No, it was a bird I know." I sat up, lighting my palm and looking at his concerned face. "He was trying to tell me something."

"A bird?" Nassir asked.

"Window!" I shot to my feet. "Nassir, you called it a window. I need to get there."

"Slow down, the hole? Well, or window. Or whatever it is."

"Yes, yes, can you show me?"

"Of course I can, come on."

Nassir took me to where the water source was. It was painstakingly slow. While the light helped me to see where I was going, it did nothing for Nassir, so he still had to rely on his clicking tongue trick to get around.

My heart sped up when the cavern around us began to take shape. Light, more than just my little flickering palm flame, showed the walls around us as we went in further than the small spring. I hadn't been in this deep before.

"Does there still appear to be some light here?" Nassir asked.

"More than that, I think there really is a way outside! It must have been night when we were here before, because there is so much more light now," I said excitedly.

"Really?" Nassir grinned. "Quick, over here. Halfway up this wall there is a hole, see if you can tell what it is."

We rounded a corner, and sure enough, the light was coming through a hole barely bigger than my arm. I held on and climbed up the wall as well as I could, shoving my face to the hole.

"What is it? What do you see?" Nassir asked.

"Not much," I said. "There's some light, so I think we're must be at the outside of the mountain. The air is very cold here. But we must be under an overhang of sorts, because all I can see is rock."

I slid down the wall, and we both took in the news. It was a strange mix of hope that we could reach the outside air and despair that we could never get through it.

I sat on the ground next to Nassir and tried not to let the disappointment slip into my voice.

"Well, at least I know what that hole is now," Nassir said.

"Yeah," I said.

Tap tap.

"Did you say something?" I asked.

"No," Nassir said. "That was the hole."

We both tilted our heads to the hole, and then I heard it again.

Tap tap.

Carefully, I got up and climbed back up to the hole. I lifted my face to it, only to be rewarded with a hard peck on my nose. "Puko! Ouch."

There was enough light that I could see he had something in his beak. I reached out my hand to catch it. "What's this?"

Puko dropped a few strands of hair in my palm and pecked me in the forehead, cawing.

"Ouch, stop that!" I rubbed my head and looked closer at my palm. I lit my other hand to see better and gasped. Four strands of deep-blue hair had landed in my hand, and they could only belong to one person. "Thain."

"What is it? What's going on?" Nassir asked.

"I think I have a way to tell my friends where I am," I said, pulling a few strands of my own brown hair off my head. I handed them to Puko, who took them and nodded once before hopping up the hole and flying out of sight.

"How?" Nassir asked.

"Puko, my raven friend, just brought me a sign of Thain, and I just sent a sign back. With enough luck, they'll be able to find this place."

Nassir was silent, a stunned look on his face.

"Nassir?" I came back down and sat beside him. "Nassir, if anyone can get us out of here, it's Thain. We can get out. You'll be free."

"He'll never let me leave here," Nassir insisted.

"He won't have a choice." I pressed on. "Please, Nassir, my mother didn't get a chance to get you out of here, let me do what it was she wanted. Will you come with me? I don't know if the friends I've made will accept me now that I'm not what we thought I was. But I couldn't leave you behind. I want to know so much more about you, and Lark, and I want to show you where I'm from. I want to take you out of here. Please, Nassir."

He was quiet a moment longer as I held my breath. I knew he could hear my crazy heartbeat, but I let him think until he finally gave me an answer.

"Okay, if your friends come, we'll leave together."

And that was that. Suddenly, we both had a reason to hope.

FORTY-ONE
PATIENCE

It killed me to be alone with my thoughts.

Thain was alive. I hadn't been too worried, I knew how strong he was, but when he hadn't caught up to Schula and me, it had been unsettling. Surely Eberon was safely with him.

But I still worried that my newfound lineage would break apart my recently healed friendship with the blue fae. And what of Eberon? He seemed to care quite a bit about status; would this sway his view of me too? Schula. She probably already knew. I didn't know where she was, but I was so worried for her. I didn't like the way Asher and DuVarick had reacted to her, and all I could do was hope she was okay.

But despite all my worries, I was still hopeful. If anyone could find us, it would be Thain. I held on to that thought.

All the highs and lows I felt were tying my stomach into a knot. I tossed and turned as I tried to get some more sleep, but it never came.

Nassir was no better. He had remained quiet since our meeting with Puko. Whatever was running through his head took up all his concentration, and he barely said a word all night. Or day. Evening? And he didn't eat much either.

Both of us were wrecks.

And then, all too soon, I felt someone outside the door.

Lying on the cool ground, I clenched my jaw and waited to see who it was.

My chest tightened when Asher's familiar presence pushed against me.

The door opened, but the light didn't blind me quite as badly as it had before thanks to my fire. I was able to see him, wearing more relaxed clothes, similar to what DuVarick had worn previously but not as embellished.

He sneered down at me where I had been trying to sleep near the doorway. I reached out with my power to feel for Nassir, but he was already long gone.

"Come on," Asher growled and grabbed one of my braids to pull me up. I bit back a scream, and he hauled me over a shoulder and carried me away.

The moment I was out the door, it felt like I had been punched in the gut. The sudden urge to go somewhere nagged at me. It was probably the panic, but I needed to get away.

"Stop squirming or I'll take one of your thumbs," Asher said calmly as though he was commenting on nothing more interesting than the weather.

I sucked in a breath and obeyed, but it was hard. The restlessness only grew stronger the further we went.

Instead of dwelling on the uncomfortable sensation, I tried to memorize where we were going. The intricate hallways made that nearly impossible, though, and there was little variation on the walls that would make memorable landmarks. The same dusty portraits and gruesome battles were depicted on canvas after canvas as Asher hauled me to my fate.

Finally, we were back at the doorway to DuVarick's office, and as we entered the chamber, Asher dropped me on the carpet.

DuVarick stood at a bookshelf, reading something with his back to the room. He didn't look up as he ordered, "Leave us."

Asher didn't argue, he simply closed the door, and I felt his suffocating, aggressive aura leave.

The Winter King was dressed more regally today. He still had no shirt, but his chest was draped with gold, and his kilt was adorned with jewels. The crown atop his head had wicked points, reminding me of the mountains surrounding Icehold. The wisps behind him were still present, even more today than last time.

I stood, but I didn't dare say anything while DuVarick thumbed through the pages of a thick tome. He let the silence drag on while he studied the pages in front of him, until finally he closed the book and slipped it back on the shelf.

"We suppose you want to know what we're going to do with you," he said matter-of-factly.

I didn't answer, but my eyes grew wide. It was an answer I both dreaded and needed but wasn't expecting to get anytime soon.

"We've nearly decided, but first we have questions that you will answer."

I swallowed and nodded.

"Why would Schula be with you? What in the Wyldes possessed Baeleon to send *her* into *our* lands?" DuVarick asked.

"My friends brought me here for my magic. Schula is my friend," I said.

"So then where is the rest of your party?" DuVarick asked in a low tone.

"I don't know," I said. Thank the Stars and the Mother and any other being that might be listening that it was the truth, because I was certain I didn't want to tell him where to find Thain or Eberon.

"Crawling back to the Autumn Lands, no doubt," he scoffed. "In light of the newfound abomination, we have sent for envoys from each crown to come witness this year's winter solstice. It's going to be very entertaining. My advisers continue to moan, saying if we killed you now without the other courts present, we would start another war."

DuVarick rolled his eyes and waved a hand in the air, dismissing the idea. "Even if we did, it would be good for the fae. The ones only a few hundred years old don't know war. Regardless, we will do this publicly. You will be revealed for what you are, and then we will lead the charge to wipe your kind out. Starting with you."

"My kind?" I breathed. Was it witches, or was it whatever else I was?

"Yes, about time too. Should have chased the lot of you down years ago, just to make sure you never came back."

The madness in his eyes slipped through the cracks. He was hungry for violence. Some part of DuVarick wasn't right, just as Nassir had said. I decided to take a risk.

If he was going to kill me at the solstice anyway, I might as well try something.

"I thought you cared for Lark! How can you want to kill her child?" I cried.

"*What did you say?*" he hissed, rounding on me. His face was close enough for me to feel his hot breath on my nose.

"H-how could you—"

"DO NOT SPEAK HER NAME!" he roared, breathing hard as his stare pierced me with hatred. "She betrayed us! And then she died a coward's death, just to spite us. He saw it, he told me!"

I was terrified to move; his anger was a thick stew in the air, and it was hard to breathe. I could only imagine what Nassir's power must be to match such a fae. If I could get him out of here, would he thrive again? Would he be this ferocious? DuVarick's magic was so strong, and it grew stronger with his hatred.

And then something clicked. His obsession. His boiling anger.

"You loved her," I whispered.

DuVarick slapped me across the face so hard I tumbled from my feet and slid into the wall behind me. I clutched my stinging face and looked up in horror at his new rage.

I should not have said that.

"How dare you speak as if you know *anything* about our feelings for Lark," he seethed. "We gave her everything, and she threw it back in our face. And you're no different with your tricks. You had no idea who your mother was a few days ago, and here you are now, suddenly informed. That means that disgrace is still alive enough to talk."

My heart stopped. Nassir.

"Oh yes, we haven't forgotten about him. Whatever delicious fate we decide to end you with at the ball, he will meet the same end. And so will any other fae in my clutches that helped you or *her*."

Schula.

She'd definitely helped me, and she was definitely in his clutches.

No. I will not let you hurt my friends.

"Should we rip out your throat? Or maybe poison you at the start of the ball, and as our people dance around you, they can watch your slow, painful death. Or should we feed you to a pit of flesh hounds?" he asked.

When he still didn't get a response from me, he sighed and walked away. "Asher!"

I swallowed, and only a few heartbeats later Asher came through the door. "My king."

"Take her back, we are sick of looking at her," DuVarick said.

"Wait," I demanded. "Where is Schula? She didn't have anything to do with this, she doesn't know!"

"Quiet." Asher kicked me, knocking the air from my lungs as he swung me back over his shoulder.

DuVarick had resumed his place by the bookshelf, but he turned slightly toward me with a grin. "Don't worry, you'll see her at solstice."

DuVarick chuckled as Asher carried me away, and I screamed my hate for him and his king as Asher took me back through the halls.

Nassir was in trouble. Schula was in trouble. I still didn't know entirely what I was, and now I had only days at the most before DuVarick's promised gruesome death.

Tears were still slipping down my face, I still felt a tug to go somewhere, and I felt one more thing I rarely felt. Anger.

I had been through a wide array of emotions since coming to the Wyldes: fear, joy, frustration, and sadness. But this was a burning, horrible anger. The unfairness of it all. The threat to my friends. The threat to me. The disgrace to the memory of my mother. And now, Asher ready to throw me back into the darkness.

Like I had been told, my powers were connected to my emotions.

Asher carried me a little longer, until I finally saw the dimming of the light. We were near the entrance to the darkness. I reached out with my powers, trying to find Nassir. I couldn't sense him. No matter, I would find him soon enough.

I glanced at a suit of armor down the hall and decided it was time to stop waiting around for Thain and do something.

Bryn's girl wasn't about to go down without a fight.

As we passed the armor, I took one look at a decorative but not particularly useful axe and decided on a plan.

A poorly thrown together disaster of a plan.

The moment we were close, I shot my arm out and yanked the handle free of the armor. I surprised myself with how fast I could do it, but I recovered enough to twist in Asher's arm as he was beginning to react and perform the one trick I had up my sleeve that they weren't expecting.

My recovered magic.

I took a breath and smacked my hand and the fist with the axe handle in it to Asher's face. He dug his claws into my side, and I screamed, but I also let out everything I had. Burning, angry, boiling fire engulfed the hallway. We were so far from the rest of the palace I could only hope it would be a few minutes before help could arrive.

Asher roared as the fire ate him. The smell was awful. I flashed back to the shores of Silver Lake where the village had burned and the blackened flesh of the villagers hung in the air. But I didn't stop.

The struggle was horrible: even burning alive, Asher was much stronger than I was, but he was fighting blinded, and I was able to free a wrist and smash the axe as hard as I could into the meat of his neck where his shoulder ended and a fleshy muscle climbed up to meet his throat. It bit deeply, and the curdled roar he let out nearly made me throw up. Hells, I couldn't guarantee I wouldn't still lose my breakfast once the action was over.

But I jumped off the burning and blinded Asher, taking the axe with me and running the rest of the way into the darkness.

There was a lock on the barred door. I shoved the bar off and screamed for Nassir as I smashed the butt of the axe into the lock as hard as I could. It wasn't working. I tried to blast it with fire, but I didn't melt anything. But I must have softened it, because I was able to break it with the axe on the next try.

I threw open the door and ran in.

"Nassir!" I screamed. "We have to go!"

I reached for him again and felt him this time. Far in, close to the water. No, past the water. He was at the window.

I ran as fast as I could, using the little trickle of power I hadn't just burned away to light the path ahead. When I was close enough, I yelled again.

"Nassir! We have to leave, now!" I called.

"Wren?" he yelled back. "Wren, wait!"

"Wren?" another voice called.

I rounded the corner into the light. Much, much more light than there should have been for that tiny window.

And that was because there was no tiny window.

In the gaping hole of mountainside, with snow blowing in around him, stood Thain. He was panting, his eyes wild and unglamoured, covered in dirt from whatever he had done to enlarge that small window, but it was him. Nassir was with him, holding Puko.

"Thain." I slowed as I got close but didn't stop even with my voice hoarse from all the heat and smoke. "We need to go. There will be soldiers here any minute."

Thain's nose flared out as he scented me, what I was. He looked surprised, but thankfully he was saving his opinions for later. "You couldn't have waited for me?" he managed to say.

I let out a breathy laugh, and Puko flapped over to me, landing on my shoulder. "Sorry."

Thain pulled me into him, a fierce hug that I returned with all the strength I had left. Pressing my face into his chest, I focused on the smell of him, the feel of him. He was *really* here.

"Schula?" he asked.

"I don't know where she is," I said, my throat tightening. "But his plans for her will take place on the solstice, so we can come back with a plan."

Thain nodded.

"What happened out there?" Nassir asked. Thain pulled away, taking his shirt off and pulling it down over my head. It felt so good to be wearing something more than the wrappings around my chest and to keep a little bit of the biting cold off my skin.

"I fought," I explained. "Backup is going to come soon."

We heard faint shouting far behind me in the cavern, and I winced.

"You have no patience." Thain sighed. "Let's go."

And we stepped out into the mountains.

FORTY-TWO
SURVIVING WINTER

Thanks to Thain's wind, our tracks were thoroughly covered, no snowy footprints or scents left behind as we ran down into the tree line and away from the mountain. I was sure Nassir had questions. Hells, Thain had to have enough himself, but it wasn't safe yet, and they would have to wait.

As the sun dipped below the clouds and we arrived at the forest's edge, Thain slowed us down enough to talk.

"I don't think we can stop for the night yet," he said.

"I don't either." I heaved, looking at my companions. "Nassir, are you okay?"

"Yes," he said, moving his head around, hearing all the strange noises of the Winter Lands around us for the first time in so long. His body couldn't keep up with us, having been misused and malnourished, but Thain had already pulled him onto his back.

"I think we should go south. Surely, they will be looking for us at the borders to the other lands of the Wyldes," I said.

"The human lands?" Thain asked.

I bit my lip and nodded. "Yes, take me back where you found me; head southwest toward Silver Lake. When we get close, I'll steer us to Mila's cabin. They might find us at your outpost, but they won't find us at Mila's, and it's covered in protection. Nassir will be hidden there." The southern border of the Winter Lands ran up against the wards to the mountains I'd called home with Bryn. Granted, we would have a few days to go, but with my newly transformed body and Thain's infallible strength, we would make better time than I would have before.

We didn't stop that night. Thain ran us through the open fields as much as he could, not through the trees where the flesh hounds and whatever else lurked just out of sight lived.

By the time the sun was over the tops of the mountains now far behind us, I was exhausted. Thain was no better, and Nassir was worn out, even though all he had done was hold on to Thain's back.

"I can nearly scent the wards from here," Thain said after slowing his pace a bit.

I caught up with him, winded, and raised my nose to the air. "That spicy scent? So does that mean we're nearly out of the Winter Lands?"

Thain nodded. "How far do you think your destination is from here? Silver Lake is nearly due south from us right now."

"Probably one long day. Do you think it's safe to stop?" I asked.

"He's out of range, I can't feel him," Nassir added.

"He who?" Thain asked.

"I'll explain when we stop." I sighed. "But I promise it's a good thing. Can you get us somewhere just on the other side of the wards to rest?"

"Yes, follow me." Thain took off again, and I grunted as I struggled to reach his pace once more.

I followed him through trees and over the rocky landscape until we came across the wards. I *felt* them. They crackled on my skin as we passed a line on the ground. The cold suddenly stopped, or at least it eased up, and the ground softened underfoot with a familiar dusting of pine needles and frosty leaves.

I sighed, releasing my muscles for the first time in so long. It felt different from the Winter Lands behind us. We were finally out of DuVarick's realm.

Thain walked us further until we came to a branch of stream trickling down the slope. There were trees overhead and a soft mound of root moss to lie on. It was perfect.

I sank to the ground with a sigh, tearing off my boots and shoving my feet into the icy water. Thain set Nassir on a comfortable patch of moss and helped him drink from the stream as well. Then the quiet, dark fae got up and began to collect firewood. I had shoved the axe in the band of my trousers when we began running, and now I pulled it out. The head of it was dull and decorative. A good blunt object in my time of need, but it didn't look like it would ever be truly useful as an axe. I set it aside and stood to help Thain find wood.

"I have the fire, you go find something to eat," he said gently. "Then, I want to hear everything."

A small pit of sorrow sank in my belly at the prospect of revealing everything to Thain, but I pushed it aside and wandered off to find food.

There were a few small fish in the stream, lean from winter and not worth the effort of getting them. I moved on and found some chestnuts that hadn't been picked clean by the squirrels, and I took all of them I could easily get. If I'd had my bow or traps, I could have tried to find an animal, but I didn't dwell on what I didn't have. I also found the tops of a few winter carrots. I yanked them out of the ground to find most already eaten from underneath, but a couple of them had survived. I brought my measly findings back to Thain and Nassir and sat down in front of Thain's pile of wood.

Thain was trying to light the kindling. I brushed my hand across a branch without much thought and lit the pile with a warm, dancing flame. Thain stared at me for a moment, then he sat back against a tree and let his body relax.

"New trick?" he asked.

"Yeah." I sighed. "Sorry I couldn't find more than this to eat."

"Tell me what happened, and when we're done here, I'll go find more," Thain said.

I took a shaky breath and grabbed a chestnut to shell. It was something for my hands to fidget with while I talked. Nassir, who had been mostly silent, reached a hand over and placed it on mine.

Thain let out a soft growl then stopped himself abruptly as Puko landed on his shoulder, surprising him with the rare attention.

Nassir just laughed. "I see some things haven't changed since I've been away."

He squeezed my hand in a reassuring gesture, then felt the ground until he found one of the winter carrots. He absently rinsed it in the water nearby. "I think more would be explained if I told my tale first."

My eyebrows shot up in surprise. "Nassir, are you sure?"

"I am." He nodded. "And I think, if this is the Thain of whom I heard tales from the battle of the two cliffs, he will be clever enough to put the rest together without you having to say a word."

Thain's serious look didn't budge from his face, but he leaned back slightly, relaxing his clenched jaw, and seemed ready to listen.

And so, Nassir spoke.

It was the same tale I'd heard from him, but Thain listened without interruption, unlike me who had stopped Nassir with questions.

He seemed unsurprised about the revelation of DuVarick's mental state. He knew who Omber was. He even accepted the notion that Nassir was DuVarick's long-lost triquetram.

Lark, however, brought a different reaction. The occasional witch attempting to make contact in the Wyldes wasn't unusual, but as soon as Nassir said she'd been allowed into Icehold, Thain stopped him for his first questions. When Nassir said she was the remainder of their triquetram, Thain was shocked but stayed quiet for the rest of the tale. And then for the timeline that Nassir gave, and his suspicions of my lineage.

I stared down at the pile of chestnuts I had accumulated and placed half of them in front of Nassir. It made me just as sad and uncomfortable to hear as it had the first time. But I felt in my bones that it was the right answer. My mother. Lark.

"Truthfully, I thought she *was* Lark when I first felt her in the darkness. I thought my mind was playing tricks on me," Nassir said.

"You're sure?" Thain asked, now looking at me as I stared uncomfortably down at my pile of chestnut shells.

"Tell me, Thain, after all this time, have you found any of your triquetram?" Nassir asked, tilting his head to the dark fae.

"I have," Thain answered.

"Then you know. You will always know. You will forever feel the echoes of them. Their offspring, their essence lingering in a place like their home or on their clothes. Even if they leave you, you will always know," Nassir said simply. "And I know that this child is Lark's."

Thain seemed to accept it, then he turned to me. "You didn't know any of this, did you?"

"No," I said quietly.

"I'm sorry, that must have been a shock." Thain leaned back, disturbing Puko, who flapped over to sit on my knee instead.

"So, what do we do now? I think I can take Nassir to Mila's cabin. You should go, though. Won't being caught with a witch get you in trouble?" I asked. "And what of Eberon? Where is he?"

Thain sighed and ran a hand through his hair. "Eb is in Thananthol. I sent him back to report to Baeleon the moment you and Schula were taken. I was still recovering from my fight with . . . from a fight. And I wasn't in any condition to take on Asher. So Eberon went back, and I followed you as closely as I could. It doesn't matter what you are. Even if Baeleon thought you deceived him, he'll come around. I've known him for a long time; he'll get over it."

"But I shouldn't go back to Thanantholl for a while," I said sadly.

"No," Thain agreed. "Not yet, anyway. Not until we sort this mess out."

"We have to help Schula," I sobbed. "DuVarick hates her for some reason. And I think he's going to hurt her, and I think it's going to happen at the solstice."

"What makes you say that?" Thain growled.

I told him about the encounter with DuVarick that had led to our escape. Nassir and Thain both listened, as this was new information to them both. The threat to me, Nassir, and Schula, and the realization that DuVarick loved Lark. Thain hissed at that.

"That's taboo," he growled.

"Loving a witch?" I asked.

"Loving your triquetram," Nassir said. "Even after all this time, that hasn't changed."

"It can't change," Thain rumbled. "Your triquetram must always remain in balance; if two portions of your triquetram are lovers, it will tilt off-center. There are roles to be played by each person, and you can't fight the will of the Wyldes that gave them to you."

"Roles?" I asked. This was the most anyone had told me of a triquetram, and I wanted to understand it better.

"One to protect, that would be me," Thain said. "One to keep the balance, that would be Schula at this time. Her job is to keep us in line if we break rules, keep us going forward. And Eberon is the peacemaker. Sort of. Our diplomat."

"Oh." I realized his triquetram was already off-balance, thanks to his lost third member. They did the best they could, but it wasn't the same. It would never be the same again, and that was heartbreaking. I leaned back against a tree and fiddled with the decorative axe, running my finger along an ornate carved design.

"Do you think Wren could have a triquetram out there with what she is?" Thain asked Nassir softly.

"It's hard to say, and I can't quite place her second half, but it's not fae," Nassir answered.

"I agree. It's definitely of the Wyldes, though. The mix of witch in there is making it hard to place," Thain said.

"Thain, I'll keep the fire up. If we want any more food tonight, I think you should go find it," I said.

He gave me a soft look and nodded. "Right, of course. I'll be back shortly."

I let him get well out of earshot before I whispered to Nassir, "I know I brought you out here, but I don't want to cause you or Thain trouble because of what I am. I'm sorry."

"Don't be, my dear. I am thankful to breathe the fresh air again. The food is a pleasure I had all but forgotten. The company of others, especially Lark's daughter, is so precious to me. Never tell me again you are sorry for taking me with you."

Tears threatened to spill, and I furiously wiped my arm across my face before that could happen. "Nassir, I think we should go somewhere and hide out. I don't want my presence to hurt Thain, or anyone else. I need to get you set up in Mila's cabin, and then I need to go back for Schula. DuVarick is going to kill her on the solstice, I just know it. I need to get her out. And if she never wants to see me again, I'll understand. But this is all my fault, and I need to fix it."

By the time I was done with my rant, tears were dripping off my chin, and Nassir had me wrapped in his arms while I sobbed.

"Shh, it's all right. I wouldn't discount your friends so easily. I'm sure we can come up with a plan to get her out of there."

"Wren," Thain said, and I gasped at his silent return. How much had he heard?

He kneeled in front of me, and Nassir made room for him to place a big hand on each of my shoulders. When I tilted my head up to look at him, his face was determined. "I promise you we *will* get Schula back. I don't want any more talk of running off on your own, do you understand?"

I nodded and wiped away another round of tears.

"Good, now let's get some sleep, get to the cabin, and come up with a plan."

FORTY-THREE
MILA'S CABIN

We woke before dawn and made our way to Mila's cabin. As we grew closer to the parts of the mountains that were familiar to me, my heart ached. With grief. With homesickness.

The smell of Mila's herb garden stung my nose long before I saw the wooden building. She had always grown strange things that weren't meant to go into the cookpot, and as a child I had been afraid to set foot in her garden. Now it was the thing that comforted me as we grew close.

Puko was restless, no doubt sensing how close we were to his old home.

A dusting of snow covered everything within sight. Thain let me lead the way as we came up the dirt path and I opened the door.

The inside was empty of life. The shelves that usually overflowed with jars of herbs and solutions were nearly empty, only scraps and a few empty containers remaining. Her books were gone, her furniture was dusty, and her wardrobe was open and bare. I was a little surprised to see that none of the mountain people had tried to take any of the good furniture, or at least the empty jars on the shelves, but maybe they were still too afraid to steal from a witch.

"What is this place?" Nassir frowned, moving his head around the room as he took in the strange smells.

"The abandoned home of Mila the witch," I answered. "And before you say anything, she was my friend. And I wonder if she was my mother's friend too."

I had begun to suspect Mila might have answers I sought, but that would mean that she'd kept those answers from me for all these years, and I couldn't bear that truth. Not yet. I pushed the thoughts away and picked up the broom she always kept by the door. I used it to brush off as much dust as I could from the chairs, table, and bed.

"Nassir, I'm sure you're tired. Can I show you to the bed to sit while we discuss our next move?" I asked.

"I will sit wherever you put me," he answered. "I am at your mercy."

"Here," Thain said as he helped Nassir find the mattress. His eyes widened as he sat on a soft bed for the first time in hundreds of years. Sorrow clenched a fist around my heart for him, then anger for what DuVarick had done.

"All right." Thain sighed, taking a seat at the wooden table and looking a bit uncomfortable in his new surroundings. "If DuVarick is really going to harm Schula at the solstice, he's going to do it publicly. There's something about Schula that you don't know. I wasn't going to say anything—Eberon and I were going to let her tell you in her own time—but I think at this point you need to know."

I took the other seat at the table and asked apprehensively, "What is it?"

"Schula is from the Winter Court," Thain started. "And she has a complicated history with DuVarick."

"What does that mean?" I asked, nervously playing with the end of a braid.

"I don't even know where to begin. I'm not sure the humans in this part of the world have this concept. Do you know of any rulers who keep many lovers for their bed?" Thain was trying to explain and was clearly a little uncomfortable with the subject.

"No, how do you have more than one lover?" I asked.

"You could consider them like the courtiers you saw in Baeleon's presence. There to bask in the edges of his power, mingling with other influential or useful courtesans. In Icehold, members of prominent families sometimes send daughters to accrue power for their families in the bedroom." Thain sighed and ran his fingers through his hair. "Stars, this is hard."

"Schula wasn't one of those, was she?" I asked, panic seeping into my voice. "DuVarick doesn't have those, does he?"

"No, no." Thain growled in frustration. "I wish Eberon were here for this. Schula wasn't one of DuVarick's lovers, but she was the daughter of one. Do you understand?"

"DuVarick has a daughter?" Nassir hissed.

"What?" I whispered.

Thain leaned forward, elbows on the table as he rubbed his temples. "DuVarick kept many courtesans in his quarters, daughters given to him as gifts from the noble families of Icehold mostly, in order to produce offspring. There would be no stronger connection to the king than that. With conception being so difficult for the fae, there is no guarantee that a monogamous relationship will grant you offspring. Even if it did, you could wait centuries for it. The practice has been around since the courts began; it's not a new concept to the Wyldes, even if it's not often used anymore. When DuVarick began collecting courtesans, no one batted an eye."

"So why would he hate Schula so much?" I asked.

"Her mother was particularly beautiful. She was smart and had a lovely singing voice. Many others in the court coveted her, so DuVarick began hiding his women away. They weren't allowed to be seen by anyone but him and his advisers. Most called them the frost flowers. A garden for only DuVarick to enjoy. When Schula's mother fell pregnant, DuVarick was suspicious that the child wouldn't be his. There was jealousy among the frost flowers, as you can imagine, and plenty of nasty stories circled Icehold about her. DuVarick treated her miserably until the birth, half-believing the whispers in his court, and when Schula came out looking just like her mother with little discernible likeness to DuVarick, he killed her."

Nassir and I gasped at the same time.

"How could he?" I cried, trying to imagine them side by side. "They had multiple similarities, didn't they?"

Thain shook his head. "As many similarities as much of the Winter Court would have with one another. Their eyes were both blue but different shades. The skin was pale on both of them, but Schula does not have his blue tinting and neither did her mother. He was looking for a clear sign the child was his and apparently did not find one."

Nassir growled. "He's not who I once called friend. He hasn't been for a very long time."

"So, is Schula his child or not?" I asked.

"We can't really say. And with the only fae who would know the truth now dead, there will never be a way to know for sure. At any rate, no one stepped forward to claim Schula, since that would be a death sentence. Not even her mother's family. Instead, just in case she showed signs of being DuVarick's blood, she was kept in the inner holdings with the rest of the frost flowers."

"But she could have been his heir!" I said.

Thain shrugged. "We don't have heirs, not in the way you're thinking. But she would have been a blood connection to the king, and that's why the families had sent their daughters to him. Schula grew up under scrutiny, never able to please him and never able to fit in with the flowers because of who she might be. One day, when she had truly displeased him, she ran off rather than face whatever punishment he had for her. I can't remember what she had even done anymore. But she ran. She explored the rest of the Wyldes, then she came to Thanantholl, and she found us. There was no returning after that. She broke her bond with the Winter Lands and joined us in Autumn."

"What did DuVarick do?" Nassir said, his voice low and angry.

Thain grimaced and scratched his jaw. "Banned her from Icehold."

My chest tightened. "But she came back because of me. And we weren't even in Icehold when Asher dragged her back. It wasn't her fault!"

"It doesn't matter," Thain said. "You have to understand the Wyldes: it doesn't matter what circumstances got you into a situation, it's up to your strength to get yourself out. What you've seen so far may have seemed peaceful, but we have a long and bloody history with no room for the weak in it."

"No." I pulled my knees to my chest, resting my feet on the chair where I sat. "So how do we get her out of there?"

Nassir shifted on the bed, fidgeting to get comfortable. "Thain, is the solstice still a ball?"

"I think so," he said. "But we should try to get to her before the solstice."

"I would agree with you, but if I know DuVarick, he has eyes on her at all times. Our best bet is when she's in motion between her prison and the ball. Is it still a masquerade ball?" Nassir asked.

"I wouldn't know," Thain said. "Even with masks on, Wren and certainly you would be recognized right away."

"Not as servants we wouldn't be," Nassir said. "The servants would always wear identical masks, and the uniforms are all the same. Or they used to be. We could go all over Icehold as servants, and as long as we stayed out of the ballroom, we should be strong enough to conceal ourselves from DuVarick."

"Hmm." Thain looked out the window into the frosted herb garden. He was quiet for a long time. "Wren, maybe, but not you. He would feel you."

I stared anxiously at Nassir. I already felt close to him, and I didn't want to hurt him when he'd just gotten his freedom, but surely him coming with us would be a burden, and his information was centuries old.

"I think we need to do a little spying first." Thain finally spoke.

"How long do we have?" I asked anxiously.

"Five days, which is why we need to move fast," he answered.

"Do you have anyone in mind that could help?" I asked.

"Yes," Thain and Nassir said simultaneously.

I blinked in surprise. "Both of you?"

"Eberon or one of his people could do it easily," Thain said, giving Nassir the same concerned look I was.

"If they survived this long, my family will help us," Nassir said confidently. "If not my father, one of my siblings or their children."

I had an idea too, but I wasn't ready to tell Thain just yet. And I certainly wouldn't tell Schula, provided we got her out. No, we *would* get her out. It was just a matter of how.

"Why don't you both try?" I suggested. "Surely more eyes would be better? We can find out what the ball will be like and maybe find out where Schula is being held."

"It's been so long," Nassir said. "If only I could get a letter to them.

I could try to reach them through meditation, but I'm so out of practice I don't know if I can."

"I can reach Eberon within a day if I go alone," Thain said. "If we do this, I have to go quickly."

"Do it," I said. "And Nassir, try to meditate. It would be good for you anyway. You're a free fae now, and you should build your strength. If you can't reach your family this way, we'll try something else."

"Will you be all right?" Thain asked, concerned.

I laughed and gestured out the window. "I'll be better than you realize. These are my mountains. I know them like the back of my hand, and I can take care of us until you get back. Go."

He nodded and left, not once looking back. When he was finally out of sight, I turned to Nassir, only to find he was already breathing evenly and trying to meditate.

I left quietly and decided to rummage through the garden for whatever I might be able to find that was edible.

The rest of the day I spent finding wood and gathering food. I even checked my old trapping spots that weren't too far away and was able to save a few of my old ropes and tools. I set them up closer to Mila's cabin and hoped for meat for breakfast.

I came back in the evening and began a stew for us. Mila hadn't taken her cooking pot; it was probably too heavy, and she wouldn't need it wherever she had gone with her coven.

After dinner, I shared a few mountain songs with Nassir. It was clear he was tired from trying so hard to meditate. He fell asleep on the bed after a while, and I searched the cabin for more supplies.

It wasn't until I came across a single sheet of paper that my earlier idea began to take real form.

I scrambled in the fading light to find something to write with. I grabbed some charcoal from the fireplace and carefully formed the letters I was looking for.

As the last rays of light left us, I folded the paper carefully and approached Puko in his window perch.

"Puko," I whispered. "Puko, do you think you can deliver a letter?"

I had seen him do it for Mila before, but I wasn't sure how she got him to agree to it.

He looked me in the eye with a soft caw and snatched the letter from my hand.

"Hey!" I hissed as he flapped around in the window and turned to face me. It was as though he was waiting for something.

I stared wide-eyed at him when I realized he was waiting for the recipient. Someone who would have a reason to enter DuVarick's court. Someone it might be useful to know inside the palace. Better yet, someone who might already be there now.

The thing about odd birds like yours, they can find their feathers again if you have need of me.

"Krissaph," I whispered.

And Puko flew away.

FORTY-FOUR
WITCHLIGHTS

Nassir slept, and I meditated.

The cabin was cold, but I'd found an old blanket for Nassir to use. He was clearly worn out from his efforts to build up his magic. As he slept, I decided a walk would warm me up. I had been meaning to see the fate of my old home, since we were so close to it. I just had to see it once more.

I used a tiny amount of my fire to keep warm as I trekked along the familiar path home.

The walk was quiet and eerie in the faint moonlight, but there wasn't anything here to be afraid of, not after what I had seen in the Wyldes.

My heart was hammering in my chest by the time I reached the bend that would reveal Bryn's cabin. I wasn't sure whether I wanted to see the cabin gone or for it to have remained untouched as the day I'd left it.

Hints of a solid structure peeked through the bare winter trees as I drew close. I bit my lower lip and held my breath as I rounded the last copse of pines to reveal a blackened husk.

I stopped in my tracks. "No." It had been burned, but not fully. I examined the remnants of the building that remained while I still had the courage to look at it. The ground had the signs of many feet on it, and the door had been splintered open.

I walked inside and looked up. The loft was gone, and where the roof should have been was just open sky. Anything of value that I hadn't taken with me was gone. Our large cooking kettle, the furniture, the chest of extra bedding.

The fireplace remained mostly intact. The lower halves of all the walls did too, as though rain or snow had come through and put an end to the fire before the cabin was entirely gone. It looked like a lightning strike got the cabin after the villagers had already taken anything of value.

I felt something uneven under my boot, and when I lifted it, I found a charred lump that had once been a carving of a bear. I closed my eyes and took a shaky breath, moving on.

The cabin had little left to it, so I went back outside and decided to walk the outside perimeter instead.

I found more footprints, and the scrape of claws where a dog had run through the earth. But when I went around to the back side, near the fireplace, my heart sank.

There, a flat river stone had been placed over blackened earth, and I knew it was for Bryn. This burning was older than the cabin fire, and I approached the stone, which had a crudely carved axe on it. Smaller stones were scattered around it in respect. They must have brought him here for his burning separately.

That was when the tears started. It wasn't the loud sobbing I had done the day he died but a flow of silent tears that fell down my cheeks and dripped off my chin. No matter what the humans around here thought of me, they'd loved Bryn.

I looked around for a tribute for Bryn on the ground. Usually, you would leave a precious rock, or a gem if you could afford it. Since I had neither in my possession, I had to settle for an interesting brown rock. I gave it a kiss and placed it under the edge of the larger stone.

I walked away, feeling this place lift off my shoulders. Any remaining connection I'd had to these mountains was now gone for good.

I wiped my face and sighed, turning back the way I'd come. I rounded the remains of the cabin and left the clearing. I was numb to the cold, and since this would be my last trip through this part of the mountains, I decided to take the longer, winding path back to Mila's. I walked past the stream I'd once bathed in. The last patch of oak Bryn and I had started clearing. My feet wandered without thought, and I found myself in the spot Bryn had found me. Many times he had brought me here, and many others I had come to sit and think by myself. I sat again now, looking for the same peace it used to offer.

Did Mila know Lark? Did she know Lark was my mother? How did she not sense I was part witch? Or maybe she did, but she never told me for some reason.

Maybe I could try to find Mila after all this was over. Maybe I should just leave the Wyldes for good. I could take Schula, and we could get far, far away from DuVarick and the Winter Lands and everything else.

Shifting, I faced in the direction of Silver Lake, if the forest wasn't in the way.

Then I saw it.

It was a curious stone. It was carved with a number of strange symbols, and it was half buried in the soil.

And it glowed a soft purple.

Witch magic. Mila?

I snatched it from the ground and sat up wide-eyed as it glowed brighter and then—

I was standing on the cliff, my arms outstretched as I enjoyed the breeze. The sun was high overhead, and my black dress billowed around my legs. A cawing bird overhead drew my attention, and I looked up to see a sleek black raven gliding in lazy circles above me. He circled down and landed on one of my outstretched arms.

"Puko! Welcome back," a voice that wasn't mine said.

The light flashed again.

I inspected the sapphire bracelet on my wrist, watching as the little stones caught the candlelight. It brought me both joy and sorrow to look at. I was in a tavern, sitting in a dark corner with a very handsome figure on the other side of the table. He had a cloak drawn over most of his face, but his smile was enough to melt hearts.

"Lark, my love," he murmured. "Come back with me to Eidelhein. I wish I had never let you leave in the first place. Surely the Mother never meant you to have this heartbreak. We can go back and build that greenhouse you wanted and forget this ever happened."

I sighed and played absently with my wineglass. "I can't just leave Nassir like that. There must be a way to get him out of there."

"You barely got out yourself," the figure whispered. "Please, I don't know what I'd do if anything happened to you. We can get you back safely, and I'll come with a few warriors to get him out. We can bring him back to live with us; we can treat his eyes."

I looked down and rubbed the growing bud that was my stomach. The warm thought of our future brought a smile to my face.

"All right, my love. If you promise to come back for Nassir, I promise to come to Eidelhein. And there is something else I think we need to discuss . . ."

The light flashed a third time.

Weak from the sickness, I handed my sleeping baby to a dark, scarred man with concern in his eyes. I sat resting on the forest floor under my favorite tree.

"I can't go back without you, Lark," he said. "I will wait for you."

"Do as I said!" I cried out desperately. "Do not wait for me. The Mother calls me to her, but I have one last task before I can go. Lay her gently where I told you and play the whistle. If I can give her nothing else, I can let them know her name. They will come, and they will call her Wren."

"I will not leave you!" the man commanded. "Enough have died on this quest. I will not lose you as well."

My voice strained and my face wet, I reached out a hand and pushed the man's chest. "You will have no choice, my friend. I'm sorry."

A flash of heat and purple light moved through my fingers. The man stood, his motions stiff even as he carried the baby.

"No. Lark, no!" he cried.

"And you will not speak of this to anyone." My voice shook. "None will know until the traitor is found."

"Lark!" the man pleaded, but another flash of light overtook my vision.

The man steeled his face and nodded before turning away. I watched him go, then I turned to Puko.

"I'm sorry, old friend. Please find Mila; she will take care of you." I removed a small scroll from my pocket with labored breath and shaking

hands. "This will tell her what to do and shield them both from what has come to be. Fly swiftly, fly safely."

I kissed his beak, and he nodded once, taking off in the dawn sky.

Feeling a smile on my lips, I picked up a stone from the ground and squeezed it as more purple light flickered out of me. "If you know these mountains in your life, I hope you one day find this, my Wren. When the seal is gone and you are safe, I hope you will be able to see this. South, you'll find . . . them . . ."

The light faded, and I stumbled backward on the hard earth, barely catching myself before I fell. I sucked in a sharp breath and stared at the now lifeless stone in my palm.

Was that Lark?

I tucked the rock into the top of my boot and ran for Mila's cabin. There was a reason Lark had wanted me to see this, and I hoped Nassir might have some answers.

FORTY-FIVE

ANOTHER PIECE OF THE PUZZLE

By the time I reached Mila's cabin again, the sun was starting to rise, and Nassir was wide awake.

He sat on the floor in front of the fire, meditating. I startled him when I came in.

"Sorry, how long have you been up? Do you need anything?" I asked.

"I just got up," he said. "Don't worry about me. See? I found the wood."

Indeed, he had knocked over a portion of the wood I had brought in and set next to the fireplace. He seemed to have gotten some of it in the fire too, and the flames that had burned low overnight were now full of life and dancing on the logs.

I smiled at how quickly he'd adapted to the new surroundings, then I tugged the stone from my boot. "Nassir, I'm going to hand you something. Do you think you could tell me if you've encountered it before?"

"Hmm, let's find out." He reached out and let me place the stone in his palm, then he went rigid.

I was afraid something had happened to him. His face was in shock, and he didn't move for several heartbeats. I knelt beside him and whispered, "Nassir?"

He didn't react. I sat back on my heels and bit my lower lip, wondering what my next move should be, when suddenly he gasped and fell backward.

"Nassir!" I rushed to help him back to a sitting position, then I grabbed a cup and filled it from a bucket of water I had gathered the previous night. "Here, drink something."

He nodded, still catching his breath, and held out a hand for me to help him find the cup. He drained it in a moment and turned his head toward me. "Visions from Lark."

"Yes!" I exclaimed. "I saw them too. I found it in the place where I was left as a baby," I explained. "I wonder why I didn't see it before."

He sighed and tapped his chin, a habit I had started to notice since we'd come into the light where I could see him. He sighed and crossed his arms. "I'm wondering if you weren't meant to see it as a small child. Perhaps this was meant for you once you came into your powers."

"That would make sense," I said. "That was quite a risk, though. How did she know I would come back this way when it was time? I could have moved far away from these mountains. I could have never wanted to see this place again."

"That I don't know," Nassir said. "But rather than dwell on what did not happen, why don't we look at what did. What is it you plan to do with this information?"

"First, I need to rescue Schula," I said, and Nassir nodded. "Then, I want to get far away from here. I think . . . I'm not sure, but I think my father could be that person in the cloak. Or at least he was Lark's lover."

"I think you're right. She mentioned to me only once that she had a love, but she didn't tell me more than that," Nassir said.

"There has to be a reason she wouldn't have told you about him," I wondered out loud.

"I think I know who, or at least what, was under that cape," Nassir said. "And I'm not sure what that would mean for you, but you don't smell like a fae, or a dryad, or a sprite, or any number of other things I'm familiar with in the Wyldes. It's very hard to place with the witch blood mixed in there, but now I'm more and more sure of what your other half could be."

I sucked in a breath, my heart pounding. Finally, the last piece of the puzzle. "Who is the one in the cloak?" I asked.

"In the vision, they speak of it as a place, but I know it as something else," Nassir said. "*Eidelhein* is the elvish word for 'last stand.' The last cry of the elven king before he was killed in the War of the Wyldes."

The elves.

I remembered Cosimo's lessons. A memory flashed across my mind of my fingers brushing the great mural in the Autumn library The one depicting a group of exiled elves.

Cosimo's voice still rang in my ears. *The elves were nearly decimated. Heh, now there was a faction that left cursing our names. They were banished, and our kind doesn't live well outside the magic of the Wyldes. I think they numbered only five males anyway, so even if they live there remain only five.*

It felt like the wind had been knocked out of me. Eidelhein. Last stand.

"Nassir." I swallowed. "Can the elves have children with any other races? The fae? Or . . . or humans?"

"Before today, I would have told you no," he said softly. "Now, I'm not as sure."

We sat in silence while I mulled over the implications.

"I think I need to take a walk," I said. "I won't be gone long. I'll go find us some more food."

"Take all the time you need, little one," Nassir said. "I will continue my meditation."

I nodded and stood on shaky legs. The more questions I answered, the more new ones arose. I left the cabin, closing the door behind me, and walked toward a patch of trees where I could sometimes find late-season walnuts. It was a mindless path for my feet to take, and I let my mind wander.

I reached up and felt the curve of my ears. They'd grown longer than I'd expected, but I hadn't had much time to dwell on it since Asher had captured me quickly after that. Were they different than Thain's? Eberon's? Schula's? I still hid them under my mass of hair, so I doubted Thain had had a good look at them during our wild escape from the Winter Lands.

I pictured Thain and Nassir, the two fae I'd most recently looked at, their ears swept back in a curve. Tracing my fingers along my newly formed ears, I realized they were perfectly straight, and at a higher angle, as if to point to the crown of my head instead of curling back.

I briefly wondered what my fae friends would think of me. Half witch, half elf, if that was truly what I was. Though it was starting to make sense. I gave a humorless laugh, my breath clouding in the crisp air before me.

Half enemy, half mistrusted neighbor. Wonderful. They had no reason to stay with me now. Even if they did, there was no way I could stay with them in the Wyldes.

I sighed as I came up to the walnut grove and began kicking the leaves on the ground, searching for whatever nuts the squirrels hadn't gotten to already. I gave up after a while, guessing they had been eaten or hidden already, and sat down under a large tree. I picked up a leaf and played with it for a minute before calling up my fire and burning it. It went up in an instant, leaving plenty of smoke in its wake since the leaves were damp. I sat there for a while, burning up leaves one by one. I knew at some point I had to go back, but I wasn't sure what to say. Or do, for that matter.

I stood up and brushed the fallen leaves and dirt off my pants then began to walk back to Mila's place. The trail didn't seem long enough for what I wanted to ask at the other end. I hadn't known Nassir long, but already I felt close to him. Would he come with me? His knowledge would be valuable for finding this place.

I sighed as the cabin came into view. I kicked a pebble in the path and headed toward the door. Then, on the light winter breeze, I caught a familiar scent.

Thain was back.

My heart skipped a beat, eager to see him, and then sank when I realized I had some new truths to tell him. I squared my shoulders and grimaced as I pulled open the door.

"I am sorry, Wren. I told him everything," Nassir said. "He touched the stone with the witching magic and had questions."

Thain was quiet as he stared with that stony expression of his.

"Thain," I began, but I didn't know how to finish. I reached up to touch my ears under my hair, and he stood slowly to stand in front of me. His hand, much the same way it had on the day we met, moved the hair out of the way so he could see my ears.

"This changes nothing," he said.

I gasped. "Thain," I choked out.

"This changes nothing. You are you, we will figure it out."

"How?" I managed.

"I don't want you to worry about this right now," he said. "Right now, we finish our plans for Schula. Here, I brought you something."

He turned to the table for a moment and grabbed a bag I hadn't noticed before. He pulled out a black tunic in the style Schula and I had taken to wearing when we trained. I was beyond caring about changing in front of anyone since I had been paraded through the Winter Court in a breast band and torn pants. I happily threw Thain's borrowed shirt on the table and pulled the tunic over my head.

"There are fresh clothes for you and Nassir in there, and cloaks, and a set of Winter Court servant uniforms," Thain said. "Courtesy of Eberon, who sends his regards."

I bit the inside of my cheek, and I knew the worry had slipped onto my expression when Thain interrupted my thoughts. "Eberon will not hate you. Schula will not hate you. We need to go over the plan, and that is *all* we need to worry about for now. All right?"

Nassir reached over and squeezed my hand.

"All right," I said. "Let's hear the plan."

FORTY-SIX
FINDING SCHULA

"Are you ready?" Thain asked.

I nodded. We were hunched behind a large outcropping of rock, downwind and a good minute of running to the steps that led down to the Icehold gates.

"Let's go get her," I said.

Stepping out from behind the rocks, I carried a large basket with jars of sap that we had spent the better part of the previous day collecting. It had been no small feat in the midst of winter. I kept my eyes turned down, watching so as to not spill anything and conveniently hiding my face from anyone who might recognize me. Not that many had seen me, but just in case.

I walked carefully in the snow: my new tight-fitted boots were a bit too short for my feet, and the matching white-and-blue servant's dress was uncomfortable and exposing. A small pouch hung from my neck, a common token from what I'd been told, but this one held a mix of magic and spices to conceal my scent, which would surely arouse suspicion.

Thain would remain some distance behind me and sneak in another way when he could. He was too recognizable to disguise, and one lone servant would more easily be allowed inside without question than two of us. Besides, splitting up would double our chances that at least one of us would get to Schula.

I steeled my nerves as I approached the warriors guarding the entrance to the steps.

"State your business," one of them grunted.

"Supplies for the bow-makers," I mumbled, trying to add a tremble to my hands. I remembered the skittish nature of the common people here as I had first passed through Icehold and tried to mimic it.

The shorter fae leaned in to glance through the jars for a moment, then waved me through without another word.

I thought my heart was going to burst through my skin waiting to be let through or discovered, but I managed to hold myself together as I began my walk down the long, carved staircase.

The gate at the bottom was no different, to my relief. Once I was waved through, I found a secluded tunnel that would lead me to the servants' hall.

I pulled out a scrap of parchment on which I had written notes and a rough map. Nassir, who had helped design much of the layout of Icehold as it stood now, was able to give me quite a bit of useful information. I was sure much had been added on over the years, but the base of the plans would still get me where I needed to go.

Nassir was frustrated that he couldn't come but agreed it was for the best. I frowned at the thought of him putting himself in harm's way. He had been trying for days to reach out and find any family he might have left, but his connections weren't as strong now, and he hadn't gotten anywhere.

I looked at my map and ensured I was on the right path, then hid it once more and walked with purpose down the corridor. Thain had told me if I walked as though I belonged there, no one would question me. I had passed very few other creatures so far, but as of yet it was working.

I kept a good pace, occasionally double-checking my map. There were indeed new halls and rooms carved that weren't included in Nassir's descriptions, but thankfully nothing that he'd expected to be there was missing or boarded up, and I was able to go swiftly to my designated meeting place.

I reached a carving of a beautiful fox sleeping in flowers and smiled at Nassir's handiwork. Then I ducked into the doorway beside it. The old washing room looked like it had gotten little use in recent years. There was dust everywhere, and the lone wooden stool that remained was rotting from age.

"Little bird?" whispered a shadow from the dark corner of the room.

"Washing maid?" I replied.

A short sprite danced from the shadows with a sly smile. She did in fact wear a washerwoman's apron and carried a basket of laundry.

She quickly set down her burden and began pulling garments loose from the pile. I set down my own basket and began to undress.

"Down the hall and to your left you will find a stairwell that will bring you up to the training fields. You will find her there, but you must hurry. There are many eyes on her." She spoke quietly and rapidly, and I had to concentrate to hear her.

She helped me strip and quickly outfitted me with a padded training uniform. It disguised me nicely, and the smell of sweat was already on it. I nearly gagged as she pulled a stained leather gorget over my head, but it would help to further mask my scent.

"Do not—*do not*—stray from this path." She looked sharply into my eyes, pressing the importance of her warning on me. "This corner of the holding is as far from the ballroom as you could possibly be, but we still do not know how far he can sense. The moment you remove her, you must prepare to *run*."

"I understand," I said firmly.

"I hope so," she said. "Blue one should be arriving at his own designated point shortly, if he hasn't already. Find each other on the training grounds and judge your options from there."

"All right." I nodded.

"And, little bird," she said slowly, "tell the burning one that my debt is repaid."

"I will," I promised.

She nodded curtly and rushed out the door with my basket of sap.

Fully dressed and with my face mostly covered, I walked with confidence to the staircase she'd indicated. The itch to find something grew more desperate with every step, making my pulse race in my ears. I breathed rhythmically through my nose just to calm down.

The stairs wound up. And up. And up. Few other doors opened into the stairwell as I climbed higher and higher, and I didn't see any other living thing. At the top, a heavy wooden door opened over my head into sharp wind and snowflakes.

I opened up just enough of my magic to keep me warm and stepped into the air.

It would have been breathtaking if it weren't for the reason I was up there. A portion of the mountaintop was flattened. There were long stretches of stone courtyard for running and sparring. There were targets for the archers, and wooden dummies for weaponry. A few strategically placed firepits attempted to warm some of the area but failed miserably under the falling snow.

I needed to act like I belonged until I could find Schula and hopefully Thain. Searching a nearby rack with wooden practice weapons, I grabbed a war axe. Now was as good a time as any, I supposed, to start learning how to properly fight with one.

I went to the most unoccupied area I could find to try to strike at a dummy while watching the field. A few warriors sparred, stripping off their shirts and practicing hand-to-hand combat. Others stretched or shot arrows.

But one knot of soldiers on the far side of the field was not training. I narrowed my eyes and tried to see what it was they were doing.

My jaw went slack, and my stomach twisted.

A snow-white figure had been tied to a small watchtower, arms and legs spread as they were chained to the cold stone. Bright red splatters stood stark against the white skin around her wrists and ankles where the chains were cutting into her. She wasn't far off the ground, her stomach about head height for the warriors standing around her. Her head lolled to the side, but my breath caught as she snapped it up in a heartbeat and our eyes locked.

I thought my heart would burst. Schula, I had to run to her! I had to—

A hand grabbed my elbow, and Thain's low voice murmured in my ear. "Not yet, let's talk."

I shook my head; my heart was beating hard, and I couldn't take my eyes off Schula. I struggled in his grip to step forward, but he wouldn't budge.

"Please," I begged under my breath. "I have to go to her! I have to get her down."

"Look at me," he snapped.

I ignored his demand and tried again to walk forward. Schula was little better: she struggled weakly in her chains as the fae around her laughed. She had her eyes shut tight, but her ears were trained on me. I realized she was trying to break free without tipping off the warriors that we were here.

"Schula," I hissed, and Thain had to catch me from moving forward.

His face changed to puzzlement. "What's wrong with you?"

"Please, just let me go to Schula, we need to get to her!"

He cursed and pulled me back to the stairwell I had come from, dragging me as I struggled.

"N—" I tried to cry out, but Thain's hand cupped my mouth and held my screams in place. I continued to watch Schula as I was pulled off the grounds and shoved inside kicking and struggling.

"Wren, listen to me," Thain demanded. "Stars, your pupils are huge. When did this start? This feeling about Schula?"

"What? I've always liked Schula. We need to help her!"

"Wren, listen to me," he ordered again, gripping my face in his hand so I had to look at him and not at the door that stood between me and Schula. "I know you like Schula, we all like Schula. Tell me when this desperation started. You feel the need to run to her?"

I whined as I struggled in his hands. "She needs me."

"Wren." His grip held me in place as another tear fell down my cheek. "I know she needs us, but if you show up like this, you're going to get her killed. I need to know, when did this feeling start?"

I took a shaky breath and closed my eyes with some effort, trying to remember. "As soon as I saw her just now."

"And when Schula released your seal? What did you feel then?" he asked.

"I was overwhelmed by the fire then, I don't remember anything else," I answered.

"And Schula, what did she do after she released your seal?"

"She gave me a strange look and left to see who was chasing us," I said.

Thain huffed. "I'll bet she did."

"I think she could tell then that I wasn't a fae," I said sadly. "But I don't care if she hates me for it, we need to help her!"

Thain gripped my shoulders and looked me in the eye again as panic rose in my chest. "Wren, listen. She doesn't hate you, but I need you to calm down. This pull you're feeling, do you think you can resist it? Can you stay here, right here in this spot, until I get back?"

"I can try."

"Good." He nodded, slowly letting me go and watching for me to bolt for the door. "Change of plans. I'm going to get her for you right now, okay? Then we are going to need to run like hell, understand?"

I nodded and bit the inside of my cheek, clamoring for the distraction of pain.

"Good, now stay here, I'll be right back."

A heartbeat later, Thain was out the door, and I was staring at my white-knuckled grip on the railing as though Schula's life depended on it. And right now, it did.

FORTY-SEVEN

FIRE AND ICE

My breath was ragged, and sweat beaded across my skin despite the cold air seeping around the door overhead. I wanted to go out there, *needed* to.

But Thain had told me to stay here, and I was determined to do it. Gritting my teeth, I formed a mantra and chanted it in my head.

Stay here.

Stay here.

Stay here.

Yelling outside clawed at my self-control, and I squeezed my eyes shut, continuing the thought on repeat.

Stay here!

STAY HERE!

The railing under my white-knuckled grip bit a splinter into my hand. The top of the steps just under the door were cramped with the heavy wood closed above, and I pressed my forehead to it.

More voices. Snarling, fighting, a bellowing roar.

"Stay here." I whispered the plea, begging my bones to still. "Stay here, stay here!"

Breathing didn't help. I tried to dip into the serenity of that magic place I'd learned to go to, but I couldn't quite reach it. It took another burst of effort to force my way there.

All the air was knocked out of me. The white spark, the one I'd seen just before Nassir first met me in my cabin, was screaming. Pain. Fear. Love. Regret.

The spark sent me through a whirlwind of thoughts and feelings, and I felt her in her rawest magical state. My white spark. Schula.

My eyes popped open. I couldn't do this; the pull was too strong. Nothing was going to make the urgency in this connection ease until Schula was safe.

Gritting my teeth, I shoved the door above me open, flooding the stairs with daylight. Thain would be pissed, but I could worry about that later.

The climb out of the doorway was slick with ice on smooth stone, but even with the distraction of watching my footing, my head swiveled to the far side of the training yard. Schula, bound by chains and with a blizzard swirling at her feet, lifted her head and met my gaze.

Thain, or at least I was fairly certain it was him, was hunched over nearly on all fours in a blur of midnight fury. He was more beast than fae, his eyes almost aglow with silver fire, his fingers longer, ending in claws. His posture had lost all its civility but none of its grace. I'd seen glimpses of this from him, the fangs and claws, on more than one occasion. But this was the largest shedding of his glamour that I'd seen yet.

Thain lunged, fighting for every footstep he could gain between Schula and the enemy, but he was terribly outnumbered, and it struck my heart with fear to see a dash of red that had opened on his shoulder, dripping onto the stone.

There was no time to think before I moved. Leaning down, I scooped up the wooden practice axe I had dropped and hauled myself out toward the fight. Thain had all their attention on him and Schula, and he didn't look my way until I was right behind one of the enemy warriors.

Lifting the wooden axe, I slammed the thick edge of it into the back of someone's head, since the bladed end wasn't sharp or metal. The fae was knocked forward into Thain, who met him with a brutal ripping motion to the throat that I had to look away from. Keeping the momentum from that first blow, I swung for the next fighter and missed horribly as she turned to defend herself.

"Wren, no!" Schula managed a scream as I stumbled, and the fighter bared her teeth.

If it hadn't been for the fact that my opponent was turning around at the last second, I wouldn't have bloodied her nose the way I did. The snap of cartilage rang clear as she fell to the ground, clutching the slippery mess of her face.

Keep going.

Two more fighters tried to turn on me, but Thain was faster, taking a swipe at one of them, leaving me with only one to deal with. And if I had been a trained fighter like they were, maybe I could have. My few weeks of work with Schula were not going to help me here. Not against the giant in front of me with arms like tree trunks and a nasty snarl on his face.

I took a wild swing with the axe and missed horribly. This fae was much more ready for a fight than the one whose nose I'd broken. He landed a punch right in the soft spot under my rib cage. The wind was knocked out of me as I rolled across the stone training grounds.

"No!" A weak cry came from Schula, who struggled against her chains.

That made me angry. They'd chained her up. They'd chained up what could quite possibly be DuVarick's own daughter and done who knew what to her while she was helpless. Did they know why they tormented her? Did they care?

What else has she endured here? Not only now, but before she left in the first place?

I unclenched my fist and let the wooden axe clatter to the floor. I watched, panting, as the big fae came after me for another attack. And then I set the world on fire.

No control, no holding back. I let it out. I roared as my back arched on the cold stone beneath me, and I threw flames out around me. I knew I caught the fae charging at me because he screamed as the heat and flame hit his clothing.

I hoped I hadn't hit Thain, but I was pretty sure I was well away from him at this point. My little show got the attention of more than just my attacker. Several heads turned my way. Thain took the opportunity to attack anyone who was distracted. Schula's eyes bored into me with a desperate want, and I was sure my face mirrored hers as I called out, "I'm coming!"

I climbed to my feet, slightly shaky but mostly intact. A few of the fae tried to use their magics against me, but no wind, rain, snow, or anything else was able to penetrate my radius of fire. I quickly positioned myself behind Thain, who took up the mantle of protecting me and Schula, though he didn't look too good. There had been an awful lot of warriors to fight, and as powerful as he was, Thain was only one person amid them. But my eyes were locked on Schula. Up close, I could see healing-over bruises, and the scars on her body that I had seen in the bath were joined now by new lacerations. I snarled as I attacked the chains. "Let go!"

I reached out with my hands and grabbed the links, burning them, melting them, pulling them off her and off the tower that held her. Schula whimpered, but I was being as careful as I could. I tried a little harder to be gentle as I pulled the metal from her wrists and ankles. I sagged with relief when she fell into my arms, extinguishing my fire, then both of us fell over. She was in my arms, finally, and she was safe. And she would never be hurt like this again as long as I drew breath. She buried her face into my neck.

"Wren," she sobbed.

"We have you now," I whispered, stroking her hair. "It's going to be okay."

"Wren, you beautiful fool." She let out a choked laugh among her tears. "If anything happened to you . . . You shouldn't have come for me."

"Why?" My heart tightened.

She does hate me after all, doesn't she?

No matter, she was safe.

She placed a soft kiss on the tip of my nose. "Wren, you're mine, and I'm yours. Of course I don't want any harm to come to you, you're my triquetram."

Triquetram.

It hadn't occurred to me that somewhere out there I might have one. To have found one of them, and for it to have been Schula all along, was unbelievable.

I blinked at her.

"I finally found you," Schula whispered.

An angry roar brought us back to the world around us. Thain was furiously fighting the Winter Court warriors, more of them pouring into the open grounds from wooden doors like the one I'd come through.

"Shit." Schula coughed.

I took off my training coat and slipped it over her. She needed the padding more than me. I discarded the helmet and was left with boots, padded pants, and the undershirt from my servant disguise.

"We need to go," I said. She nodded, and we turned to see how Thain was faring.

He had taken several blows but was still standing. Blood dripped on the ground around him, mixing with the snow and making his footing treacherous and slippery. I turned my head, trying to find a closer door than the one on the other side of the training grounds. There were several, but they all had at least one fae between us and escape.

Since there was little difference between them, I chose the closest one and ignited my flames again. I made a sudden push for the door, but the warrior wasn't surprised by my actions. I flung one arm out before me, the other supporting Schula. Fire spat toward the big fae and threatened to engulf him, but his own powers were just barely pushing mine back.

Schula threw an arm out to mirror my own, and my eyes grew wide as the air around us gathered into little ice crystals and reinforced my attack tenfold. It knocked the warrior aside as though he were a doll in a windstorm.

I felt it, her presence and powers supporting mine. This was what Thain had meant all along. Her strength was my strength, and my weakness was her weakness. I could see how in DuVarick's madness he could lock Nassir up, though it didn't quell my anger at him for it.

I trusted Thain to follow when he was able and pulled Schula to the doorway. Inside, without the elements barraging us, I looked her over again. She was tired, and she was hurt, but it was survivable.

"Can you walk?" I asked.

"I think so," she said. She stood but kept a solid hold of my hand. I was happy to let her have it. I pulled us along blindly, not knowing where I was going but knowing we needed to leave Icehold entirely.

The tunnels were nothing like the servants' ones I'd traveled before. These had less decoration and had probably been added long after Nassir had been imprisoned.

"Do you know where you're going?" Schula panted.

"No," I answered.

We walked quietly, as fast as I thought Schula could be pushed. I heard the distant sounds of Thain fighting on the roof, until I didn't.

"Do you hear that?" I asked.

"What?" Schula whispered.

"Nothing. Thain was fighting, and now he isn't," I said.

She tilted her head to the side, pointing one ear to where we had come from. "Nothing. You're right."

Neither of us wanted to ask the question, but we were both thinking it.

Is Thain okay?

"Hey," I whispered. "We're nowhere near the ballroom, right?"

"I—oh!" Schula was snatched inside a darkened room, and the surprise of it caused me to lose my grip on her hand.

"Schula!" I hissed and pushed into the room, only to be pulled further into it by a thin hand with long, claw-like nails.

The room was black. I panicked and brought up a flame to my hands as I searched desperately for Schula.

A pink figure closed the door swiftly and pressed a hand to my mouth firmly.

"Shh," it whispered.

I was about to lose it when I spotted a wide-eyed Schula sitting on a bed.

She was unharmed, sitting there in shock. I noted the nature of the room. I would have thought it was someone's living quarters, but there were no chests or wardrobes, and candles lined every corner, flickering temptation and secrets making the room look eerie. There was a seductive musk in the air that reminded me of something. This room had one purpose, and the bed being the sole furniture in it attested to that. I was about to pull the hand from my mouth when the footsteps started.

Right outside the door, six or seven beings were running.

My heart pounded for Thain. Was he okay? Was he being chased?

The footsteps slowed, and I distinctly heard doors being opened and closed around us.

Panic started to set in when I was gently tugged to the bed. I was urged, along with Schula, to get under the blankets, and then I turned and recognized the pink figure with short black hair and crystal-white eyes. She was naked as the day she was born, save for a diamond collar and a golden ring.

Krissaph? I mouthed.

She winked at me and pulled the blankets over my head, covering me and Schula in one swoop. I heard her blow out a few of the candles before I heard the door pull open.

"Oh, excuse me, Ambassador Krissaph," a rough voice said. "Have you seen a white fae and an accomplice come by here?"

I began to sweat under the heat of the blankets. Schula reached out and held my hand, which helped my nerves.

"No, I've been quite *busy*." She paused, and I could swear the hum I heard meant she'd turned her head toward the blankets. "Getting ready for the ball, of course. I haven't noticed anyone else."

"You're sure?" the voice asked.

"Would you care to join us, Captain?" Krissaph asked. "I'd be delighted to help you find out just how distracting I can be."

"No," the voice said curtly. "Go about your business, but alert us if you see anyone suspicious."

"Your loss," Krissaph purred. "I'll let you know, Captain."

"Right," the captain said, and then I heard the none-too-gentle closing of the door.

The opening and closing around us continued for several minutes before fading. Krissaph finally pulled the blankets from over us and peered down at us with a sly grin.

"Hello, you two," she mused. "I got your birdie, and I'm here to help."

FORTY-EIGHT

A BOND BEYOND UNDERSTANDING

Krissaph blew a kiss at me and Schula before turning to pull something from a basket by the door. She slipped on one of the body-length veils the Winter nobility wore and held it in place with a delicate silver headband. But while the outfits I had seen previously seemed to be in competition with one another to wear as little as possible under the veil, Krissaph won by a landslide by not wearing a stitch of clothing at all. Her ensemble was topped off by an ornate lace masquerade mask, presumably for the ball.

"I don't understand," Schula said skeptically. "Why are you helping?"

Krissaph shot her a cheeky grin as she answered. "Despite whatever animosity we have between us, I like Wren. Or rather, I like her more than I dislike you. When her little birdie came calling with a note promising to stir up the winter solstice, well, of course I had to come be a part of the mischief. By the way, Wren, love the new look. Haven't seen your kind in centuries. I'll bet there is a delicious story there."

It was an uncomfortable reminder of what I was going to have to deal with from now on, assuming I got out of Icehold alive.

Schula looked at me, holding my hand a fraction tighter and biting her lower lip. Her eyes roamed over me, taking in my new shape. I knew she had seen me when she'd unleashed the witch seal from my back, she knew what I was, but she hadn't seen me after my ears grew and my body took on a few more subtle changes.

She looked more unsure than I had ever seen her, and I hated it. Schula was the strongest female I knew, but I would have to be the one to step up and get us through this. She was on rocky ground and had just gone through so much; it was my turn to be the strong one.

"Krissaph, we need to get out of here. Do you know if there is a safe way to do that?" I asked.

"Oh, I'm certain there isn't," she mused. "But if you mean to avoid the ballroom, I can point you in the right direction."

I sighed in relief. "Great."

"Although . . ." She tapped her chin and looked up toward the ceiling in thought. "There are all those soldiers roaming around looking for you."

I looked over at Schula, who still wore nothing but my padded training jacket. The cuts and bruises stood out starkly on her skin, though they were healing now that she was off that tower and out of the elements. And I was dressed half as a servant and half as a warrior. There was no way we were going to walk down the hall without being accosted.

"Schula," I muttered. "Do you remember how to get out of here?"

She shook her head. "It's been a long time, and a few things seem to have changed since then."

I nodded and squeezed her hand, then turned to the succubus. "Do you have any suggestions?"

"Well, *I* plan on going to the ball," she said. "I'm certain it's going the be the best place to view the aftermath of your escape."

I could feel Schula's annoyance through our newly formed connection.

"Well, we need a way out, and we need it fast," I said. I looked around the room. There was no more clothing or veils in Krissaph's basket, and there wasn't anything else in the room to wear unless we wanted to steal the bedding.

"The kitchen," Schula whispered. "We can't be far from the kitchen. I don't know if anyone I know is still there, and I don't think they'll help, but I don't think they'll call the guards on us either."

"Perfect," I said. "And is there a way out from there?"

"There's a shaft that goes to the surface," Schula said. "It's used for raising and lowering large orders of food from the farms to Icehold. If it's still running, we can go out that way."

"A solid plan," Krissaph mused. "The last pieces of the puzzle are falling into place. Now you just need a handsome male to escort you there safely, and I think that can be arranged."

Schula immediately shot her a skeptical look, and I had to admit I was tempted to do the same.

"What do you mean, Krissaph?" I asked.

"Just listen," she said.

We did, and I heard him. Thain's grunts were coming down the hallway, and he must have been in bad shape.

I ran to the door and flung it open, not thinking about who else might be on the other side until it was too late. Luckily, only two living creatures were in the hall, and one of them was Thain.

He looked like he'd been on the sour end of a fight, but he was well enough to walk, which was encouraging. What I wasn't expecting at all was who was helping him down the hallway. In a fresh white Spring Court waistcoat with his long hair neatly braided down his back was Caldon.

Caldon's eyes widened as he took in my appearance. A problem I'd undoubtedly have to address later.

"Thain!" I hissed and ran to his side. "Caldon, what happened?"

"Inside first," Krissaph chirped from the doorway.

We pulled them inside and shut the door tight. Schula ran to Thain, and they embraced in a tight hug, Schula on the verge of tears.

"You came," she whispered. "You, and Wren, and now you're hurt."

"Shh." Thain, arguably the one in worse condition, comforted Schula in his arms as Caldon helped them sit on the edge of the bed.

"What happened?" I asked again.

"Some of the warriors got around me and went after you," Thain said.

Krissaph nodded. "Yes, they've been here and gone."

"That left few enough that I was able to finish them off," Thain said. "It wasn't long after that when I was yanked into a room and hidden by this one."

I bit my lower lip, remembering the last conversation Thain and I had had about Caldon. Or rather, about what it meant that Caldon had given me the necklace and how Thain felt about it. Caldon seemed to sense my thoughts, and he looked over at me with that gentle smile that had enticed me those weeks ago in Dwellonmar.

Had it only been weeks? It felt like years.

"After we heard from your bird, I came with Krissaph to the solstice. She's rather fond of you, and I'll admit you've piqued my interest too. It was lucky we're staying in this corridor because we were nearby to hear the soldiers running. Of course, our first assumption was that it was your doing, so I came to help, and Krissaph stayed to watch for signs of what happened."

"You came with Krissaph?" I asked, surprised.

The room looked at me, each with knowing eyes that suddenly made me realize they knew something I didn't.

"Wren," Caldon started, "Krissaph and I—"

"Oh, hush now, lovey." Krissaph rushed to Caldon on the bed and sat in his lap, draping her arms around his neck. I blushed, remembering she was naked under the sheer veil. "Don't spill all our secrets at once."

Caldon rolled his eyes and lifted her off his lap. "I've told you not to do that, you'll make people think things."

Krissaph cackled and walked back over to the doorway, leaning on the frame.

"Relax, Cal." She turned her attention to me. "Caldon and I are triquetram."

To say I was surprised was an understatement. A small, amused grin tugged at Thain's lips, and Caldon seemed a touch frustrated with her antics.

"Right." Caldon sighed. "So of course we came, and I'm glad we did. From your letter, it sounds like I'll be needing to make a report to King Diamid about DuVarick's current state of stability."

I bit my lower lip. "And that report would include my newly found heritage?"

Caldon looked at me softly for a long heartbeat, then shook his head. "No, it won't."

I let out a slow breath. "Thank you."

"That's all well and fine," Krissaph said. "But you should keep moving, and we should get to the ballroom before we're missed."

"Thain, we're going through the kitchen to a cargo shaft unless you've got a better plan," Schula said.

"No, our plan has already changed too much to recover it. Let's go through the kitchen," Thain agreed.

We whispered our goodbyes and snuck out the door. Krissaph blew a delighted kiss to us as she hooked an arm around Caldon's elbow, and they walked to the festivities as though nothing was amiss.

Thain took the lead, Schula followed, and I trailed at the back as we wound through the halls. Thain had been to Icehold, and Schula of course had been familiar with it decades ago, but neither of them had more than a gut feeling that we were going the right way.

I was astonished that we didn't run into any servants for the first few twists and turns. Presumably they were all occupied by the solstice ball. It wasn't until we turned a corner and the smell of roasting meat hit me that I realized they were right, and we were by the kitchen.

"Keep on your guard," Thain whispered.

Schula pushed ahead of Thain silently and took us through a small doorway. A few fae, a dryad, two sprites, and another creature I couldn't name paused what they were doing to look up.

Schula held her head up and looked one of the sprites in the eye. They had some kind of silent conversation before the sprite finally looked away as though she had seen a ghost.

"Get back to work," the sprite growled, returning to her cleaver, which was breaking down a lamb on a large butcher block. "There's nothing to see here."

I was so relieved that I thought my knees would give out, but I recovered and quickly followed as Schula took us through the back pantry to an old brick shaft full of pulleys and ropes.

"Stars, it's still here," she sighed.

"Can we pull ourselves from the inside, or does someone need to stay here and work the ropes?" Thain asked.

"It will have to be one at a time, but we can do it from inside," Schula said. "I got caught more than once doing it as a child."

"Get in then," I said nervously. "I won't feel any better until we're all far from here."

We helped Schula in first. She began to pull herself up, and Thain gestured for me to go next. We watched her slowly rise to the light above.

I looked back at the kitchen workers, all of them quietly doing their jobs with their eyes glued to their stations.

Good. They owe her that much.

Schula was nearly to the top when the hairs on the back of my neck stood straight up.

Something was very not right.

Thain was one step ahead of me. He whirled around with a low growl, and in that instant every sound of kitchen work stopped except the crackle of the fires. Every servant scattered to the nearest exit. Through the doorway stepped a gray fae that I had never wanted to see again. With a nasty smirk on the burnt, scarred remains of the left side of his face, the eyes of a true enemy bored into me with intense hate.

Asher.

FORTY-NINE
WITH YOU OR NOT AT ALL

Asher stepped through the doorway, moving slowly and keeping unblinking focus locked on me.

"*You*," he seethed. "And Thainalan the Ravager. This is an act of war."

"The act of war was when you tortured a fae of the Autumn Court!" Thain roared, starting to grow into the beast I'd seen him as on the training field. "Wren, run."

Thain shoved me behind him into the bottom of the lift, but the shelf lifting Schula was still at the top, not yet lowered down again for the next passenger.

"You will not escape me again!" Asher roared.

I took in a sharp breath as Asher came at us at a frightening speed. But Thain met him in the middle of the room, claws out and eyes blazing silver as the two hulking fae crashed together with a terrible sound.

The butcher-block table that had been between them was in splinters and thrown to the side, narrowly missing a cart holding an elaborately decorated cake.

The shelf hit me with a dull thud, and I whipped my head up in the shaft to see Schula.

"What?" I began.

"We're all getting out," Schula said. "All three of us."

My eyes flicked over my shoulder to the kitchen door where two more fae had arrived. Both were dressed in brown fighting leathers and bore the Winter crest on their shoulders. One of them held a sword, and the other a bow. The archer nocked an arrow and aimed for the scuffle between Asher and Thain.

"No!" The word ripped from my throat before I recognized it had come from me. I gripped either side of the entrance to the lift and flung myself out toward the new fae. I let out all the rage I had toward the Winter Court in the form of a stream of fire.

Protect Schula. Protect Thain.

That was all that could run through my head as I released my fury on them.

Unlike anything I had created before, this was white-hot fire. The heat from it suffocated the room. I just hoped it wasn't affecting Thain. The bright flames licked at the warriors as they tried to jump away. Still, I knew I'd burned the archer's arm, and it satisfied me that she could no longer draw an arrow.

I yelped as my legs were pulled out from under me and I slammed into the stone floor. Over me, one of the Winter fae sneered and held his blade high, ready to strike. I flailed and clawed, trying desperately to roll out of the way or at least conjure more fire, provided I hadn't spent everything with my last display.

"Wren!" The screech like a banshee chilled the hall and lifted my heart into my throat. I felt her before she reached me, ice creeping on the floor in her path and sending jagged shards at the male standing over me.

I turned to Thain, who now had Asher pinned under him, a bloody hand half buried in Asher's chest as he roared in anger. Asher wasn't giving up, though. Despite the line of blood at his mouth, he drew back a clawed hand, striking for Thain's throat.

Thain growled as an arrow sprouted from his collarbone, and Schula and I gasped.

Schula ran to Thain, and I ran for the doorway where more fae were coming into the kitchen. I spotted the offending archer right away and snarled as I released more white-hot fire into them.

Asher recovered somewhere behind me, or that was what it sounded like anyway, and he retreated into the line of incoming soldiers.

"Can you get him to the lift?" I shouted at Schula over the sounds of fighting.

"I'm *fine*," Thain grunted as he grabbed the arrow protruding from his collarbone and snapped it off near the base of the wound. Then he stood, not taking his eyes off the wounded Asher, who was already being tended to by the Winter Court fae who had been arriving in a steady flow. By now, we were dreadfully outnumbered.

"Go," Thain said. "Now."

I gritted my teeth and looked at Schula, who was just as resolved as I was. She nodded at me and wrapped an arm around my waist.

"We all go or none of us go," she said flatly.

Thain looked like he was about to argue, but then something in him hardened. "Schula, Wren, it has been an honor. If you will not run, then help me bring it down."

I looked at Thain, who promptly cleaved the arm of a large green soldier in a gory mess. His chest was heaving, his eyes gleaming wildly, his wounds bleeding slowly. He was in the battle now, mind and soul, and from his words it seemed like he thought it would be his last.

"Always, old friend." Schula just gripped me harder and added her ice to my powers.

I was afraid to look at her face, but I was resolved to end with her, if that was what she wanted. I didn't want to run either, so I couldn't blame her for standing by Thain as we tried to tear Icehold down.

Once again, the pressure exploded around us. Something about the hot and cold didn't mix well, or mixed too well, I supposed, depending on the results you wanted. The flames and ice licked the walls and chased out all but the most hardened warriors. But still more came to take their place.

During our assault, Thain had felled the enemies before him and gone to another doorway in the crumbling wall. With a low rumble, he called on the gale he had summoned before and began hurling his might down the halls.

The cracking and creaking overhead were surely heard in more parts of Icehold than just the kitchen, but Schula and I tore through the few warriors left in our path and left the kitchen entirely.

A rumble in the distance told us that our efforts were working elsewhere. That or Thain was to blame.

"We're not done yet," Schula breathed. "DuVarick has this disgusting gauntlet, it's his favorite punishment."

She ran a finger down her hip. A place, if I remembered correctly, that held one of her nastier scars. She grinned, but it was filled with no warmth. "If I go down, so does that damned thing."

"Show me."

And she did.

There was a great deal of rubble to handle now as we picked our way through what was obviously a forge and an armory. It took us to a tunnel, then another, then another. Screams around us told of more soldiers looking for us, but our destruction was everywhere, and there was no clear path to where we were.

The mad gleam in Schula's eyes told me she would welcome the destruction of this gauntlet if it was the last thing she did. I had few regrets. Not having more time with Schula, Thain, and Eberon was one. I'd also wanted to search for the witches, or maybe the elves, for more answers about my parents, and though it would not break my heart to not find out more, it did sadden me. Puko, I would miss. Nassir, I would miss. Perhaps whatever afterlife awaited an elven witch would allow me to see Bryn again. Or Lark.

Schula flung ice periodically, destroying weapons and rooms as she saw fit in her path to the gauntlet, until finally she stopped before a giant iron doorway at the end of a long, empty hall. It was heavily decorated and stood out from the corridors around it.

She let out a slow breath and pulled the door open with a grimace.

Shouting behind us told of more soldiers approaching, but we stepped inside the room, ignoring them. For this was it, this was the gauntlet.

A long tunnel of grotesque iron sculptures and tools. Pits of spikes, swinging blades, and heavy chains. Every bit of it had the brown splatter of old blood on it. My mouth opened in horror as I looked into the nearest pit, where several mostly whole skeletons now rested, a little meat still on the bones.

"What is this place?" I whispered.

Schula looked over the room darkly, her eyes resting on a golden throne at the back of the room.

"A place to suffer. Bring it down."

She turned suddenly and hugged me tightly, twisting our bodies as she cried out in pain.

"Schula!" I screamed as an arrow struck her arm. She had used her body to block it.

"Now!" Schula kissed my cheek, tears in her eyes as she turned us to the gauntlet.

I was now the one with tears in my eyes. It would have been nice to have more time with Schula. It would have been nice to see Thain once more.

We raised our arms and let out everything. Let it out as it burned my skin, let it out as it cracked walls and froze the iron around us. As it melted the door and blew out the walls. The ceiling screamed overhead with the burst of pressure and loss of supports.

In a palace of DuVarick's warriors, sometimes you had few choices.

And our resolve was strong as we brought the gauntlet down.

FIFTY
TOGETHER

I had always thought being buried would be a terrible way to die. Surely something quick would be better. A beheading, maybe. Or poison, if it were the right sort. But slipping into unconsciousness wrapped in Schula's arms beneath the rocks, it was hard to argue with the dark, comfortable sleep that beckoned.

I was floating in the dark.

It was like meditating, but I wasn't in my cabin.

Wherever I was, it was definitely magic. It wasn't water, because I could breathe just fine.

I was in my body. Or maybe I wasn't. Whatever I was, I was purple. And I glowed.

I giggled.

It occurred to me that my thoughts were jumbled, and I was having a hard time keeping them straight. If Bryn heard my thoughts right now, he would think I was mad with fever.

A white glow next to me drew my attention. It wasn't shaped like anything; it was just there.

I wanted to reach toward it, and I pushed myself that direction. Apparently, the white glow wanted to come to me too, so it did.

We floated slowly to each other, and as we finally touched, it all came rushing back.

The fight. Our last stand. The soldiers. The gauntlet.

The ceiling crumbling down around us as Schula delighted in its destruction.

I wrapped myself around Schula, and she wrapped herself around me.

I tried to speak, but no words came out.

She squeezed me tighter, and I relaxed into her embrace. At least we had each other.

But where exactly were we?

I tried to look around. Everything was slow, as if I were wading through thick mud, only there was no mud, just nothing. Emptiness. Darkness.

Then I felt it. A light brush against us. I stiffened, and Schula shivered.

We faced the direction it had come from, and that was when I felt it again.

Smooth and warm and old. A consciousness that had spanned an impossible distance to reach us.

I shuddered. It was overwhelming.

It was the black spark. The one I had first seen from a great distance when I met Nassir. I now knew the white spark I had seen at that time was none other than Schula. But who or what the black spark was, I still didn't know, and I wasn't sure if I wanted to.

It reached out again, firmer this time. It seemed curious, inspecting us.

I held Schula tighter.

Then it suddenly drew back. I wasn't sure what to think. A part of me was glad the overwhelming presence was gone, but another part of me was saddened by it.

I gently reached out but fell much too short to reach it.

Schula added herself to me, and we both reached out again. This time, we made it much further, but still impossibly far from the presence. But our actions didn't go unnoticed, and the black glow came back to meet us again.

I was a little happy to feel it again. I didn't have a particular reason to be, I just was.

And then it did what we hadn't been able to do yet. It communicated.

I felt the intentions more than I heard anything, but the message was clear.

Wake up.

Find me.

Find them? But how? As far as I knew, I wasn't even alive anymore. We had put everything into toppling the parts of Icehold that were a danger to others. A permanent reminder to DuVarick that he wasn't invincible. An act to shake up the city and hopefully alert the other courts.

We had done it, but at the cost of our lives.

Right?

But the presence didn't like my thoughts on the matter. It just pressed into us harder.

WAKE UP.

FIND ME.

This time, it was almost painful. I clung to Schula's white glow as the presence receded once more, but not before it sent us a final parting thought.

WAKE UP.

Air was forced into my lungs. My real lungs. Lungs I hadn't realized weren't being used until this very moment. My eyes flew open but were met with only darkness. I thought I was back in that place again, but everything hurt far too much for that to be the case. Surely if I were dead I wouldn't hurt?

I tried to move and immediately regretted it. My leg was either pinned or broken. The rest of my body was in agony. One big throbbing injury with no discernible parts. A groan next to me caught my ears, and I tried to turn my head.

"Schula?" I asked softly. I noticed the sound in my left ear was muffled. I tried to reach it to scratch at the irritating feeling, but I couldn't move my arms far before they ran into rock.

"Wren?" she whispered.

"We aren't dead?" I asked.

"I suppose we aren't," she said.

We lay there quietly for a moment before Schula spoke again. "Can you move at all?"

"My arms somewhat," I said. "We're under the rocks, aren't we?"

"I think so," she said. "Light?"

I tried to call up some fire. Even a flicker. Nothing.

"I'm spent." I let out a breathy laugh. Then it turned into a full-blown fit of giggles.

"What is so funny?" Schula asked tiredly.

I laughed a little more until it ended in a coughing fit. "Ow. Um, we survived DuVarick's soldiers, Asher, the training grounds, and pulling Icehold down around us, and we're going to die from hunger under these rocks."

Schula giggled too. "You're right."

"Or suffocation," I added.

"We might have concussions," Schula said.

Then we were quiet again. In the distance, I heard more rock fall. There would probably be a lot of that over the next few days.

"Hey, Wren?" Schula broke the silence again.

"Mmm?" I sighed.

"Do you think we're alive because of that black thing?" she asked.

"Maybe," I said. "What do you think that was?"

"Nothing of the Wyldes," she said. "Not even close. It was old. And strong."

A loud clattering of rock and iron grating against each other screeched in my ears. Schula winced, and I was thankful for the muffled hearing in at least one ear.

"*Where is she*?" The boom of a terrible voice echoed around us, shaking the ground.

"No," Schula whispered.

I took in a sharp breath, realizing too late who it was that boomed over us.

DuVarick.

"Find her!" he demanded, and dozens of feet obeyed.

The rock must have settled enough that the Winter Court could investigate. I heard them now, far overhead. They moved rock and pulled bodies from the wreckage. The problem was, from the sounds of it, that there was a lot of wreckage. It would take days, even for the fae, to move it all.

And we didn't want to be found. Not like this. We had no magic, no strength, and no fight left in us.

Then I realized that he was looking for "her" and not "them." Who was *her*? My first thought was Schula, but then I remembered his obsession with my mother, and I wondered if it was actually me.

All I knew was that I didn't want him to get hold of either of us.

"Schula," I whispered, barely loud enough for her fae ears to pick up. "They're going to find us eventually, alive or dead. What's our next move?"

"They aren't close yet," she said. "It sounds like they are still way over by the kitchen where this all started. It's going to take time to get here."

"Are you suggesting we could possibly get away?" I asked.

She laughed. "Stars, no. I can't move at all, and you're little better."

"I don't want them taking you alive," I said sadly.

"And I don't want that for you either." Schula sighed. "Maybe if they take long enough we can get enough magic back to . . . Huh?"

Silence.

"Schula?" I asked.

"What is that? Who is that?" she asked.

"Who?" I asked, but she didn't need to answer. A familiar magic brushed my mind. I sank down into my head, into the magic place, and found him again.

"Nassir!" I whispered.

"Who?" Schula asked.

"Shh, let me talk to him. A friend."

I reached out to him with my mind. It shocked me to see how little reach I had right now, but it was probably due to my empty magic reserves.

Nassir's yellow form reached out to me from below.

Stay, I will get you down.

How? I asked.

But Nassir didn't reply.

Instead, I felt a shifting of the earth under me. Rocks broke and rolled away, soil shifted around me, and I sucked in a breath. My eyes popped open wider than they ever had when I felt my whole body sink as though I was in a pond and not a crumbled mountain. It was excruciating.

"Ooh!" Schula squealed next to me.

Down and down we sank, eventually falling out of the rocks and into open air as we dropped into a cavern beneath the ruins of the gauntlet.

I sucked in a breath as soon as I hit the air, my heart pounding as I fell into nothingness. I clenched my jaw, trying to hold in the scream and readying myself for impact.

But the floor never came.

Instead, strong arms caught me as I sank into a deep-blue embrace.

I blinked and looked into Thain's silver eyes. They swirled with emotion as he searched me for signs of injury.

"Thain, you're alive," I whispered.

Those silver eyes locked on mine, and promptly my mouth was covered by his. His lips pressed against mine; his arms pulled me in close to him as he gently set me on the ground. He noticed my leg and was careful to set me down as painlessly as he could. I slid my arms around his neck, getting as close to him as I could. My eyes fluttered shut as his warmth encompassed me. I felt the tear slip from my face; I hadn't realized what almost losing each other would do to me. I was not ready to let go of Thain, I realized. There had been a lot of unspoken words between us since he'd found me. Maybe I should start changing that.

He drew back from the kiss, and I was breathing hard as I looked up at him. The gash on his forehead was ugly and swollen. I wasn't sure how he'd caught me without hurting himself; he looked pretty bad and favored his left leg and left arm over the other side of his body. I was glad he hadn't been near us at the center of the collapse.

A gasp from the ceiling was what finally turned my eyes away from Thain as Schula fell from the rock above and was caught by Nassir, who had been standing next to us this whole time with Puko perched near him.

I blushed at the realization that, though he couldn't see it, he'd definitely heard our kiss.

"Wren!" Schula squealed, then, upon looking around and seeing Thain, she calmed down. "Thain?"

She turned to Nassir with a wary look.

"Schula," I said. "Let me introduce you to Nassir."

"You feel familiar," she said hesitantly.

"You as well," Nassir said, then his lips parted as he took in a sharp breath. "You are the child of DuVarick?"

"That answers that old debate," Thain muttered.

"You're an earth-shaper?" Schula asked, still looking at Nassir.

"I suppose I am," he answered. "It has been a long time since I have done it."

Thain went over to take Schula from Nassir and set her down by me. I wrapped my arms around her, taking in the arrow wound, the gash on her neck, a wrist that must be broken, an ankle that was swollen, and a pile of bruises and cuts. She moved like I did, as though everything hurt. I was little better off, and a pain in my lower side told me I probably had problems that couldn't be seen on the surface.

"You see, Wren, this is why I argued for you to bring me with you," Nassir chided.

"I see you didn't listen." I groaned.

"Good for you that I didn't," he said.

"What in the Stars is going on?" Schula asked.

"There is a lot to discuss," Thain said. "But not here."

"Where are we?" Schula asked.

"Some caverns far below the city," Nassir said. "I had always meant to put some rooms down here but never got to them. I'm glad to see they were of use."

"I can't believe we're alive." I sighed.

"Neither can I," Thain said softly. "I felt it when you caved in those floors."

I looked over Thain's shoulder to Schula. We were both thinking about the same thing, the black presence. She shook her head slightly, a clear *don't mention it* look in her eyes.

I nodded. This would require investigation later. For now, we had to get out of here.

"I seem to be the only one who can walk," Nassir said. "Which does pose a problem, as a blind fae can't carry three injured warriors by himself."

"Eventually, DuVarick is going to move his search out from the wreckage and find us," Schula said softly. "We can't stay here."

"It would take a very long time for me to move you one by one," Nassir said. "But if we cannot find another way, that is what I will do."

We sat quietly for a moment, trying to think of a plan, a difficult act through the distraction of the pain.

Then the high, soft note of a bird echoed lightly.

"He's here," Thain murmured.

My heart shot into my throat, and I turned toward the exit of the caverns expecting to see our enemy. I heard several footsteps bounce lightly off the walls.

Instead, I saw a face that had me melting in relief.

"Stars, there you are!" Eberon rounded a corner with a torch in hand. He had three Autumn fae with him.

He ran to Thain and immediately bent down to embrace him. Then he bared his fangs and hissed at him. "Don't you ever pull this shit again!"

"I missed you too, Eberon." Thain smiled tiredly before lying down to rest.

"You're going to tell me what in the hells happened," Eberon chided. "But first, let's get out of here." He smiled and stood up, brushing the dust off his pants. "All right then, let's get you four to a safe location. We need to move quickly, and we have a long way to go."

FIFTY-ONE

ONE LAST PUSH

The trio that Eberon had brought with him pulled supplies from their packs and made harnesses for the three of us. The cloth and ropes were wrapped in a way that allowed each of the newcomers to carry an injured one. Our injuries were tended to as well as they could be on a cave floor. My leg, which I was told had been broken in two places, was set and tightly wrapped. I passed out the moment they pushed my bones together. A small blessing that I wasn't conscious for the remainder of my treatments, because I was told there were a lot of them.

I finally came to when we were being situated in the harnesses. I glanced over at Schula, whose brow was slick with sweat, her face scrunched in discomfort, despite the fact that we had been given a thick, sweet syrup to numb the pain.

As soon as they were done with us, we fled the mountain. With the help of a few scouts Eberon had also brought with him, we dodged any more Winter Court fae as we proceeded. We went as fast as possible, trying to get out of the Winter Lands as soon as we could.

Despite the luck we'd had at the start, eventually we heard the distant sounds of yelling. I supposed that was bound to happen: our group was far too big to hide all of us. When a scout caught up with us, I knew things were turning for the worse.

"A large unit is on your tail. How do you want to proceed?" a lanky fae asked Eberon.

I might have been a bit delirious from everything, but a stray thought trailed into my mind.

"Are we passing by the crater?" I asked.

Eberon looked at me softly. "We'll be not too far from it; it's the straightest route."

"Keep the course straight," Thain suggested. "Send scouts to weave footprints around, away, and through our path. It won't fool them, but it might slow them down."

Eberon gave a curt nod to the scouts who were listening. "Do it."

The fae sprang into action.

I, on the other hand, meditated.

I did what I could to bring myself to my safe place, to my little cabin.

I let myself idle there. Recover. Grow strong. If I was counting our distance correctly, I had only a few hours to build up strength for one last push of magic.

The journey was bumpy, and long, and tiring. I was vaguely aware of orders being given, unseelie creatures being fought, and the occasional quick stop to check our bandages.

I was pretty sure I even fell asleep a few times.

But my sleep and meditation was interrupted when an arrow whizzed by my ear.

Eberon let out a string of curses. Thain, finally fed up with the harness, climbed out of it against Eberon's protests.

"Bring in the scouts leaving false trails," Thain said. "Focus on movement. Switch out the ones carrying injured and get fresh legs to do the carrying. Make a straight line for the closest reach of the Unclaimed Wyldes."

No one even looked to Eb; they all deferred to the most notable and senior warrior. We paused immediately, and I was transferred to the back of an impish-looking sprite with a little black beard and sly yellow eyes. But he was big, and strong, and carried me easily.

It was all done as quickly as the fae could go. As the scouts were being called back in, there was an exchange of arrows, then we were off again.

Ahead of our group, ahead of the trees, was an expanse of ice and emptiness. We were getting closer, but not quite close enough.

A scream behind us bounced off the trees as one of our fae was hit.

"At the tree break, we head south!" Eberon called.

"No!" I yelled. "Please, stay straight."

"We need to at least try to shake them," Eberon said, but he drew closer to me with a frown, carrying the injured fae on his shoulder.

"Please trust me." I looked at him, then at Thain, hoping the blue warrior would take my side. "Please. Just take us by the crater. If it doesn't work, I'll shut up, and we can go wherever you want. Please, Eberon."

It was Thain who spoke first. "Go straight."

I sighed, relieved, then sank into my mind immediately to reach out again.

As soon as I reached a state of meditation, I threw myself forward, reaching for the crater. Reaching under it. Reaching.

An ancient presence sat under the ice, which had partially refrozen but was not fully back to the way it had been before I'd melted most of it. It was old. It was furious. It was terrifying.

It was perfect.

It had chased me under the ice when I'd scrambled out of the crater before, and I'd been afraid it would break the surface and devour me. Hells, it almost had. But I'd gotten away once, and chances were it was still hungry. I was counting on it.

My body jolted as the sprite carrying me leaped over a fallen tree. Puko puffed out his feathers and took to the skies ahead of us. I could tell he didn't care for the creature I had just found. I blinked and saw another arrow fly dangerously close to one of the fae helping us.

I gritted my teeth and threw everything forward, determined to get the thing's attention. I felt it stir, and my heart thundered in my rib cage. It turned its attention to me, and it roared, shaking the ice, shaking the ground, throwing me back into my mind.

I slammed back into the real world and looked around. Eyes were wide, looking around for an unknown assailant. Its presence was thick in the air. Old, cold, and angry.

Thain's eyes found mine, knowing immediately. "What have you done?"

I opened my mouth to respond, but a loud snap covered up my words. The creature was ramming the ice, and some of it was breaking.

I looked forward. The crater was coming into view, and we had to act now.

"Eberon, take us to the back side of the crater. Do not set foot on the ice inside the crater, whatever you do."

"I hope you're right about this, little bird." Eberon sighed and gave the orders.

I dove back down into my mind.

The thing was close now. It was hungry, and it wanted my fire. Not just my fire, any fire. It was almost through the surface. I couldn't gauge the size of it, or the shape, but it was massive.

While we were on this side of the crater, I threw everything I had at it. The tiny reserve of magic I had built up made a meaningless flame, but it was enough to get its attention.

It roared, furious and hungry. Perfect.

I made sure to use every drop I had. Every tiny ember I could muster.

Now I was well and truly spent, and the thing couldn't find me by my magic any longer.

I blinked my eyes, my real eyes, and looked around. We were rounding the back side of the crater now, and the creature was slamming itself into the ice.

"Run!" I cried out, my throat dry. "Get out, it's almost here!"

Our group pressed on harder, creating space between us and the crater.

Our pursuers were doing the same, or trying to, but they were much closer to it than we were, just at the front of the crater now.

I gasped, looking back at the huge group of Winter fae that had come after us. If they caught up, we would be vastly outnumbered. DuVarick must have sent all his soldiers who had survived the collapse of the barracks.

There, in the front, was Asher. His injuries were minimal enough that he could lead this charge. He looked like a rabid animal, crazed and deadly.

If he caught up to us now, I had no doubt my death would not be quick.

CRACK.

SPLASH.

In one earth-shattering moment, the surface broke, and all hells broke loose with it.

I sucked in a breath, craning my neck painfully and watching as a smooth, black head threw itself out of the water. It was serpent-like in shape, but with the slick, wet body of an eel or a worm. It had no eyes; it didn't need them in the dark depths of the crater. What it did have was a maw full of teeth that could swallow an army. I couldn't look away.

It thrashed, sending huge ice shards from the surface of the crater's underground lake flying through the air. Several landed just behind the fae bringing up our rear. Several more splintered into the Winter army behind us.

Asher roared as a shard of ice sliced into his leg, but he charged at the thing, blinded by rage.

My newly elven eyes were a curse as I watched the horror and dismemberment the great serpent inflicted on the army. It flailed its body, landing on several fae and snapping its huge jaw and rows of blade-like teeth into them.

Asher was nothing before it, barely a morsel between its teeth as in one massive bite, he disappeared into the depths of the serpent. And he didn't come back out.

The serpent snapped its jaw, and each time bursts of blood splattered in the white snow as it devoured more and more.

Some got away, but not many.

We continued our retreat across the Sangolins, but the screams of the Winter Court followed us.

Long after I stopped hearing them, they rang in my memory.

Icehold's army was now in shambles.

Asher was no more.

If I was certain of nothing else after today, I was certain that DuVarick would hunt me down to the ends of the earth.

I didn't remember much of the rest of the journey after that. I was spent and injured, and it wasn't long before shadows took over and I passed out.

FIFTY-TWO
SOUTH

I woke up in Mila's bed, next to Schula. Puko sat perched on the bedpost at our feet.

The cabin was too small for everyone to fit, but Eberon had organized things beautifully. A triquetram had been sent back to Thanantholl to give a preliminary report to King Baeleon. The rest had been set as lookouts and hunters for now.

Nassir sat quietly in the corner.

Early reconnaissance reports of Icehold were bleak. We had managed to avoid damage to the residential areas, and thanks to the solstice masquerade, most of the population of the city had been on the other side of Icehold, away from the destruction.

We had, however, decimated the kitchen, barracks, armory, training rooms, and equipment workshops.

After a few days, with the help of magic and rest, Schula invited me out for a walk alone.

She let me lead us somewhere, and I took us to the hill where my mother had left the stone for me.

Schula had been mostly quiet since our retreat to Mila's cabin. Today, she played with a strand of hair that had come loose from her long white braid.

"Is everything all right?" I asked softly.

She shook her head. "It's not. It may never be all right again."

I nodded, giving her another moment of silence before I tried again. "It seems you've had something on your mind."

Schula sighed and turned my way. "I'm DuVarick's daughter. But I don't want to be. And even if he somehow came to accept it, I could never forgive him. I know he's not right. I know his mind is foul, but I can't forgive him."

I bristled at that. "I wouldn't want you to."

She nodded, a melancholy smile on her lips. "I know what we did will have repercussions."

"Yes," I agreed. "But it's high time the other kings realized what is going on in the Winter Lands. DuVarick *isn't* right, and he's not kind to his people."

Schula gave a dark laugh. "Don't let the other royals fool you. The fae aren't a peaceful people. We put on a pretty show, but that's where it ends. Though DuVarick is definitely the worst of them."

Puko fluttered overhead, landing heavily on my shoulder, and I stroked his head absentmindedly.

"I don't want to go back to Thanantholl," Schula whispered.

Ah. That was what was bothering her.

"I don't either."

She looked at me, startled. "You've made friends there."

"I know what they'll call me behind my back. The elf witch. That's all I'm going to be to them, and I'd prefer not to waltz up to Baeleon if he's going to react the way DuVarick did. I don't belong in the Wyldes, not anymore."

Nothing could hide what I was from the two dozen creatures of the Autumn Court that Eberon had brought with him. They had easily pieced together that I had called the serpent from the crater, and they had questions.

Her eyes softened. "Then where?"

"The wards are deteriorating. And the witches are the ones who built them in the first place. And they might know more about Lark."

"It sounds like we could get several answers from one place," Schula finished. "What about the elves?"

"I don't know where to start. I think the witches would be easier to find. I've grown up knowing them, and I know where to find information on them, but the elves have been hidden for a long time, right? I don't know how to find them."

"Well, we can start with the witches then," Schula said. "Maybe they can lead us to the elves."

"Maybe," I said. "And one more thing. I want to bring Nassir with us, if he wants."

"Of course," Schula said instantly. "I couldn't imagine going without him. How would he survive a big city? He's too used to quiet. And I know it sounds silly, but I've grown fond of him, though I've only known him a few days."

I smiled. "He has that effect, doesn't he?"

"All right," Schula said, much calmer now. "An adventure it will be, then. My lovely Wren, our wonderful Nassir, and we'll find the witches and the elves and see distant lands and maybe find the black . . ."

She trailed off, and I chewed on my lower lip in thought. "It told us to find it. Do you think we should?"

"I don't know," she said quietly. "I feel like we're supposed to. It's frightening."

"I feel the same way."

We sat, enjoying the peaceful breeze for a while. It was quiet times like this that made me notice the difference from the Wyldes. The air wasn't thick with magic and life. I might miss the Wyldes someday, but for now I was content to be far out of its reaches.

We stood, disturbing Puko for a moment, and headed back.

There was a pair of fae that we needed to talk to, and one particular goodbye that I wasn't looking forward to.

"So, you're leaving soon then?" Eberon asked softly.

Schula nodded.

We had taken Thain, Eberon, and Nassir with us away from the bustle around the cabin. We walked a deer trail near one of my old fishing spots, and as we told them about our plans and concerns, they listened patiently.

Still, the sorrow in Eberon's eyes cut deep. Thain's stony expression didn't reveal anything he was feeling.

"A war may very well start in your absence," Eberon said.

"And if we leave, DuVarick will split his resources and leave himself weakened," Schula said. "You can't believe that he would leave us alone after all that."

"Which is all the more reason you shouldn't go alone." Thain spoke for the first time since we'd started our walk.

Schula and I looked at each other, surprised.

"Lord Eberon and you will be needed in Thanantholl," Nassir said quietly. "These two have proven capable of taking care of themselves. They will return to you once they have found the answers they seek, Lord Thainalan."

Thain glowered at Nassir, though the older fae couldn't see him do it.

"He's right, Thain." Eberon laid a hand on him gently. "We would be miserable apart like that, and we're going to be vital in the pursuit of DuVarick. We're needed by Baeleon's side."

"And if he harbors us in Thanantholl," Schula added, "it will only cause trouble."

Thain's attention landed on me, his silver eyes melting my heart as he resolved himself.

"I think I should gather some provisions," Schula said.

"I'll help you," Eberon chimed in quickly, and they both left.

"I will simply leave, as it seems you need a moment," Nassir said honestly, a smile on his face as he slowly walked back. Puko took off and landed on Nassir's shoulder, startling the old fae as he walked back toward the cabin.

I looked up at Thain, not knowing what to say. Thankfully, he broke the silence first.

"I will find you," he promised.

Shaking my head, I swallowed down the ache already forming. "I'll be back."

"I will find you anyway," he swore, his tone firming. "Once my duty to the Autumn Lands is completed, I will find you."

I still didn't know how. There was no telling where the journey to find these answers would take me. The quiet swirled between us, the calmness of the air in stark contrast to the war inside me.

"I will miss you," he said softly.

He put his hand up to my face, and I leaned into it. His warm palm was a comfort as I held in the tears trying to escape.

"What gave you interest in a plain girl like me?" I had always wanted to ask.

"There's nothing plain about you," he murmured, now rubbing his thumb in small circles on my cheek while he held my face. "Kindred souls, perhaps? I admire your resolve, though it irks me right now as it's taking you away from me."

He drew back a moment and pulled a thin silver chain from under his shirt. It was long on Thain, and as he slipped it over my head, it dropped nearly to my belly button. I lifted the chain; on the end of it was a tiny stone. It was dark blue, as dark as Thain's hair, with specks of silver in it.

"What is this?" I asked.

"I had been meaning to give it to you since that fight we had. But then you came back from Dwellonmar with that quartz from Caldon, and I never did." He took the chain from me for a moment to look at the stone. He whispered, leaning down to my ear, "I like that color of blue against your skin."

Heat bloomed on my face, and I pulled in a breath. "I think I do too." He held my wrists gently and pulled my hands away. Then he leaned in and gave me a slow kiss.

It wasn't like our first one; it was slow and passionate. It spoke more words than either of us could have said out loud. It was a promise. A promise to pick back up where we'd left off when I came back.

He deepened the kiss, making me gasp as his tongue slid into my mouth. I met him with more warmth, and he growled playfully before pulling away again.

I was breathless and hot when he pulled away. His eyes were full of emotion as he watched me recover from him.

"Let's get you back. We have things to do."

"Right," I breathed. "Let's go."

Thain laughed and led us to the cabin.

It was dawn when we left. Schula, Nassir, and I carried packs filled with supplies. I'd asked Eberon to take my smoky quartz for safekeeping. I had no romantic intentions toward Caldon, at least not anymore, but he was still a friend, and I didn't want it destroyed. I wasn't sure what Thain might do with it while I was gone.

Schula gave Thain the key to her apartment. He would move her things into a guest room in his home, and Mama Flori could rent the place to someone who would be there, since we had no idea how long our trip would be.

Nassir, with food and meditation, was now able to get around much better. He walked in a meditative trance, sensing the objects around him and skillfully navigating the mountain terrain. He said he didn't want to be more of a burden than he already was, and he'd progressed quite a bit over the few days we had been here.

The three of us walked in quiet contemplation as the Autumn creatures behind us said goodbye, watching us leave their sight.

There would be hard times ahead, and hopefully good times too. But with Schula and Nassir by my side, and Thain to come home to, I was ready for the challenge.

I needed answers. Not just for me but for the good of the Wyldes and the humans who lived south of the wards.

As we stepped from the tree line toward the plains below, I held my head high.

I was Wren.

Witch. Elf.

Bonded to Schula. Daughter of Bryn.

I would find the witches. I would find the elves.

I might even find the black presence.

And then I would save the Wyldes.

ACKNOWLEDGEMENTS

Half Wylde has been such a long time coming. My other books have been filled with me trying to tell an entertaining story. Sure, they may have included themes or social commentary, but mostly, I wanted to make people smile. That's it. That was my goal. This book was much less of my usual writing and much more selfish. Cathartic, in many ways. I could thank a lot of people who made this story what it is, but that would be me thanking people who made my life harder. If you think I'm funny, just know it's the trauma. It makes me a delight. Hi, Ashley, if you're reading this: I can't wait to hear what questions you have for me in my next therapy session. Anyway, let's jump into who supported this book while it was being written. Those are much better people to be thanking.

Wattpad readers. You, first and foremost, kept me going. Some of your usernames have been household conversation for me. Telling my husband that you commented on the new chapter, that you sent me a message or asked me questions; that you cared, honestly, is the core of why I have this finished book to share with the world. You are the reason for the first draft of the story, so thank you.

All the industry people behind me are amazing. I'm truly lucky to have the team that I have: Deanna, Fiona, Delaney, Austin, the marketing team, the cover designer, the social media team, and everyone who had hands on this book. All of you made this book happen the way it did, and I'm so glad to be working with you.

To my agent, Ali, you're the best. The twist of luck that put us together is a blessing for me, and I appreciate your guidance so very much. Thank you so much, and thank you to Spencerhill for all the support. I couldn't wish for a better group of people on my side.

To my husband, Josh, you and our son are my biggest supports and reasons for trying. And my mom, who supports every book I write. Thank you.

And thank you to all the readers who have been with me and those who have just found me. You make being an author the best job in the world.

ABOUT THE AUTHOR

Sabrina Blackburry writes romantasy escapes about passionate women finding their place in the world, witty side characters, and love with a touch of magic. From Wattpad to bookshelves, Sabrina's debut novel, *Dirty Lying Faeries,* kicked off her career in 2022. She remains a staunch believer that anyone can become a writer if they have the heart to make it happen.

From central Missouri, Sabrina lived with her grandparents throughout her childhood where her love of reading and taste for fairytales took root. Her hobbies include gardening, walking nature trails, and getting involved with the local renaissance festival, but none of these take priority over a cat, a coffee, and a good book.

Don't miss book two in

THE WYLDES

COMING SOON